Starring...
JOHN DILLINGER

Starring... JOHN DILLINGER

Bill Walker Brian Anthony

FOREWORD BY DAVID MAMET

DELARGE BOOKS
2021

Copyright © 2021 by Bill Walker & Brian Anthony

DeLarge Books Edition 2021
ISBN-13: 978-1-7358796-4-2

This is a work of fiction.

Cover Design: Andy Carpenter Design
Colorization: Birgit Kreps
Typesetting and Design: Alexander DeLarge
Printed in the United States of America

To my literary mom, Elizabeth Butler Klungness (1924-2015),
whose brush with history inspired this book.

—BW

To my wife, Kim, who stole my heart.

—BA

FOREWORD

Ah, publicity.

I was playing Movie Trivia with a friend, and challenged him to name a famous actor who had actually killed his wife. He named four.

Dillinger was the most famous man in America for eighteen months. Three way-stations of his run have become staples of our beloved National Gangster Myth: the shootout at Little Bohemia, the escape from Crown Point Jail, and his death outside the Biograph Theatre.

I've always felt a close connection to Dillinger. I spent summers in Northern Wisconsin, close to Manitowish, the site of Little Bohemia; I lived for years around the corner from the Biograph, and went there weekly; and I am the discoverer (and you may be reading it here as the first to share the gem) that, *at* the Biograph, prior to his death in the alley, he was watching a film which makes reference to him.

Think about it. A year and a half from his entrance, and Clark Gable is playing him, *and* joking about his exploits. The film was, of course, MANHATTAN MELODRAMA. At one point Gable, Dillinger, is joking with William Powell, who plays a Public Prosecutor. Powell says he is going to arrest some criminal, and Gable says, "Just don't get your picture taken with him. You know what happened to that guy at Crown Point."

When he got nabbed at Crown Point, Dillinger got his photo taken with his arm around the prosecutor, Robert Estill, the two and the attendant fuzz all buddied-up.

I got hired, some years back, to write a Dillinger film, and the script was gangbusters. Then I got fired. But I got to spend some time reveling in the myth. At one point in my script, Dillinger realizes that he has become nationally famous, and, so, has nowhere to hide.

Aristotle teaches us that the Hero cannot simply "get the idea." So how, using film, which is, you will allow a pictorial medium, does our Hero receive *information* which changes the course of his journey.

Enter Burma Shave.

He is driving down the highway and comes across the Signs:

John Dillinger
Was bold and brave
He always had
The closest shaves.
BURMA SHAVE.

P.S. As I have your attention, whore that I am, and should the Burma Shave folks be reading, I expanded the conceit thus:

How did Al Capone Escape
From positively every scrape?
and
Baby Face Nelson
Watched this Space
And learned how to keep
His Baby Face.

I got to elaborate (and so participate in) the myth. And, now, so have Bill Walker and Brian Anthony, in STARRING... JOHN DILLINGER.

It is as tasty as a hot beef sandwich.

—David Mamet
August, 2021

7

PROLOGUE

I was in the summer of my tenth year when John Dillinger met with my father to discuss the terms of his surrender, a summer so hot you felt as if you were burning from the inside out. A summer so hot it made a man reflect upon his past and whether he had any future at all. In the year he'd spent at large robbing banks in the Midwest, John Dillinger had grown into a legend admired by poor folk all over the country, and he'd grown tired of being hunted like an animal.

My father, Robert Butler, was a newspaperman, a profession that used to mean something far more than it does today. Back then people read the paper, talked about what they read, and took pride in knowing what was going on. And people took men like my father at their word, trusted them, looked to them for guidance and advice, welcoming them into their living rooms and kitchens every morning like a favorite uncle with a good story to tell.

My father was a feature writer for one of the major Indianapolis dailies, and a Robert Butler byline meant you were in for the unexpected. His articles were read as far away as Washington DC, for my father had opinions on the great issues of the day that great men found of value. But it was the simple folk for whom he wrote, using plain-speaking prose that made you feel as if he were sitting right next to you with his arm around your shoulder, whispering in your ear, telling you secrets just between you and him. At the same time, he would let you know that his opinion was just one of many, that he wasn't—and couldn't be—always right, that he expected you to take what he wrote and think for yourself. Those simple people, those humble readers he loved so much, for whom he toiled endless late nights, took him at his word. They trusted him.

John Dillinger trusted him too.

Dad wrote several articles about Indiana's most infamous son, but he'd always tell the truth—that John Dillinger couldn't have robbed two banks in the same day a hundred and fifty miles apart; that maybe one of those bankers was hiding something. And we lived only seven miles from the Dillinger farmhouse. My father knew Johnnie, would see him around from time to time, and knew Dillinger wasn't as bad as everyone painted him out to be.

The call came in a little after noon that mid-July day. We lived in a small, one-story brick house in Plainfield, a bedroom community twenty miles outside of Indianapolis, where my father had his office in the back bedroom. He liked being able to keep his own hours and write whatever stories interested him without having an editor constantly telling him what to do. That meant Dad was home for lunch every day, and I couldn't wait to hear about what he was writing, because I wanted to be a writer too.

The phone rang, and my father continued eating his soup, content to let it ring. My mother never could.

"We should answer it, Robert," she said. "It might be important."

Dad calmly took another spoonful of soup. "Might be, might not. Might just be folderol."

Mom rolled her eyes and grabbed for the receiver, bringing it to her ear. "This is the Butler residence."

It was never "hello." My mother always loved the way the servants answered the phone in those movies about the rich and the well-to-do. She said the greeting was used by the well-bred and she wanted to bring a little bit of that elegance into our home. That day was different. As soon as those words left her mouth, her countenance changed, the soft planes of her face shifting into an expression of unease. A knot formed in my stomach.

"I'm sorry, what did you say? I'm getting a lot of static on my end. Oh, wait, it's clear now. Can you repeat what you said?"

She listened, the frown lines between her dark brown eyes deepening.

"All right, sir, hold on a minute." She pulled the receiver away from her ear and covered the mouthpiece with her other hand. "It's John Dillinger Senior. He wants to speak to you."

My father hesitated for only a moment before putting down his spoon and rising from the table. I watched him take the receiver from my mother, marveling, as always, at his height. He was a large-framed, physically imposing man whose hands still exhibited the hard calluses of a youth spent toiling on his parents' farm, yet they were soft and gentle against my skin. His face was permanently wind-burned from those years in the searing sun, leaving him with a fine web of crow's feet around his eyes that crinkled when he laughed. He had dark brown hair just going gray at the temples and a square, angular face that on another would have looked hard and bitter, but on him gave the impression of sincerity, an impression that he was a man who would listen to your confessions and take them to his grave.

"Hello, Mr. Dillinger, what can I do for you?" he asked.

He listened, his lips pursing, while the man on the other end spoke his piece. He nodded as the man talked, keeping his bright blue eyes on me as I sat at the kitchen table and pretended not to eavesdrop.

"Yes, sir, I understand what you're asking . . . No, it's no trouble at all . . ."

He winked at me then, letting me know not to worry, that everything was under control. I hadn't realized until that moment that I'd been holding my breath—terrified that something awful had happened.

"All right, Mr. Dillinger." My father glanced at his watch. "It's half past twelve. If I leave now, I should get there a little after one . . . Yes, sir, I'll see you and your boy then. Thank you."

Dad hung up the phone and stood a moment staring at it, a curious little smile on his lips.

"Robert?"

"Yes, Millie?" he said, his gaze still locked on the phone.

My mother rolled her eyes. "Do I have to pull everything out of you like some two-bit dentist?"

That broke the spell, and my father went for his jacket and his hat, both hanging on a wall rack next to the front door. "John Dillinger wants to surrender," he said. "Told his father I was the only man he could trust to make that happen safely."

Mom's eyes widened. "Oh my Lord. Why'd he call *you*?"

"He liked what I wrote about him."

"Are you leaving now?"

"John's holed up at the farm and he can't stay there long. Too risky."

"You be careful then, okay?" she asked, giving him a quick peck on the lips.

Dad smiled and let her help him slip on his linen jacket. Then he plucked his straw boater off the hat hook and placed it on his head with a rakish tilt that brought a smile to my mother's face.

Then he turned to me. "You ready to get the scoop, Lizzie?"

I leapt up from the table. "And how!"

Mom's eyes widened. "Robert, have you lost your mind? Dillinger's a killer, and you're going to take your ten-year-old daughter to meet him?"

Dad chuckled and grasped my mother's shoulders. "Honey, the man trusts me because I always wrote the truth about his exploits. I never pandered, and he knows that. He figures with a newspaperman bringing him in, they won't shoot him. And he's never killed anyone, Millie, it's all made up."

"You don't know that."

"I do. I know the family, and I have my sources."

"You always say that," Mom snapped. "Sources can lie, can't they?"

Dad sighed. "Millie, I don't have time to argue. I need to go."

"Then leave Lizzie with me."

"No, I want to go!"

My mother ignored what must have been a look of profound disappointment in my eyes, but my father saw it as clear as a drop of blood on white silk sheets. He never missed anything.

"I thought you had your Women's Club meeting today."

"I do, but—"

"Do you think it's appropriate to take her? She'll be bored stiff."

"It's a lot more appropriate than taking her to a meeting with the most notorious bank robber in America! What if the police show up?"

"They won't."

"And how do you know *that*?"

"Because they never look in the obvious places."

"Robert . . . please."

Instead of answering, my father stared back at her with that stark, implacable gaze he had.

Mom sighed and shook her head. She knew my father would get his way, but she could never let him have it without speaking her mind, and that was why he loved her.

"John Dillinger wants my help—he wants to do the right thing. Lizzie and I will be fine."

She chucked him on the arm. "I know . . . but I don't have to like it."

My father grinned and kissed her cheek, eliciting a tiny smile despite her frustration and annoyance.

"Come on, Scoop, let's go."

Even though we lived on a shady street, Dad kept his LaSalle in a rented space in a garage two blocks away on East Main. That 1933 LaSalle Coupe was his most prized possession, the first new car he'd ever owned. He loved the power of its V-8 engine, said it was like driving some untamed beast. And that's what he called it, the Beast. I loved to watch him drive it, feeling the vibrations of the engine and the road through the springs in my seat. I didn't often get the chance to ride with my father, especially while he was working.

The sun felt as if it were pressing down on me, baking every inch of my body. My father never noticed the heat. He liked to walk at a fast pace, dodging slower pedestrians with swift, adroit movements that reminded me of football players I'd seen in the newsreels. I followed in his wake, skipping to keep up with him.

When we reached Vinny's Garage and Body, I felt as if I'd taken a bath with my clothes on. My father looked as fresh and dry as if he'd simply walked across a room.

14

Vinny Iazzi, the owner of the garage, slid out from under a Hudson and sat up with a wide grin on his chubby, grease-stained face. "How ya doin' Mr. B?"

"Just fine, Vinny, just fine. Is the Beast gassed up?"

Vinny nodded, still grinning. "Sure thing, Mr. B. It's always ready to go. I even patched that tire you was talkin' about last week."

My father threw Vinny a silver dollar and waved me over to the car, which sat in the corner without a speck of dust or grime, its black paint gleaming in the glare of the overhead lights. We both climbed in, and a minute later we shot out of the garage onto East Main.

We turned onto Route 267 and took that gently winding street the entire way. The air blowing in through the open windows was still warm, but pleasant. The one thing that wasn't pleasant was seeing all the abandoned farms, the roofs of the houses sagging like the backs of old nags, tractors rusting in the middle of fields gone to weed.

We kept ourselves entertained by singing our favorite silly songs. Dad had a rich baritone that I loved to hear, so I let him do most of the singing, as my untrained voice sounded like a cat screeching.

We reached the Dillinger home on Northridge Drive just before one o'clock. The house was modest—one and a half stories with a peaked roof and a small front porch with a swing. As Dad braked the Beast in the short, graveled driveway, he turned to me, his expression grave. "Now, Lizzie, you need to do everything I'm going to tell you to do, okay?"

"Yes, Daddy."

"Good," he said, running his fingers through my curly hair. "While I'm meeting with John, you need to wait on the porch, and if you see anything coming down that road, no matter what it is, you need to give a holler. Understand?"

"I'm going to be a lookout?" My eyes must have lit up, because my father's serious expression vanished. "That's right—a lookout. Can I count on you, Lizzie?"

I nodded, and he caressed my cheek.

"You're looking like your mother more and more every day."

We climbed out of the car just as an older man emerged from the house, the screen door banging shut behind him. He was shorter than my father, whippet thin, and he wore overalls with white long johns underneath. The long johns were yellowed with sweat stains and the overalls were faded and patched. The old man wore a battered straw hat above a face that was all sharp angles with dry, weathered skin stretched over jutting cheekbones. His gray eyes looked as if they'd seen all the sorrow in the world.

He lifted his hand in a languid wave. "Afternoon, Mr. Butler. Thank you for comin'."

I followed my father up the drive and onto the porch, where he grasped the older man's hand, giving it a quick, emphatic shake. "Mr. Dillinger, it's nice to see you again. And this is my daughter, Lizzie."

The elder Dillinger bent down, his thin, chapped lips creasing into a gap-toothed smile. "Well, ain't you a pretty little thing."

"Thank you, sir," I said, trying to keep from gagging on the man's odor, a combination of sour sweat and manure.

He stood and looked to my father. "Johnnie's inside," he said, motioning with his head.

My father moved to the screen door and opened it, turning to me. "Remember, Lizzie, if you see anything at all, you holler, okay?"

"Okay, Daddy," I said, not wanting to be left alone with the old man.

My father walked into the house, and before the door slammed shut, I caught the dim outline of a man reaching to shake his hand.

"Come on over and set with me, child," the elder Dillinger said, heading for the porch swing. He plopped his rangy body into it, and it swayed in a lazy arc, the chains squeaking like frightened mice.

I looked at it dubiously, as the chains were rusty, and the white paint was peeling off the swing in huge patches. I didn't want to sit next to him, but I didn't want to be impolite either, so I joined him on the swing, sitting as far away as I could.

From where I sat, I could view the road in either direction, and I kept my eyes on it for the first few minutes, until I was distracted by a swaybacked horse in a nearby corral. How fun it would be to ride it.

"Is that your horse, Mr. Dillinger?"

"Yep."

I turned and looked at him, and his eyes held that thousand-yard stare I'd read about in some of the Zane Grey westerns I liked.

"Sure would be nice to ride him," I said, being pitifully obvious.

Dillinger Senior didn't take the bait. "It might be, except he's a plowin' horse and too tetchy to ride."

I saw movement in the corner of my eye, and I panicked when I realized it was a car coming down the road. I could hear the blood rushing through my ears, and for a split second I imagined the worst, until I realized it was a dusty pickup truck belching out clouds of oil smoke in its wake. The truck honked as it passed, and Mr. Dillinger raised his hand and waved.

As if sensing my fear, Mr. Dillinger said, "That's just old Judd; he's not after Johnnie."

I kept my eyes on the road from then on. Voices reached me from inside the house and I tried to overhear what was being said, but they were too indistinct to make out any of the words.

Ten minutes later, the screen door opened a crack. "Lizzie?"

"Everything's okay, Daddy," I said hurriedly, feeling a knot of guilt in my stomach about the horse.

Dad smiled. "That's good," he said, motioning to me. "Come on in. Someone wants to meet you."

I stood on wobbly legs and my father held the door open for me.

Inside, I was blind for a moment, bright stars swimming in my vision, until my eyes adjusted to the shadowy gloom.

A man sat on a brocaded couch, wearing a white dress shirt open at the neck and a charcoal-gray vest and matching pants. He stood and came over to me, an easy smile creasing his face. That smile did something to me, and it wasn't until I was a teenager that I understood what that feeling meant. All I knew then was his smile made me feel all rubbery inside.

Dillinger knelt, so he and I were eye to eye, and the smile widened. I saw a darkened tooth, which was the only fault in that smile. His face was stubbled with the beginnings of a beard, and he sported a Clark Gable mustache, and his hair was combed straight back and gleaming with pomade. I noticed these details in passing because it was his gaze that held me, steel-gray eyes that spoke of danger and excitement.

"So, this is my little lookout."

"Y-Yes, sir," I managed to stammer.

He chuckled. "Sir? You can call me Johnnie. What do I call you?"

"Lizzie."

Dillinger's grin widened. "Well, Lizzie, I want to thank you for helping your dad today. You made me feel really safe."

That made me smile, despite my guilty conscience. "You're welcome . . . Johnnie."

Dillinger laughed. "So, what do you want to be when you grow up, Lizzie?"

"A writer."

Dillinger eyed me with a look tinged with equal measures of curiosity and amusement, then turned to my father, who was smiling proudly. "She's pretty good already," Dad said.

"I'll bet she is," Dillinger said.

"You don't look like a bank robber," I blurted, feeling foolish as soon as the words left my mouth.

Instead of being upset, Dillinger gave me an appraising look. "No? What do I look like then?"

My face flushed as I answered. "A movie star—like Clark Gable."

Dillinger laughed.

"Well, aren't you the sweetest thing. You think I missed my calling?"

I nodded solemnly, not sure if I was being kidded or not.

"Maybe in another life," he said, standing up. He shook my father's hand. "I sure am grateful for your help, Mr. Butler. I couldn't do this without you. They want me dead."

"Just stick to the plan and we'll get you to the police station in one piece."

We left soon after, and for the drive home Dad and I didn't talk, nor did we sing. I think both of us were thinking about Johnnie too intently to amuse ourselves with silly songs. I know my father was going over his plan in his mind, trying to discern if there were any flaws. As for me, I kept seeing Johnnie's easy smile and feeling aglow. He'd talked to me like I was a grown-up, something no one had ever done before.

And now that I'm an old woman and setting these thoughts

to paper, I've begun to wonder if what I said to Dillinger that day changed something, if his fate would have taken a different turn had I not accompanied my father that day, or if he hadn't been curious to meet his little lookout.

To my dying day, I'll always wonder if John Dillinger would have died that day at the Biograph Theatre.

Elizabeth Butler Klungness
Yuma, Arizona
July 22, 2014

LIGHTS!

1

Chicago, Illinois
July 15, 1934

He left the motor running.

Even though leaving it that way made perfect sense in this far-from-typical situation, Robert Butler was nervous walking away from his beloved LaSalle Coupe, and leaving it to the mercies of any ne'er-do-well who happened by and cared to take the shiny late-model car for a joyride. And in this neighborhood, someone stealing his car was more likely than not. The supreme irony was that he was waiting for the most notorious criminal in the world, the man J. Edgar Hoover wanted to bury.

Butler had arranged to meet him in front of the Lincoln Avenue Rexall Drugstore, where he now stood, sweating profusely. And that was the strange thing. The heat never bothered him, even when it was over a hundred, as it was today. He knew it wasn't the heat—just good old-fashioned nerves. What an old Vaudeville friend called flop sweat.

Well, he had no intention of flopping today. He'd picked that location because it was a Sunday and most people would be at home or in church and the police station would be less hectic, with fewer men on duty. He hoped that was the case, as one never knew what could happen. The other reason he'd picked that location was because they had so little time. If he didn't get Dillinger to the police station today, he might not be alive tomorrow.

Butler took up a position on the corner and noted the hour on his watch.

Ten minutes to go . . .

All Dillinger had to do was walk up and get in and they'd be off to the police station five blocks away. The problem was there'd been no parking directly in front of the store. His LaSalle sat rumbling in front of the Dorchester Hat Emporium next door. A few extra steps, but those extra steps might make the difference between life and death for Dillinger.

Butler leaned against a light pole and lit a Lucky Strike with a flick of his new Zippo, inhaling the acrid smoke and trying to blend in with the half-dozen unemployed men he saw loafing about on the street.

He checked his watch again.

Five more minutes.

Butler looked behind himself and down the side street. Traffic was light, even for the lunch hour, which was a good thing. Dillinger would be coming from that direction any moment, from a secret address he wouldn't reveal.

"Better you don't know it, Bob, just in case," he'd said with his characteristic smirk.

And that was fine. After today, it wouldn't matter.

Butler tried to imagine what it would be like, parking in front of the police station and walking in with his charge. He found himself smiling as he pictured the fat desk sergeant's eyes bugging out when they presented themselves. He intended to hold nothing back from the article he planned to write. The world would know that John Dillinger voluntarily surrendered without incident. And while his career would get a huge boost from what would be considered a historic event, that was of secondary importance. He just wanted to see Dillinger get a fair trial rather than a federal agent's bullet.

A movement on the street caught his attention, and he froze.

A police car cruised the block, creeping right toward him. He threw away his cigarette and looked down the side street, trying to keep his movements inconspicuous. The sidewalk was empty.

No Dillinger.

That was good.

But not good enough.

Instead of cruising past the corner and continuing up the street, the police car stopped short, double-parking right next to his La-Salle—blocking it. The overweight cop in the passenger seat heaved himself out and stood staring at Butler's car. He moved closer, shaded his eyes, and scanned the coupe's interior before straightening up and shaking his head.

"Car's running. This guy's asking for it, Jimmy."

Butler strained to catch the other cop's reply but couldn't discern what was being said over the street noise.

He resisted the urge to move closer.

A moment later the cop shrugged and started for the Rexall, then stopped and turned. "Vanilla or chocolate?" He listened and nodded. "Okay, but don't come cryin' to me if you slob it all over yourself like you done the last time."

The cop inside the car flipped his partner an obscene gesture, and the fat cop laughed as he disappeared into the drugstore.

Ice cream. The cops were stopping for ice cream.

Another check of his watch verified it was just after one.

And there came Dillinger, sauntering toward him, his straw boater at a rakish cant and a confident smile on his face. The Clark Gable mustache he'd started was now grown in, and he looked less like the man in the wanted posters plastered all over the city. Butler wanted to signal for Dillinger to stop and wait, but the cop sitting in the car was watching him with more than casual interest.

When Dillinger was a hundred feet from the corner, the other cop was still in the Rexall getting the damned ice cream.

Butler had to do something fast.

He began to turn, with the idea of heading Dillinger off if only to have him hang back in the red brick niche of the Rexall's recessed side door. At the same time, the cop exited the drugstore carrying two chocolate cones, the ice cream already starting to run over his hands in the sweltering heat.

When he looked back at Dillinger, he saw the outlaw had stopped, his eyes glued to the fat cop with the ice cream. Then he stared at Butler with a look of anger and betrayal in his eyes. A chill washed through Butler's body.

My God, he thinks I've set him up!

He wanted to holler that it wasn't true, but all he could do was stand helplessly as Dillinger turned and hurried off and the cops—unaware of their infamous quarry being so close at hand—licked their cones and drove away.

Butler fought off a wave of dizziness and collapsed against the lamppost, a river of sweat pouring down his face. He clutched his stomach, feeling it roil and rumble.

Christ, I'm going to be sick.

He bent over and threw up into the gutter, some of his stomach's contents splashing onto the pristine white-walled tires of an Essex-Terraplane. Staggering toward the LaSalle, he used his handkerchief to wipe off the sweat stinging his eyes and the remnants of the vomit from his lips.

Inside the LaSalle, he leaned over the steering wheel, waiting for the wave of dizziness to subside.

What was he going to do? Dillinger must think him the worst of traitors. He threw the car into gear and turned down the side street, hoping to catch sight of the outlaw. But Dillinger was nowhere to be seen, no doubt having scurried back down the bolthole from which he'd emerged.

Disgusted with himself, Butler drove home, cursing his incompetence for the entire three-hour drive. He should have foreseen the possibility of having to wave Dillinger off, should have planned for it, but he'd had little choice except to play the game Dillinger's way, as the outlaw wouldn't reveal where he was living and thus Butler couldn't pick him up there and run the risk of leading the cops right to him. He didn't blame John for his caution one bit. His life was at stake.

Butler dropped off the LaSalle at Vinny's garage and walked home, grateful that Millie and Lizzie were still out of the house at a double-feature matinee. He needed the time to think. Perhaps his plan could still be salvaged; Dillinger deserved the chance to pay his debt. During their brief meeting at his father's house, one of the things they'd discussed was the murder charge. A police patrolman named O'Malley had been gunned down during a robbery at the First National Bank of East Chicago, and while witnesses claimed Dillinger had been the shooter, John swore he had not fired that shot.

"It was Red Hamilton," Dillinger had said that afternoon. "That poor son of a bitch almost got his hand shot off. Those witnesses are lying, Bob. I just need someone good to prove it."

In the two days since that meeting, Butler had spent his spare time trying to arrange for a top criminal attorney to defend Dillinger, having told the outlaw that his current attorney, Louis Piquett, was bush league. "If you want to beat this charge, you need someone as good as Clarence Darrow."

"So, let's get him," Dillinger had said without a trace of irony.

And that had lit the fire of inspiration inside Butler. Darrow was world famous, having gone head-to-head with the great William Jennings Bryan during the famous Scopes Monkey Trial, as well as defending the "Thrill Killers" Leopold and Loeb in two landmark trials. And even though Darrow was in his late seventies, he was reputed to be a sharp as ever.

After making a few calls, he'd reached the venerable attorney at his Chicago home. When he explained the situation and what he intended to do, the old lawyer had laughed. "That Dillinger's a smart rascal. After what they say he's done, surrendering is the best step he could take. A crafty attorney will make mincemeat of those so-called witnesses."

"I was hoping you'd say that, Mr. Darrow," Butler said, feeling a wave of relief wash over him. "Will you take the case?"

The older man sighed. "As tempting as that is, Mr. Butler, I have to decline. I'm getting a little too old for the rigors of a case such as this. However, I know just the man. You need Sam Leibowitz—his acquittal record is unmatched."

Butler thanked Darrow and placed a call to New York. Within five minutes of reaching Leibowitz, the attorney agreed to take Dillinger's case.

"I've read a number of your articles, Mr. Butler. Most impressive. If you can bring Dillinger in, I'll do it."

"What about the fact that you're from New York? Will that be a problem?"

"I can apply to the court to represent Mr. Dillinger. It's done all the time."

They'd hung up a few minutes later with Butler feeling that he had the situation in hand. Now, all of that effort was wasted unless he could reach Dillinger and convince him that what had happened that afternoon was a fluke—an accident.

Inside his office, Butler reached for the phone and tried to reach Dillinger's father. The phone rang and rang and rang.

He must be outside, working.

Butler grabbed a sheet of typing paper and dashed off a note.

Millie: I had to take a ride down to Mooresville. Will be back after dinner. Love, Robert.

He left the note on the kitchen table under the salt and pepper shakers and returned to the garage.

"Goin' out again, Mr. B?" Vinny asked.

"No rest for the weary, Vinny. I'll be back by six thirty."

"No problem, I'll be here. Just knock on the door, and I'll let you in."

By the time he reached the Dillinger farm just past five o'clock, the sun had dropped lower in the sky, casting stark shadows that mirrored Butler's anxious mood. When he pulled into the driveway, Dillinger Senior emerged from the house, looking much the same as he had two days before, as if he'd not even bothered to change his clothes.

"Johnnie's not here, Mr. Butler."

"I had a feeling he wouldn't be," he said, stepping up onto the porch, "but I need to get word to him."

The older man frowned. "Somethin' the matter?"

Butler tried to keep the embarrassment from showing on his face as he related what had happened earlier that day. "I just don't want him to believe that I set him up."

28

The old farmer shook his head slowly. "Johnnie'll know it weren't your fault, Mr. Butler. He trusts you. If he didn't, he'd never have allowed me to call you in the first place."

Butler sighed. "You didn't see the look he gave me, Mr. Dillinger, as if I'd stabbed him in the back. If he calls you, would you please tell him it was all just lousy luck? Tell him we can still get this done. I'll meet him anywhere he wants, and we'll go in together, just like we planned."

"If Johnnie calls, I'll tell him. I wish my boy'd had friends like you before any of this happened. Maybe things would've turned out different."

Butler shook the older man's hand and drove back home. He'd done all he could. It was all up to Dillinger now.

2

Chicago, Illinois
July 22, 1934

The heat pressed down on Dillinger as he approached the Rexall Drugstore at the northeast corner of Fullerton and North Racine, making him feel as if he were walking under water. Thermal waves floated off the sidewalk, undulating in the sultry air like sloe-eyed hula girls, further enhancing the aquatic illusion. He wiped the sweat from his brow with his already-drenched handkerchief and smiled at the thought. Sitting on some nameless beach would be far better than where he was, in a city suffering its worst heat wave in a decade. It was better than thinking about his current situation, which was worse than ever. And though he was only a mile from Anna Sage's apartment where he'd been staying for the past month, he felt exposed, as if he were an insect squirming under a magnifying glass.

As he passed a hat store half a block from the Rexall, he stopped and studied the displays through the plate-glass window, admiring a straw boater similar to the one he now wore. He'd paused at the store window to admire the latest fashions—and to make sure no one was tailing him. Using the store window's reflection, he studied the people strolling along the sidewalk immediately behind him and across Fullerton. Some hurried, as if late for an appointment, while others took their time, as if they had nothing better to do. None of them paid him the slightest attention, and that was good. Even better, there was no one standing around pretending they weren't looking at him.

He'd stayed too long in this neighborhood and repeatedly felt his survival instinct urging him to move on. Then why the hell didn't he just go? Because he still had faith in Robert Butler.

Moving away from the hat store, Dillinger crossed North Racine and entered the Rexall. The store had an odd, yet pleasant smell, a combination of fresh-ground coffee, perfumed soap, and sap from the newly installed pine floor. The place was stocked full of all manner of sundries, and the narrow aisles felt claustrophobic. The last place he wanted to be trapped. The air inside the store was only a little cooler than the sweltering air outside, but the fans overhead, spinning to beat the band, provided only a little relief. He headed toward the phone booth at the back of the store, nestled next to the magazine rack, mindful of the store clerk's owlish gaze.

Probably thinks I'm gonna steal his aspirin.

He'd made it a point to visit different drugstores over the last several days to stave off suspicion, but this one was closest to the apartment, and it was too damned hot to walk any further than necessary.

When he closed the phonebooth door, the bare lightbulb snapped on and the tiny fan rattled in its housing with a regularity Dillinger found annoying. Ignoring it, he reached into his pants pocket and cursed. He'd forgotten to pick up the change off his dresser before leaving the apartment.

Now he had no choice but to break a dollar, putting himself a lot closer to the clerk than he wanted to be.

Sighing, he left the booth and strolled to the front counter with a friendly smile he didn't really feel pasted onto his face. The clerk, a mousy man in his early forties, regarded Dillinger with raised eyebrows perched above a pair of round rimless glasses.

"Need to make a call. Can you break a dollar?"

The man nodded and took the dollar, and gave Dillinger back three quarters and five nickels.

"Thanks, pal," Dillinger said, and returned to the booth. He could feel the clerk's gaze boring into his back and steeled himself. He'd call his father, get Butler's number, and get the hell out of this rat trap.

The nickel clinked and clanged as it made its way down through the guts of the phone, and a moment later the operator chimed in. "Number please."

Dillinger gave her the number of the Mooresville house and waited while it rang.

"H-Hello?"

Dillinger breathed out a sigh of relief. "Pop?"

"Johnnie? That you?"

"Yeah, Pop, it's me. I've tried to call you five times over the last few days. Where've you been?

"Tendin' the crops, Johnnie."

Dillinger shook his head, feeling foolish. *Of course.*

"Listen, Pop, I can't stay on long. I need Bob Butler's number."

"He called here the other day lookin' for you. He was real sorry things turned out like they did—"

A note of impatience crept into Dillinger's voice. "I know, Pop. I'm sure he was. Can you get me his number?"

"Sure, Johnnie, I got it here somewhere. Hold on a minute."

The handset clunked as his father put it down on the little mahogany table under his mother's photograph in the hallway. Dillinger couldn't hold back the pang of homesickness that washed over him, his heart aching so bad, he thought it would burst. If only things had been different. If only he hadn't been such a reckless kid who thought he knew everything, maybe he'd be home now with no need to be looking over his shoulder.

Stop thinking like this! You can't change it.

Through the phone, Dillinger could hear his father rummaging through drawers, muttering to himself.

Hurry up, Pop!

His father picked up the phone. "Johnnie, I know it's here somewhere, I just can't seem to lay my hands on it."

Sweat popped out on Dillinger's brow. "Did you check the Bible? You're always squirreling things away there."

"First place I looked, Son. I'm sorry. I'll keep lookin'."

"Okay, Pop, you do that."

Dillinger peered through the smudged phonebooth window towards the front of the store and noticed the clerk staring directly at him.

"Gotta run, somebody's casting their lamps on me. I'll try and call you tomorrow."

"I'll find it, Johnnie, don't you worry none. Stay safe, Son."

"I will, Pop. I love you."

"I love you, too, Johnnie."

Dillinger hung up the phone, his mood darkening. For some unfathomable reason he felt as if this was the last time he'd speak to his father. It was crazy, but it persisted nevertheless.

He left the store and returned to the street, taking a different, more roundabout route back to Anna's apartment. It gave him time to think.

Without Butler's number, their plan for his surrender was dead in the water. It was time to find another way out—if there was one. Dillinger's thoughts turned to Butler's daughter, Lizzie. He smiled as he recalled her awed expression as she shook his hand. She was a cute kid. And that line about him looking like a movie star was a corker.

Me? A movie star?

Dillinger laughed as he entered the apartment, putting thoughts of his young admirer out of his mind.

※　※　※

Dillinger tried to keep his annoyance in check as he watched Anna and Polly make ready to leave the apartment. While Polly's company was pleasant, she didn't make up for the hole in his life Billie's absence had left behind. She was still languishing in jail because of him, because of who he was, and because of J. Edgar Hoover. That bastard wanted him to feel his wrath in every way possible.

He'd moved into Anna Sage's apartment right after the last job and the money was still holding out, which was fine with Anna, a thieving mercenary if ever there was one. When he'd first arrived, he'd stayed in his room reading the papers and listening to the tinny radio and had food brought in, but that routine had gotten to him quicker than he'd imagined. He realized that tiny room, as comfortable as it was, was no different from being in stir. A ten-foot square box with a single dusty window overlooking a rusty fire escape and an alley strewn with uncollected trash. The hideous, ancient red-and-yellow flocked wallpaper made it seem as if the walls were creeping toward him, making the room feel smaller and smaller with each passing day. And when Anna had introduced him to Polly Hamilton, he was ready to walk out then and there, but the girl's sweet nature won him over. He missed Billie—he missed everything about her—

but he was a healthy man with appetites, and he knew Billie would understand.

Dillinger mopped his forehead with a handkerchief and glanced at the clock. They were going to be late if they didn't hurry up, and he was looking forward to seeing the new Gable picture. He also was looking forward to sitting in the blissfully cool theatre for the length of the two-hour show. The Biograph had installed air conditioning a few months earlier, touting this technological marvel on a big banner hanging from its brightly lit marquee: *Cooled By Refrigeration! Iced Fresh Air!*

Refrigeration.

Like a meat locker . . . or a morgue.

Dillinger sighed. *Put that thought right out of your head, Johnnie.*

If getting out of this oven of an apartment and into a cool theatre made him feel like a cold side of beef for a couple of hours, that was just fine by him.

He watched Anna—the one he called the Bolshevik behind her back because of her Slavic features and thick Romanian accent—as she slipped into a bright orange skirt.

"You really gonna wear that thing?" he asked, wiping the sweat from his forehead again.

She scowled with annoyance. "Why? What is wrong?"

Dillinger shook his head; it was too hot to argue. "Nothing, it's fine. Tell Polly to hurry up."

Anna shot him a nervous smile and sashayed into the adjoining room where Polly was getting dressed. Truth was he'd noticed Anna had been acting strange for nearly a week, and that made Dillinger nervous. He didn't need the cops raiding her operation only to net him as a bonus. Maybe it was time to bid these two ladies farewell and find some new digs. Maybe it was time to take a powder.

Just then Anna and Polly entered the room, and Dillinger turned and smiled. "You look like a million bucks," he said to Polly, who grinned with innocent pleasure.

They left the apartment a few minutes later, joining the throng crowding the sidewalks on Lincoln Avenue. It was one of the more prosperous Chicago neighborhoods, but the broken sidewalks emitting the stench of sewage, and the vacant storefronts—with their white-washed windows—were harsh reminders of the desperation that had overwhelmed the nation a few short years before.

Dillinger acted cool and casual, putting on the airs of a man without a care in the world, a happy and contented citizen out for a Sunday night stroll. On the inside, he was tuned as tight as a piano string, and when he found himself relaxing too much, the .380 Colt automatic in his right pocket would thump against his thigh to remind him to maintain his vigilance. They reached the Biograph five minutes before show time, and Dillinger bought three tickets and ushered the two women into the theatre.

Inside the lobby, the air was nowhere near as cool as Dillinger had hoped, but it still felt good, and he'd stopped sweating. The auditorium was mostly filled, and Anna took a single seat near the back, while he and Polly found adjacent seats on the aisle near the right side. He was glad of that, as he didn't relish the thought of having to flee a trap, if need be, by having to climb over other patrons. Their seats were situated ten rows back from the screen, and the rear exit lay a few feet beyond that, the crimson light from the exit sign a glowing beacon of reassurance.

Settling back into his seat, Dillinger put his arm around Polly and finally began to relax, allowing the muscles in his neck and back to go slack. Two minutes later the lights dimmed and the show started. The cartoon was a Popeye, which Dillinger enjoyed, and a newsreel followed. He was thankful that it concerned the goings-on in Nazi Germany and there was nothing in it about him. He recalled the time his gang had met in a crowded theatre for cover, only to have a newsreel with audience participation, participation that meant looking at your neighbors to see if one of them was John Dillinger! He thought it funny now, but it took him weeks before he considered going to the movies again.

Finally, the newsreel ended, and *Manhattan Melodrama* began. The story was about two orphans who grow up on opposite sides of the law and fall in love with the same woman. It was classic Hollywood claptrap, but Dillinger found himself engrossed in the drama, especially the character of Blackie Gallagher as played by Clark Gable. And while Gable was good, Dillinger couldn't help imagining himself up there on the screen, saying Blackie's lines and romancing Myrna Loy.

I could do this . . . I could do this better than Gable. And with me they'd get the real McCoy....

Dillinger chuckled at the thought, and Polly nudged him to be quiet. He turned to her. "You want something to eat?"

"Gimme a popcorn," she whispered, her eyes glued to a gigantic close-up of Myrna Loy on the screen.

"Sure thing," he said.

He rose from his seat and made his way toward the lobby, scanning the faces of the other patrons as he strode up the aisle, trying to determine if anyone looked even remotely out of place. No one met his eyes or even looked his way.

Out in the lobby, a few patrons waited in the concession line, including a young, dark-haired girl. She turned to him and smiled, her cute nose wrinkling as she frowned.

"Do I know you?" she asked, tilting her head just so. "Are you someone famous?"

Dillinger chuckled. "Sure, kid."

"Really? Can I have your autograph? I'll treasure it always!"

She held out a leatherette autograph book and a pen. As a lark, Dillinger took the pen and the book. "What's your name, kid?"

"Frances. Frances Gumm. My sisters and I have a Vaudeville act, and tonight's our night off."

"Well, everyone deserves a night off," he said. "Even famous people like us."

Dillinger grinned and wrote in swift slanting strokes: *Knock 'em dead, Frances! John Dillinger.*

He closed the book and handed it back to her, along with the pen. She grinned and said, "Thank you, mister," and ran back into the theatre.

Still grinning, he got his popcorn and made his way back to his seat, handing the buttery treat to Polly just as a feeling of despair stole over him. He sighed then closed his eyes. Why the hell had he signed his real name like that? Why didn't he sign "Jimmy Lawrence," the name he'd been using for the past month? He knew why. The girl was adorably cute, and he couldn't resist giving her a thrill, couldn't resist the flair for the dramatic, the same flair he showed when he vaulted the counters of the banks he robbed, leaping over them like Douglas Fairbanks. Fortunately, the girl had been in a hurry to get back into the auditorium, hadn't even waited to buy herself a snack. She might not look at that autograph for hours yet.

But what if she did?

What if she was looking at it right now and decided to do the civic-minded thing?

Christ, Johnnie, you can be such a dope.

Dillinger forced those thoughts from his mind and watched the film as it moved toward its climax: where Blackie refuses a pardon and goes to the electric chair. It was silly, yet watching Gable's character walk that last mile hit Dillinger squarely in the gut. What, he wondered, would he do in the same situation?

As the lights came up, Dillinger surveyed the auditorium. He didn't see anyone that looked even remotely like a cop. Certainly no one who resembled Melvin Purvis, J. Edgar Hoover's golden boy, whose photo he'd seen in the papers and whom he knew was spearheading the special Bureau of Investigation unit tasked with capturing him.

And while everything looked normal, Dillinger couldn't shake the uneasy feeling that had crept over him during the last third of the movie. Maybe that was it. Maybe the movie was spooking him. He looked again toward the exit doors behind the screen and was about to pull Polly in that direction when he spotted Anna motioning for them to walk up the aisle.

Something's up with that woman.

"Jimmy? Is everything okay?"

Dillinger ignored Polly and stared hard at Anna, who met his gaze with a blank expression.

"Jimmy, let's go!"

Dillinger reluctantly let Polly lead him up the aisle, feeling like a steer walking through the stockyard gauntlet to the slaughter.

Outside, the air was leaden, a steam bath, wrapping its humid arms around him in a suffocating embrace. They turned south on Lincoln, and the two women on either side of him chattered away about the movie. All Dillinger could think was that something was wrong, as if the entire world were tilted at a crazy funhouse angle only he could see. The same feeling he'd had hurrying away from the Rexall Drugstore last week hit him again, the sensation that someone was aiming a gun at the back of his head. They were approaching the alley just past the theatre when the urge to cut and run grew so strong, the muscles in his legs tensed up like they used to do when he was about to steal a base. And then a tiny voice spoke up in his head.

Surrender. Give up right now!

Dillinger stopped walking and raised his arms slowly over his head. The two women, who'd kept walking for a couple of steps, stopped and stared at him as if he were nuts, and then their attention was diverted by something behind him. He grinned and slowly turned around.

"I give up, boys!" he said, loud and clear over the clamor of the streets. "I surrender!"

In front of him stood three Bureau of Investigation agents with their pistols drawn. To a man, they looked as if they'd seen a ghost.

One of the agents, a short, stocky man with a round face and beady eyes, raised his .45 automatic, taking aim.

"Agent Hurt! Stand down!"

The command came from a man walking up behind the agents. He bulled his way through the growing crowd and physically grabbed Agent Hurt's arm, forcing him to lower the pistol.

Hurt glared at him. "Sir, those aren't our orders."

"He's surrendered, Clarence, and I'm telling you to stand down. Those are *my* orders."

Hurt holstered his weapon and walked away, while the other agent stepped closer to Dillinger. Dillinger smiled, recognizing him from his newspaper photos: Special Agent in Charge Melvin Purvis.

"Good evening, Melvin. Hot enough for you?"

Purvis looked amused then turned to one of the two agents nearest him. "Hollis, search and cuff him."

The one he'd called Hollis patted Dillinger down and found the Colt, which he handed to Purvis. He then locked Dillinger in handcuffs. By now the crowd had grown into an unruly mob, everyone yelling and jostling to get a better look.

With a nod from Purvis, Hollis and the other agent each took one of Dillinger's arms and followed their chief as he plowed a path through the surging crowd to the curb, where a black Ford V-8 now waited, its engine rumbling. They pushed him inside and Hollis followed, sitting next to Dillinger. The other agent ran around to get in on the other side. As Hollis reached to close the car door, Dillinger caught sight of the young girl with the autograph book. She stood motionless amid the raging crowd, staring at him with saucer eyes, the autograph book clutched in her delicate hands. He laughed and blew her a kiss, the chain between the handcuffs jingling.

"See ya in the movies, kid."

A moment later, the Ford roared off into the dark and sultry night.

3

The verdict was in.

At least that's what one of his guards had told him half an hour before. He'd used the time to change out of his jail overalls and back into his suit. Once he was dressed, all there was to do was wait. He ran a hand over his beard stubble, wishing he could shave, but they wouldn't let him have a razor, and the barber they brought in twice a week wasn't due until tomorrow.

Probably won't be here, anyway.

He turned and studied one of the guards, a stoic Indiana farm boy in a rumpled uniform, holding a freshly oiled Thompson submachine gun, his carrot-colored hair shaved to the scalp underneath his peaked cap.

"Hey, Mac, what's the holdup?"

"That's Officer Murphy to you, bub."

Dillinger swallowed his annoyance. "Sorry. What's the holdup, *Officer* Murphy?"

If the guard was irritated by Dillinger's sarcasm, he didn't show it. More than likely, he hadn't even picked up on it.

"The judge is finishing his lunch," the guard said, not even looking at Dillinger.

Dillinger sighed and shook his head. It figured. The judge was a bit of a prissy pants, a stickler for protocol and the like. Well, he'd waited this long. He could wait a little longer. He'd done his best through the trial and he had to admit his lawyer had presented the case as well as any man could. You just could never know for sure what the twelve men on that jury were going to do. They might set him free, though he doubted that, or they might give him the chair if they hung the murder rap on him. It didn't matter that he hadn't shot that bank guard. All that needed to happen was for the jury to *believe* he did. At this point, he'd be relieved if it were just some jail time.

Two minutes later, a new contingent of guards entered the basement room where they'd constructed his private cell. All were armed with Thompsons, save for the potato-faced sergeant who approached the cell, a pair of handcuffs jingling in his pudgy hand.

"Time to go, Johnnie," he said. "You know the drill. Stand up and put your arms through the bars."

Dillinger complied, as he'd done all throughout the trial. The sergeant cuffed his hands and then opened the door. Dillinger stepped out and was immediately surrounded by the guards. He felt a swirl of butterflies in his guts and did his best to put on his trademark bravado.

"Okay, boys," he said. "It's showtime."

※　※　※

Melvin Purvis stood in the back of the packed courtroom, watching the twelve-man jury file in, trying to read their faces, trying to see if any of them had that look he'd seen before, the look that spelled acquittal, an outcome J. Edgar Hoover dreaded. The courtroom was deadly silent, not even a cough or a sneeze from the hundreds of spectators and press alike, as if every soul in that room were holding their breath. A brace of newsreel cameras on tripods stood to Purvis's left, the cameras silent and the studio lights darkened. The judge, a conservative man by nature, had nevertheless allowed cameras to record the verdict, recognizing the historic importance of the moment. It also didn't hurt that he was running for reelection in November.

Dillinger sat slouched in his chair, dressed in a white shirt and gray vest and pants set off with a red tie, looking for all the world like a man enjoying a quiet day in the park. His defense attorney, Sam Leibowitz, sat up straight, his white hair gleaming, staring at the jury as if he too were trying to divine their intentions. They would all know soon enough.

The night Dillinger had surrendered, Hoover gave Purvis a thorough dressing-down, berating him as if he were child. The long and short of it—he was being reassigned to the Washington office to chase tax evaders. It was all Purvis could do to hold his temper. This was his punishment, his penance for not killing Dillinger.

"When would you like me to report, sir?" Purvis asked when Hoover fell silent.

"Not until after Dillinger's trial. I want you there as my eyes and ears, Special Agent Purvis."

And so he'd remained in Chicago these last few months, awaiting the start of the trial. In the office, Sam Cowley had taken over as Special Agent in Charge, an action that left Purvis with exactly nothing to do. It was a bitter pill to swallow, as was the prospect of permanent reassignment to Washington, DC, a city he loathed. Sighing, he thrust those morbid thoughts from his mind and glanced over at the phalanx of reporters, recognizing one of them.

While most of the press rotated from day to day, Robert Butler of the *Indianapolis Herald* remained a constant presence. It had been that way from day one. And Purvis had to admit, from what he'd read, the man was a hell of a writer. Intrigued, Purvis had conducted an unofficial investigation and learned Butler had met with Dillinger prior to his capture at the Biograph and had tried to facilitate his surrender at a local police station. What would have happened, Purvis wondered, if Butler had succeeded? And then he knew. Hoover would have thrown a tantrum, and his career would still be in the toilet.

As for Dillinger, because of his spectacular and unprecedented escape from Crown Point Jail the previous March, it was decided that he would be held in a special cell contained within the Superior Court Building in downtown Indianapolis. A special construction crew had worked around the clock to fabricate a cell that looked— some said intentionally—like a cage in a zoo.

Situated in the basement and centered in an otherwise empty twenty-by-twenty-foot room, the ten-by-ten-by-eight-foot cell was built upon a raised reinforced concrete slab and consisted of four walls of steel bars and a ceiling of riveted steel sheets, all welded together on the spot to form an impregnable enclosure. Dillinger could be watched from all sides, even while he used the small toilet bolted to the floor in one corner. The only other furnishings were a cot that was welded to one of the walls, on which rested a thin mattress, blanket, and pillow.

Rotating shifts of guards with Thompson submachine guns sat watching him twenty-four hours a day, and his food was slipped through a slot at the bottom of the door. Utensils were collected and counted after meals.

The most amazing aspect of all this was that Dillinger had surrendered on a Sunday and by the day of his arraignment on Friday, July 27th—five days later—the customized cell was ready to receive him. Purvis was there for the arraignment, which consisted of Dillinger pleading not guilty to murder and bank robbery and Sam Leibowitz filing several motions the judge immediately denied. Trial date was set for October 2nd at nine o'clock a.m.

The trial itself had lasted four weeks, with the prosecutor bringing in witness after witness and Sam Leibowitz adroitly discrediting them one by one. On October 30th, the trial had concluded with two impassioned summations by two skilled attorneys, and the jury had retired.

Now, after deliberating for eighteen hours, they were back.

Purvis watched as the jury took their seats. Every one of them turned and stared at the judge, who seemed to be preoccupied with a document lying on his desk, but Purvis knew this was simply part of the man's theatrics. This was his big moment, and he was going to make the most of it. After another long and agonizing pause, the judge looked up and cleared his throat. "Gentlemen of the press, you may start your cameras—quietly," he said.

As if someone had thrown a master switch, all the studio style lighting snapped on, and Purvis heard a gasp from the spectators. It was as if a small sun had ignited in the room, and Purvis could feel the temperature inching upward. Soundmen repositioned their microphone booms and the cameras began to turn, filling the silence with the soft whir of clockwork machinery.

The judge looked at Dillinger. "The defendant will rise."

Both Dillinger and his attorney rose to their feet and looked toward the jury.

The judge said, "Gentlemen of the jury, have you reached a verdict?"

The jury foreman, gaunt and stringy like the farmer in Grant Wood's *American Gothic*, stood up.

"We have, Your Honor."

The judge nodded to the bailiff, who took the folded paper and handed it to the judge, who opened and read it with an expression as rigid as that of a cigar store Indian. He handed the paper back to the bailiff, who returned it to the jury foreman.

"Mr. Foreman, please read the verdict," the judge said.

The foreman's hands shook as he unfolded the paper, the rattle sounding like the rumblings of a distant storm. "In the count of the indictment of robbery in the first degree, we the jury find the defendant . . . guilty."

Several spectators gasped but silenced themselves instantly when the judge glared at them.

The foreman looked even more nervous now, as his bloodshot eyes scanned the crowd then returned to the wrinkled paper in his hands. "In t-the count of the indictment for murder in the first degree, we the jury find the defendant . . . not guilty."

The courtroom exploded.

Dillinger turned to Sam Leibowitz and grasped his hand in a warm handshake as reporters shouted questions and spectators gabbled excitedly to each other. The judge, stunned into momentary immobility, slammed his gavel against its sounding block.

BANG! BANG!

"There will be order!" he shouted as he continued banging away with his gavel.

Moments later, the courtroom finally grew quiet.

The cameras continued to turn.

"Any more outbursts like that and I will clear the courtroom," he said, his voice booming. "The press included."

"Your Honor?" All eyes turned to Sam Leibowitz, who had remained standing. "If it pleases the court, I would like to move for immediate sentencing."

The judge glowered at the attorney, as if this was the last thing he'd expected to hear, yet Purvis noticed an undercurrent of impatience in the judge's expression. *Perhaps he's had enough of history for one day*, Purvis thought.

"Motion granted," the judge said. "Defendant will rise."

Dillinger rose to his feet, a look of relief on his face.

"It is the sentence of this court that you be remanded to the Indiana State Prison in Michigan City for a period of ten years of solitary confinement."

Dillinger gaped at the judge, and the courtroom buzzed.

"Silence!" the judge yelled, banging his gavel.

"Your Honor," Leibowitz said, "while we appreciate your leniency with regard to the length of his sentence, solitary confinement is simply barbaric—"

"Counselor, your client has committed serious crimes against this state, not the least of which was aiding and abetting an escape from the very institution where I'm sending him."

"Your Honor, there has been no evidence submitted in this trial to support that allegation."

The judge pointed his gavel at Leibowitz. "That may be so, Counselor, but nevertheless it is my sentence that he have no contact with any of the general population of the aforementioned institution, and therefore no chance to formulate and facilitate another escape."

"But Your Honor, there's no precedence for this."

"And there's no precedence for Mr. Dillinger, either," the judge said, eliciting laughter from the spectators and a grin from Dillinger.

"Your Honor, I must protest this."

The judge shot Leibowitz a merciless grin. "Why, Counselor? You asked for this."

"Not for this, Your Honor. This is a mockery."

"Would you care to see him serve fifteen to twenty?"

Leibowitz was about to speak when Dillinger put a hand on his shoulder, leaned over, and whispered something. Leibowitz appeared to deflate, and then gave his client a vigorous nod. "Your Honor, my client says that he will accept his sentence and that he very much respects your fairness and impartiality throughout these proceedings."

The judge turned to Dillinger, his eyebrows raised in a questioning look. "Is this true, Mr. Dillinger? Do you accept the court's determination?"

Dillinger nodded. "Yes, Your Honor, I do, and I hope this'll be the last time I'll ever have to say that."

Purvis had to admit the judge appeared impressed by Dillinger's forthright attitude.

"Very well then, Mr. Dillinger. I appreciate your candor, and hope this occasion marks the end of your criminal career."

The judge banged the gavel and so ended the most famous trial in Indiana history.

Purvis watched as the bailiffs cuffed Dillinger and took him away, and then he returned to the field office.

Later that night while lying in bed, smoking his last cigarette of the day, with his wife, Rosanne, sound asleep beside him, Purvis kept replaying the moment the bailiffs led Dillinger away. The outlaw had turned and caught Purvis's eye with a smile and a wink. At the time, he'd chuckled to himself, thinking, *Still the same old Dillinger!*

Now, as he watched the headlights from a lone car sweep across his bedroom ceiling, he began to worry Dillinger might be planning something, something that would render pointless all of Purvis's efforts to put him behind bars. If John Dillinger did escape, there would be no second chances, no more reprieves. He would be dead.

Whatever you're planning, Johnnie, I hope you'll think twice.

Purvis stubbed out his cigarette, rolled over, and let sleep steal over him, having had no inkling that Dillinger's plans went far beyond anything he could have ever imagined.

CAMERA!

4

John Dillinger finished the last sentence of Dickens's *A Tale of Two Cities*, closed the book, and placed it on the shelf containing his growing collection. This one had taken some time to get his mind around, and the ending bothered him. That a man would willingly go to his execution in place of another man left him scratching his head. He wasn't sure if Sydney Carton was a fool or the noblest man who ever lived. It reminded him of Gable in *Manhattan Melodrama*.

"You need to stop sending me books like this, Mr. Butler," he said out loud. He was only half kidding. When the books had started arriving from the reporter a couple of weeks after he'd begun his sentence, he'd turned up his nose, thinking that reading books was for sissies. Then the boredom got to him, a lot faster than he'd expected. And that's when he realized he was more of a social person than he would have thought, a man who thrived on interaction with his fellow humans. Take that away, and he'd start to go mad. And one could only sit in a cell thinking about one's mistakes for so long. *What the hell*, he thought, *it'll pass the time.*

The first book he'd cracked was a collection of Edgar Allan Poe's poems and short stories. It was hard reading at first, with so many words he didn't know, but Bob had also thought to send along a dictionary, and that was a godsend. Every time he came to a two-dollar word he'd look it up, fascinated to learn that it meant something completely different from what he'd initially thought. After a while he needed to consult the dictionary less and less, the new words becoming second nature. He even found himself just looking through the dictionary when he was between books, content to learn new words for the fun of it. He soon realized these words were more than just fancier versions of other words; their placement in the pages he read created sounds and rhythms all their own. That rhythm was evident in Poe's stories, but in his poetry it bloomed and flowered in a way Dillinger would never have noticed in the past—or cared to notice. He loved the eerie cadence of "Annabelle Lee," and Dillinger thought "The Raven" the scariest thing he'd ever read.

Next came a five-volume set of Dickens, an author whom Dillinger found the most entertaining, his characters sly, vivid, and unforgettable. Now that he'd finished the latest one, he sat back on his bunk, letting the images of the story run through his mind. Doing this helped him relax. It also allowed him to segue into the latest version of his plan. The judge had been right to keep him away from the rest of the prison population. He would have been scheming and planning with the boys from the outset, until he figured out how to bust out.

But solitary had taught him a few things about himself—that escapes were short-term thinking—that getting oneself out for a short exhilarating period and then being hauled back to the slammer and cold, hard reality wasn't worth the attendant risks.

There had to be a better way. And he now believed he'd found it.

What Dillinger had been thinking about for the past few weeks was something completely different, a way to show the screws and everybody else that John Dillinger had learned his lesson—that he'd changed for the better.

When the idea had first occurred to him, he'd thought it was so far out in left field he'd laughed out loud, but he couldn't seem to shake it. And the more he thought about it, the more he realized it might make for the greatest escape of all.

A sound at the door drew Dillinger's attention. He didn't have a watch, but the grumblings of his stomach told him it was time for lunch. A moment later the food slot opened, and Dillinger saw it was the captain of the guards. He shot off his bunk and approached the door with a friendly grin. "Hey, Cappy, you're back! How was Daytona?"

The guard, an older man with white hair, leathery skin, and gin blossoms on his bulbous nose, gave Dillinger a toothy grin. "A hell of a lot warmer than this hellhole," he said, chuckling. "The fishin' was pretty good too."

"I'll bet," Dillinger said, taking the tray. He stopped when he saw there was extra food. He turned back to the guard. "What's this for, Cap?"

The older man shrugged. "Just thought you'd appreciate it. That tip you gave me on the ponies really paid off."

Dillinger grinned. Captain Hauser was a good egg, which was a rare thing when it came to the screws. "Glad I could be of help."

Cappy nodded and reached up to close the slot. "Anything you need, John, just let me know."

Dillinger knew this was the time to act. "Hey, Cap?"

The guard slid the slot back, his bushy eyebrows shooting upward. "Yeah?"

Dillinger put the tray down on his bunk and leaned against the door, his voice growing quiet. "I have something I'd like to talk to Warden Cushing about. Any chance you can set that up for me?"

Cappy looked dubious. "I . . . don't know, John. He's a pretty hard-boiled egg . . ."

Dillinger nodded. "I know, but if you'd just mention that I'd like a word with him, I'd really appreciate it. And I'll make it worth your while."

"Oh, yeah, how's that?"

"Just get me the form and I'll eyeball the races for you."

Cappy turned to check his surroundings then nodded. "Okay, John, I'll put in a word, but I can't promise anything."

"Neither can I."

"Well, you called 'em right the last time," he said with a wink. "So I think maybe you're my lucky charm. See you."

The slot slammed closed, and Dillinger returned to his bunk and the food.

Later that afternoon, there was a knock at the door and the rattle of keys.

As required by the rules, Dillinger stood to the side of his bunk at attention as the door swung inward. Captain Hauser entered with two other guards. "Warden wants to see you, Dillinger," he said in a voice that was all business, but there was a twinkle in the older man's eyes, and Dillinger relaxed. Cappy had come through.

Dillinger allowed them to handcuff and escort him out of his cell. From there they walked down the hall toward the door that led from the Isolation Unit to General Population. They stopped at the door and the turnkey threw the lever, and Dillinger heard the familiar hum of the motor as the heavy steel door slid open on its track. They stepped through and there was an immediate increase of noise, the sound of hundreds of yammering voices. He'd forgotten how noisy a prison could be. All alone in his little cell, it was eerily quiet. They headed down the main hall and Dillinger began hearing other prisoners calling out his name. Some were catcalls, but many were cheers and good wishes.

They reached the administration wing two minutes later, where they passed through another lever-activated door and into what looked like a floor in any office building in America: shiny linoleum floors, mahogany wainscoting, and plaster walls painted in what some decorator would call "eggshell." The warden's office lay straight ahead at the end of the hall.

When they reached the warden's door, Cappy knocked.

"Come in," a feminine voice intoned.

Inside, Dillinger saw a blonde-haired secretary seated at a modest desk with a typewriter, a phone, and little else. She looked up, and Dillinger thought he saw a flash of an admiring glance. Cappy smiled at the girl.

"Prisoner John Dillinger to see the warden."

The girl smiled back.

"You may go in, Captain."

Cappy turned to the other guards and said, "You boys go get some coffee and be back here in fifteen minutes."

"Right, Captain," one of them said, and they both left the room. Cappy waved Dillinger forward and the two of them entered the warden's inner sanctum.

Warden Cushing, a middle-aged man of slight build, reminded Dillinger of Calvin Coolidge. He had the same earnest expression and pomaded hair. The office reflected a Spartan air, the only decorations being a photo of his wife and daughter. Dillinger noted the warden's daughter was a looker.

"Please sit down, Dillinger," the warden said in a soft voice. "Captain Hauser said you wanted to see me."

Dillinger took a seat in a leather-covered chair that hissed under his weight. "That's right, sir."

"Is there a problem?"

"No, sir, no problem," Dillinger said with a friendly grin. "Just an idea."

"Really." The warden had said it in a way that made it sound as if this was the last thing he would ever have imagined.

"I know you expect inmates to complain, sir, but I think you run a square joint, Warden."

The man looked both pleased and wary at the same time. "Well, I appreciate that. So, what is your . . . idea?"

Dillinger sat up and leaned forward, prompting the warden to do the same. Dillinger smiled inwardly, knowing this was a good sign.

"When the judge sentenced me, I told him I wanted this to be the last time . . ."

Warren Cushing nodded. "I remember reading that."

"Well, I meant it, but I've also had some time to think, and I want to do something more than just sit in my cell. I want to do something good, something that'll count . . ."

Dillinger could tell he'd piqued the man's interest.

Now for the pitch.

"What I want to do is appear in a newsreel, a movie that'll be me talkin' to the kids of America. I'll tell them I was a sap for what I did and that they should listen to their parents and do what's right, so they don't end up like me."

Warden Cushing exhaled a rush of breath and sat back in his chair, looking as if someone had pulled the rug out from under him. "You want to be in a film?"

"That's right. Something they'll show in all the theatres across the country, especially on Saturdays and Sundays when the kids are in the audience. I've done a lot of bad things, Warden. Maybe this'll start to make up for it."

The warden steepled his hands and fell silent, and Dillinger willed his pulse to slow down. He didn't want to appear desperate.

The older man withdrew a cigarette from a humidor on his desk and lit it, not bothering to offer one to Dillinger. He appeared unconvinced and Dillinger knew it, so he played his last card.

Lay it on thick if you're gonna lay it on at all!

"The way I figure, they'll start by showing your prison, the only joint that can be trusted to hold Public Enemy Number One. They'll mention you by name." Dillinger grinned, adding "*If they're smart.*"

The warden sat back, and Dillinger saw the wheels turning in his head. "Something of this nature is unprecedented, and I'm not sure I can make this kind of decision unilaterally."

Hooked him like a trout!

"And, obviously," the warden added, "there would be costs involved. I will have to consult the Bureau of Prisons and seek their permission."

"So you'll consider it?" Dillinger asked, keeping his voice steady.

The warden nodded. "I think it's an admirable idea, and I'll give it my recommendation, though I don't know if that will help with my superiors."

Dillinger smiled. "That's all I can ask, Warden. And thank you."

Ten minutes later, Cappy led Dillinger back into his cell and removed the handcuffs. "A movie, John?"

"Sure, Cap, and I want you in it with me."

The guard blushed. "Me? I ain't no actor."

Dillinger laughed. "I don't want an actor, I want the toughest guard I know, and you're the man."

Cappy grinned. "Well, I guess I could. Somebody's gotta keep an eye on you, after all. Might be fun."

"Let's just hope the warden can swing it."

After Cappy locked the cell door and left, Dillinger lay down on his bunk and picked up his new book, *The Prince* by Machiavelli.

Now he had to be patient and wait for things to go through their proper channels. It was frustrating, as Dillinger had never been a patient man, but he had a feeling his idea was going to find acceptance in all the places that counted.

Things were looking up.

5

The letters had been sitting on his desk for a week now, and J. Edgar Hoover still didn't know what to make of them. One was from Warden Cushing of Michigan City State Prison to Superintendent Radford Hurley at the Indiana Bureau of Prisons, the other letter from Hurley to him, dated a week after Cushing's. From the gushing quality of the man's prose, it was obvious Hurley was trying to curry favor, but since Hoover had no authority over any prison, it made him wonder why. Once a criminal was captured, prosecuted, and imprisoned, his job was done.

Hurley seemed to feel otherwise, his letter ending with, "although this is outside your bailiwick, I thought you should know . . ."

Dillinger had made a request to make a short public service film, and while the idea of it appealed to Hoover—he could think of no other public enemy he'd like to humiliate in front of a camera more than Dillinger—the fact that the outlaw had thought of it and made the request is what rankled him.

It should have been my idea!

Still, there might be a way to capitalize on this. Again, it was

Hurley's decision, and the cost for this would come out of his budget, but it was obvious to Hoover that Hurley wanted his approval and his involvement—was begging for it, in fact—without outright stating it.

Hoover reached for his intercom. "Miss Gandy?"

"Yes, Mr. Hoover?"

"Put in a call to Radford Hurley at the Indiana Bureau of Prisons, and then I want you to call Special Agent Purvis and place him on hold. I'll want to speak with him right afterward."

"Yes, sir."

Hoover only had a moment to formulate his thoughts before the phone rang. He snatched it up. "Hello, Radford, how are you?"

"Very well, Mr. Hoover, very well. I'm quite frankly surprised to hear from you."

Hoover rolled his eyes. The man had fawned all over him at a party when he'd been in Washington last year. Had gone on and on about how the Bureau of Investigation had done such a great job capturing Dillinger . . . blah, blah, blah. Hoover wallowed in the adulation but had to admit the man's incessant platitudes had worn thin well before dinner was served.

"You wrote me a letter, Radford," Hoover said.

The man sighed. "Of course, I just didn't expect a phone call."

"What are you going to do about Dillinger's request?"

The man sighed again, deeper this time. "I'm not sure, Mr. Hoover. It's very unusual."

"So is Dillinger."

"Well, you're right about that. What I mean is I don't know how to go about it, or even if I should, which is why I sought your advice."

Hoover glowed. "I appreciate that, Radford. But what's your gut telling you?"

"That we should turn him down."

Hoover cracked a cobra grin. This was the opening he was waiting for.

"Radford, I would consider it a personal favor to me if you would grant his request."

"Y-You do?"

"I do, indeed. Dillinger is a symbol, a rallying point for members of the criminal element. Putting him up there on the screen like a rat in a cage will drive another nail into their coffins, and you and I will be standing together at the vanguard."

"Mr. Hoover, I had no idea—"

Of course you didn't, you cretin!

"Will you do me that favor, Superintendent Hurley?"

"I'd love to, Mr. Hoover, but my budget . . . I don't think we have the money for it."

"You let me worry about that."

Hoover heard the man's intake of breath. "Are you sure . . . ?"

"Absolutely. And I'm going to send someone to help you set that up."

"That would be great, Mr. Hoover—thank you."

Hurley became effusive and Hoover cut the call short as quickly as he could, then hit the intercom button.

"Is Special Agent Purvis on the line, Miss Gandy?"

"Yes, Mr. Hoover, I'll put him right through."

The phone rang as he was reaching for it.

"Special Agent Purvis?"

"Yes, sir, I'm here," came the reply with its deep Southern lilt.

"I have a job for you, one for which I think you're ably suited."

Over the next few minutes, he brought Purvis up to speed. When he finished, there was silence on the line.

"Are you there, Agent Purvis?"

"Yes . . . sir, I'm here. I'm just trying to understand. Dillinger actually *requested* this?"

"Yes, and I think we can turn this to the Bureau's advantage."

"I know nothing about making movies."

"Leave that to me. I have some contacts at Warner Brothers. Just get to Michigan City as soon as possible and I'll keep you apprised."

"Yes, sir."

They hung up a moment later and Hoover clapped his hands together, feeling euphoric.

"Miss Gandy?" he said, hitting the intercom button again. "Please put in a call to Jack Warner."

"Mr. Hoover, it's six a.m. in Los Angeles."

"Right." He glanced at his watch to confirm it. "He'll be there in an hour. Call him then."

6

Michigan City State Prison
Common Room 5
January 28, 1935

Melvin Purvis sat smoking his fifth cigarette of the morning as he watched Dillinger interact with the film crew. True to his word, Hoover had called in a favor and Warner Brothers had sent out a small crew consisting of a cameraman and his assistant, a soundman and boom operator, two lighting technicians, and a make-up man. There'd been a director, too, but Dillinger had sent the man packing.

"Listen, pal," Dillinger had said, poking the little man's chest with his finger. "This here's my picture and we're doing it my way."

"But you have no idea what you're doing!" the director said.

Dillinger had just stared at the man, who finally threw up his hands and stalked out of the room, saying how Jack Warner would hear about this, Hoover or no Hoover.

Purvis had marveled at the director's monumental ego, though in truth he'd been embarrassed by the tantrum.

All this was forgotten while he watched Dillinger directing the crew. To the lighting men he said, "Guys, I want this room to look like the hellhole it is. Lots of shadows. Chiaroscuro, you got me? And put some shadows of bars on the wall behind me."

The lighting men's eyebrows had risen at that, as had Purvis's.

Chiaroscuro?

From where on earth had he gotten that?

As the lighting technicians went about their work, Dillinger approached the cameraman and his assistant, who were placing the Mitchell camera onto a heavy wooden tripod. To Purvis, the young men looked as if they were fresh out of college, but looks could be deceiving that way.

Dillinger put his arm around the cameraman, whose expression was a mixture of fear and amazement. "Kid, when we're ready to go, I want you to start all the way back near the door when they bring me in and sit me down in that chair." He pointed to a lone hard-backed chair sitting in the middle of the room. "Once I'm sitting down, you start moving the camera in on me until you get halfway then stop. You'll be at that point for a little while, then, when I raise my hands to show the cuffs—that's when you start moving again, real slow, until a little before I finish talking my whole head is filling the picture."

The cameraman looked nonplused.

"Uhh, Mr. Dillinger, I'm sorry, but we don't have a dolly. W-We didn't bring one."

"You don't have a—" He stopped speaking and appeared to be considering his options. "That's okay, kid. Hang on for a minute," he said, patting the cameraman on the back. He then turned, as if he were looking for someone. "Hey, Cappy?"

Purvis watched as an older man, one of the half-dozen guards in the room, loped over to Dillinger. "Yeah, John?"

"You think we could fit that camera on one of those hand trucks from the loading dock?"

Cappy squinted at the camera, turning his head first one way then the other. "Hmm . . . Maybe . . ."

"Okay, would you do me a favor and send one of your boys to get one?"

"Sure thing."

Ten minutes later, one of the other guards returned, pushing a four-wheeled hand truck consisting of a hardwood platform mounted on four small rubber tires with a U-shaped railing to push it. What was more surprising is that after a moment of uncertainty, and a switch to a shorter tripod, the camera fit perfectly. Moments after that, the assistant was pushing the cameraman and his camera fluidly back and forth, rehearsing their move.

Dillinger took his seat in the chair while the lighting technicians made final adjustments. To Purvis's amazement the view now resembled a scene out of a Hollywood gangster film, all stark shadows and bright highlights. The shadow of bars slanting across the wall behind the chair was chilling.

Dillinger sat down on the hard-backed chair and studied the script he'd written himself earlier that week, while the makeup man went about his business. Instead of making Dillinger look better, Purvis realized the former outlaw had instructed the man to give him a haggard, unkempt look, which combined with his two-day's growth of a beard made him look as if he hadn't had a good night's sleep in weeks. The wrinkled black-and-white striped shirt and trousers he wore underscored the effect.

Twenty minutes later, the camera was loaded, the soundman had adjusted the microphone level, and they were ready.

Dillinger stood up while the guard he'd called Cap placed him in leg irons and handcuffs. When they were done, he handed his script to the older man, who escorted him to his starting point behind the camera near the door leading into the room. Everyone's eyes followed Dillinger as he shuffled, the leg irons clanking, amazed at the transformation.

"Okay, boys, I know we want to get this done as quickly as possible. So, we're gonna film the rehearsal. That way, if we get it right off the bat we can all go home . . . or at least you guys can."

Everyone laughed, including Purvis.

"All right, boys," Dillinger said. "Roll camera!"

Purvis was riveted to his seat. His throat had gone dry, and the burning cigarette in his left hand was momentarily forgotten as he watched Dillinger go through his moves and say his piece. He hadn't known what to expect when Hoover had assigned him this duty, thinking it was all a waste of time—more punishment for his failure to kill Dillinger when he had the chance.

Now he held a different opinion, and the thought of it brought a mirthless smile to his face.

John Dillinger in front of a camera was as deadly as a Thompson submachine gun, and J. Edgar Hoover had just made the biggest mistake of his life.

7

Jack Warner watched the other executives file into the crowded screening room, the buzz as thick as the clouds of cigar smoke swirling in the air above the red velvet-covered seats. They'd had to turn people away, as the room only held thirty-five. The only notable absence was J. Edgar Hoover, having begged off the invitation due to an issue of extreme urgency.

Baloney. The extreme urgency was the old poof was shacking up for the weekend and couldn't be bothered.

And that was just as well, as the thought of the FBI director gave him indigestion. Even now, Warner felt the burning sensation in his gut ratchet up a notch, and he wished he'd taken another dose of milk of magnesia before leaving his office suite.

Hoover—that man was a bastard and *meshugga*, to boot. He didn't trust him, but he knew a good idea when he heard it, and Hoover's was a dilly. Imagine, putting John Dillinger on the screen saying he was sorry for all he'd done. "The Jackrabbit" had stayed at large for over a year, had thumbed his nose at the authorities and then surrendered with a grin on his face. Millions followed the ensuing trial in the papers and the newsreels, and the public never seemed to tire of the man. And so it seemed today. Warner allowed himself a tiny self-satisfied grin as he contemplated the possibilities. If the anticipation for this little film was anything like the commotion he was witnessing right here in his private screening room, then the public would flock to every Warner theatre just to see Dillinger, making even more money for all their current releases—even the turkeys.

Of course, the downside would be if Dillinger came off like a wooden Indian, but he'd seen newsreel footage of the outlaw, and the man appeared confident and at ease in front of those cameras.

We'll know soon enough.

"Mr. Warner?"

He turned toward the voice behind him and saw the young projectionist. "Yes, Grady?"

"We're ready when you are."

"Wait another couple of minutes and then flash the lights."

Grady nodded and brushed a lock of oily brown hair out of his eyes. "Yes, sir. Will do."

The kid disappeared back into the projection booth, and Warner sat back and thought about lighting up a cigar but decided to forgo it. His stomach was already doing flip-flops, and he didn't need to tempt fate.

He saw his brothers Harry and Albert enter together and head up the aisle, taking the seats adjacent to his.

"We miss anything?" Albert asked with a chuckle.

"Just the boat," Jack said.

Harry patted his younger brother on the shoulder as he took his seat. "Do us a favor and leave the quips to the comedians, Jack."

Warner was about to offer a juicy rejoinder when the house

lights flashed and the atmosphere in the room turned electric, as the normally jaded executives and their secretaries rushed to take their seats, laughing and shouting at one another. He spotted his own secretary down toward the front and briefly wondered who was covering his office, but he pushed that thought from his mind as the lights dimmed and the projector started. The room grew silent, as if someone had thrown a switch.

At first, there was only darkness on the screen, and then he heard sounds of jingling chains. A moment later the screen faded up on a nearly empty room, except for a lone hard-backed chair sitting in a pool of light, the shadows of jail bars on the wall behind it. The sound of chains grew louder, and just then a man dressed in stripes, accompanied by a lone guard, walked into the frame, his movements a shuffling gait because of the leg irons he wore. The sound of those chains grew louder as the man walked farther into the room. When they reached the chair, the guard pushed the man into the chair then moved out of frame.

The camera started to dolly in, slowly creeping up on the man as if it were a lioness stalking its prey. The man sat with his head bowed, as if in weariness or prayer, Warner couldn't tell which. He realized the sound of chains had ceased when the man had sat down, but now he could hear the clanging of doors and the angry shouts and terror-filled screams of men in captivity, sounding as if they were coming in through the walls of the screening room itself. It was unsettling.

And then, without warning, the man raised his head, sitting up and leaning back, his careworn face speaking volumes of sorrow and pain. It was John Dillinger, and Warner's heartburn was now completely forgotten.

"Kids, you may not know my face, but I'm sure you've heard

my name. I'm John Dillinger. And I asked to be here today 'cause I thought we should have a talk. You see, I was once like you. I had a mom and dad who loved me and wanted all the best for me, but I was full of moxie, and thought I knew what made the world tick."

Dillinger leaned forward, a world-weary smile on his face. "You know what I mean, don't you? Your mom and dad tell you to do this and do that and all you want to do is tell them where to get off, right? Well, let me tell you, boys and girls, I didn't know *anything*. I was just an ornery kid who wanted to grab life by the scruff and shake it for all it was worth.

"First thing I ever did was steal a car for a little joyride. Got away with it, too, which maybe was the worst thing, 'cause it made me hungry for more. So I upped the ante and robbed a decent man of his hard-earned money just because he had it and I didn't. I didn't get away with it this time, and I went to prison for ten years.

"You think that's nothing at your age, but ten years in a hole like this is a lifetime." Dillinger held up his handcuffed hands and shook the chain, jingling it, and the camera resumed its slow creep toward the outlaw. "These are the only reality in here," he said, lowering his hands. "In this place they tell you what to do, where to go, what to eat, when to sleep, and what to think. And, mostly, you think about what you did—every day—you think about it over and over again, and you come to wish you'd never done it and that things had gone different.

"But in here you also learn things you never learn anywhere else. You learn that when you get out, there's no forgiving and no forgetting. You're marked, and no one will give you an even break—ever. And that's when it all starts again. You think to yourself, 'The hell with them. I'll show those sons of guns, I'll get 'em back—every one of 'em—take them for all their worth.' But all you'll be doing is digging your own grave. And someday, maybe sooner than you think, you'll end up rotting in that hole and it'll all be for nothing!"

Dillinger's entire head filled the frame now, and Warner stole a glance at the rest of the audience. Both Harry and Albert were staring, slack-jawed, and everyone in the room leaned forward on the edges of their seats.

"This doesn't have to be in your future, kids. You don't have to go and do what I did. Your parents love you and want the best for you. Listen to them and do your best in school, 'cause that's where you'll learn the things that *really* count in this world.

"And one more thing. Think you're tough? Gonna be a big shot? You'll probably end up in a cell here, right next to me. But don't you ever speak to me, tough guy, not so much as a howdy-do, 'cause I'll spit in your eye for being so dumb. You've been warned."

Then a loud electrical hum was heard on the soundtrack and the lights in the room dimmed. A moment later the sound died down and the lights came up, then it happened again.

Dillinger looked up.

"That," he said, "is another story."

Dillinger's shadow-rimmed eyes blazed, and then the screen went black.

The lights came up and Jack let out the breath he'd been holding.

Nobody was talking. Silence hung in the air like the curtain of cigar smoke above their heads. And then . . .

"Holy crap!"

. . . the room exploded into excited chatter.

Jack turned to look at his brothers, whose expressions mirrored his own. "My office. Ten minutes."

❋   ❋   ❋

Warner had downed the rest of his milk of magnesia by the time Harry and Albert wandered into his office. They'd taken their time, which annoyed him, but he let it go.

"Take a seat, boys," he said. Both of his brothers plopped themselves into the leather easy chairs, and Warner dropped into the swivel seat behind his desk.

"What'd you think?" Warner asked, finally succumbing to temptation and lighting up a cigar. He blew out the smoke, and Albert wrinkled his nose.

"I think you need to stop smoking those," Albert said. "They smell like crap and they'll play hell with your ulcer."

Warner smiled. "You're right, Al, but I want to know what you guys think of our little public service film."

It was Harry who answered. "We're not sure what to think, Jack. It was pretty grim."

Warner rolled his eyes. "That was the point, fellas. Some of these kids think that bum walked on water. Now, when they see this, they'll think twice. That's what we want. More important—that's what Hoover wants."

"Screw Hoover," Albert snapped. "You show that to the kids and we'll have every mother in America up in arms and calling for a boycott!"

"I'm not so sure about that."

"Well, I am," Harry said, moving to Jack's dry bar and pouring himself a Scotch and water.

"A little early for that, don't you think?"

"Jack, since when did you turn into our mother?" Harry asked.

Warner stood up and started walking around the room. "Didn't you guys see how our little audience was reacting?"

"That's *your* job, Jack," Albert said.

73

"That's right, it's my job to judge talent and to gauge an audience to see if a film is working or not. That's why I attend all the screenings, when you mugs can't be bothered."

"Somebody's gotta count the beans," Albert said.

Jack scowled. "If it weren't for the talent I find, there'd be no beans to count."

"All right, all right, that horse has run." Harry threw back the rest of his drink and poured another. "What's your point?"

"My point," Jack said, "is that fucking hoodlum's got a boatload of talent, and if I could sign him today, I would!"

"Christ, Jack, it was just lighting and some halfway decent direction," Albert said. "*I* could've done as good too."

Warner laughed, and Albert looked insulted. "Dillinger threw our director out of the room five minutes after he got there. *Dillinger* wrote and directed that little ditty, gentleman."

Both of Jack's brothers now bore the same dumbfounded expression. "You're pullin' our legs, Jack. Come on . . . You're tellin' us John Dillinger *directed* that?"

"That's right, and as I hear it, the crew was pretty damned impressed. They only did two takes."

The three men fell silent, and Warner let his brothers stew in it. Finally, Albert broke the silence. "So, what do we do with it—the film, I mean?"

"Isn't it obvious?" Warner asked. "We're going to put John Dillinger into every Warner theatre in America with his name on the marquee. And we're going to put him on *after* the feature."

Albert threw up his hands. "Jack, you're out of your goddamned mind! No one'll stay for it."

"You're wrong, Al. *Everybody'll* stay for it. If we treat it like any other featurette, it'll be forgotten in a week. If we play it up and make 'em wait for it, make it like *it's* the feature, they'll be lining up around the block, even in theatres where we've got underperforming pictures."

"You mean the stinkers, Jack?" Albert asked. He tried to look bored, but Warner could see a 24-karat gleam in his brother's mercenary eyes.

"Yeah, the stinkers."

"Okay, let's say we do that," Harry said, leaning forward in this chair, his gut spilling over his belt. "What's next? What do you do for an encore?"

Warner smiled and relit his cigar, enjoying his brothers' impatient glares. "We sign him to a seven-year contract. This guy's *got* something, boys. He could be bigger than Robinson—bigger than goddamn Cagney!"

"But the fucking guy's in jail, Jack!" Harry said.

Warner sat back. "Let me worry about that."

"Now, wait a minute. The only way Dillinger's gonna get out early is if he gets a pardon from the governor of Indiana. I don't know about you, Jack, but I don't know the guy, so why should he do us any favors?"

"We don't need the governor, Harry. You're forgetting something. Dillinger was convicted of bank robbery, which is now a *federal* crime. It's the president we need to talk to."

"I don't care how cozy you are with Roosevelt. He'll never do it—not in a million years."

Albert was nodding in agreement. "It'll never happen, Jack."

"Then we got nothin' to lose if I try, do we? In the meantime, we put this film out the way I just outlined. You'll see I'm right."

The two brothers stood and began moving toward the door. "Fine, Jack," Harry said, placing his empty tumbler back on the dry bar. "You go on and give it a try. If you manage to get Dillinger out and put him under contract, I swear I'll never question another thing you do."

"Is that a promise, Harry?"

When they were gone, Warner buzzed for his secretary. She strode in moments later carrying her steno pad, taking her customary seat in one of the easy chairs.

"Yes, Mr. Warner?" she said. She had a businesslike look in her eyes, but Warner knew better.

"What did you think, Molly?"

Her carefully constructed façade crumbled. "I'm sorry, Mr. Warner, I was just so darn curious, you know, with him being in jail and all—"

Warner held up a hand, silencing her. She looked terrified, and he felt a twinge of paternal guilt.

"It's quite all right, my dear. You do a fine job, and there was no harm done."

Her entire demeanor brightened. "Thank you, sir. I appreciate that."

"But I really do want to know what you think."

"About the film?"

"Yes, about the film."

Molly looked thoughtful for a moment, biting her full lower lip, the marcelled waves in her blonde hair catching the sunlight beaming in from the tall windows behind the desk. "It was scary. I mean, who would want to end up in a place like that?"

Warner nodded and bade for her to continue.

"Well, I guess the most surprising thing was that Dillinger looked kind of dreamy, if you know what I mean."

Warner grinned. "I think I do, Molly, but why don't you elaborate?"

"He's got something, is all. You can see it in his eyes. It was like he was looking right through my clothes!" For a moment she looked as if she might swoon, then quickly regained her composure. "Is that what you wanted to know, Mr. Warner?"

"Yes, indeed, but before you go back to your desk, I need to ask you one more question—the most important one."

"Sure thing, Mr. Warner."

"Would you go see a gangster film starring John Dillinger?"

Her eyes widened. "Oh, gosh," she said. "That would be really swell. I'd go see that in a New York minute!"

8

The Apollo Club
Washington, DC
February 26, 1935

L unchtime traffic crawled at a pace that quickly grated on
Hoover's nerves. Even though he anticipated the delay and
brought paperwork with him to pass the time, he found the stop-
and-go movement of the Lincoln Model K was making him queasy.
Then again, he'd had that unsettling feeling ever since Jack Warner
had requested this meeting at the Apollo Club in Georgetown.

The club was known for its posh décor and its exclusivity.
Hoover had applied for membership back when he'd begun his career, figuring it would help his advancement. The stuffy old coots
who ran the place had turned him down flat, and he'd vowed never
to set foot in the place. They let in the Hollywood riff-raff, but not
the man who ran the greatest investigative agency in the world. If it
wasn't such a travesty, it would be laughable.

Now, here he was going into the lion's den to meet with a man
who'd refused to reveal the purpose of the meeting, other than to

say it concerned John Dillinger. And that had sealed it for J. Edgar Hoover.

"How much longer, Special Agent Hughes?" Hoover asked, flipping a page on the report he was reading.

"Not long now, sir," the agent said with a studied earnestness that brought a smile to Hoover's face.

The young man was a newly minted agent and eager to please, and he liked that—very much.

"We should be crossing Rock Creek shortly, and the club is about half a mile from there."

"Very good, Special Agent Hughes. Carry on."

True to the young man's estimation, they reached the club ten minutes later and still early for the meeting. Just the way he liked it.

Housed in a brownstone that was part of a row of similar buildings, the Apollo Club went out of its way to be unobtrusive, the only discernible flair being the scalloped forest-green awning stretching from the entrance to the sidewalk. No signage of any kind.

The agent leapt from the car and swept open Hoover's door with a flourish.

"Be back here in one hour," Hoover told him. "I have a meeting with the president."

The young agent's eyes widened. "Yes, sir."

He entered the club and found Warner relaxing with a whiskey and soda in the mahogany-paneled lounge, which was surprisingly empty for a weekday. When he'd spotted Hoover entering the room, Warner had stood and extended his hand, a warm smile on his face.

"Mr. Hoover, so glad you could make it," he said, shaking the FBI director's hand. "Please, have a seat."

Hoover had been disarmed by the man's friendly manner, but felt there was an undercurrent of something else, something on

79

which he couldn't put his finger. Warner wanted something, and Hoover would have to be patient.

He didn't have long to wait when a few moments later they were approached by a tall man in a short white serving jacket.

"Mr. Warner?"

"Yes, Barney."

"Your private room is ready, and lunch is served."

"Thank you, Barney, we'll be right along."

The waiter inclined his head. "Very good, sir," he said and walked away.

Hoover frowned. *A private room? What was going on here?*

He was still wondering when Warner rose to his feet and led him to a scaled-down version of the lounge on the second floor. And although there was room for half a dozen tables, there was only one, centered under the crystal chandelier and impeccably set with expensive Wedgwood china and sterling silver cutlery.

"You probably know this, Edgar, but the steaks here are the best in town."

"So I've heard," Hoover said, taking his seat and unfolding the starched white napkin, which he spread across his lap.

He'd expected Warner to reveal the purpose of the meeting once the drinks and food were ordered, but the studio head surprised him by keeping the conversation going, expounding upon a variety of subjects. Hoover found himself engrossed in Warner's scandalous stories about several of his major stars, stories the studio head, through his power and influence, had kept out of the press. Hoover's expression remained neutral, but inwardly he reveled in it. Information such as this was potentially useful in the future, and he made mental notes of all the salacious details.

The steaks were as good as advertised, but Hoover rushed

through his meal, anxious to get to the point of the meeting. Warner, as if sensing his guest's mood, ate all the slower, savoring the meat with a gastronome's delight. Finally, it was over, and Hoover eschewed dessert for a black coffee. Warner ordered an empty glass into which he poured milk of magnesia. He drank down a large gulp and sighed.

"I'm sure you must be wondering why I asked you here, Edgar. It concerns the Dillinger film."

Hoover gave an inward sigh of relief. So, this was the reason, a congratulatory meal. Perhaps he'd misjudged the studio head, after all.

"I've heard the reaction is unprecedented," Hoover said, sipping his coffee.

"Have you seen it?"

"Yes . . . it was disturbing and very effective."

Warner smiled, giving his head a vigorous nod. "Yes, it was. And did you know that Dillinger wrote and directed it?"

"No, I didn't," Hoover said, remembering those blazing eyes before the fade-out at the end. He suppressed the shiver he felt and picked up his coffee cup.

"Forgive me, Jack, but what's your point?"

"My point is that Dillinger's got talent and I'm going to make him a star. I need your help to secure him a pardon."

Hoover nearly choked on the coffee. "You what?" he said, smacking the cup back down onto the saucer, sloshing coffee onto the spotless linen. "You want to put him in the *movies?*"

"That's exactly right, and I've got the perfect property for him, *The Petrified Forest*. It's a hit on Broadway and he's perfect for it."

Hoover stared at Warner, scarcely believing what he was hearing. This had to be a practical joke, the most tasteless joke imaginable. Hoover picked up his glass of water and gulped half of it, then looked the studio head directly in the eyes.

"Mr. Warner, while I have the utmost respect for your studio and its accomplishments, I have to say that this is the most outrageous thing I've ever heard. John Dillinger a movie star?! It's an insult to all the people he's hurt and stolen from over the years. Dillinger is a dangerous man, and even the thought of him as a *celebrity* disgusts me. I won't allow it."

Warner was still smiling as he picked up a small silver bell and rang it. "Just a little dessert, and then we can talk about this."

Hoover's brow furrowed, and he rose to his feet. "I don't want any dessert, and there's nothing to talk about. Now, if you'll excuse me, I have a meeting with the president."

"Come now, Edgar, I had the chef prepare something special. It's quite unforgettable."

On cue, a waiter entered the room, bearing a large silver tray covered by a domed bell-cover. He placed it in front of Hoover, who retook his seat with reluctance.

Warner's smile turned feral. "I call it food for thought."

He nodded to the waiter, who gave a curt bow and left. Warner then removed the bell-cover to reveal a spread of black and white photographs showing Hoover dressed in women's clothing, dancing with his deputy, Clyde Tolson. Hoover felt as if someone had sat on his chest. He took a breath, hating the wheezing sound it made.

"How did you get these?" he said, his voice low and terrible.

The question was more rhetorical than not, as he'd seen them all before clutched in the hoary claws of Meyer Lansky, whose lackeys had set up the party and the one-way glass behind which they'd been taken. Lansky's threats were simple and direct. Stay off the mob's back or they would go public.

Hoover slapped the table. "How did you *get* them?"

Warner shrugged. "I've got friends," he said. "I take care of my friends, and they take care of me."

"You only *think* they're your friends. You have no idea what you're mixed up in here."

"Maybe. Maybe not. You can't run a studio without the unions on your side, and the mob runs the unions. To think otherwise is suicide. I treat 'em well and they return the favor."

Hoover closed his eyes and shook his head. "So you want me to talk to the president?"

"That's right. I've already mentioned it to him, and not surprisingly, he passed the buck."

"To whom?"

"Paul McNutt, the governor of Indiana. It seems that while bank robbery is now a federal crime, the robberies Dillinger committed were still state crimes. McNutt is the man who can pardon him."

"Then what the hell do you expect *me* to do? I don't even know the man. I have no leverage."

Warner flagged the waiter and asked for a brandy. "Anything for you, Mr. Hoover?"

"No."

Warner waited until the drink arrived then sipped it with relish.

"While I know you have no influence with McNutt, you do have leverage with Roosevelt. I want you to have the president talk to McNutt, promise him a post after his term ends. He can always back out of it later."

"You're out of your mind."

"Perhaps, but I know talent when I see it, and Dillinger's going to be the next big thing. You're going to help me, or by God you're going see those photos splashed all over the papers." He leaned clos-

83

er to Hoover. "Wouldn't it be better to have the upper hand with the president? Wouldn't it be better to make sure you have your job for life?"

"What do you mean?"

"Let him see his file. Eleanor's, too . . ."

He knows about my files!

Hoover started to stand then sank back into his chair. He wanted to sweep the table clean of china, break everything breakable in the room—Warner included. He was in a bad position, and he knew it.

"So you know about his wife?"

"Let's just say that she got along famously with one of my starlets when they last visited Los Angeles. I made sure of it."

Hoover nodded. He knew he might one day have to resort to his files, but he'd never imagined he would be doing so against his will. "All right. If Roosevelt agrees, I won't stand in your way. When do you want him out?"

"As soon as possible. We start shooting in six months, and he'll need some grooming."

Hoover gathered up the photos and placed them in his jacket pocket, and Warner laughed. "That's fine. You keep 'em, I have copies."

Hoover left the club moments later, returning to his darkened office where he burned the photographs to a fine gray ash. It was only a symbolic act, as he knew the threat still existed—now from *two* enemies.

Later at home, while he readied for bed, he wondered what he would say to Clyde and how he would take the news that now it wasn't only the mob who had access to those photos. The mob could be relied upon to live up to their end, as it involved their very survival. Such was not the case with Jack Warner. It was pure, selfish greed on his part, which meant that this was not the end of the blackmail.

It was the beginning.

He would do what Warner asked because he had no goddamn choice, but if Dillinger thought his new career would proceed without incident or scrutiny, he had another think coming. Once Dillinger was out, Hoover intended to reassign Melvin Purvis to the Los Angeles office, where his sole responsibility would be to keep an eye on the soon-to-be former felon. It was then only a matter of biding their time. Dillinger would show his true colors eventually. He was as sure of that as death and taxes.

ACTION!

9

The Indianapolis Herald
Newsroom
March 8, 1935

The scrawny copy boy dashed into the newsroom just after ten o'clock, his spindly legs scrabbling for purchase on the slick linoleum floor, his hands grabbing the doorframe. "Turn on the radio, guys! Right now. Governor's making an announcement."

Robert Butler looked up from the story he was getting ready to file, an expression of bewilderment on his face. Rafe Ellis, the sports reporter, stopped pecking at his battered Underwood portable and gave the boy a sour look. "Who fucking cares what McNutt has to say?"

The boy ran to the radio and snapped it on. Butler put down his blue pencil and waited with the rest of the room for the Zenith console to warm up and for the boy to tune it in.

By all rights, Butler shouldn't have even been there, but Daugherty had asked him to fill in as city editor while his regular man was on vacation in Florida. He'd been happy to help out, grateful for the regular paycheck, even if he had to put up with the sweltering heat and the clouds of cigarette smoke generated by a city room full of yammering reporters, all of it punctuated by the incessant clacking and dinging of typewriters. He missed the blessed silence of his home office and the freedom it afforded, but for once he was glad to be on the front lines.

The copy boy spun the dial and the radio squealed and crackled then centered in on WMAQ. ". . . the governor is just coming to the podium now. Stay tuned," the announcer said in a gravel-voiced hush.

Butler could hear the murmur of the crowd diminish and the scratch of shuffling papers.

"Ladies and gentlemen of the press," Governor McNutt said in a clear, ringing voice. "I called this conference to announce that as of noon today, I have acted within my powers as governor of Indiana by granting John Herbert Dillinger a full pardon for the crimes of bank robbery, for which he was convicted late last year. I am granting this pardon in recognition of Mr. Dillinger's good behavior and in recognition of the public service film he recently appeared in. I am proud to report that overall crime statistics are down by fifteen percent nationwide, in part a result of Mr. Dillinger's commitment to help educate our younger citizens. It is for these reasons that I grant Mr. Dillinger a second chance to continue this exemplary work and to show the world that Indiana stands behind its citizens one hundred percent. Thank you."

The radio exploded with the sound of reporters hurling questions, and Rafe motioned for the copy boy to shut it off. The resultant silence was almost too much to bear. Butler had seen Dillinger's film on a night he'd taken Millie and Lizzie out to the movies. The strangest part of the experience was that it came on after the feature, as he was getting up to leave. It was then he'd noticed no one else had budged from his seat. In fact, the guy behind him had groused for him to sit down. He'd done so, and watched the short film, shocked that it was so grim and visceral, and taken aback that Dillinger had been so effective—so charismatic. As the film was ending, he'd stolen a look at a young couple seated next to them, and the look on the girl's face was nothing short of rapturous.

And now that performance had gotten him pardoned.

"Butler!"

Butler snapped out of his reverie and looked up, spotting Jed Daugherty, the editor-in-chief, standing in the doorway to his glassed-in office. He indicated for Butler to join him with a jerk of his head then turned and dropped his lanky frame back into his desk chair.

With a sigh of resignation, Butler rose from his desk and walked into Daugherty's inner sanctum.

"Close the door," Daugherty said in his flat, Midwestern growl.

Butler complied and then sat down on one of the two hard-backed chairs facing the desk. "Everything all right, Jed? We weren't playing the radio too loud for you, were we?"

Daugherty shook his head as he lit a Lucky Strike. Butler noticed the ashtray was overflowing. "No, you weren't," Daugherty said, followed by a short hacking cough, "but it does have to do with what you heard."

"Dillinger?"

"Yeah, Dillinger. I can tell you now, but I knew this was coming for the better part of a week."

This shocked Butler, who stared back at his boss with what he hoped was a neutral expression.

"You *knew*? Why, Jed? Why'd you sit on it?"

The editor exhaled a cloud of smoke then reached into a desk drawer and withdrew a bottle of Jack Daniels and two tumblers. He poured two fingers into each and pushed one across the battle-scarred desk. When Butler hesitated, Daugherty said, "Go on, you're gonna need it."

With mounting trepidation, Butler picked up the glass and tossed back the drink, grimacing as the sour-mash whiskey burned its way down his esophagus. He put the glass down and Daugherty refilled it. "You know I've been friends with Paul for a long time," he said, referring to the governor.

"You helped him with his campaign, didn't you?"

"Where I could without compromising my journalistic integrity," Daugherty said. "He called last week and asked me to meet him in his office. He sounded funny on the phone, and I thought it was going to be some kind of scandal he was involved in."

"But it wasn't."

"No, it wasn't. He told me that FDR had called him and asked him as a personal favor to grant Dillinger a pardon."

"What?"

"Yeah, that's what I said."

"Why would Roosevelt do that?"

"Paul didn't know or wouldn't say. My guess is he didn't even ask. I mean, who's going to question the president of the United States? Right?"

"I would," Butler said.

Daugherty laughed. "Yeah, you would."

The editor knocked back his second drink, and Butler eyed his own glass. "FDR then told Paul that he was considering him for the ticket in thirty-six."

Now it was time for that second drink. Butler took it and drained the glass then waved the bottle away when Daugherty moved to refill it. "He offered McNutt the vice presidency?"

Daugherty nodded.

"Nothing certain, but the president did bring it up."

"Well, I guess the cat's out of the bag about FDR running again."

Daugherty leaned forward. "We can't say *anything*, Bob. Not about that."

"Then why are you telling me all this, Jed? What's the point?"

"Because there's a bigger story here."

"A bigger story?"

Daugherty shook his head with a heavy sigh. "Aw, hell, I'll just say it. Dillinger's going to Hollywood."

Butler was silent for a second and then burst out laughing. "Oh, Jesus, that's a good one, Jed," he said, blotting the tears in the corners of his eyes.

When Jed's stern expression didn't change, Butler's laughter died. "And you found this out . . . how?"

"I pulled in a favor from a stringer in Los Angeles. It seems a producer he's friendly with at Warner Brothers told him Jack Warner himself is angling to make Dillinger a star."

Butler sat there—the two shots of rye making his temples throb—trying to fit this square peg into his round mind. And it wasn't working. "Christ, Jed, this is nuts."

"Maybe so, but Dillinger will be out in three days, and I want you in Chicago to get an interview before he leaves for LA on The Chief."

"And . . . ?"

"And then I want you to follow him out there and cover the story as it develops."

"Jed, I've got three major stories I'm working on—"

The editor held up a hand. "You won't have to leave right away. From what my source tells me, Warner's going to spend some time grooming him. When you *do* go, I'll pay you a hundred fifty a week."

STARRING... JOHN DILLINGER

Which was exactly fifty dollars more than he made now.

Instead of saying anything, Butler grabbed the bottle of Jack Daniels and poured himself another. Millie was going to skin him alive when she smelled the booze on his breath, but to hell with it. This was nothing compared to what she was going to say when he told her about his new assignment. There was no question he was going to take it—the story was too good to pass up. The real question was how to keep his family life from flying apart at the seams with him a thousand miles away for what could turn out to be months. Butler's pulse raced as he thought about the book idea he'd all but abandoned after the trial. Here now was the real hook, a new direction that would be irresistible to publishers and readers alike. And he would be there every step of the way.

"What do you say, Bob? I know it's a lot to ask."

Butler sipped the rye and looked Daugherty squarely in the eye. "If I'm going to do this, Jed, I want carte blanche."

"You got it," Daugherty said, pouring another drink for himself. "Whatever you want to write. I just want you filing a story *every* week."

"I've also been thinking about writing a book."

"That's great!"

Butler held up a hand. "The paper will have no claims on that, Jed, and that's ironclad."

Daugherty slugged back the whiskey. "Okay, okay, you write up an agreement and I'll look it over."

Butler had a feeling he should be doing that right now, or certainly before the day was out, as the rye was no doubt making Daugherty more pliable than he might otherwise be. He decided to push for one more concession, an idea that just occurred to him.

"One last thing. To do this story justice, I'm going to have to be away from my family for months at a time—"

"I understand, Bob. You'll want me to pay for travel back and forth for holidays and the occasional long weekend, right?"

"Wrong. The only way this is going to work and keep me out of divorce court is for Millie and Lizzie to go with me, and it'll cost you less money in the long run. You'll only have to pay for three round trips. Once the story's run its course, we'll come back."

Daugherty chuckled. "Is that it?"

"That, and two hundred a week."

"Two hundred!"

"I'm going to have to rent a house out there. The extra money will help cover that, 'cause I'm not sticking my wife and daughter in some fleabag hotel."

"I hear the Westside is pleasant," Daugherty said as he stuffed the cork in the bottle of Jack Daniels and placed it back in his desk drawer. "If I have any more of this I'll be giving away the store. Go on and get out of here before I reconsider all of this."

Butler grinned and rose to his feet, feeling a wave of lightheadedness pass through him. He moved toward the door.

"Bob?"

Butler turned back to the editor, who was looking at him with an excited expression that matched his own. "The increase in our circulation will be worth every penny I'm paying you."

"And a Pulitzer wouldn't hurt, either."

Daugherty laughed, and Butler returned to his desk, his mind ricocheting like a ball in bumper pool.

10

Michigan City State Prison
John Dillinger's Cell
March 11, 1935

*T*oday is the day . . .
Dillinger lounged on his bunk, feeling the anticipation course through his body on a wave of adrenaline. Judging from the angle of the sun out in the yard, it was just past nine. Two hours after breakfast and another hour to go before that cell door swung open for the last time.

Good riddance.

He couldn't wait to put this damp, flea-bitten pile of rocks behind him. Leibowitz had been in yesterday afternoon and had completed the paperwork with the warden. All on the up and up. It was hard to believe he'd be walking out . . . instead of tunneling. Now, it was just a matter of watching the clock, which would be a whole lot easier if he had a clock to watch. Glancing across the cell, he saw the pile of boxes containing his books. He'd decided to take them on the train, rather than have them shipped out later. No sense in trusting the screws to do the right thing if they didn't have to. He'd just finished *Great Expectations*, which he decided was his favorite of

Dickens's novels. He liked the rags-to-riches aspect of the story and found he identified both with Pip and Magwitch, the boy's ex-convict benefactor. Jack Warner was no Magwitch, but Dillinger was grateful just the same.

A door opened at the end of the cellblock and Dillinger heard a series of rapid footsteps. A moment later, Captain Hauser appeared in front of the cell with three royal blue boxes marked with the brand name of Hart Schaffner Marx in gold.

Dillinger sat up on his bunk. "Hey, Cap, what's this?"

The old guard nodded his head toward a business-sized envelope attached to the top box. Dillinger took the envelope and Cappy placed the boxes down on the floor long enough to open the cell door.

Inside the envelope, Dillinger found a sheet of letter paper bearing the Warner Brothers logo embossed in black and gold.

Dear Mr. Dillinger:

Today is a momentous day for you, the beginning of an era of great expectations.

Please accept these garments with my compliments. After all, if you're going to be a star, you need to look like one.

Best Regards,

Jack L. Warner

When Dillinger looked up from the paper, Cappy was placing the boxes on his bunk. One was definitely a hatbox, and the other looked as if it might hold a suit. The third one—an in-between size—he could only guess at.

"Well, go on, John, open 'em up," he said, the sparkle in his eyes reflecting the same eagerness Dillinger was feeling. He pulled the lid off the suit box and found a charcoal double-breasted suit. He liked the fact that the pinstripes were subdued, rather than the bold ones on the cheap suits his former associates tended to favor. And while Dillinger was sure it was off-the-rack, its quality impressed him nonetheless.

"Jeez, those are some classy duds."

Dillinger grinned. These clothes explained why an assistant accompanied his lawyer during a visit two weeks earlier. The little gray-haired man had patiently measured him without saying a word, marking the measurements down in a little leather-bound notebook.

Next came the in-between box, where he found two shirts, two ties, some boxer shorts, socks, shoes, and a belt. The third box revealed a dove-gray Borsalino fedora in a fur felt that was even silkier to the touch than the suit. The wide black grosgrain ribbon gave it the finishing touch.

Cappy moved to the cell door. "I'll leave you to change," he said, and walked away, leaving the cell door ajar. Dillinger felt a tiny electric jolt through his body. He could walk out right now—just open the door . . . Chuckling, Dillinger shucked his prison clothes and began changing into his new wardrobe.

Warner seemed to be a right guy, and Dillinger especially liked that the studio head had used the phrase *"great expectations"* in his little note. He took that as a good omen.

The clothes fit perfectly; even the wing tip shoes with their buttery-soft leather felt as if they had been made for his feet. Everything hugged and draped in just the right places, a far cry from the clothes he'd worn during his bank-robbing days. They were nearly always purchased on the fly and were never of the best cut or quality. And while he appreciated the finer things, it didn't make sense to waste all his dough on something that might end up being left behind in some seedy apartment because he had to scram at a moment's notice. Now he could afford to indulge himself a bit, or at least he would once he got to Los Angeles.

Dillinger stepped in front of the mirror above the sink. Rather than glass, it was a thin sheet of highly polished steel secured to the wall with one-way bolts, making it impossible for it to be removed and used as a weapon. The reflection was optically imperfect, fraught with distortions like a funhouse mirror, but he could see well enough to notice that the clothes looked sharp, the Borsalino cocked just so being the icing on the cake.

Cappy returned twenty minutes later with another guard trailing behind him pushing a hand truck. Cappy didn't say anything because of the other man's presence, but Dillinger could tell the older guard was impressed by the dashing figure Dillinger cut in his new clothes.

The other guard began loading the boxes of books onto the hand truck.

"Time to blow this pop stand, John," Cappy said, unable to suppress a grin.

"And not a moment too soon." Dillinger shot his cuffs and turned to look at his cell one last time before turning back to Cappy with a purposeful gaze. "I'm not coming back, Cap," he said with his patented smirk.

"Damn right you're not," the older man said. "I gotta good feelin'. Just wish I was goin' with you."

Dillinger grasped the old guard's shoulder. "Listen, you ever get tired of this joint, you come on out to Hollywood and look me up. If they don't give me the bum's rush, maybe I can find you something to do. Hell, they got guards at the studio. And the only difference is you gotta worry about keepin' the riff-raff out, not in." Dillinger laughed and patted Cappy on the back as the two men left the cell and walked down the hall for the last time.

Warden Cushing and another half a dozen guards met them at the exit, which was a large steel door painted black, inset with a small window of bullet-proof glass.

The final obstacle between him and freedom.

"John, there're a lot of reporters out there between you and the car the studio sent over. If you want, I can have the boys clear them out."

Dillinger shook his head. "Not on your life, Warden. From now on the press and me are gonna be thick as thieves, if you'll pardon the expression."

Warden Cushing laughed and was joined by Cappy and the rest of the guards behind him.

The warden stuck out his hand. "I don't normally see the former prisoners off, but I had to make an exception in this case. Best of luck to you."

Dillinger grasped the older man's hand in his. "Thanks, Warden. As I said that last time in your office, you run a square joint. Just don't expect me back." Everyone laughed, and one of the guards grabbed the lever controlling the door and pulled it back. As the door slid open to the sound of grinding gears, the bright sun forced Dillinger to squint. After a moment, his eyes adjusted.

The warden had been right. Beyond the short, barred corridor leading to the outer gate, Dillinger could see a large crowd of men. Many had cameras, and he could also see the newsreel photographers had set up their equipment on a makeshift platform off to the right of the car. Grinning, he turned back to the warden, Cappy, and the others, and said, "See you at the movies, gents."

He walked out into the bright morning sun, followed by the

guard with the hand truck loaded with boxes. The crowd of report-ers shouted questions, jostling each other for a better view of Dil-linger. Warden Cushing signaled the other guards to join their two nervous colleagues at the outer gate and formed a cordon around Dillinger. The gate began sliding open on its track, and the guards forced the crowd of reporters and curiosity seekers back, forming a ten-foot clearing for the former outlaw. Dillinger watched the spec-tators with a lopsided grin on his face, and the crowd quieted down long enough for one of the reporters to shout a question.

"Hey, Johnnie, you ready for Hollywood?"

Dillinger's grinned widened. "Don't you mean is Hollywood ready for me?"

The crowd burst out laughing.

"Honestly, boys, I aim to click in pictures. I just hope you all will enjoy them, otherwise I won't know how to make a living. And you know what that means."

The crowd laughed again, and Dillinger motioned for the guards to begin clearing a path. As the mob of reporters parted like the Red Sea, Dillinger marched forward. Flashbulbs went off in his face and the questions came so fast and furious that it sounded like a contin-uous, unintelligible roar. Up ahead he spotted the Warner Brothers car, a late-model Ford with a super-charged eight-cylinder engine.

Sweet.

The guard with the boxes of books hurried to the trunk and began loading them in.

Seeing Dillinger's approach, the driver alighted from the car and opened the rear door in one fluid motion. Dillinger turned and posed for one last round of photos then disappeared inside the car. That's when he noticed he wasn't alone.

"How are you, John?"

Startled at first, it was a moment before he recognized his companion. "Bob! How's it hangin'?"

"Just where it should be, John," Butler said, returning the smile.

The driver started the car and Dillinger felt the smooth rumble of the engine through the padded leather seats.

It was really happening. No more dreams!

The Ford started moving a moment later, and Dillinger ignored the reporters running alongside. "So, what the hell are you doing here, Bob? And how did you wangle a seat in this car?"

"My editor had to pull more strings than Geppetto. He wants me to interview you before you head out and then follow you to Tinsel Town in a few months. I'm to be your Boswell."

"You know, if you'd said that to me a couple of years ago, I would have asked you, 'Boswell, who? What mob is he with?'" He laughed. "So, how long you going to be in LA?"

"For a while. Millie and Lizzie will be joining me. I just need to tie up some loose ends here then find a place to hang our hats."

"That's swell. I'm going to need every friend I can get," Dillinger said, watching the passing scenery as the car raced towards Chicago and the Dearborn Avenue Station where the Chief Transcontinental Express awaited. "So, you said you needed an interview."

"If you don't mind."

"Sure, go ahead."

Butler removed a steno pad and a pencil from his jacket pocket.

"So, what's the first thing you're going to do when you get to Hollywood?" Butler asked.

"You mean besides looking up Jean Harlow?"

"Yeah, besides that," Butler said, grinning.

"First stop is the dentist."

Butler frowned. "The dentist?"

101

Dillinger pointed to the canine tooth on his right side, which exhibited the dark mottled gray of a tooth with a dying nerve. "Mr. Warner wants me to get this fixed. Cameras notice that kind of thing, and so do the ladies. And the truth is it's always bothered me." Dillinger frowned. "You know, maybe you shouldn't use that. The studio might want to keep those kinds of thing on the QT. Christ, I'm gonna have to get used to watching what I say, for a change."

"I wouldn't worry about it, John, just be yourself," Butler said. "That's what readers want. But anything you tell me not to use, I'll keep mum about it. You have my word on that. I'm here to help, not to hinder. Okay?"

Dillinger grinned. "Thanks. You've always played it square with me, and I appreciate that." He looked down at his hands, his expression turning wistful. "My mother died when I was only three . . . Did you know that?"

"No, I didn't," Butler said.

"Well, as you can imagine, that's something I hadn't thought about for a long time. But that's what you do in stir, Bob, you think about anything and everything—your whole damn life.

"Anyway, they had her laid out in the living room, like they used to do back in those days. You know what I did? I pulled up a chair and climbed on it, and grabbed her shoulders and shook her, trying to wake her up." Dillinger's voice caught in his throat. "That's what they told me I did—I really don't remember it at all.

"What really gets me is when I think about how my father must have felt. He's had it rough all his life and he deserves a break. Maybe with this Hollywood thing, I can get him set up and sitting pretty. He's getting too old to be working the fields . . ." There was a silence and then Dillinger added, "And *that* is not for publication."

Butler nodded and waited a moment before asking his next question. "So, what are you going to do after you look up Miss Harlow?"

Dillinger's mood changed, and he chuckled. "They've got me set up with some old Russian dame for acting lessons. I think her name is Open Sky, or something like that. Sounds more Indian than Russian."

"Maria Ouspenskaya?" Butler asked. "Acting lessons? I thought you looked pretty good up there."

"Thanks, but you know I've never done anything halfway. Maybe this old Bolshevik can teach me a thing or two and I'll give John Barrymore a run for his money." Dillinger laughed, then turned pensive. After another long moment of silence, he turned and looked Butler in the eye. "I'm gonna show these mugs I've got what it takes. I was the best bank robber there ever was, and if I have anything to say about it, I'm gonna be the biggest star in Hollywood. Just you watch."

Butler smiled and closed his notebook. "That's what they're paying me to do. And knowing you, I'd say that's an even money bet."

11

Dearborn Station
Chicago, Illinois
March 11, 1935

Butler spent the rest of the hour-long ride into Chicago quizzing Dillinger about his future, what he wanted out of it, and how he thought the Hollywood community would take to him.

"I tell you, Bob, everybody has their opinion of me, most of them formed out of a lot of hogwash they read in the papers. Some of those stories had me robbing two banks in one day a hundred and fifty miles apart!" Dillinger laughed. He paused a moment. "I expect some people will always make me out to be a bum, no matter what I do in Hollywood. I could win a dozen Oscars, give all my dough to charity, walk on water, and I'd still be a mug to them. But I think there'll be plenty of others who will give me a chance. Did I tell you I already have a fan club?"

Butler smiled and shook his head, furiously scribbling in his notebook.

"Got a letter from this sweet kid in Dallas. Said she'd just formed the club and already had five members. All of them girls." Dillinger laughed and shook his head.

"Well, there's the old saying that you reap what you sow."

Dillinger sighed. "I'm sure some will say I made that film for my own personal gain, but honestly, Bob, how was I to know it would go anywhere? I was just trying to do something good for once."

They reached Dearborn Station on West Polk Street just before eleven, which he confirmed with a glance at the station's six-story Romanesque Revival clock tower. The sidewalk in front of the station was sprawling with a crush of reporters and travelers spilling over the curb and into the road. Chicago's finest was doing its best to hold back the crowd long enough for the Ford to pull up and disgorge its passengers.

Dillinger hopped out first, and the crowd went wild. A young blonde woman pushed through the crowd, screaming hysterically. "I love you, Johnnie!" she shouted, tossing something that landed on the former outlaw's shoulder. It was a pair of red silk panties. Dillinger lifted them up and gave them a kiss. The crowd roared, and the woman screamed.

Butler, having seen this, scribbled in his notebook and then climbed out of the car. Dillinger was talking to the driver. "Make sure these boxes get on the train, okay?" He reached into his pocket then rolled his eyes. "Hey, Bob, you got a buck for this guy? It seems the big movie star is flat broke," he said with a glint of humor in his eyes.

The driver held up his hand. "That's okay, Mr. Dillinger. Everything's on the house. Mr. Warner's orders."

Dillinger shrugged. "He's the boss."

The driver then pulled something from inside his jacket and handed it to Dillinger. "Your ticket, sir."

"Thanks, pal. Come on, Bob." He turned and strode through the stone archways, waving to the crowd as he walked.

Butler followed Dillinger into the station, crossing the cavernous lobby with its thirty-foot ceiling of stout crossed beams, and out onto the tracks. The Chief, with its streamlined locomotive belching plumes of steam, stood on the nearest set of tracks, conductors checking tickets and helping passengers board.

Dillinger walked up to one of the conductors, a short middle-aged man with a salt-and-pepper mustache, and handed the man his ticket. The conductor glanced at it, punched a hole, and handed it back. "You're in a private car at the end of the train, sir," he said with a thick Irish accent.

"Thanks, pal. Say, when are we leaving?"

The conductor pulled out a heavy-looking Hamilton railroad watch from his vest pocket, his bushy brows wrinkling in thought. "The train's scheduled to leave at exactly eleven fifteen a.m., eight minutes from now."

Dillinger nodded his thanks and strode off toward the end of the train while Butler hurried after him. The car at the end of the train turned out to be a sleek private Pullman devoid of any markings. Instead of another conductor, there was a tall black man in a white coat who exited the car, his lean, angular face creased with a toothy grin.

"Aft'noon, Mr. Dillinger, my name is Woody," he said in a deep voice graced with a southern lilt. "Your boxes is bein' loaded right now, and the rest of your luggage is already aboard."

"I don't have any luggage," Dillinger said.

The man's grin widened, and he leaned toward Dillinger conspiratorially. "It looks like you do now, sir."

Dillinger laughed.

"I like this guy," he said to Bob. "Reminds me of Reed Youngblood."

Butler recalled that Youngblood was a black man who aided Dillinger in his escape from Crown Point Jail. He was gunned down days later in a sleazy bar, after flashing a roll of money Dillinger had given him.

"Thank you, sir. Now, let's get you aboard. Yo' friend can come along, but he's got to be off the train in seven minutes or he's goin' to Hollywood." He laughed and led the way onto the Pullman car.

The first thing that struck Butler was the smell of the food. As they passed the galley, Butler spotted a tray laden with a lavishly prepared meal with a thick Porterhouse steak as its centerpiece. Past the galley was the dining area, which consisted of a single table that could normally hold four people but was instead set for one. Nearby stood an ice bucket holding two bottles of beer, beaded with condensation, and a bottle of Jim Beam bourbon leaning out of a gift basket set off to the side. Beyond the main dining area came a private sitting room and then the sleeping quarters. Dillinger slipped inside, and Butler saw two leather suitcases stacked at the foot of the bed. The narrow closet, the door of which stood ajar, contained a set of dinner clothes.

Dillinger gave a low whistle. "You'd think I was Adolphe Menjou or something."

Butler laughed and made a notation in his notebook. "Now all you need is Jean Harlow."

"Maybe she's hiding under the bed," Dillinger said with a grin.

They made their way back to the dining area and Dillinger plopped himself down at the table. Woody appeared and asked, "Can I get you gentlemen something to drink?"

"Why don't you pop the cork on that bourbon, Woody, so Bob and I can toast our good fortune?"

"Very good, sir."

Woody grabbed the bottle and expertly removed the cork, filling two tumblers and handing one each to Dillinger and Butler.

"Here's to the future, and good fortune for the both of us."

They clinked their tumblers, but instead of taking a sip, Dillinger stared at the faceted glass.

"Anything wrong, John?" Butler asked.

"No, I was just thinking how not so long ago, in stir, we used to pour a little bootleg hooch onto a painted surface, and if it didn't take the paint off, it was probably safe to drink. Times are changin', Bob." He tilted his head and knocked back the entire drink.

Butler had barely brought his glass to his lips when Woody announced, "Train's leavin' in a minute, sir, and lunch is served."

Butler put down his drink and extended his hand. "Have a safe trip, John. I'll be seeing you in a few weeks."

He stepped off the train a moment later and stood watching it huff and chug its way out of the station, disappearing around a curve in the tracks. As he walked through the lobby, he thought he saw someone he recognized but dismissed it, the view of the man too fleeting to make a connection.

The Ford dropped him at the *Herald*'s front door and Butler tried once again, unsuccessfully, to tip the driver for going above and beyond. As before, the money was politely refused, and Butler thanked the man and went inside to his office. Even though Daugherty didn't expect him to file the story for a couple of days, he wanted to get his thoughts down on paper. He would probably rewrite it half a dozen times, but sometimes that first draft contained a spark of something special that might otherwise be lost if he waited. Millie would be upset that he was late getting home, but that couldn't be helped.

He wrote for an hour and a half, finally throwing in the towel when he saw the streetlights snap on outside his window. Realizing the time, he picked up the phone and dialed home.

"You're at the office, aren't you?" his wife asked in a tone of annoyance.

"Yeah, I'm sorry, but I needed to get some thoughts on paper."

"Last time I looked, we had paper here too."

Butler chuckled. "Okay, okay, I'm guilty as charged. Am I late for dinner?"

"Actually, no. I figured you might be late, so I started late."

Butler grinned. Millie was one in a million. "All right, I'm leaving now. Promise me not to char the roast too much."

"Don't push your luck," she said, playing coy.

"I love you," he said, and hung up.

Putting on his jacket, his gaze wandered out through the window to the street. He noticed a lone man wearing a white fedora and a dark overcoat leaning against a lamppost across the street, his posture casual yet wary, as if he were waiting for someone. Butler was turning away from the window when he saw the man light a cigarette, the flair of the match briefly illuminating his handsome face. It was the same man he'd seen at the station. And he now realized who it was.

Special Agent Melvin Purvis.

Purvis was gone by the time Butler made it out to the street. He looked both ways, but the wily agent was nowhere to be seen. He walked to where his car was parked, his mind brooding over Purvis's appearance in two places he'd been today. That obviously meant he was being tailed. A flare of anger coursed through him, tempered by the realization that Purvis had *let* himself be seen. He *wanted* Butler to know he was under surveillance. The question was *why?*

Climbing into his LaSalle, he started the car and pulled away from the curb, his eyes watching the rearview mirrors for anything even remotely suspicious. No one seemed to be following him, which in no way relieved his anxiety. After all, it wasn't as if the FBI couldn't look up his address in the phone book. They knew exactly where he lived. Purvis had allowed himself to be seen, either because he wanted to rattle Butler, or he simply didn't care.

Arriving home, he parked the LaSalle in the driveway and climbed out, retrieving his jacket from the passenger seat. When he glanced at the street, he noticed an unfamiliar late-model Ford sedan nestled next to the curb in front of his house.

He fought off the wave of anger washing over him and marched up the flagstone walkway to the front door.

Inside the house, Millie greeted him with a kiss, but her normal cheerful demeanor was nowhere in evidence. She nodded toward the parlor, her mouth pressed into a tight line. "He said he's from the FBI. I didn't know what to do—"

Butler silenced her with a finger to her lips. "I'll take care of it. Just keep a plate warm for me. Okay?"

Millie nodded and walked back into the kitchen, glancing back over her shoulder before disappearing from sight. She looked frightened, and that made Butler all the angrier. Without missing a beat, he walked into the parlor and found Melvin Purvis seated on his favorite chair.

Another annoyance.

Butler smiled, extending his hand. "Agent Purvis, this is a surprise."

Purvis stood up and shook Butler's hand, a gentle smile playing across his face. "I do hope I am not inconveniencing you and your family, Mr. Butler," he said, his grip dry and firm. The agent's deep, resonant voice held a hint of a southern accent, and his courtly manner was in keeping with it.

"That's okay, Agent Purvis," he said, indicating that his guest should retake his seat. "What can I do for you?"

Purvis eased himself back into the leather easy chair while Butler sat on the adjacent love seat and crossed his legs, hoping that made him at least *appear* more relaxed than he felt.

"It's *Special* Agent, Mr. Butler, but I admit that can be a bit of a mouthful at times." There was that easy smile again. "Suffice it to say, Mr. Hoover is taking an active interest in Mr. Dillinger's new career."

"Surely the fact the man's been pardoned would render that interest unnecessary," Butler said.

Purvis stared back at him, saying nothing, and Butler started to sweat.

"What is it you want from me?"

Purvis pulled out a small notebook, flipped it open. "From your articles in the *Herald*, you stated that you were trying to arrange for John Dillinger's surrender, is that correct?"

"Yes, his father contacted me and asked me to meet with him."

Purvis nodded and made a notation in the notebook with an expensive mechanical pencil.

"And the result of this meeting was . . . ?"

Butler was growing annoyed, but he swallowed the anger and said, "The result was he was going to meet me at a predetermined location and I was going to escort him to the police station."

"And that's your statement?"

Butler frowned. "Yes, that's my statement."

"And there was no talk of helping him elude capture?"

"I'm a credentialed journalist, Agent Purvis, and a law-abiding citizen. I got a phone call from an old acquaintance and I acted on it in good faith—and I resent your implications. There's no way in hell I would ever aid and abet. You have a lot of nerve—"

Over the FBI agent's shoulder, Butler saw Millie waving from the kitchen. The slow shake of her head was enough to convince him to take a deep breath and calm down.

Again, Purvis waited him out, saying nothing.

"Why didn't you?" Purvis asked, breaking the long, uncomfortable silence.

"Why didn't I what?"

"Meet with him."

"Surely this is all old news now."

Purvis nodded. "Nevertheless, Mr. Hoover likes his files complete."

By that Butler took it to mean that he had no choice but to answer Purvis's questions.

He sighed and shook his head. "A police car showed up on the street unexpectedly and he ran."

"Mr. Dillinger must have suspected a double-cross."

"Is that a question, or an assumption?"

Purvis shrugged. "Go on, Mr. Butler . . ."

"That's it. A week later he surrendered to you outside the Biograph. The rest you know."

Purvis smiled and closed his notebook, placing it back inside the jacket of his double-breasted suit.

"Mr. Hoover would very much appreciate it if you would keep us informed of Mr. Dillinger's activities, both on and off camera, while you're in Hollywood."

Butler was stunned. Only his family, his editor, and Dillinger knew about his upcoming assignment, which left exactly no one who could have leaked that information. Unless . . . "Did you get that from someone at the paper?"

"We have our confidential sources, Mr. Butler, just as you do," Purvis said, his voice oily smooth. "And we'd like you to be one of them."

Butler's knuckles turned white as he gripped the sofa's arm. He wanted to throw this smarmy bastard out of his house, consequences be damned. But something held him back, partly fear and partly his journalistic instincts. "You want me to spy for you?"

Purvis shook his head, and for a moment Butler could have sworn he was going to shake his finger and say "Tsk, tsk."

"I wouldn't call it that, but you must look at it from our point of view. Pardoned or not, Mr. Dillinger has exhibited dangerous and illegal behavior in the past, and Mr. Hoover feels his good intentions are just another facet of his manipulative personality."

"You think Dillinger's pulling the wool over our eyes, is that it?"

"Exactly, Mr. Butler. The director feels it's only a matter of time before he reverts to his true nature."

"Is Sigmund Freud one of your sources, too?"

Butler was only half-joking, but Purvis didn't laugh, didn't even crack that mint julep grin of his.

"If a man's been pardoned, then he deserves the second chance he's been given," Butler said, shaking his head. "I won't do it."

Purvis started to speak, then his gaze shifted as Millie entered the room, bearing a tray containing a coffee pot, three cups, as well as the cream and sugar.

"I thought you two men might need a pick-me-up," she said, placing the tray onto the coffee table. She shot Butler a warning glance then turned to Purvis. "Mr. Purvis, would you like a cup?"

Disarmed, Purvis smiled and nodded. "Please, ma'am, I'd appreciate that. It's been a long day. Cream and two cubes."

Millie served them all coffee and then sat next to Butler. He was about to ask her to leave when she surreptitiously squeezed his hand. "You'll have to forgive me for overhearing, Mr. Purvis, but I think you've put my husband in a very awkward position."

"Millie . . . " Butler started to say, then shut up when she mashed her left foot onto his right one.

Purvis smiled. "I apologize if I've given that impression, Mrs. Butler. I have only the highest regard for your husband's work, and all I really wanted was a chance to read his Dillinger stories before they're officially filed."

He knew that wasn't what Purvis truly wanted, but he realized Millie's appearance and her knowledge of what they'd been speaking about had necessitated a change of tactic. Butler wanted to give his wife a big fat kiss. Instead, he seized the opportunity before it slipped away.

"If that's all you want, I have no objections, if my editor doesn't. I'm sure he's as patriotic as the next man. I'll talk to him about it and let you know."

Knowing there was nothing left to say, Purvis drained what remained of his coffee and stood up. "I won't take up any more of your time," he said, extending his hand. "Thank you for your co-operation." Butler shook Purvis's hand and then saw him to the door. After he was gone, Butler turned to his wife and took her in his arms.

"You're a genius," he said.

Millie shook her head. "I heard what that man was trying to do, and I knew you'd refuse. Do you realize what he could do to us?"

"Yes, I do, but should I be expected to throw my integrity to the wolves? If it ever got out that I was spying for the FBI, my career would be over."

"If I hadn't intervened, it would have been over anyway," she said. "All Hoover has to do is pick up the phone and you'll be out of a job."

"There's always freelance work."

"Do you really think anyone will buy a Robert Butler story after that?"

Butler sighed. Millie was right.

"Mommy?"

They turned to see Lizzie standing in the doorway to the kitchen. "What is it, sweetheart?" Millie asked. "Mommy and Daddy are talking."

"Can we have dinner now?" It was said in such an adorably plaintive voice that Butler felt a stab of guilt and a rush of love for his daughter. He could see the same feelings reflected on Millie's face, as well. They looked at each other and laughed.

"Sure, honey," Butler said, moving toward the kitchen. "Let's eat."

Later that night, as he and Millie lay in bed entwined in each other's arms, Butler thought about Purvis's visit and decided that if the agent wanted to read the stories prior to publication, he would accommodate him. He was grateful for Millie's intercession, for he had a feeling Purvis had been about to make the very threats his wife had feared. Besides, the stories were for public consumption, in any event, so what harm could there be in letting the FBI agent read them first? Still, in the back of his mind Butler had the feeling that once he crossed that line, there was no going back.

12

The Roosevelt Hotel
Hollywood, California
March 15, 1935

The train ride from Chicago had taken exactly fifty-three hours and forty-five minutes to reach Union Station in Los Angeles, precisely at five o'clock in the evening. And while Dillinger had been expecting some fanfare, like the send-off he'd received in Chicago, when The Chief pulled in there was a reporter each from *Daily Variety* and the *Hollywood Reporter*, as well as the *Los Angeles Times* and a small crowd of curiosity seekers. No panty throwers.

"The people out here are a little more jaded when it comes to movie stars, Mr. Dillinger," Woody had said. Dillinger had shrugged it off and received the reporters in the car's dining room, laughing and joking and posing for photos.

The bigger surprise occurred after the reporters left, when Woody reappeared dressed in chauffeur's livery and carrying Dillinger's luggage.

"I don't work for the railroad," he said. "I work for Mr. Warner, and you."

"So, you're my majordomo, eh?"

"I prefer valet, but that's pretty much what I do."

They'd left the train and Dillinger followed Woody to another smart, late-model eight-cylinder Ford parked just outside the main door to the station. As they approached, a young man wearing thick tortoiseshell glasses and slicked-back hair climbed out of the car, smoothing his dark blue suit with his delicate hands. "Mr. Dillinger," he said, extending a hand. "I'm Gerald Connors. Welcome to Los Angeles."

"Thanks, kid," Dillinger said, shaking Gerald's hand. "Are you from the studio?"

"Yes, sir. Mr. Warner wanted me to help you get settled."

"So where are we going?"

"We have you booked in a room at the Roosevelt. We're heading there now. Once you're checked in, we have a seven o'clock dinner reservation at The Brown Derby."

"Is Jack going to be there?"

Gerald looked embarrassed. "Regrettably, no. Mr. Warner's in meetings until late this evening and regrets that he cannot see you until your meeting at the studio tomorrow morning."

"Then I'm dining alone?"

Gerald smiled. "No, sir."

"So, who am I having dinner with, Gerald? You?"

"No, no, I'll just be there to make the introductions," the young man said, his smile widening. "I can assure you your dinner companions will be a lot more interesting than me."

"So, why the mystery?"

"It's a surprise—courtesy of Mr. Warner."

Dillinger shook his head and laughed. "Your boss likes doing that sort of thing, doesn't he?"

"He lives for it, Mr. Dillinger."

They'd left a few minutes later, negotiating the early-evening traffic and arriving at the Roosevelt Hotel just after six. According to the fussy manager who led them up to the room, it had just been vacated by a couple who'd thrown a party the night before. "We've only just straightened up, so I do apologize for any inconvenience," the manager said, shooting worried looks at Dillinger.

"That's okay, pal," Dillinger said. "I just need a place to hang my hat."

The manager gave the former outlaw a dry grin and a nervous titter then handed Gerald the keys. "Do let me know if you need anything—anything at all," he said, and scurried off.

"You think he's worried I'll steal the silverware?" Dillinger asked.

Woody shrugged his shoulders and Gerald looked embarrassed.

Once they were inside, the room proved to be a modest suite. It was airy and comfortable, with two bedrooms, a small kitchen, and a view overlooking Hollywood Boulevard. Woody brought in the bags and set about unpacking and putting Dillinger's clothes away in a spacious closet adjoining the bedroom.

Gerald watched for a few moments then headed to the door. "I'll leave you to relax until dinner. Woody will drive you."

After Gerald departed, Woody emerged from the other bedroom, now dressed as a butler. Dillinger had to laugh. "How many disguises do you have, Woody?"

"One for every occasion, sir," he replied with a grin. "I've drawn you a bath and laid out your clothes for the evening. I'll have the car brought around at a quarter to seven."

"That's swell. Say, is there anything to drink around here?"

"Yes, sir. What would you like?"

"You know, I'll stick to bourbon. I'm sentimental when it comes to old friends."

"Right away, Mr. Dillinger."

Clapping his hands with relish, Dillinger made his way into his bedroom and spotted the clothes Woody had laid out on the bed, consisting of a white dinner jacket, black vest, black trousers, starched white shirt, and black bow tie. Nodding his approval, he went into the bathroom. The black porcelain tub was full, and tendrils of steam rose from the water's placid surface, reflecting the overhead lights like an obsidian mirror. He disrobed and left his old clothes on the floor then stepped into the water, sending ripples to the tub's edges. Easing himself into the water, he sighed with contentment. The water was deliciously hot, and the steam opened his sinuses.

Woody walked in and handed Dillinger a crystal tumbler containing a double shot of bourbon.

"These guys think of everything," Dillinger said, grabbing the bottle and perusing the label. "Where's your glass?"

Woody looked nonplused. "That wouldn't be right, Mr. Dillinger."

The former outlaw shot him a look of annoyance. "The hell with that. I'm not drinkin' alone. Go grab a glass and let's have us a toast."

Woody nodded and left the bathroom, returning with another tumbler, which he then proceeded to fill with bourbon. Dillinger clinked his glass against Woody's and said, "Here's to fast cars and faster women."

"I'll drink to that." He downed his glass then made ready to leave.

"Hold on a second. Sit down," Dillinger said, pointing to the toilet seat. Woody sat down.

"Where you from?"

The valet remained silent as Dillinger picked up the bottle and gave him a questioning look. Woody held out the glass and Dillinger refilled it. "I'm from Saint Tammany Parish, just north of New Orleans," he said after draining half of the glass. "My daddy was a sharecropper—grew cotton mostly. He was a good man, worked hard, but we was always dirt poor, and with six mouths to feed, I decided as soon as I was old enough I'd be gone.

"Left when I was fifteen and hopped a freight to the Big Easy. Had these visions I was gonna be a famous bluesman, 'cept I can't hold a tune worth a damn." He laughed and took another sip of bourbon. "You can pretty much guess the rest. Fell in with the wrong crowd, and after we tried to rob a liquor store, I wound up on Parchman Farm for a five-year stretch."

"I heard about that place. Must have been tough."

Woody nodded, absently passing the empty tumbler between his rough-hewn hands. "It was hell on earth, Mr. Dillinger. Hot, muggy, and full of every kind of vermin that wanted a piece o' your hide. They worked you to the bone, too, and sometimes those bones got broke." He put the tumbler down on the edge of the tub and held up his hands. Dillinger saw that none of the fingers were perfectly straight. "I made a promise to God and my mama that I was gonna make it through that five years and turn myself around. Just like you done."

Dillinger held up his glass, which still held a splash of bourbon. "My hat's off to you, Woody. You're all right."

Woody smiled. "Thank you, sir." Then his expression changed as he turned and looked at a small gold clock sitting on the vanity. "Oh, Lord, you got twenty minutes to get yourself dressed and out the door or we gonna be late."

Dillinger scrambled out of the tub and Woody handed him a towel. Fifteen minutes later, dressed to the nines in his new finery, he crossed the lobby, drawing a few appreciative stares from a couple of elegant women standing near the registration desk. He smiled at the ladies and exited to Hollywood Boulevard, struck first by how warm it was in the evening and by the crush of traffic both on the street and the sidewalks. Just as he was beginning to draw the attention of several bystanders, Woody rounded the block and pulled up in the Ford. He started to get out of the car, and Dillinger motioned for him to stay put as he climbed into the back, noticing with increasing admiration that his valet had changed back into his chauffeur's livery.

"Is it far?"

Woody grinned. "About a mile straight down this here street and a right turn on Vine."

When there was a break in the traffic, Woody eased the Ford away from the curb and Dillinger sat back for the short ride to The Brown Derby.

The car pulled up to the restaurant, and Dillinger looked out at the big tawny-colored derby and grinned. *There was never anything as ridiculous as this in Chicago*, he thought. Somehow, here it didn't look the least bit out of place.

Woody opened the door and Dillinger climbed out of the car, giving a classy-looking couple waiting for their car the once-over. The woman, a dazzling redhead in a bottle-green gown, gave Dillinger a saucy smile, while her companion, a callow-looking man in tails, glared at him with ill-concealed malice.

Just then the door to the restaurant opened and Gerald Connors emerged, a look of relief on his face. "Right on time, Mr. Dillinger," he said, guiding him toward the door. "This is the place in Hollywood to see and be seen, so don't be concerned if you draw some attention."

"Isn't that the point, Gerald?"

The young man grinned. "I don't have to worry too much about you, do I?"

"No, you don't." Dillinger turned and fixed Woody with a look. "You gonna be okay?"

Woody nodded. "I'll be here when you're ready to leave, Mr. Dillinger."

Dillinger let Gerald lead him into the restaurant, through the foyer, and into the main dining room. Despite the round, derby-like exterior, the dining room was more conventionally shaped, the most striking aspect being the absence of freestanding tables—only booths—their tables covered in starched white linen and the seating a luxurious hemisphere of dark brown tufted leather reaching shoulder height. The walls were festooned with the hundreds of framed caricatures for which the restaurant was famous.

Gerald threaded his way through the room, nodding and saying hello, but not stopping. Dillinger felt every eye in the room was on him.

They arrived at a corner booth, and Dillinger did his best to remain calm and cool. It seemed his dinner companions were none other than Jean Harlow and William Powell.

"Jean, Bill," Gerald said. "I'd like you to meet John Dillinger."

Powell looked at him with an expression Dillinger could only define as a frank appraisal, then he stood and extended his hand. "A singular pleasure, Mr. Dillinger."

Dillinger took Powell's hand and gave it a firm shake. "Call me John."

Jean Harlow remained seated, smiling that dazzling smile of hers, holding out her delicate hand, the light from the overhead chandeliers gleaming in her platinum locks. "So, Jack Warner tells me you're a big fan of mine," she said as Dillinger took her hand.

"Yes, ma'am. I thought you were swell in *Red Dust*."

"Ma'am? So formal and polite. Come on, Johnnie, sit down and take a load off."

Dillinger laughed and slid into the booth, followed by Gerald. Harlow moved closer to Powell, who put his arm around her. Dillinger felt a twinge of jealousy then let it go. It was obvious the two were deeply in love. Who was he to muscle in on that? He was just a reformed mug. "You know, Jean, I have to thank Mr. Powell, here."

Powell's eyebrows arched. "Really? Whatever for?"

"It was one of your movies that convinced me to surrender."

Powell's amused half-smile turned genuine. "Really? I had no idea. Which one?"

"*Manhattan Melodrama*," Gerald interjected.

"That's right, I remember reading that," Powell said, leaning onto the table. "I'm flattered, old boy."

Harlow gave Dillinger a wink. "Flattery will get you everywhere with Bill."

The actor gave her a mock pout. "Come now, I'm not that easy."

She poked him in the ribs. "Actually, you are."

Dillinger grinned.

A waiter approached and took their orders for drinks: a gimlet for Harlow, Scotch and soda for Powell, and a Manhattan for Gerald. Dillinger stuck with water.

"So, what I want to know," Harlow said, sipping her drink, "is where you learned your craft."

Dillinger looked surprised. "Craft?"

"Your acting. Bill and I saw that little film of yours, and you hit it out of the park."

"Absolutely riveting, old boy," Powell said, lighting a cigarette.

"Surely you didn't have an acting coach while you were out robbing banks?" Harlow asked with a mischievous glint in her green eyes.

"Truth is I've never had any training, not yet, anyway."

"Mr. Dillinger also wrote and directed that film," Gerald offered.

Both Harlow and Powell looked at each other, taken aback. "That's astounding," Powell said. "You mean to tell us you did that right out of the gate?"

Dillinger shrugged, feeling a little embarrassed. "Just wanted to give the kids who thought I was a big shot the straight dope."

"Well, you scared the pants off me," Harlow said, raising her glass and finishing the rest of her drink.

The waiter was heading back to the table to take their orders. Before he reached their booth, he was shouldered aside by a man who looked as if he'd had way too much to drink. It took a moment to realize he was looking at James Cagney, the star of *Public Enemy*.

"So, you're the tough guy's gonna show us how it's done, is that it?" Cagney swayed, looking like a caricature of himself. "Big bad John Dillinger gonna show us pansy actors the real deal?"

Dillinger stared back at the actor, every muscle in his body tensed . . . waiting.

"Come on, big boy, why don't you give me one right on the kisser. Right here." Cagney jutted out his chin and touched it with an index finger. "Show me how tough you *really* are. Or are you just a mug with a smart press agent?"

He laughed and lost his balance, slamming into the table and knocking over the glassware, which doused Powell with the remnants of his drink.

Powell, livid, stood up. "You've had too much to drink, Jimmy. Go home and sleep it off before you do something you regret."

Cagney straightened up, giving Powell a lopsided sneer. "I'll take you both on, fancy pants."

Powell's eyes bulged. "Fancy pants!"

Harlow grabbed him by the elbow. "Sit down, Bill," she said, glaring at Cagney.

"Yeah, you listen to that dame of yours. She's a real peach, but I bet there's times she could use a grapefruit in the face, too!" Cagney started to laugh and bumped into another waiter carrying a tray of food that went clattering to the floor.

A middle-aged man came rushing up. "Mr. Cagney, please, please, I must ask you to leave."

Cagney shook the man's hands off his jacket and glared at him. "Hey Cobb, why don't you go and make a salad or something." He giggled, and the man he'd called Cobb rolled his eyes in exasperation.

Dillinger had just about enough. He pushed the table away, stood up, and moved into the aisle, his eyes never leaving Cagney's. "The man asked you to leave, pal. I suggest you do so."

Cagney grinned. "Yeah, and what if I don't, pal?"

Without another word, Dillinger hauled off and threw a right cross that sent Cagney to the floor, where he lay in a heap of broken crockery and spilled food.

The room fell silent and, for a moment, no one moved, every eye on Dillinger. And then someone began clapping and the room erupted into cheers. Two burly men came and pulled Cagney to his feet, and from somewhere a flashbulb went off.

Cagney shook his head, looking dazed. "Jeez, that guy can really hit."

The two men led him away and Dillinger rejoined Gerald, Harlow, and Powell at the table. The rest of the evening went well, and

Dillinger realized that Hollywood wasn't so different from the places where he'd been. Sure, the clothes and booze were better, but it was still a dog-eat-dog business. He understood that.

As Dillinger dug into his steak and listened to Jean Harlow and William Powell's stories, he knew he was going to do just fine.

13

Warner Brothers Studios
Burbank, California
March 18, 1935

By morning, the fight at The Brown Derby had hit all the papers, with large boldface headlines:

PUBLIC ENEMY KAYOS PUBLIC ENEMY!
DILLINGER DECKS CAGNEY!
DILLINGER SHOWS CAGNEY WHO'S BOSS!

It was all a bit silly, Dillinger thought, but the real kicker were the photographs, each publication having their own version, taken from several different angles, as if the photographers had been lying in wait. When he pointed this out to Woody, the big man had shrugged as he served Dillinger his bacon and eggs.

"That's how those fellas earn their keep. They hang around the fancy joints where the stars likes to go, hopin' somethin'll happen."

"Well, it certainly did." Dillinger tossed aside the *Los Angeles Times* and picked up *Daily Variety*. The front page had a particularly crisp shot of his fist connecting with Cagney's face.

"I'd say that was the best one, Boss. You look real fierce—like Max Baer with that right cross." Woody fell into a fighter's stance, throwing a punch into the air.

Dillinger rolled his eyes and picked up his fork. "Maybe. But this ain't exactly a great first impression."

Woody laughed. "It is in Hollywood."

Dillinger had thought his valet's comment was a joke, but the accompanying stories had been anything but scathing; they'd been downright laudatory, praising his prowess and how perfect he was for his upcoming role in *The Petrified Forest.*

He spent the rest of the weekend in his suite, reading a copy of the screenplay for *The Petrified Forest* that Jack Warner had sent over. Warner had attached a handwritten note that read: "See you on Monday."

❆   ❆   ❆

Dillinger arrived for his appointment with Jack Warner early, the guards waving his car through the main gate off West Olive Avenue. The drive "over the hill," as the natives termed it, was scenic and relaxing, though Dillinger still harbored a case of nerves, not knowing what to expect in the wake of his dust-up with Cagney.

Dillinger had seen photos of the movie studios, but being on one was something else altogether. Warner Brothers Studios occupied dozens of sound stages and bungalows, sprawled over sixty-two acres surrounded by farmland and orange groves.

He walked down the main street, taking everything in, getting a feel for the unfamiliar terrain.

Almost like casing a bank.

There were the unnaturally wide streets just beginning to hum with activity and building fronts that for all the world looked like hundred-year-old brownstones but were in fact perfectly crafted facades only a foot or two in depth. There was even the fuselage of an old British SE-5A biplane, minus its tail section, being trucked through the massive doors of one of the largest of the sound stages.

At the appointed hour, he perused the map that was given to him by the gate guard, and made his way to a two-story stucco building abutting a soundstage. Shielding his eyes from the glare of the morning sun, Dillinger walked into the building and asked the guard the way to Jack Warner's office. It turned out to be a large corner suite with a panoramic view overlooking the backlot. Warner's secretary, a pert blonde named Molly, gave Dillinger a warm smile and offered him a seat. "He's just finishing up with someone," she said.

"That's fine," he said, sitting on a leather-covered chair and picking up *The Hollywood Reporter*. Just like the others, there was a nice big photo of him and Cagney on the front page. The secretary's intercom buzzed as he was rereading the story.

Molly pushed one of the buttons. "Yes, Mr. Warner?"

"Send him in, Molly," came the tinny reply.

Molly nodded toward the door marked "Private," and Dillinger put down the paper and stood up.

Here goes nothin'.

Jack Warner's office was a study in calculated effect. The teakwood desk, instead of being directly across from the door against the wall, was set at a forty-five-degree angle from one of the room's corners. It allowed the occupant the full view of the room yet kept the visitor off-balance. Dillinger did his best to ignore that and strode across the room as Jack Warner smiled, rose from his seat, and extended his hand.

"Mr. Dillinger, it's a pleasure to finally meet you face-to-face."

Warner's grip was dry and firm. This guy was no pushover. "Pleased to meet you as well, Mr. Warner."

Warner beamed, his pencil mustache curving with his lips, giving his mirthful expression a piratical flair. "Please, call me Jack, and I'll call you John. Sit down, sit down," he said with a paternal wave of his hand. "Is everything all right at the Roosevelt? Is Woody treating you well?"

Dillinger knew this wasn't a casual question—he knew the valet's future hung on whatever he said. "The room's first class, and Woody is too." Dillinger lit a cigarette. "I read the script you sent over. Duke's a real corker. Could be a lot of fun. The problem's that Alan Squier character. A high-tone mug—too preachy. Nobody talks like that."

Warner nodded. "I know, and I agree. But since Leslie Howard has an interest in the property, there's not much we can do about it. Besides, the ladies love him."

"He's the guy playing Squier?"

"That's right."

"He's going to be a problem."

"Why do you say that?" Warner asked.

"The way I hear it, he wants some other guy for my part."

"You mean Humphrey Bogart?"

"That's the name I heard."

Warner shook his head with a rueful smile. "Bogart was very good in the play—excellent, in fact."

"So, why aren't you using him?" Dillinger asked, locking eyes with Warner.

"Because he's not you, John. Because the play's author modeled the character of Duke Mantee after you. And when I saw that film you did, I knew there was no one else better."

Dillinger remained silent.

"We'll find something for Mr. Bogart. The studio just signed him to a long-term contract. I'll admit Mr. Howard was difficult—"

"How so?"

Warner hesitated a moment, and for a split second Dillinger thought the man would clam up, but instead he sat back and smiled. "Mr. Howard thought he could strong-arm me by saying 'No Bogart, No Howard,' but I told him in no uncertain terms that you had the part and that if he wanted off the picture, there would be no hard feelings."

Dillinger grinned. "And what did he say to that?"

"Let's just say he became very pragmatic. And when I offered to sign Bogart as a consolation prize, he saw the light." Warner's smile now had a feral edge to it.

Dog-eat-dog.

"I'm glad to hear that, as I wouldn't want to be the cause of any bad blood. It's bad enough I'm splashed all over the papers because of Cagney."

"Don't feel too badly about that, John. You did good."

Dillinger straightened up in the chair. "What?"

Warner shrugged. "My publicity department arranged for that little show, and Jimmy was only too happy to oblige."

Dillinger felt like a first-class fool. Those photographers *had* been lying in wait, and he was just too dense to figure it out.

"Why didn't you clue me in?"

"John, you're a natural actor, but if we'd told you ahead of time, you would have put too much thought into it. It would have *looked* staged."

"Yeah, I got that. But I didn't pull my punch, Jack. I nailed him good."

"I know. And I can tell you feel badly about that." Warner pushed his intercom. "Molly, go ahead and send him in."

Dillinger turned as the door opened and in walked James Cagney, sporting a black eye and a grin like the Cheshire cat's. "How ya doin', tough guy," he said, strutting across the room. Dillinger stood up, feeling even more foolish.

"Sorry about that punch. I had no idea."

"And that's the way we wanted it," Cagney said, winking his good eye then sticking out his hand. "Where'd you learn to hit like that?"

Dillinger grinned as he shook the actor's hand. "On half the street corners in Indianapolis."

"I should've known," he said, laughing. "Listen, I know they've got you set up with Ouspenskaya. She's one of the best, but she'll run you like a racehorse. If you ever want some pointers—the straight dope—you come and see me, okay?"

"I appreciate that," Dillinger said, genuinely touched.

"Helping you helps us all. Right, Jack?"

"Right, Jimmy. Say, why don't you take our newest star for a tour of the lot? Show him the new stages."

Cagney grinned. "Why the hell not? With this shiner I've got a couple of days off, anyway."

※　※　※

Outside the building, Cagney commandeered one of the numerous electric golf carts and they set off on their tour. Their first stop were two adjacent soundstages under construction, 25 and 26, both of which appeared to be nearing completion.

"These are the latest ones. Over twenty thousand square feet and fully air-conditioned. And believe you me, when you're under those lights, that cool air makes a difference."

From there they headed to the other end of the lot, where Cagney showed him a warehouse as big as any of the soundstages that held nothing but props and wardrobe. "You can outfit anything from a caveman to Buck Rogers," Cagney said.

As they turned around to head back toward the commissary, Dillinger spotted a large Wells Fargo armored truck lumbering past them, heading for one of the administration buildings, the heavyset driver giving him the gimlet eye.

"What's with that?" Dillinger asked.

"Payroll truck. When you have ten thousand people working for you, you gotta bring their pay in a truck like that every week."

Dillinger shot Cagney an incredulous look. "Every week?"

"Yep, six hundred grand every week."

"Looks like I got into the right business, after all," Dillinger said, shaking his head in admiration.

"Yeah, so do I. But hands off the truck, my paycheck's in there too." Cagney grinned and both men laughed.

※　※　※

After lunch at the commissary, where Dillinger indulged in a thick hamburger and one of the best malted milk shakes he'd ever had, they hopped into the golf cart and headed over to a live set.

Climbing out of the cart, Cagney led the way to a large sliding door where a uniformed guard watched the comings and goings of the actors and crew. He smiled when he saw Cagney. "How you doin', Mr. Cagney?"

Cagney clapped the guard on the shoulder. "Just peachy, Joe. If you don't mind, I'm gonna show my friend the set."

The guard turned to Dillinger, his sleepy eyes widening. "Gosh, are you—"

Dillinger stepped closer and shook the guard's hand. "Nice to meet you, Joe."

The guard looked even more star-struck than he had with Cagney. "You can go on in. They're between setups."

Cagney led Dillinger through a maze of disassembled sets and various freestanding lights and related equipment. Cables were stretched across the floor in all directions, and Dillinger tripped up twice until he learned to watch the floor as he walked. In a few moments they came to an area bathed in light. The set resembled the exterior of a New York City tenement and consisted of a ground-floor restaurant and a second floor with sash windows. The set ended just above the second floor, where a grid of overhead lights hung from latticework of two-inch piping. An actor stood at one of the windows, holding what looked like a .45 automatic pistol.

Dillinger's gaze shifted to the camera, which was mounted to a crane suspended about six feet off the ground and focused on the actor in the window. The crew swarmed over the set, making adjustments to the lighting, while the actor and the camera crew rehearsed their moves. Dillinger watched as a crewman dressed in coveralls hefted a Thompson submachine gun.

"What's with that guy?" Dillinger asked.

"He's the marksman. My guess is there's supposed to be shots that'll just miss one of the actors. That guy will fire it."

Dillinger looked shocked. "You mean you guys are using live ammo?"

Cagney laughed. "You're one to talk, tough guy!"

"It's one thing to have some mugs shooting at you when you're stealin' their dough. That comes with the territory. It's another thing to just stand there and let somebody *try* and miss you with a Tommy gun." He shook his head.

Still smiling, Cagney said, "I can't speak for robbing banks, but these guys know what they're doing."

"I remember that scene in *Public Enemy* where you ran around a corner and a machinegun shot up the wall right where you were just standing. You mean that was real?"

"Yeah. It's the only way to make it look real."

"Maybe so, but couldn't you put explosives in the wall? That way you could fire them off whenever you want and there's no chance of anyone getting shot."

Cagney's stunned expression made Dillinger want to laugh.

"Jesus Christ, that's a hell of an idea," he said. "But those marksmen aren't going to like being out of a job very much, and they're the last ones you want sore at you!"

"They can plant the explosives," Dillinger replied with a grin.

Just then the assistant director called for quiet and everyone took their places. Somewhere, a bell rang, and all the noises he was hearing—talking, hammering, sawing, and drilling—stopped, as if someone had thrown a switch.

Dillinger watched the scene unfold, which as Cagney had guessed, consisted of the actor firing blanks out the window and screaming, "Come and get it, coppers!"

Dillinger stifled a laugh, as he would have never shouted anything of the sort. He'd just fire and, if he had the chance, duck and run. There was no shame in not getting killed. Just as the actor finished shooting, the marksman with the Thompson took aim and let off a burst that snaked a line of holes right above the window.

"Cut!" the director yelled. "Print it!"

The bell rang again, and the hammering, sawing, and drilling started up immediately.

They left the set a few moments later, taking the golf cart back to the building housing Jack Warner's office. Woody waited with the Ford idling at the curb. Cagney thrust out his hand and Dillinger shook it.

"I meant what I said. You need anything, you just holler."

"I appreciate that, Jimmy."

135

Cagney shook his head. "There's a lot of crazy people in this business, and it takes smarts to rise above it and not lose your head. You're not like these mugs and they know it. They'll fawn all over you to your face, but given half a chance, they'll spit in your soup. They're just biding their time, waiting for you to screw up."

"I'm not gonna screw up," Dillinger said, his jaw tightening.

"Good. Just do your best and don't bump into the furniture."

During the ride back to the Roosevelt, Dillinger brooded. He knew exactly what Cagney was getting at. As nice as everyone was, which was surprising when one took his background into account, he knew there were those who would like nothing better than to trip him and see him fall flat on his face. Well, that wasn't going to happen.

It was late afternoon by the time Dillinger returned to the hotel. Crossing the lobby, he recognized a white-haired man smoking a cigar seated near the elevator, staring at him.

"Hello, Mr. Sennett."

"Hello, Mr. Dillinger," Mack responded.

Dillinger knew Sennett was down on his luck and now considered a has-been by the industry. Still, he wanted to pay his respects to the man many still considered "The King of Comedy." Sennett appreciated Dillinger's kind words and offered him a cigar.

"They won't let me chew tobacco in this dump," Sennett explained with a tired sigh. "Won't wash out of the rugs."

"Thanks," Dillinger said, pocketing the cigar, "I'll save it for later."

"Smoke 'em if you got 'em, John," advised the old man, his gaze locked onto Dillinger's. "Otherwise . . ." The older man shrugged and smiled. Just then the elevator doors opened, and Dillinger bid Sennett a good evening.

On the way up to his suite, Dillinger pulled out the cigar and held it under his nose, inhaling its robust aroma. It was a hand-rolled Cohiba and must have cost Sennett at least a buck. Smiling, he bit off the end and stuck the cigar in his mouth.

"Smoke 'em if you got 'em . . ."

Probably the best advice I'll ever get out here.

SIX MONTHS LATER

14

Warner Brothers Studios
Burbank, California
September 11, 1935

"Again!" the old woman said, pounding her cane upon the polished hardwood floor. In the bare twenty-by-thirty-foot space, the sound echoed like a rifle shot. The room was situated in one of the many squat stucco buildings dotting the Warner lot, occupying the entire second floor. It was ostensibly a dance studio, with waist-high polished wooden railings and mirrors on every wall, save for the front bay windows where the sun blasted through, casting bright rectangles of light on the floor. The room was an oven, too, and Dillinger was soaked in sweat as much from his efforts as from the heat.

The heat didn't seem to bother the old woman, though.

Maria Ouspenskaya stood ramrod straight, swathed in a high-necked black dress, a woolen shawl, and a turban in gold lamé. Barely five feet in height, she nevertheless exuded an imperial presence that made her seem larger. Her steel-blue eyes and wide, flat nose gave her the look of a stern taskmaster who brooked no impertinence. She lit a new cigarette with the butt of her last one, throwing the discard onto the floor, where it smoldered.

Dillinger had heard she was a terror to work with, making un-reasonable demands and consulting astrologers before consenting to be filmed, holding up entire crews for hours. Yet she and Dillinger had formed an immediate bond, she sensing his raw talent, and he drawing from her the inspiration for discipline and hard work. There was also a maternal element. He wanted to please her, for her compliments were few and far between, and when they came, he felt honestly rewarded.

Now, he wanted only to wring the scrawny old bird's neck. For the last hour, she'd made him crawl about on the floor, pretending to be various animals. First, he'd been a monkey, then a dog, a snake, and now a lion stalking its prey. And while he enjoyed the simian im-itation, the novelty quickly wore thin. He felt silly, and the sweltering heat had frayed his nerves to the breaking point.

"Again!" she said, the cane striking the floor.

He stared back at her, and Dillinger saw a flicker of understand-ing in her eyes, acknowledging that she'd gone too far. Without a word, she hung her cane from one of the railings and walked the length of the room to a small sink, where she filled a glass of water. She returned to Dillinger and handed it to him, watching him gulp it down in two swallows. It wasn't all that cold, but it felt like a little draught of heaven nonetheless.

"Thanks," he said, wiping his mouth with his sleeve.

Maria sank gracefully to the floor next to him in a move that re-minded Dillinger of a ballet dancer. She crossed her legs and looked at him with an indulgent smile.

"You t'ink I am torturing you, eh, Johnnie?"

"It seems like that at times," he said with a rueful smile of his own.

"Acting is more than reciting one's lines, my child. It is a way of life. When I was younger, I traveled with a company of actors performing in the provinces for any audience that would sit for us. Sometimes, we played in grand palaces for thousands, and other times in *shtetls* for audiences no larger than what I could count on my fingers," she said, holding up a leathery hand gnarled by arthritis. "And I learned quickly that the one thing every audience had in common was the desire to leave their lives behind, if only for a little while, and live as if they were someone else. To do that, I had to become those characters, to live those make-believe lives as if they were real. Do you understand what I am saying?"

Dillinger nodded. "Yeah. I'm just not sure I can *do* that."

The old lady waved off his comment with a flick of her wrist. "Bah! You can, and perhaps better than others I have taught. You have a spark, Johnnie. You need only believe this, and you will light the fire in the hearts of your audience."

Dillinger felt something akin to the moments before he would step into a bank, pull his gun, and order everyone to raise their hands—that indescribable rush of adrenaline that was better than any drug or booze. He gazed into Maria's ancient eyes and saw that feeling reflected in them.

"One more time?" he asked with a sly smile.

The old woman nodded, rose to her feet without the aid of her hands, and walked back to where her cane hung from the railing and stood there . . . waiting.

Dillinger sat for a moment, his eyes closed, his thoughts racing across the world to a patch of sun-blasted savannah in west Africa. He rose on his haunches, his eyes never leaving his prey, the gazelle that stood drinking at the watering hole fifty feet away. He moved through the stalks of bone-dry grass, feeling every muscle rippling along his body, tendons taut and ready to spring. He stopped, frozen in place, crouching in the tall grass, his yellow eyes watching as the gazelle sniffed the air. The animal looked as if it might bolt at any second, and he crouched lower in the grass.

He waited, his stomach growling in anticipation of the hot blood and warm meat. A moment later, the gazelle dropped her head to the stagnant brown water and took another drink.

And then he pounced!

"Excellent!" Maria shouted, pounding the floor repeatedly with her cane.

Dillinger smiled and sat back, basking in the glow of her approval, still tasting the warm blood of the gazelle in his mouth.

※ ※ ※

After a shower and a quick lunch at the commissary with Cagney, who was in the midst of shooting *Frisco Kid*, Dillinger headed over to Stage 15. Today was the first table reading for *The Petrified Forest* script. As Cagney had explained, this was the opportunity for the cast to meet and go through the screenplay from start to finish. Any awkwardness with dialogue or stage business could be ironed out, as the writer or writers would also be in attendance. While Dillinger saw the logic in this, a part of him was wary, as he had no idea how his fellow actors would receive him. Cagney, Harlow, and Powell might be good eggs, taking him at face value and welcoming him into the fold, while others might snub him or be downright hostile— judging him for his past deeds rather than keeping an open mind. As he walked into the cool darkness of Stage 15, he let these feelings peel away from him like the skin of a snake. Truth be told, he was John Dillinger, and people would judge him no matter what he did. For some he would need to continually prove himself before that old persona was forgotten, and even then, there would be some who would never forget.

As he moved deeper into the stage, he saw carpenters and painters putting the finishing touches on the exterior set of *The Petrified Forest* Bar-B-Q and Filling station, his feet crunching on the edges of the sand that covered the floor from the front of the building. Through the windows he could see the interior set. A group of men and women were sitting around a long table littered with ashtrays, clouds of smoke hanging over their heads. He glanced at his watch, steeled himself, and walked through the front door, nodding to one of the painters as he passed through.

The set fell silent as all eyes turned to look at him, making him feel like a lab specimen. "Am I late?" he asked, noticing the empty coffee cups and half-eaten pastries on tin plates.

A stocky man with pomaded black hair stood up and smiled. "Not at all. I'm Archie Mayo, the director. It's a pleasure to have you aboard, Mr. Dillinger."

Dillinger shook his hand and smiled, then the director took him around and introduced him to the writers and his fellow cast members. Most greeted him warmly, with Bette Davis and Leslie Howard being the exceptions. Davis had given him a cool appraising look, her handshake as limp as a dead fish. "Charmed," she said, and that was it.

Howard's greeting had more frost to it, but Dillinger understood where that was coming from, having displaced the actor's choice for the role of Duke Mantee. He'd said nothing, given Dillinger a perfunctory shake of the hand then returned to his folding chair and picked up the script. "Ready when you are, Archie," he said.

Mayo gave Dillinger a wink and pointed to an empty chair between his own and Joe Sawyer's, the actor playing Jackie, a member of Duke's gang. "Leslie's all right," Mayo said, patting Dillinger on the back. "Once we get going, he'll come around."

Dillinger took his seat and picked up his copy of the screenplay. The rest of the actors settled down and opened their copies. "All right, everybody," Mayo said, putting on a set of tortoiseshell glasses. "Since we all know who we are and presumably know whom we're playing, let's get right to it." He cleared his throat and began reading. "Fade in on a close shot of a manuscript entitled "Exiles," by Alan Squier. Dissolve to . . ."

Dillinger watched as Mayo read the scene headers and descriptive action, and then each of the actors in the scene recited their lines. Some of them really put themselves into it, as if they were "on" at that very moment, while others merely read the lines in a token manner, as if they were saving themselves for when the cameras actually rolled. Dillinger decided then and there he wasn't going to be in that camp. If Maria had taught him anything, it was to give his all every time. It's what he'd always done, whether it was playing baseball or robbing banks. And he had a distinct feeling he needed to make a big impression right off the bat. He needed to show the Bette Davises and the Leslie Howards of the world that John Dillinger was no slouch.

It took nearly an hour before the cast reached the point of his entrance on page fifty-four. He reminded himself not to read the parentheticals above the dialogue, the little bits of text that instructed the actors how to deliver their lines. Quite a lot of the dialogue had these, and Dillinger saw that not only did no one read them out loud, most of the cast tended to ignore them, interpreting the lines as they saw fit.

Mayo, the director, didn't seem bothered by that, so Dillinger decided to add a little interpretation of his own.

"Medium Close Shot," Mayo read. "Mantee approaching camera toward road. The automobile is dust-covered, has been apparently driven off the road into an arroyo. A group of four men are standing beside it but are not identifiable in this shot. They listen to the car's radio as their leader walks from the car to the road. The announcer's voice is distinctly audible as we realize the description fits the man approaching the road."

Dillinger looked up from his first line and saw everyone looking at him. He stared daggers at Leslie Howard and let the moment hang in silence. And then . . .

"Kill that radio," he said, knowing it sounded wrong as soon as the words left his mouth.

"Cut," Mayo said. "Try it again."

Dillinger stole a glance at Leslie Howard, who watched him with a smug grin.

"Kill that radio."

"Better, but you need to feel it, John." And then Mayo stomped on Dillinger's right foot.

Dillinger cried out and rocketed to his feet, his face flushed. "What the hell did you do that for?"

Mayo remained calm, his gentle eyes now steely. "*That's* what I want. Now read the line as if someone stomped on your foot."

Dillinger retook his seat, still seething. He never took his eyes from Howard, letting his gaze burn a hole in the actor's forehead.

"Kill that radio!"

Next to him, he felt Joe Sawyer jump in his seat at the sound of his voice.

Dillinger leaned back in his folding chair and glanced at Bette Davis, who now regarded him with a look of guarded curiosity. Howard merely blinked and gave him a cursory nod.

"Well done, Mr. Mantee," Mayo said, and the cast burst out laughing.

The rest of the reading went well, with Dillinger right on top of all his cues and delivering his lines with conviction, the dull ache in his foot a constant reminder of Mayo's admonishment. When it was over, Dillinger sat back and allowed himself a soft sigh of relief.

"All right, everyone," Mayo said, closing his script. "We need to let the carpenters finish their jobs or we'll never start on time. I'll see you all back here bright and early Monday. Six o'clock call, people." He turned to Dillinger. "A word?"

Mayo waited until the room cleared. "I hope you're not too angry with me, John. It's an old director's trick, but it works. I can't have you pulling punches when you read the lines."

"Got it," Dillinger said, picking up his script. He watched Mayo leave.

The only punch I pulled was the one I should've planted on that guy's kisser.

As Dillinger left the set, a voice called out.

"Archie's a good egg, but he can be a little dramatic."

Dillinger turned to see Joe Sawyer regarding him with a broad grin.

"Him and Howard should start a fan club."

"Ah, don't mind Leslie. He's a bit stuck-up, but whaddya expect—he's verrry British."

All this came out in a thick Irish accent, and Dillinger laughed. "That's good," he said. "And by the way, I like your work. I've seen some of your pictures."

The actor's grin warmed. "Thanks. I never get tired of hearing that. You won't either."

"That's assuming I hear it at all."

Sawyer's eyebrows arched. "Are you kiddin'? You're a natch."

"A natural screw-up, you mean."

"It's just nerves. You'll get into the swing of things. I'm bettin' on it. Besides, I hear you and Ouspenskaya have been goin' at it—in a manner of speakin'." The grin was back.

"Mazie's a hot pistol to work with, but she knows her stuff."

"That she does, boyo, that she does. Just don't ever let her hear you call her Mazie!" Sawyer laughed and clapped Dillinger on the shoulder. "Say, there's a great little gin joint not far from the lot. How about we go and grab us a couple of beers and talk about the show?"

"Sounds good to me," Dillinger said, "if you don't mind me picking your brain a bit."

"You're gonna need a pick *and* a shovel, but you can try."

※ ※ ※

The two men were the last to leave, as the crew of carpenters moved in and began hammering together the last of the set. A bland-looking young man with a pencil mustache put down his hammer and broke away, heading toward the studio wall where a bank of telephones was mounted.

One of the other carpenters, an older man with the harried look of one in authority, shouted after him. "Hey, McGillicuddy, where do ya think you're goin'? We got work to do!"

The young man turned. "Checking on the wife, Jack! Baby's due any day."

The older man rolled his eyes and shook his head, as if remembering and feeling foolish for it. "Sorry, Ben. I keep forgettin' about your missus. Make it quick, all right?"

"Sure thing, Boss."

The young man went to the phones, picked one up, and dialed. It was answered on the first ring. "Hiya, honey, just wanted to check in and see how you're doing," he said, looking around to see if he was being overheard. ". . . Ah, that's good. I'm glad you're feelin' okay. You know how I worry. Hey, just thought you'd like to know they're starting to shoot on Monday. Yeah, I'll try and get Dillinger's autograph, but I can't make any promises. They might have me working on another stage by then . . . Okay, see you later, sweetie."

⁂ ⁂ ⁂

"And don't forget the milk," Melvin Purvis said with a wry grin as he hung up his phone. The smile slipped from his face and the moment of mirth was gone as quickly as it had come. With a sigh, he stood up from his desk and moved to the window, gazing down six floors to the intersection of Hollywood and Vine. It was just after noon, and the traffic was snarled due to a road crew tearing up half the street.

"What on earth am I doing out here in this cesspool?" he asked himself, placing his forehead against the cool pane of glass.

In the six months since he'd been assigned to watch Dillinger, Purvis had done his level best to keep busy, the truth being there was precious little to do when his main quarry was minding his own legitimate business. And he had no mandate nor any authority to launch any other investigations for the Bureau. Hoover had been emphatic about that. Purvis was to keep his attention on Dillinger and concern himself with nothing else. He'd been fine with that, at first, but now he felt like one of those seedy private eyes sitting in a flyblown office, counting his debts and waiting for some seductress in a slinky dress to show up and an adventure to begin. If only his life was more like the movies, or at least more like it was before being sent out here. Even chasing tax evaders was more exciting than this.

He was also, quite frankly, not surprised that Dillinger was behaving himself. Six months ago, Purvis would have bet his eyeteeth the former outlaw wouldn't be able to resist the pull of his former life. That was before he saw how taken the Hollywood people were with Dillinger. In all the months he and his small staff were shadowing the former outlaw, he'd seen Dillinger attending parties and premieres, hobnobbing with the likes of Jean Harlow, William Powell, and Jimmy Cagney. The irony was he seemed to fit right in with that bunch. And the most infuriating thing was that Dillinger was now making more money than he'd ever gleaned from any of his robberies, all while being fawned over by these Hollywood big shots. Purvis had even managed to finagle a copy of Dillinger's studio contract, which among other things stipulated a weekly salary of $750.00, whether he was shooting a film or not. That was more money than Purvis took home in three months! It was little wonder the son of a bitch was behaving.

None of this information had persuaded Hoover to change his mind or his tactics. In the director's mind, Dillinger was a menace to be watched and eventually neutralized. That meant there was nothing Purvis could do except soldier on in the hopes Dillinger might slip up.

The phone rang, and it was Rosanne asking him not to forget the milk when he came home. Purvis had to laugh. Who was the sap here? Dillinger? Fat chance. He'd only need to glance in a mirror to see the truth. It was time to turn up the heat—he needed access to that set. If Dillinger saw him there, maybe it would rattle him, make him think twice if he was planning anything. He also had to admit that he was curious to see his old nemesis in action.

Purvis reached for the phone and dialed the home office. As much as he disliked speaking with the director, he knew Hoover was the only one who could get him on that soundstage.

After a brief conversation in which Hoover expressed grudging approval and promised to see what he could do, they hung up, and Purvis headed to the Brown Derby for lunch.

As he tucked into his steak seated in a corner booth, Purvis noticed a young starlet sitting with an older man in a booth across from him. By his manner and his flashy diamond pinky ring, Purvis assumed the man was her agent. She was ignoring the old goat as he prattled on, gazing at Purvis with a brazen look and coy smile, every curve of her ample body straining the seams of her dress. Purvis smiled back and sighed inwardly. He was a happily married man, though he had to admit the view in Los Angeles was far better than the one in Washington.

15

Dillinger brooded during the ride to the studio, his dog-eared and coffee-stained copy of *The Petrified Forest* clutched in his hand. It was more of a security blanket than a necessity, as he could recite the entire document from memory, having learned everyone else's lines in addition to his own. He was ready, but his gut was twisted into knots nonetheless. It struck him as strange that he would be so nervous. He'd never been that way before a robbery. He'd been excited, but never fearful. The only thing that made any sense was that he was feeling this way because a part of him felt that he didn't really know what he was doing—despite Maria Ouspenskaya's coaching and the words of encouragement from Joe Sawyer and Cagney.

In the old days, when he walked into a bank, everything was planned down to the smallest detail, and he was in control. And maybe that was the crux of the issue. Though he knew the script backwards and forwards, he was not calling the shots. When he'd made that short film, he'd known exactly what do to, as if he'd always known it. Dillinger shook his head, letting out a heavy sigh.

He glanced out the window just as they passed a Bank of America on the corner of Hollywood and Argyle and longed for the bygone days when things were simple.

"You all right, Boss?" Woody called out from the driver's seat.

Dillinger met the valet's eyes in the rearview mirror. "I'm fine, Woody. Just anxious to get on with the job."

Woody grinned, his teeth a fluorescent white in the predawn light. "I hear you, Mr. Dillinger."

They were winding their way along North Cahuenga Boulevard, the wooded hills crowding the narrow two-lane road. Homes on either side were nestled into those hills, some of them behind imposing fences and gates. Others fronted the street, with most of their living space hanging off the edge of a cliff. And while the homes were beautiful, no amount of money in the world would ever convince him to live in one.

Woody guided the Ford onto Barham Boulevard for the descent into the valley. The sun was just peeking over the Santa Monica Mountains to the west, and the entire San Fernando Valley spread out before him bathed in a golden glow. *Well, maybe the view is worth it*, he thought with a smile.

The guard at the studio's main gate glanced into the Ford, nodded, and waved them through. Woody slowed the sleek car to a crawl as they wound their way toward Stage 15, so as to avoid bumping into the throngs of extras and crewmembers streaking this way and that on urgent errands. Dillinger glanced at his watch.

Five forty-five a.m.

At least he wasn't late. He rubbed his three-day stubble of beard, still feeling uncharacteristically grubby. The director had asked him not to shave over the weekend, as Duke Mantee wouldn't be shaving while on the lam. It made sense, but when he'd asked how he was supposed to keep it that way, Archie had smiled and told him the makeup people had a special razor for that. Imagine that, a razor that would keep your three-day beard looking the same day after day.

Woody steered the car into a space outside Stage 15 and Dillinger made ready to get out.

"You gonna do just fine, Boss. I can feel it in my bones."

Dillinger grinned despite his nerves. Woody had sensed his employer's uncertainty over the past weekend and had gone out of his way to be supportive. Dillinger had noticed and appreciated it.

"Thanks. I'm almost getting to believe it."

Woody laughed. "Well, you go on and bring 'em to their knees, as my pappy used to say, and I'll be here when you're ready to go."

"I'll do that," Dillinger said, slapping the top of the front seat.

Moments later he was inside the stage and caught up in a whirlwind of activity.

The entire set and surrounding area of the stage swarmed with an army of people. Some of them were assisting members of the cast, while others were engaged in adjusting the lights hanging from the overhead grid, or readying the enormous Mitchell camera, which sat mounted on a dolly. He smiled, remembering how they'd improvised on his short film. This was the real thing. This was the belly of the beast.

"Mr. Dillinger?"

He turned at the sound of the high-pitched voice and saw a tall, skinny young man dressed in an argyle sweater and wrinkled khaki pants. He used one hand to push his coke-bottle glasses up his nose, his other hand clutching a battered clipboard. He looked nearly as nervous as Dillinger felt.

"Hiya, kid, what's up?" Dillinger asked, extending his hand.

The young man shook his hand, looking relieved. "I'm Bob Noll, the second assistant director. Let me get you to makeup and wardrobe. Mr. Mayo wants to roll the first shot at six thirty."

Dillinger nodded and followed the assistant to a windowless room filled with rolling pipe racks on which hung the wardrobe for every member of the cast. Each garment was tagged with the character's name. The wardrobe mistress, a short, stocky brunette, smiled and handed Dillinger his costume, consisting of a gray work shirt, a charcoal-gray pinstriped vest, and matching pants. Every item was covered with smudges of dirt, and the brown wing tip oxfords she handed him next looked as if they'd been wrested off a hobo.

The wardrobe mistress pointed to an open changing room, and Dillinger disappeared into it, emerging five minutes later with his street clothes clutched in hand. "What should I do with these?"

"Give 'em here," she said, holding out her hand. "I'll have 'em pressed and ready for you at the end of the day. You go on now and break a leg."

"Thanks," Dillinger said, handing her his clothes with a grin. "Just don't steal 'em."

Noll shot a nervous glance at his watch and said, "We need to get you to makeup right now, Mr. Dillinger."

The makeup area turned out to be just off set in a group of folding tables clustered together, each one topped by a lighted vanity mirror. Joe Sawyer sat in front of one of the mirrors, wearing his dusty costume and a gap-toothed grin, pieces of Kleenex tissue jutting out from his shirt collar. A young woman hovered nearby, applying powder to his face.

"Am I sexy yet, John?"

"I think you need some more rouge. Maybe a bucket's worth," Dillinger said, easing his body into the folding chair next to the beefy actor.

Sawyer chuckled. "How's it feel so far?"

Dillinger leaned back and watched in the mirror as another young woman placed Kleenex around his collar and began dabbing his face with powder. "Like my heart's running the fifty-yard dash."

Sawyer gave him a nod. "That's normal. You gotta worry if you *don't* feel like that."

"Why?"

"It means you give a damn."

Yes, Dillinger supposed he did. And the first shot was going to be a doozy. As he'd found out from Sawyer during one of their talks, films were shot out of sequence to maximize efficiency, clustering camera setups for scenes in one location that might appear throughout the film. While most of the action took place inside the restaurant, it would be impractical to film it in a linear fashion. Therefore, as luck would have it, the call sheet delivered by the studio the night before listed the first shot as scene 270. It occurred on page 101, where Duke Mantee has learned that four of his compatriots, including his girlfriend, have been apprehended, throwing him into a moment of profound crisis. It was a dramatic high point, and Dillinger would have preferred something easier for his first moment on camera. But he wasn't running this show; he was just a hired gun.

When the makeup girl was finished, she removed the Kleenex, and Dillinger stared at himself in the mirror. The makeup artist had made him look dirty and haggard.

"Everything okay, Mr. Dillinger?" the girl asked in a hushed voice.

He patted her on the arm. "Everything's jake, kid."

He rose from the chair and followed Sawyer to the set, where Archie Mayo was instructing Leslie Howard and two of the other actors in the scene. Dillinger noticed chalk marks on the floor and realized this was where they were supposed to stand in relation to each other and the camera, which had now been moved to what appeared to be a medium shot.

"Leslie, when Joe says his line, I want you to jump in a little quicker than we did in rehearsal. Your character's afraid Duke might surrender, and you don't want that. Okay?"

"Yes," Howard agreed, looking thoughtful.

Archie turned to Dillinger and gave him a squeeze on the shoulder. "I know this shot is sort of like jumping into the deep end of the pool, but you can do this. Do you trust me?"

Dillinger nodded. "Yeah."

"All right, then. Keep this in your mind: you've just heard that your girl's been arrested, and you've got all these people yelling at you and you're at the point where you just can't take it anymore. You'll make a half-turn to your left and the camera will move in on you. That's when you hit us with your line. Got it?"

"Got it."

"All right, quiet for rehearsal!" Mayo yelled.

As Mayo rehearsed their blocking, and the grips made final adjustments to the lighting, Dillinger looked off and caught sight of a well-dressed figure standing in the shadows behind the camera. There was something familiar about the man—and something out of place. The way he stood stiff and straight when he could've been lounging in one of the folding chairs was at odds with the straw boater he wore at a jaunty angle. Just then a 5K-light snapped on, briefly illuminating the man before the grip on a ladder underneath it swung the light to face the set. In that brief moment he recognized him.

It was Melvin Purvis.

Dillinger felt a rush of mixed emotions. Anger that the man was still hounding him, however peripherally, and a curious feeling of regret. In those brief seconds, he'd caught Purvis's eye and saw on the FBI agent's face an expression of the most profound sadness, as if the man had lost his dearest friend. For a second, he considered walking over to him and saying something, but he honestly couldn't think of anything to say to his former nemesis. It was at that moment that Archie Mayo called for quiet on the set and Dillinger's attention returned to the rehearsal.

They rehearsed the scene and he recited his lines. He felt juiced, as if his entire body were humming with an electric current. The dialogue flowed effortlessly from his mouth, and in that instant, he *was* Duke Mantee, feeling every emotion as if it were his own.

"Cut!" Mayo said. "Excellent, Mr. Dillinger. Okay, everyone, let's go for a take!"

As the assistant director called for quiet and the camera rolled, Dillinger stole a glance back to where he'd spotted Purvis.

He was gone.

16

It was just past seven o'clock in the morning when Purvis tossed his boater onto the coatrack and slumped into the swivel chair behind his desk. He'd left the studio just after watching Dillinger rehearse his first scene, realizing in that crystalline moment that his entire reason for being in this godforsaken city was pointless. He'd left right then, driving over the hill and into the smoggy haze of Hollywood, grateful the traffic was light. It was too early for him to be there—too early even for his secretary, who prided herself on beating her boss to the office every morning—but he realized that he had nowhere else to go. He couldn't go home, not at this hour. If he did, his wife would start asking questions—questions for which he had no ready answers. There was already enough contention in their relationship. Rosanne hated Hoover with a passion that belied her sweet, vivacious nature, and she could plainly see the effect this assignment was having on him when he trudged through the door of their home every night. The worst thing was seeing that troubled expression on her lovely face, putting worry lines where there had once been none at all. It was a knife in his heart.

With a heavy sigh, he pulled open the bottom drawer of his desk with a screech of wood against wood and hauled out a bottle of Jim Beam and a cheap glass tumbler. He'd kept the bottle in his desk due to some misplaced notion right out of a Hollywood potboiler. The bottle was still sealed, the red and white tax stamp glued across the cap unbroken. He hesitated for only a moment before twisting the cap and pulling the cork, which gave a satisfying *thunk* as it cleared the rim. He brought the bottle under his nose and inhaled. He'd always loved the smell of whiskey but hated what it did to his father, who'd wasted most of his life drinking it. It was why Purvis rarely drank, remembering the old man's belligerent bellowing as the front door to their apartment burst open every night.

The thing was he'd never asked himself *why* his father drank. It certainly wasn't because it made him happy. He wasn't—drunk or sober. And then in that moment, with the fumes of the bourbon tingling his nose, he suddenly understood *exactly* why. The old man had outlived his usefulness, had lost his purpose in life—had come to the inescapable conclusion that his best years were behind him. Purvis felt like that right now, that awful realization stealing over him as he recalled Dillinger playing his short scene like a master.

Like his father, he had lost *his* purpose.

Dillinger was going to be a star—even a half-wit could see it. Whatever talent he possessed was compounded by his undeniable charisma, something Purvis himself had experienced when he'd been face-to-face with the former outlaw.

Purvis reached for the tumbler and poured in a generous two fingers of the smoky liquid, which he downed in one gulp. As soon as he swallowed, it felt as if a bomb had gone off in his chest, the warmth spreading to every extremity and making his eyes water and his head swim.

Jesus Christ!

He coughed and poured another drink. He sipped it this time, allowing his palate to savor the flavor and his mind to study the problem at hand, because there very definitely *was* a problem.

Hoover wanted Dillinger on a silver platter, signed, sealed, and convicted of a crime that would put him behind bars for as many years as possible; Purvis knew this to be a forlorn hope. Why on earth would Dillinger do anything illegal now, when the world was his oyster and he was making real money? Why would he be *that* stupid? The answer was he wouldn't be, which brought his thoughts back around to his boss. Why was Hoover so obsessed with this man, a man who'd paid his debt to society and was getting on with his life? Could the director be *that* petty and *that* vindictive?

Purvis already knew the answer to that one.

He finished the drink and poured another, not caring a whit if his secretary came in and found him in his cups. What the hell did it matter, anyway? He was finished. Hoover had never forgiven him for allowing Dillinger to surrender. The order to kill the outlaw had been clear, but was issued in secret, thereby preventing the director from openly firing him for insubordination. Instead, he'd been put out to pasture, left to rot chasing deadbeats attempting to evade their taxes, a tedious task any rookie could have performed.

He was even late with his weekly report because he'd run out of things to put in it. For a while he'd entertained the notion of making it all up, to let his imagination run wild as he did with the detective fiction he'd started to write in the wee hours of the evening. He loved dashing off these fast-paced tales and had even sold a hard-boiled short story to *Black Mask* under a pseudonym the previous month. But he couldn't allow himself to lie in a report. His pride wouldn't let him.

The phone rang at ten minutes before eight. His secretary still wasn't in, so he picked up the receiver.

"This is the Los Angeles office of the Federal Bureau of Investigation. Special Agent Melvin Purvis speaking."

He sounded robotic, the bourbon making his head spin and his gut churn.

"Special Agent Purvis."

It was Hoover.

A bolt of panic shot through him, and he straightened up in his chair. "Yes, sir."

"I tried to reach you at home, but I see you're in early," Hoover said, a hint of grudging approval in his voice. "I didn't receive your report this past week. I assume it must have been delayed in transit."

Purvis eyed the quarter inch of whiskey in the glass and was this close to allowing Hoover to believe that assumption, but instead he said, "I'm sorry, sir, but I'm still composing it."

"I see . . ."

He doesn't see at all!

" . . . then perhaps you'd better explain."

Purvis winced as a sharp pain lanced through his head. Hoover wanted a plausible excuse accompanied by the requisite amount of groveling, something for which Purvis no longer had the stomach. "There's nothing to explain, Mr. Hoover, as there is nothing to report."

"That's nonsense. We all know what this man is capable of; it's only a matter of time."

Purvis slugged back the last of his drink and decided that he should be completely truthful. "I just came from a visit to Warner

Brothers Studios and the set of *The Petrified Forest*, where I saw Dillinger rehearse his first scene like a pro—"

"I fail to see how that is relevant to what we're discussing," Hoover said in an irritated tone.

Purvis grimaced, the knuckles of the hand holding the phone whitening. "It's relevant because the man is embarking on a new and lucrative career that is completely and utterly legal. You may not like this, sir, but it's the truth. Dillinger's reformed."

"No, he's not!"

Purvis yanked the phone away from his head, Hoover's vitriol still ringing in his ears. The man continued to shout, his high-pitched voice sounding like an angry insect. Not listening anymore, Purvis grabbed the bottle of Jim Beam and took a long swig directly from it, wiping his mouth on the sleeve of his jacket.

"Special Agent Purvis, are you still there? Answer me!"

Purvis brought the phone back to his ear. "I'm here, sir, and I respectfully request that you take me off this case. I cannot find what is not there."

Purvis hadn't meant to sound like he was begging, but he couldn't keep that plaintive tone out of his voice. This was his last shot at keeping what was left of his dignity, if not his job.

"Absolutely not, you're the man for this."

"Then at least assign me another case or two. I can handle the load. You *know* that."

"No."

Purvis closed his eyes and swallowed the bile in his throat. There was no changing Hoover's mind once it was made up. Whether the director believed Dillinger was still dangerous was irrelevant. The fact of the matter was that J. Edgar Hoover was going to punish Melvin Purvis for his sins. The real question was why he was continuing to allow it. And as he sat there, his life passed before his eyes, the entire stinking cliché of it, like some sordid B-movie in a dirty rundown theatre on skid row.

"I want that report, Special Agent Purvis," Hoover said after a lengthy silence. "And I want you to shadow that son of a bitch night and day."

Purvis poured himself one last drink and gulped it down.

"Did you hear what I said, Special Agent Purvis?"

"Yes, sir. And now I want you to hear this— I resign!"

The ensuing silence stretched on far longer than he thought it would, and Purvis wanted to scream. Instead, he just let his mind concentrate on that glowing warmth in his chest.

"What did you say?" Hoover asked finally. His voice sounded hoarse and strained.

"I said, 'I quit,' Mr. Hoover, I resign—effective immediately."

"Your resignation is *not* accepted! Do you hear me, Special Agent Purvis?"

"Loud and clear, sir, and you can go to hell."

Hoover began to sputter more vitriol, and Purvis grinned, feeling the weight of the world lifting off his shoulders.

"You are a disgrace to the Bureau, Mr. Purvis, and I will make sure you never work again in law enforcement. Am I making myself clear?"

The shift was subtle, but unmistakable. Hoover had called him *Mister* Purvis.

It was done.

It was finally over.

He hung up the phone, cutting off Hoover in mid-rant, then reached for a blank sheet of typing paper and a fountain pen. The phone started ringing again, and Purvis ignored it. He wrote out his resignation, signed and dated it, and stood up, feeling taller in this moment than he'd felt in a long, long time. He walked into the outer room, where he placed the note on his secretary's desk along with instructions to mail it to Hoover first thing. For a moment he felt a pang of regret for her, as she really needed the job and was good at it.

Returning to his office, he saw the half-empty bottle still resting on the desk. He took it into the men's room and poured it down the sink. Unlike his father, he didn't need this, and already felt the effect of the alcohol receding. Once he sobered up, he would probably regret what he'd done, but right now it felt good. He was J. Edgar Hoover's whipping boy no longer. His wife would come to see that eventually, once he told her about all the shenanigans that had gone on during his years of service, something he didn't feel at liberty to discuss before today. She would come to understand that Hoover was more dangerous than many of the men he put behind bars.

Purvis threw the empty bottle into the trash and returned to his office, grabbed his straw boater and took one last look around, noting how bare and devoid of personal items the room was, which was just as well—that much less to take with him. Perhaps, on some subconscious level, he'd known he wouldn't be there for long.

Good riddance.

He was still too drunk to drive, so he locked up and walked to a diner two blocks over and treated himself to a second breakfast of sinkers and sausage. That and two cups of hot coffee took the edge off the effects of his early-morning imbibing. And it gave him a chance to think.

He knew Hoover's threat was not an idle one. Any future employment opportunity, whether in law enforcement or the private sector, would entail obtaining a reference from his previous employer. That's where that bastard would nail him. There would be nothing overtly stated, nothing that would give Purvis grounds to sue the man for slander. Rather, it would be a campaign of innuendo, of damning with faint praise. Hoover would do his level best to hold Melvin Purvis down without exposing his true motives.

Perhaps it was time to write that novel he'd been thinking about, a novel with main characters much like himself and John Dillinger. Now that he was out of the Bureau, he could publish it under his own name. He was still well-known as the man who'd captured Dillinger, which would be of incalculable aid in the book's potential for success. He even had a couple of ideas for motion picture scripts. He would need to study the style, structure, and format, but how hard could it be? He'd spent his life telling stories, and he was certainly in the right place for anything lucrative to emerge. He just had to sit down and see if he could write them.

I'll be fine, as long as I don't write about Hoover!

Purvis shook his head and laughed, feeling a little better than he had only moments before.

There *was* a silver lining in all of this. Being over-cautious and something of a pessimist, he'd socked away a fair percentage of his salary over the years, knowing someday there might come the proverbial rainy day. Well, it was about to pour buckets. If they were frugal, he and his family would have enough to tide them over for at least a couple of years while he wrote that book and those scripts. He just hoped he could sell them. If not, he would have to find something else to do—God willing, and Hoover be damned.

Pushing those bleak thoughts from his mind, he paid his check, retrieved his car, and slowly drove home to deliver the news to his wife.

SIX MONTHS LATER

17

The Roosevelt Hotel
Hollywood, California
February 1, 1936

Dillinger leaned against the open window and watched the crowds surging in the streets below, the starched collar of his shirt chafing his neck. He hated these monkey suits but had to admit the reason for wearing it excited him. Tonight was the premiere of *The Petrified Forest.* After a grueling three-week shoot, which had drained him far more than he'd expected, the studio had ramped up an unprecedented campaign, building steadily to the film's February 6th release.

Tonight, the cast, crew, VIPs, and critics would get a first glimpse. Dillinger looked down at Graumann's Chinese Theatre, marveling as searchlights swept the sky overhead, their white-hot beams criss-crossing in an endless figure-eight pattern, adding to the magical glow created by the banks of Klieg lights bathing the spectators lining Hollywood Boulevard. Warner had ordered bleachers built that stretched for half a block, and a bright red carpet extended from the street through the courtyard with its world-famous cement imprints of the stars' hands and feet, up the steps and into the theatre.

He was especially keen to see the finished film, as the director had good-naturedly barred him from preliminary screenings. "I want you to see this for the first time with a real audience, John," he'd said with his characteristic half-cocked grin. "At least as real as Hollywood royalty can be."

Watching from his window high above Hollywood Boulevard, Dillinger could feel the anticipation of the crowd. "Hope you're right, Archie. Hope I didn't embarrass myself."

He felt his valet's presence behind him. "What is it, Woody?"

"Miss Davis's car is waiting out back, Mr. Dillinger."

Dillinger turned and saw his valet regarding him with a paternal gaze. "Do I look okay?"

"Lookin' like a pair of aces, sir," Woody said, his dark eyes lighting up.

They left the suite moments later and descended to the loading dock via the hotel's freight elevator. Dodging crates of produce and other sundries, Dillinger nodded to one of the workers who'd offered him a thumbs up and descended a short set of concrete steps to the alley floor. Bette Davis's car, or rather her limousine, idled at the curb. It was a Rolls-Royce Phantom II in silver and black, and Dillinger could hear the inline six-cylinder engine purring.

Nice wheels.

Woody moved ahead and opened the door to the rear compartment, which was closed off from the driver by a thick glass partition. "Good luck, sir," Woody said.

Dillinger climbed in and eased himself into the plush leather seat, his nostrils filling with the heady odor of rich leather and saddle soap mixed with Bette's Chanel perfume. As soon as Woody shut the door, the driver pressed the accelerator and the Rolls moved toward the mouth of the alley. Dillinger glanced at Bette Davis, who so far had not uttered a word, her gaze riveted on some point far beyond the windshield. Because of the unique traffic issues that occurred during a premiere at Graumann's, the chauffeur turned right out of the alley and took Orange to Hawthorne then to Highland and finally back to Hollywood Boulevard. The police had a roadblock, but the chauffeur held up a special placard and the Rolls was waved through. Now they sat in a long line of Cadillacs, Duesenbergs, and other swanky automobiles inching forward at a snail's pace, all of them holding stars and other Hollywood personalities waiting their turn to strut their stuff on the red carpet.

While Bette stared out the window, Dillinger stretched out his legs, luxuriating in the soft carpeting and the extra room the silver Phantom's passenger compartment provided. He cast another glance at his date and then, confident and relaxed, he began singing softly to himself.

"Yippy ti-yi-yo, get along little doggies, it's your misfortune and none of my own, Yippy ti-yi-yo, get along little doggies, you know that Wyoming will be your new home."

Bette's shoulders hunched in annoyance. "What the hell are you singing?"

"Just a little ditty I used to hum to relax me after a robbery," Dillinger said, suppressing a grin. "Kind of like a good-luck charm."

Bette frowned and turned back to the window.

"This wasn't my idea, you know," she said, a moment later.

"Oh? Whose was it?"

"Jack's."

Dillinger grinned. Old Jack Warner was up to his usual tricks, all for the benefit of the film and ultimately, of course, the studio.

"So, he thought if everyone sees us together that'll get us more publicity?"

Bette's plucked eyebrows arched. "You catch on quick, I'll give you that. But let's be perfectly clear. There's nothing between us, not now, or ever, and if it were up to me, you'd be walking."

Dillinger felt a flare of anger, but let it go. This woman hadn't given him so much as an inch of slack during the shooting of the film, but he'd sensed a grudging respect from her as the production wore on. He was always on set on time and knew his lines. And while she could display an acid tongue, he admired her talent, which she had in spades.

"Well, just the same I appreciate the ride," he said, staring through the glass partition. "And you don't have to worry about me, Miss Davis, you're not my type."

In his peripheral vision he saw her eyes widen and then something even more curious, her mouth twisting into a satisfied grin.

So that was it, she had no respect for pushovers. Where she'd gotten the idea that *he* was a pushover he had no clue, but one thing was certain: he'd just scored some points.

She sat in silence as he continued humming his little cowboy tune. The car idled forward inch by inch, the crowds outside the window shouting and screaming.

"What was it like?" she asked.

Dillinger turned and found the actress regarding him with a relaxed grin.

"Robbing a bank, I mean."

Dillinger chuckled. "You really want to know?"

"It might come in handy someday."

Dillinger laughed out loud. "Knowing you, it might."

Bette's smile widened. "Go on . . ."

Dillinger squinted, as if he were looking off into a vast distance. And maybe he was. He'd come so far from where he'd been. "Every job was different, but I think what they all had in common was this feeling deep in my gut that I was putting everything on the line, that anything could happen. Those two minutes we spent inside those banks were the most exciting moments in my life." He nodded toward the crowds clamoring for a better look at them. "This is exciting too, but not even close."

Bette Davis studied him a moment. "And it never became routine?"

"Routine? No, never."

"I truly love what I do, but I'd be lying if I didn't find it all so boring now and then."

"Maybe you should try having someone shoot at you," Dillinger said.

Bette looked shocked then began to laugh. "He'd better not miss, 'cause he wouldn't get a second chance."

It took her a couple of minutes to compose herself, and by that time their car was third in line from the red carpet. Seeing they were almost there, she laid a hand on Dillinger's arm. "I owe you an apology, Mr. Dillinger. I've behaved in such a dreadful manner; my mother would be appalled. Will you forgive me?"

"I will if you'll call me Johnnie."

Bette grinned. "Johnnie it is." A moment passed and then she said, "Are you going to Jack's party after the show?"

"Do I have a choice?"

"Of course not, but they're usually fun, and you'll ride with me."

"Beats walking."

Bette Davis said nothing, her expression both coy and amused.

The car stopped in front of the red carpet and it seemed that every light in the area was now trained on them. A man dressed in a red uniform with brass buttons and a cape ran forward and opened the car door. Bette turned to Dillinger and said with a gleam in her eyes, "Let's give them something to talk about."

Even though he'd watched the crowd from his hotel room and studied their faces as Bette's Rolls-Royce glided past them, he was unprepared for the sheer bedlam that erupted when he and Bette alighted from the car. Hundreds of men and women screamed, pushed, and shoved, wanting to get closer to the two of them. In front of this surging mob were a line of LA cops, arms linked, their faces strained and sweating as they did their best to hold back the human tide threatening to overwhelm them at any moment.

Dillinger waved, and the crowd screamed louder. Up ahead, he spotted a cluster of microphones and newsreel cameras. A short, smiling, wavy-haired man dressed in a tuxedo was greeting each party of stars, joking with them, and then coaxing them to make a comment for the live radio audience.

Time to pay for the soup.

"Just follow my lead," Bette whispered, then turned on her thousand-watt smile. "Hi, Bert!" she said as the two of them reached the mikes. "You're looking dashing tonight."

Dillinger recognized the man as none other than Bert Wheeler of the comedy team, Wheeler and Woolsey.

"Thank you, thank you! Hey, everyone, we've just been joined by one of the brightest stars in tonight's show, Miss Bette Davis. Bette, what's it like playing opposite the legendary John Dillinger?"

Bette shot Dillinger a wink then said, "Well, Bert, I'll tell you, he's probably the most professional player I've ever worked with, and after tonight, everyone's going to see why."

Bert laughed. "You know, they say Dillinger's gone straight, but I bet after tonight he'll have stolen a million hearts!" The crowd around them laughed, and Bert put his arm around Dillinger, who gave him a look of tolerant amusement. "You know, I've known Johnnie a long time. He's a great guy, but you don't want to get on his bad side. Nope. Get him mad and he's more coldly calculating than an adding machine at the North Pole!" More laughs, and Dillinger rolled his eyes and shook his head. "And talk about tough?" Bert continued. "Why, we went fishing last week and the bait was laid out, right there on the pier, and Johnny took out a penknife and cut his worm in two. I asked him why he cut the worm in half and he said, 'It looked lonely!'"

Wheeler, Davis, and the crowd burst out laughing, and Dillinger grinned.

"Well, there you have it, folks," Wheeler said, drawing an apple from out of his pocket and taking a bite out of it. He gave Dillinger a chuck on the shoulder, and Dillinger, still grinning, shook his head. Bette touched his arm and nodded toward the lobby, and after one last wave to the crowd the two of them disappeared into the theatre.

The lobby was wall-to-wall people milling about and gabbing a mile a minute. The doors to the auditorium were closed, and Dillinger noticed uniformed waiters weaving through the crowd, bearing trays laden with canapés and flutes of champagne. Dillinger grabbed two glasses and handed one to Bette.

"Thank you, kind sir," she said, and took a sip. "You nervous?"

Dillinger shrugged. "I'd be lying if I said I wasn't, but I've got a good feeling."

"Me too," Bette said, taking another sip. She looked off, smiled, and waved at someone she knew. Then she frowned. "Don't look now, but someone's watching us."

"Isn't that what they're supposed to do?"

"Not like this. He looks very intent. He's just to the left of the lobby entrance."

Dillinger used the excuse of reaching for a canapé from a passing waiter and let his gaze wander over the crowd. He spotted the nattily dressed man standing next to a pillar, holding a flute of champagne. Melvin Purvis.

Dillinger turned back to Bette Davis and whispered, "It's someone I know. Excuse me for a moment."

She nodded her assent and Dillinger made a beeline for the FBI agent.

"You've got a lot of nerve showing up here," Dillinger said, his gray eyes like two sparking flints.

Purvis held up a hand. "Hold on, it's not what you think."

"No? What the hell am I supposed to think? I kept imagining I was seeing you everywhere I went. I put it down to nerves about the picture, but I can see it wasn't my imagination. It was you at the studio the first day of shooting, wasn't it?"

Purvis nodded. "Yes, but things are different now." This was delivered with a warm smile, and Dillinger's brow furrowed.

"What do you mean, things are different now?"

"I'm here by invitation. I work in the Warner Story Department now."

Dillinger couldn't hide his surprise. "You're not working for that bastard Hoover anymore?"

Purvis shook his head. "He never forgave me for not shooting you."

Dillinger remained unconvinced. "So, what happened?"

"Hoover sent me out here to watch you. He was convinced you were up to no good. When I told him that in my opinion you were on the up and up, he wouldn't listen, so I quit. That was six months ago."

Dillinger remained wary. "You better not be pulling my leg, pal."

"I'm on the square, John, and as glad to be done with Hoover as you are."

"I don't know what to say, Agent—" Dillinger frowned again. "What the hell *do* I call you, anyway?"

Purvis smiled. "Melvin will do."

"Okay, Melvin," Dillinger said, relaxing a bit. "Did you come to see me make a fool of myself?" Dillinger nodded toward the auditorium.

Purvis sipped his champagne. "I have a feeling you're going to prove a *lot* of people wrong tonight, John, and aside from wanting to see the show for myself, I also wanted to wish you all the best, and no hard feelings." Purvis stuck out his hand and Dillinger shook it.

"Thanks. I hope you're right. Say, you going to Jack Warner's party afterwards?"

"My invitation doesn't extend that far, I'm afraid. Besides, I have a wife waiting for me at home."

Dillinger looked wistful for a moment then smiled. "Well, okay, but if you're working on the lot, come and see me. I'm starting a new picture next week. Stage Fifteen. We'll catch up. What do you say?"

Purvis nodded, and Dillinger headed back to Bette Davis, who was talking to a well-dressed man. The man had his back turned to Dillinger, but there was something familiar about the guy. When he rejoined her, he got his second surprise of the night.

It was Robert Butler.

"Bob! How the hell are you?" Dillinger said, clasping the reporter on the shoulders.

"I'm fine, John, and it looks as if you're not doing too bad either."

"Well, let's hope I'm feeling that way in a couple of hours. How long have you been in town?"

"We arrived a couple of months ago. A lot of interesting stories out here."

"So, you're still my Boswell?" Dillinger asked with a grin.

Butler laughed. "I am if my editor has anything to say about it—and he does." He turned to Bette. "And as I was just telling your lovely date, I'm here to review the film, but I'd like to get an interview from you when you have a chance."

"Sure thing," Dillinger said. "I'm starting a new picture with Cagney next week."

"Johnnie, they're seating us," Bette said.

Dillinger looked up and saw the doors to the auditorium were now open and the crowd streamed through them.

"Just give me a minute and I'll join you," he said.

Bette nodded and started for the door.

Dillinger turned back to Butler. "You know, Bob, the strangest thing. I saw Melvin Purvis here too. Told me he's working at Warner's as a writer."

Butler nodded. "I heard about that and some of what happened with Hoover. He's actually pretty good, published a couple of stories in the detective magazines."

"So, you think he's being square with me?"

"I do," Butler answered. "I think he likes Hoover about as much as you do."

"Well then here's an angle for you, why don't you interview us both?"

"At the same time?"

"Why not? Might make for interesting reading."

Butler looked thoughtful. "You're on. Let me run it by my editor and I'll get back to you and set it up."

Dillinger bid his friend goodnight and joined Bette in the auditorium. She'd saved him a seat on the aisle—his favorite spot—at least it used to be. He didn't need to worry about making a run for it anymore. Then again, if everyone hated the movie, maybe he would. He chuckled, shook his head, and settled into his seat.

"What is it, Johnnie?" Bette asked, managing to look both amused and puzzled.

"Oh, it's nothing. Just thinking what a crazy world this is."

✖ ✖ ✖

As the curtains closed on the "End" title and the house lights brightened, there followed a profound silence, and Dillinger would swear his thundering heartbeat was audible to those around him. Bette was staring at him with an expression of frank admiration. After what felt like an eternity, the theatre burst into a sustained applause that grew louder and more ardent with each passing moment.

The shock of it left him immobile, his mind reeling from a potent mixture of emotions. On the one hand, it was exhilarating, and on the other it was frightening. Part of him, deep inside, doubted everything he was seeing and hearing, a tiny voice telling him it was all a crock—and that little devil on his shoulder was hard to ignore. Yet the oddest thing was he felt pride in what he'd accomplished.

The theatre audience rose to its feet chanting his name, the applause growing even louder. Bette tapped him on the arm, her voice urgent in his ear.

"It's for you, big man. Take a bow."

He looked at her and saw his own feeling reflected in her eyes—and maybe something more carnal, too.

"Speech!" someone called out, and that became another chant.

Bette continued to prod him good-naturedly, and after a moment of indecision he stood up to a renewed wave of applause. He basked in it for a moment then raised his hands for silence.

"Thank you . . . thank you," he said as the room settled down. "I really want to thank you for that, because until this moment I had no idea if I would make the grade."

"Aces, Johnnie!" someone called out, followed by a smattering of laughter and a few "Hear, hears."

Dillinger grinned. "And to think I only gave him five bucks to say that."

The room erupted in laughter. When things quieted down, Dillinger continued. "Seriously, though, I'm glad you enjoyed the film. It was a lot of hard work, and I enjoyed every minute of it. I especially want to thank Archie Mayo, our director, for keeping me from bumping into the furniture." More laughter. "But there's one person in this theatre who deserves all the credit for my performance, and that is Miss Maria Ouspenskaya."

She was sitting four rows back, wrapped in a lace shawl and a turban studded with rhinestones, looking very much like the gypsy queen she often played. When the applause again erupted, she beamed, nodding her thanks to Dillinger with eyes brimming with tears.

"I'm telling you, people," he said, extending a hand toward the diminutive woman, "this little lady is tougher than any of the mugs I ever ran with. Thank you, Maria. If I ever pull another job, you're riding shotgun."

The room laughed again.

"Anyway, enough gab, let's go have a party!"

18

1801 Angelo Drive
Beverly Hills, California
February 1, 1936

The tension inside Bette's limousine during the ride to Warner's mansion was so thick, Dillinger thought he would choke on it. A few times he started to say something then thought better of it, sensing her somber mood. As they crossed into Beverly Hills, he could take it no longer.

"What's wrong, Bette?"

She turned from the window, a look of guilt on her face. "Nothing."

"You and I both know it's anything but nothing. What is it, trouble at home?"

"Am I that transparent?"

Dillinger offered a warm smile. "I wouldn't say that."

"You remember my husband, Ham?"

Dillinger nodded, recalling the man from the few times when he'd visited the set. "Seems like a decent guy."

"He is, and that's the problem."

"Why?"

"Because I married him for all the wrong reasons."

Dillinger sensed where this was going but said nothing.

Bette sighed and leaned her head back against the seat. The passing streetlights made her eyes seem to glow in the dark. "I thought he was 'the one.' I—I don't know anymore."

Dillinger didn't know what to say for a moment. "Sorry to hear it."

"You should be," she said, her voice nearly a whisper.

"Why should I be sorry?"

She stared at him now with a look of coy amusement. "I hated you, you know, coming in and replacing Bogie. I wanted you to fail, even if it meant the picture would fail too. But as we worked together, I realized you weren't just some hooligan riding on reputation rather than talent. You proved me wrong. You were perfect for the part."

"You don't have to apologize—"

"Shh," she said, placing a finger against his lips. Her skin was so warm, and he could feel her racing pulse beating in her fingertip. "Let me finish. You also showed me that Ham isn't the man for me."

Part of him, the part with the logical mind, tried to come up with something to say that would put her off gently, but those limpid eyes enthralled him, making him want to forget everything else.

And then all at once she was in his arms, her burning lips crushing his, her tongue exploring his mouth. Her hands seemed to be everywhere at once, caressing him, her soft moans arousing him to a fever pitch. His manhood was so hard, it hurt.

She broke away. "Take me back to your suite, Johnnie—right now. I don't want to see anyone or be with anyone . . . but you."

"Warner is expecting *both* of us."

"Don't you want me?" she asked in a sultry tone.

Dillinger looked into her eyes once again, his resolve faltering. "Yeah, I do. But we can't ditch this party."

Bette fell back against the seat. "Damn it, you men are all the same. Always by the book—always duty first."

"Not always," Dillinger said, offering her a knowing smile.

Bette threw him a sidelong glance, a saucy grin curling her lips. "Fine. Have it your way then. We'll go to the party, but you'd better behave yourself."

Dillinger's grin widened. "And what's that supposed to mean?"

Bette slid back across the seat and leaned against him with a sigh. "Oh, nothing . . . except I'm sure some of those shameless hussies who call themselves actresses will throw themselves at you with heedless abandon."

Dillinger laughed. "I think I can take care of myself."

"See that you do," Bette replied with a laugh. "Tonight, you're *mine*."

Just then the Rolls pulled into the gate of the Warner estate, gliding past two guards who gave the car a cursory once-over. As they wound their way up the long driveway, Dillinger caught sight of the home, which looked like a Greek temple sitting atop Olympus. And maybe in a way it was. He'd finally made it to the top.

The Rolls turned into the circular drive and eased to a stop in front of the portico, behind a Duesenberg and a Stutz Bearcat. Dillinger watched as other elegantly dressed couples alighted and hurried inside the house. Through the car window he heard the strains of a string quartet, the open doorway radiant with a welcoming amber glow.

When the Rolls made it to the head of the line, a man dressed in a gold-braided uniform opened the rear passenger door and extended a hand to help Bette exit. Dillinger followed her out.

The night was alive with music and the sounds of crickets chirping across the manicured grounds. He was struck by the odor of jasmine and other exotic flowers suffusing the air, enough to make his head swim. Bette slipped her arm through his and the two of them strolled into the house.

Inside, the music was louder, as was the sound of chatter from the living room across the wide foyer. Dillinger could see uniformed waiters passing trays of various hors d'oeuvres and champagne. His stomach growled in response to the enticing odors of the food.

Crossing the foyer, they entered the plush living room with its George III décor, and to Dillinger, it felt as if they'd walked into a museum. He spotted Jack Warner dressed in a black and white tuxedo, standing with his wife and two other couples. One of them was Leslie Howard and his wife, the other he was surprised to see was none other than Clark Gable and a woman whom Dillinger assumed was Gable's wife. He let Bette lead the way over.

"Hello, Jack!" Bette said.

Warner turned and held out his arms. "Here are my golden boy and girl! I was beginning to wonder if you two were going to stand me up." He grinned, his eyes gleaming. "Come on over and say hello," Warner said, taking Dillinger's arm and making the introductions. Dillinger shook hands all around, noting the variety of expressions, from Leslie Howard's cool cordiality to Mrs. Gable's nervous titter.

"I'm especially glad to meet you, Mr. Gable."

Gable gave Dillinger a look of cool appraisal. "I hear *Manhattan Melodrama* inspired you to surrender."

"That and four guns pointed at my head," Dillinger said. "But your performance was the icing on the cake."

Gable leaned toward Dillinger and spoke quietly. "Just so we understand each other . . . I don't like you. As far as I'm concerned, you're just a two-bit hood who got lucky, so stay away from me. I'm not Cagney, and given half a chance, I'd gladly knock your block off. And that's a standing offer."

Dillinger stole a glance at Bette Davis, who was laughing and joking with Gable's wife. She hadn't heard a thing. He turned back to Gable and fixed him with a flinty gaze.

"I don't take that kind of guff from anyone."

"Maybe not in Chicago, but this is Hollywood, you sap."

Gable laughed and clapped Dillinger on the shoulder, as if they were the best of friends.

Dillinger felt the bile rise in his throat, and he continued staring at Gable, wanting to take the man apart. And then he remembered within whose house he stood and let his anger leach away.

"By the way, I'm letting everyone know," Warner said, "that I'm running John's public service film in my screening room. If any of you are curious, the next show's about to start."

"I've heard so much about that film," Leslie Howard's wife interjected. Her voice was a sexy contralto made more so by her upper crust British accent. "Leslie, let's go see it."

Dillinger could tell Howard was annoyed, but he grinned and let himself enjoy the moment. There was no winning this man over, not after he'd supplanted the actor Howard felt should have played Duke Mantee. After a few more pleasantries, the Howards moved off toward the screening room and Warner motioned to Dillinger. "John, there's something we need to discuss."

Dillinger raised an eyebrow. "I thought you didn't like talking business after hours, Mr. Warner."

Warner sighed. "I know, but something's come up."

Dillinger leaned over and whispered into Bette's ear and she nodded. "Remember, behave yourself," she said, trying not to smile. Dillinger nodded and followed Warner into his private office, the studio chief closing the door behind them. The music and the chatter cut off abruptly.

Warner chuckled when he noticed Dillinger's reaction. "I truly wanted a private place where there would be no distractions. It's my favorite room in the house. Come on, have a seat," he said, indicating a tufted leather couch. Dillinger sat, and the couch sank under his weight with a soft sigh.

"You want anything to drink?"

"Sure, and I wouldn't mind some of that grub too," Dillinger said.

"You're hungry?"

Warner went to his desk and pressed an intercom button.

"Yes, Mr. Warner?"

"Melba, can you bring us a tray of some hors d'oeuvres and—" he turned to Dillinger. "What do you want to drink? Champagne okay?"

Dillinger nodded.

"And two glasses of champagne."

"Right away, Mr. Warner."

Warner clicked off the intercom, rounded the desk, and took a seat at the opposite end of the couch. "So, what did you think of the picture? Be honest, now." Warner was smiling, but Dillinger sensed the man wanted to hear superlatives, not honesty. Fortunately, superlatives seemed to be the order of the day.

"I think we nailed it."

Warner beamed. "I think you're right. No small thanks to you."

Dillinger flushed with embarrassment. Praise was not something he was used to receiving, but it felt good nonetheless. "Let's see if the critics agree."

Warner shrugged. "Good notices help, but the public really doesn't care what Hedda Hopper or that witch over at Hearst thinks. They'll go see it, and if they like it, they'll tell their friends. Can't buy that kind of publicity."

A moment later, a knock sounded at the door.

"Come in, Melba," Warner called out.

The door opened, and a uniformed maid walked in carrying a tray laden with two flutes of champagne and a platter consisting of two of every type of hors d'oeuvres being served that night. The young black woman set the tray down on the coffee table and handed a flute of champagne to Dillinger and then another to Warner.

"Anything else, Mr. Warner?"

"This should be fine, Melba. Is dinner on schedule?"

"Yes, sir. We should be serving in about an hour."

"Thank you, that'll be all."

The maid left the room, and when the door shut, Warner lifted his glass and said, "To our mutual success," and clinked his flute against Dillinger's.

The champagne was good—better than good, in fact. He took another sip and placed the flute down onto the coffee table and regarded Warner with a level gaze. "So, what's so important to pull us away from the party?"

Warner's jovial expression dimmed. "I hate to tell you this, but we've got to postpone your next picture."

Dillinger felt the room tilt, and it wasn't from the champagne. "What are you talking about? We start shooting on Monday."

"I know," Warner sighed, "but it can't be helped."

"Why not?"

"Cagney's exhausted, John. He's been working like crazy for the last year and a half and he begged me for a break. I couldn't say no."

Dillinger sighed. It was true that his friend had been working like a dog, and the last time the two had met for lunch, the normally energetic actor looked haggard.

"Is that why he's not here?"

Warner nodded. "He's in Palm Springs. I told him to soak up as much sun as he could stand and not to sweat it. You understand, don't you?"

"Sure, I do. But to tell you the truth, I was kind of looking forward to working with him."

"And you will," Warner said, popping an hors d'oeuvre into his mouth. "And that's a promise. I've got plans for you, John, which brings me to the other reason I brought you in here."

"There's more?"

Warner popped another tidbit into his mouth and shook his head. "Don't look so glum. This is good."

Dillinger had a feeling "good" wasn't quite the word for what he was about to hear, and watching Warner eat with such gusto was making him queasy to boot.

"I just got an offer from Fox. They want you for their next Shirley Temple picture."

"You're loaning me out?"

"You're saying that like it's a death sentence. Gable got loaned out to Columbia, and look what happened! He got an Oscar for *It Happened One Night*."

"But Shirley Temple and *me*? Don't you think that's a bit nuts?"

Warner held up his hand. "Hear me out. The tyke asked for you, Johnnie. She's the biggest thing Fox has got, and she asked for you."

Dillinger shook his head, as if to clear it. "Why, Mr. Warner? *The Petrified Forest* isn't even released yet."

"It's a small town. Word's out about you."

"How long has this been in the works?"

Warner spread his hands in a mea culpa gesture. "What can I say, John, it's business."

Dillinger rubbed his temples. "Well, that's just great, but don't you think me and this little kid will be like oil and water? Even W. C. Fields said never work with kids or animals."

"Oh, what does that old souse know? He was born a curmudgeon."

Dillinger felt as if he were trying to climb an icy slope and getting nowhere. "What if the film's a turkey?"

"Let me tell you something," Warner said, his expression turning serious. "Every one of that little kid's movies has made a bundle. And I mean a *bundle*. Fox offered good money for three weeks of your time."

Dillinger picked up his champagne and drained the glass. "So, you want me to do it?"

"Yes, and I'll sweeten the deal for you, but you've got to swear you'll keep it zipped."

"You've got it."

"I'm prepared to give you a five-thousand-dollar bonus for three week's work."

Dillinger didn't know what to say, but his stomach told him his appetite was back. He reached for one of the hors d'oeuvres, a cracker with caviar and cream cheese topped off with what looked like a pimento. It was salty as hell, but right now it was the best thing he'd ever tasted.

"What's the story?" he asked, settling back on the couch.

Warner responded, the devilish grin returning. "It's about a father-daughter confidence team who go around conning crooks out of their dough."

"What's the angle?"

Warner laughed. "They're successful because it's the little girl who's able to charm these crooks out of their money. She's the talent, but something happens. I think she gets hit by a car and ends up in the hospital—touch and go—a real tug at the heartstrings. The father realizes he's been using his kid, and now she really needs him. He has to come up with the money for her operation or she's kaput. He finally comes through in the end, and the two give up their life of crime."

It was pure Hollywood hokum, but Dillinger was savvy enough to understand this was what audiences wanted—feel-good fare that let them forget about their troubles—if only for a short while. And sitting there just now he was reminded of something Maria Ouspenskaya had said to him during a break in one of their sessions. "No matter what part you play, Johnnie, give the audience the truth; let them see into your character's heart."

It was solid advice, and this was a chance to put that into practice, a chance to show the world he was more than just a tough guy with a gun.

"I'll do it on your say-so, Mr. Warner, with one condition."

It was Warner's turn to be surprised. "What, five grand isn't enough?"

Dillinger smiled. "It's more than enough, and I'll take it gladly, but it's not the money."

"So, what is it, then?"

"I want to direct."

Warner laughed. "Your first movie isn't even out yet, and you want to direct?"

Dillinger leaned forward, intent. "You saw what I did with that film I made in prison. I can do it, Mr. Warner—you *know* I can. And I'll star in it too."

Warner remained silent, his expression thoughtful.

"You have a script in mind?" He asked.

"Not yet, it's just in the idea stage. But I swear it'll be a corker."

Warner sipped his champagne and chuckled. "Okay, John, show me a script and I'll think about it."

Dillinger rose to his feet and stuck out his hand. "Fair enough."

✖ ✖ ✖

When Dillinger rejoined Bette, she was looking at him with an expression of mild annoyance. "What were you boys talking about? It took forever."

Dillinger leaned close to her ear and said, "I'll tell you later, I promise."

"What makes you think there's going to be a later?" she asked with a haughty arch of her left eyebrow.

Dillinger grinned and backed her against the wall. "I've got a feeling."

Bette looked into his eyes, her expression filled with desire. "So do I . . ."

For the rest of the evening, Dillinger made small talk, keeping a captive audience in stitches with stories of his bank-robbing days.

Later, when he and Bette returned to the Roosevelt, she seemed subdued while Woody fussed over her wrap and an offer of refreshments, as if the valet's presence made her uncomfortable.

"That'll do it for tonight, Woody," he said.

To his credit, the valet not only took no offense, he even smiled and bowed. "You two have a good evening."

Bette watched him leave.

"Can he be trusted?"

Dillinger hid his annoyance. "Woody's a good egg," he said. "What's wrong?"

Bette sighed. "It's just the papers would love to print gossip about us."

"Well, right now there's nothing to gossip about."

"That doesn't keep them from making things up."

Dillinger closed the space between them and took her in his arms. "Then let's give them something to talk about."

She laughed. "That's my line."

And then he kissed her, his hands running down her back and cupping her firm buttocks through the satiny sheen of her gown. She moaned, her mouth pressing harder against his lips, her own parting to offer him her tongue. He pulled away, picked her up, and carried her into the bedroom. The bed was already turned down, and Woody had left a bottle of champagne cooling in a silver bucket next to the bed, a cloth napkin tied around its neck.

Dillinger smiled.

I'm going to have to give that man a raise.

Bette's blue eyes shone with a feverish gleam, and she didn't take her gaze off Dillinger as she slipped the shoulder straps of her gown off her shoulders and let it slide onto the floor. Dillinger felt a rush as his heart sped up. She was wearing only satin panties and no bra. Bette kicked the gown aside and then she made a coy move to drop the panties, giving Dillinger several false starts, before turning her derriere toward him and dropping them to the floor.

"You like torturing me, don't you?" Dillinger said.

Bette laughed, her back still toward him. "You ain't seen nothin' yet."

Then she turned.

Her body was nothing less than exquisite, a true Hollywood goddess, her sylph-like frame sculpted from the purest alabaster. Dillinger stared, and Bette noticed his glances moving from her

191

blonde hair to the dark patch of her pubic hair. She moved closer to him and began untying his bow tie. "Did you expect the carpet to match the drapes, good sir?"

"I've never been much for interior decorating."

She laughed and kissed him again, prompting him to tear off his shirt, his lips still glued to hers. She backed off and slithered onto the bed and watched him undress, her eyes widening when she saw his erection.

He joined her on the bed, his mouth covering her body with greedy kisses. She moaned and arched her back, her nipples as hard as erasers. "Oh, God, don't stop doing that," she said, gasping.

Never one to refuse a lady, Dillinger complied, losing himself in the task.

❊　❊　❊

Dillinger awoke with the late-morning sun dazzling his eyes, memories of the previous night reeling through his mind. Yawning, he turned his head and saw Bette lying on her stomach next to him. The sheets were bunched halfway down her body, exposing the delicate curve of her spine and the deep cleft of her buttocks. She slept with a smile of contentment on her face, blonde hair splayed across the pillow.

They'd made love the entire night until the sun had peeked over the mountains, and she'd been insatiable, as if she were making up for lost time. Her screams of pleasure, while arousing, eventually made him wonder if Woody could hear them and think he was killing her. Dillinger chuckled.

"What's so funny?" Bette mumbled, her voice husky from sleep.

"Nothing. Just feeling good."

Bette lifted her head off the pillow and stared at him, her hand grasping his manhood under the sheets. "I can make you feel better," she cooed.

"What about your husband, isn't he going to wonder where you've been all night?"

"He's away on business," she said, fondling him.

"You're going to wear me out."

Bette giggled. "Well, I do aim to try."

A knock sounded at the door, startling them both.

"What is it?" Dillinger asked, not bothering to hide his annoyance.

"I'm sorry to bother you, Mr. Dillinger, but there's somebody at the front door."

He glanced at the bedside clock and saw it was just past noon. "Woody, we had a long night. Tell whoever it is to come back later."

"I did, sir, but it appears to be urgent."

Bette's head disappeared under the sheets. "Wait," he told her in a hushed voice. "What makes it so urgent?"

"The young woman said it was important."

"Woman?!" Bette said, letting go of him and sitting up in the bed. "What the hell are you trying to pull, Johnnie? I don't like that kind of thing. You want something like that, go ask Joan Crawford!"

Dillinger backed away from her, his hands held up in a placating gesture. "You've got this all wrong."

"Have I?" Her faced was flushed, but not with desire.

"Yes, you do. I have no idea who's at the door."

"Please, Mr. Dillinger," Woody pleaded.

"All right! Tell whoever the hell it is to wait a minute. Don't let her in. I'll be right out."

Dillinger went to the closet and drew out a black silk dressing gown and pulled it on. The sleek satin felt cold and unforgiving against his skin but covered a multitude of sins. He went to the door then turned back to Bette, who sat up like a haughty queen, eyes blazing.

"I'll take care of this," he said. "And I'll say this one last time. It's not what you think."

When he opened the bedroom door, Woody stood there looking sheepish. Dillinger blew past him, marching the length of the apartment, his gaze riveted on the front door, his anger rising.

He threw open the door, the irate speech he'd just composed dying on his lips.

"Hello, Johnnie," the woman said. She smiled at him shyly. "I'm sorry I didn't call first."

Dillinger stood there, stunned, hardly believing what his eyes plainly told him. "Billie?"

Billie Frechette smiled, her dark brown eyes shining. "I thought maybe you'd forgot I was getting out this month."

She was dressed in a simple print dress a couple of seasons out of date, yet it detracted not a whit from her natural beauty. Her short black hair, most of it hidden under a cloche hat, shone in the dim light of the hallway. She took a hesitant step toward him. "I heard about you going to Hollywood, Johnnie, so I took a bus with the money they gave me. And here I am," she said, with an expression that gave away the uncertainty no doubt uppermost in her mind. "You're glad to see me, aren't you?"

This is gonna be a problem.

Dillinger swallowed. He'd received a letter from his old lawyer, Louis Piquett. It had arrived during the shooting of the film and he hadn't bothered to open it. Now, he wished he had.

"Aren't you gonna invite me in?" she asked.

Dillinger stole a look over his shoulder. The door to the bedroom was still shut. When he turned back, Billie was another step closer. He could smell her perfume. It was an inexpensive fragrance that would have smelled cheap on anyone else. On Billie, it somehow

194

smelled elegant in much the same way she could make anything seem better than it really was.

Her time in jail had taken nothing away from her, and Dillinger's pulse raced like it used to every time she'd walk into a room.

"I missed you," he said.

She rushed into his arms. "Oh, Johnnie," she said, kissing him with soft insistence. He'd forgotten how lost he could get in those lush, full lips.

"So, it's not what I thought, *huh*?"

Dillinger broke away from Billie and turned to see a fully dressed Bette Davis striding toward him, screeching like a harpy. "I told you, I'm not a goddamned dyke!" She halted in front of Dillinger and Billie, her chest heaving, and gave Billie a look of superior disdain. "I might have known you'd go for some tawdry extra, you cheap hood!"

She grabbed her wrap from the closet and stormed out of the apartment, slamming the door behind her. Billie stared at the door then turned to Dillinger. "A touchy one, isn't she?"

They both started laughing, and Billie fell into his arms. A moment later she was still against him, the laughter forgotten. "I'm sorry, Billie."

She looked up at him. "I know how it is, Johnnie. You were lonely."

Dillinger shook his head. "No, not that. I'm sorry I didn't realize you were coming here. I would have met you at the station. I—"

She placed her soft hand against his mouth to silence him. "It doesn't matter. I'm here and we can finally have the life we always wanted."

"It's a little different than what we planned."

Billie smiled. "Yeah, I know."

They started laughing again, and Dillinger led her into the bedroom and closed the door.

19

1408 Tamarind Avenue
Hollywood, California
February 7, 1936

DILLINGER STEALS THE SHOW!
BOFFO BOX OFFICE EXPECTED.

Melvin Purvis shook his head in amazement as he read *The Daily Variety* headline for the umpteenth time. The attendant review on page two—which he'd only read twice—was nothing short of adoration. *"Dillinger brings consummate skill and every bit of menace to his portrayal of Duke Mantee,"* the critic extolled. *"Truly a star-making performance."*

Purvis sipped his coffee and sat back in his chair with a sigh. Beams of sunlight streamed through the curtains over the kitchen sink, dappling the remains of his breakfast. Rosanne had already left for her job at Bullock's Department Store, and Purvis was lingering over the meal so he could avoid confronting his writer's block. Another glance at the *Variety* brought a chuckle and a shake of his head. Was it only nineteen months since that hot July night in Chicago? Less than two years since the entire course of his life had changed. If he closed his eyes, he could still see the back of Dillinger's head, the barrel of Clarence Hurt's .45 automatic just inches from the outlaw's skull. One pull of the trigger . . .

One bullet . . .

. . . and everything would have changed.

Dillinger would be dead and he would be . . . And that was the real question, wasn't it? If Dillinger had died that day, would his life really be all that different? Purvis believed he'd done the right thing by sparing Dillinger, and things had turned out for the best. He and Rosanne lived in a cozy one-story house on a shady Hollywood street, and his job at Warner was certainly a lot less dangerous, even if the stress level remained high. The script he was working on was supposed to be a crime story, so it was comfortable territory, but the time constraints the producer was putting on him made it almost impossible to turn out anything more than a B-movie potboiler. Still, he would get it done and take the money. What else could he do?

"Time to sing for my supper," he said with a dry laugh.

Rising from the table, Purvis dumped the remains of his food into a brown paper grocery bag, already straining from last night's dinner, and made a silent vow to take out the trash later that day. He headed into his modest book-lined den situated in the front room of the house and sat down at his desk, a massive walnut-stained Victorian relic his wife had found at a local thrift shop. It was far more ornate than the one he'd originally wanted, but it made him feel like a writer nonetheless.

The typewriter sat atop the spotless blotter, two sheets of onionskin with a carbon sandwiched between them still rolled around its platen. He caressed the keys, willing the words to flow through his fingers.

Nothing. Not a syllable.

His thoughts returned to the review. Everything that overblown critic had written was true. Purvis had seen it for himself at the premiere, and again at a special screening he and Rosanne had attended two nights before on the Warner lot. Halfway through the film, his wife had leaned over and whispered into his ear.

"I never would have believed it, honey, but that man's got something. Don't you feel it?"

Yes, he did.

And for the rest of the film Purvis watched the audience as much as the screen, seeing in their eyes confirmation for what he knew in his heart to be true: Dillinger *was* a star, and Purvis felt an odd twinge of satisfaction knowing he'd played a part in changing the man's fortunes.

"And speaking of fortunes," he mused, "I'd better get to work."

He started writing, just to feel his fingers on the keys. He had no idea what he was writing or where he was going with it, but still it felt good. An hour later, he had the bare outline of a story about a wife scheming with her insurance agent lover to kill her husband. That old adrenaline was flowing again, and it felt great. Once he had the plot fleshed out, he'd start on the script.

A knock at the front door startled him.

He looked toward the door and the knock sounded again, a sharp rapping that bespoke urgency.

Leaving his chair, Purvis strode over and opened the door.

"Good afternoon, Special Agent Purvis."

Purvis stared at his visitor, not quite believing whom he was seeing. The last time he'd seen Special Agent Clarence Hurt, the man was aiming a pistol at the back of Dillinger's head.

"What are you doing here, Clarence?"

Hurt's mouth was set in a tight grin. "We need to talk."

"No, we don't."

Purvis attempted to shut the door, and Hurt wedged his scuffed brogan between the door and the jamb. "We can do this here or we can go downtown."

"You going to cuff me too?"

Hurt shook his head and looked him in the eye. "Aren't you the least bit curious?"

He had him there. Purvis sighed, opened the door wide, and beckoned the agent inside. "You got any more of that coffee I smell?"

Purvis motioned for him to follow and they headed into the kitchen. There, Purvis refilled his cup and poured one for the agent. "Cream with two lumps, right?"

Hurt tossed his Stetson onto the table and allowed himself a smile. "You remember." Then he coughed into his fist. It sounded bad, as if something were broken inside his chest.

Purvis added the cream and sugar and brought both cups to the table.

They sipped in silence for a moment, until Purvis lost his patience. "So, why are you here, Clarence?"

"Do I really have to spell it out?" he asked.

"Dillinger . . ."

Hurt nodded. "The director would appreciate your help in solving this matter."

"Solving what matter? Dillinger's about to become a movie star."

Hurt smiled again and Purvis knew why it was such a rare occurrence. There was no warmth contained in that awkward twist of his lips. "Mr. Hoover wants Dillinger where he belongs."

"But he's committed no crimes, there's nothing that warrants him going to prison."

"A leopard doesn't change his spots. He's a criminal, and he's gonna screw up. And we'll be ready."

"This unreasonable vendetta against Dillinger has to stop," Purvis said, his anger flaring. "It's wrong. Just plain wrong."

Hurt ran a callused hand through his thinning gray hair and closed his eyes, as if collecting his thoughts. When he spoke, his voice dropped to a deadly whisper. "Let's get this clear . . . *Special Agent* Purvis. The longer Dillinger is allowed to profit from his criminal past, the more he's going to send a message to the youth of America that crime not only pays, it'll buy you a ticket to Hollywood. And this is something we cannot allow."

Purvis forced himself to remain calm. "Did Hoover tell you to memorize that?"

Hurt glared at him, remaining silent.

"You see the irony here, don't you, Clarence?"

Hurt's face screwed up into a puzzled mask, another awkward expression for the man. "What irony is that?"

"It was Mr. Hoover's machinations that paved the way for Dillinger's success. Your boss made all this possible."

"The director regrets that."

"Oh, so he's admitting to a mistake?"

Hurt gave an almost imperceptible nod.

"Well, we should probably have a national day of mourning for that," Purvis said, moving his hand from right to left like the Zipper in Times Square. "The infallible J. Edgar Hoover has made a mistake."

Instead of responding, Hurt reached into his jacket and pulled out a well-worn wallet and placed it on the table. Purvis picked it up, recognizing it. It contained his old Bureau of Investigation badge and ID.

"It's been updated to reflect your new employment. I don't have your service weapon, but we'll get you another."

Purvis shook his head, not quite believing what he was hearing.

"You're forgetting I resigned. I've got a new career and I like it. And it also makes my wife happy that I'm not out risking my life anymore. I'm done with that. And I'm done doing that man's bidding."

The agent leaned forward, his amber-colored eyes burning with a peculiar gleam. "Mr. Hoover did not accept your resignation."

Purvis sat back and laughed. "He didn't—" Purvis shook his head and tossed the ID back across the table. "You tell him he can go to hell. I'm not interested."

"You do realize your current employment with Warner Studios is dependent upon your cooperation?"

"Oh, really? From what I hear, Jack Warner and Mr. Hoover have an understanding."

Hurt shrugged. "Things change."

A chill shot through Purvis. He'd heard through the grapevine that Warner had something on Hoover, and that's why the director had helped push through Dillinger's pardon. It had been only a rumor, until this very moment when Agent Hurt all but confirmed it, yet—rumor or not—it made an odd sort of sense. Purvis knew Hoover would stop at nothing to get his way, including ruining his budding new career. His mind raced through the various alternatives and he reached a decision.

Perhaps he should play along, keep abreast of what Hoover was planning, and put a stop to it if he could. Purvis had to admit to feeling the old thrill, but he had to play this right. If he wasn't going to end up out of a job or dead, he needed to give an Oscar-winning performance.

"What's it going to be, Special Agent Purvis?"

Purvis reached across the table and picked up the ID and opened it. The badge and ID were new, reflecting the new name of the agency: The Federal Bureau of Investigation.

"I'll do what I can, Clarence, but I'm keeping my present job."

"That's what we're hoping. With you being right there, you can keep your eyes and ears open. We know you and Dillinger are being interviewed next week. This is your opportunity to mend fences, get closer to our quarry."

Purvis frowned. "How do you know about that?"

"We have sources. After all, we're the good guys."

Hurt left a few minutes later, promising to stay in touch. As he shut the front door, Purvis felt the room tilt as a moment of dizziness overwhelmed him. He sat down until it passed, his thoughts raging.

What am I going to tell Rosanne?

And that was when he truly knew he was back in the game, for he realized he was not going to tell her anything.

20

House of Daba, Couturier
Hollywood, California
February 10, 1936

Woody steered the Ford to the curb and Dillinger gazed at the storefront with annoyance. "You sure this is the place?"

"Yes, sir," Woody said, pulling the parking brake. "I got the straight dope from the studio."

Dillinger hadn't known what to expect, maybe lots of windows with dresses on display. Instead, the front of the shop was a featureless off-white stucco inset with an ornate door carved out of solid mahogany. A polished brass plaque was mounted to the left of the door underneath the doorbell and simply stated:

HOUSE OF DABA

By Appointment Only.

For her part, Billie stared at the shop, her eyes shining with anticipation. Since arriving ten days before with one dress to her name, she'd made do with that and a couple of outfits purchased in one of the stores near the Roosevelt, but Billie deserved better. If he was going to be a star, then so was she—or at least she was going to look like one.

Supposedly this designer, some fop named Salvador Daba, was the new fashion maven everyone was raving about. Dillinger didn't know and cared even less; he only wanted to make Billie happy. She deserved that after having spent two years behind bars simply for being his girlfriend. And yet, when he'd placed the call to make the appointment, he'd been told in no uncertain terms the next available opening was a year away—in March 1937! Instead of flying off the handle, he'd simply told the woman, "This is John Dillinger, and I'd appreciate it very much if you'd let *Señor* Daba know I called."

He left his number, hung up the phone, then sat back in the chair and waited.

"What'd they say, Johnnie?" Billie asked, giving him one of her looks.

Dillinger shook his head and motioned for her to wait. Moments later, the phone rang. He picked it up and said, "Dillinger."

"*Señor* Dillinger, it is such an honor to speak with you!"

Dillinger smiled, holding the phone away from his ear. The fashion designer's strident tenor was so loud, both he and Billie could hear the man as clear as a bell.

"Well, thank you, *Señor* Daba—"

"Please, you must call me Salvador!"

"Okay, Sal, I appreciate that. You call me Johnnie."

Billie rolled her eyes and Dillinger winked. "Say, Sal, your girl said you didn't have any appointments for a year. Is that right?"

"¡Ay caramba! No, no, no, *Señor* Johnnie! She was mistaken."

"Really," Dillinger said, his smile widening. "So, you have one available?"

"For you, *Señor* Johnnie, I do. What time would you like to visit our humble house?"

"How about two o'clock this afternoon?"

There was silence for a moment, though Dillinger could hear excited whispering between the designer and someone he assumed was the girl to whom he'd spoken. A moment later he heard the man shush the other person and return to the phone.

"Two o'clock is perfect, *Señor* Johnnie."

"That's swell, Sal. And don't be too hard on your girl. I'm sure she was just doing her job."

"*Gracias, Señor* Johnnie. *Adios*, my friend. Until we meet."

Sitting in the car, Dillinger chuckled, recalling the man's incessant fawning. No doubt he'd had to call some Hollywood matron and cancel her appointment, which was fine with him. Being a hot Hollywood commodity had its advantages.

"You ready?" Dillinger asked, taking Billie's hand. She squeezed his hand and nodded. Woody took that as his signal to alight from the car and open the door for them. They climbed out and crossed the sidewalk to the mahogany door, and Dillinger pressed the doorbell. Inside, he heard a muffled *Ding-Dong-Ding*. A moment later, the door swung open, revealing a young woman dressed as if she were going out for a night on the town. The dress, a black satin sensation with white accents, fit her curvy frame like a coat of glossy paint. She smiled at Dillinger, her long dark-brown hair parted on the side and covering one eye. Dillinger returned the smile. She was a doll, all right, but she had nothing on Billie.

"Good afternoon, Mr. Dillinger, please come in."

She opened the door wider and Dillinger let Billie walk in ahead of him. When his eyes adjusted to the soft lighting, he saw an all-white room with black upholstered chairs. They were arranged in precise rows on a deep-pile white carpet, facing a small raised stage partly hidden behind a velvet curtain.

"Harlow would be right at home," Dillinger said.

The young woman smiled. "*Señor* Daba will be with you in a moment. Please, have a seat. Can I get you some coffee or tea?"

"No, thank you," Billie replied.

The woman walked away. Dillinger sat down on one of the chairs and Billie followed suit. He felt himself sink into the upholstery, which gave up the faint odor of lavender.

"Kind of reminds me of a funeral home," she said, giggling.

"Kind of smells like one too." Dillinger laughed. "At least you'll go in style."

"*Señor* Johnnie!"

Dillinger turned and spotted a short, thin man barreling toward them. He was dressed in a swallowtail coat and pinstripe trousers, his mirthful face accented with a waxed Kaiser Wilhelm mustache. Dillinger stood and held out his hand. The designer gave it a limp shake.

"Charmed, *Señor* Johnnie."

"Nice to meet you, Sal. I've heard a lot of good things about you from Jack Warner."

The little man swelled with pride. "Ah, yes, Mrs. Warner is a grand lady. Wonderful taste! And such a pleasure to work with her." When Billie stood up, the designer's eyes lit up. "Ah, this is your lady, *Señor* Johnnie?"

Dillinger stood to one side and Billie stuck out her hand. "I'm Evelyn, but you can call me Billie."

Daba studied her for a moment, his eyes roaming over her body.

"You, my dear lady, are a size two. Am I right?"

"You're right, but maybe I shouldn't be admitting that," Billie said, her grin turning coy.

"Nonsense, you are the *perfect* size." He turned his attention to the stage. "Amelia!"

The young assistant peered out from behind the velvet curtain. "Yes, sir?"

"Are the girls ready?"

"Yes, sir, just about."

"Fine," he said, turning back to Billie and Dillinger. "Let us take our seats."

As soon as they sat down, the lights dimmed and the curtains parted, revealing an empty stage lit by several spotlights. A scratchy recording of a string quartet emanated from a hidden phonograph. And then the parade began, as model after model strutted across that tiny stage. First were the evening gowns and then the everyday dresses. Dillinger couldn't help noticing that all the garments draped the models' bodies like a second skin. When he mentioned this to Daba, the designer nodded. "It is what we call bias cut. It makes the dresses love the body."

Dillinger didn't even pretend to understand what the designer meant, but he knew Billie was pleased. He watched her face, seeing her gazing at the dresses with a longing that touched his heart. When the last model disappeared backstage, Daba turned to Billie.

"You see anything that strikes your fancy, *Señorita* Billie?"

Still in awe, Billie shook her head. "They're all so beautiful . . . I don't know . . ."

"We'll take 'em all," Dillinger said.

Daba's bushy eyebrows shot upward, his eyes widening. "Surely, you are pulling the leg of Salvador Daba!"

"I never kid about money. How long will it take?"

Billie touched his arm. "Johnnie, I don't need all of this, just a couple of dresses."

Dillinger covered her hand with his. "It's time you got everything you want."

Her sunny smile was all the confirmation he needed.

"So, Sal, how long before they're ready?"

The designer frowned in thought. "We can have them delivered in one month, perhaps some of them sooner."

"She needs something for tonight. Can you fix her up?"

The designer's mouth opened and closed. "Tonight?"

"Yeah, we're having dinner with the Cagneys at the Derby."

"Ah!" Daba nodded then turned toward the stage and clapped his hands twice. "Amelia!"

The young woman emerged from the back with a questioning look.

"Please escort *Señorita* Billie to the fitting area and have her try on whatever she wishes."

Looking a little overwhelmed, Billie let Amelia lead her backstage.

"Thanks, pal," Dillinger said, then added, "and no stripes."

Ten minutes later, she emerged wearing a crimson satin gown that hugged her lean frame. Dillinger's jaw dropped, and Billie beamed. "Hope you don't mind that I'm the lady in red," she said with a laugh.

"Not on your life," Dillinger replied, his eyes twinkling.

After taking some measurements and chalking the alteration points, Daba promised to have the gown delivered to the Roosevelt by five o'clock.

As they were leaving, Dillinger halted at the door, his expression turning wary. Billie frowned. "What is it?" she asked.

"I forgot to ask him something. Wait in the car and I'll be right out."

Returning to the showroom, he found Daba on the stage, talking to his assistant. Noticing Dillinger's presence, he turned, and when their eyes met, Dillinger began to laugh.

"Nutsy Herman!" he exclaimed. "You son of a bitch!"

"Hiya, Johnnie!" said Daba, whose accent had mysteriously vanished. "I was wonderin' if you'd eyeball me with this soup-strainer on my kisser."

"You almost had me fooled. What the hell are you doing here, and in that get-up?"

Daba motioned his old colleague towards the back room and away from prying ears. "It's good to see ya, pal. Chicago was getting hotter than a two-dollar pistol, so I pulled up stakes and skedaddled out here. I was picking up extra work at First National and noticed all of the swells had dames on their arms dressed to the nines . . ."

Dillinger finished his friend's thought. "And you thought you'd muscle in on their racket."

Nutsy shrugged. "You're here, aren't you, *Señor Johnnie*?"

Dillinger laughed harder than he had in a long time. "You got me there, pal. Makes about as much sense as anything else out here. But say," Dillinger asked, a look of concern creeping over his face, "you didn't really turn Nellie, did you?"

"Nah," Daba said, "but the skirts like it."

"And you're making plenty of dough."

Daba grinned. "Got no complaints."

"Well, your stuff is top-notch, Nutsy. I think you found your calling."

"Thanks, pal. You're not doin' so bad yourself."

A moment later they said their goodbyes, and Daba offered a parting gift. "Keep your head on a swivel, Johnnie, this town's nuttier than me."

When Dillinger returned to the car, Billie grabbed him and kissed him hungrily. "Thank you, Johnnie," she said. "I never thought I'd own such beautiful clothes."

"My pleasure, kiddo. You deserve it."

"What did you forget to ask him?"

Dillinger shrugged. "He reminded me of someone I knew."

When the Ford pulled away from the curb, she leaned against him and caressed his thigh.

"Maybe we should give Woody the afternoon off," she whispered.

Dillinger caught the valet's wink in the rearview mirror. He was definitely going to have to give that man a raise.

※ ※ ※

Dillinger stood at the open window overlooking Hollywood Boulevard, absorbing the sights, sounds, and smells. Cars jammed the thoroughfare, jostling for position, horns honking like angry geese— the clouds of exhaust fumes somehow blending with the scent of the jasmine growing in the hotel's flower boxes into a fragrance that was uniquely Hollywood. What he saw on those streets was a far cry from the controlled insanity of premiere night, yet the sidewalks below were alive with clusters of tourists, would-be actors and actresses, the well-heeled and the destitute, a tapestry of humanity on display. The fact that it was a Monday evening made little difference. This was the hub of the universe, and Dillinger felt the steady throb of its pulse even from his hotel room.

He glanced at his watch; it was ten after six. They were due to meet the Cagneys in twenty minutes, and Billie still wasn't ready. He'd treated her to the hotel beauty salon after their return from the House of Daba. Now, she was locked in the bathroom, primping and preening. If she were any other woman he would have lost his patience, but with Billie that patience was boundless.

"Should I bring the car around, Mr. Dillinger?"

Breaking from his thoughts, Dillinger turned and saw Woody

dressed in his chauffeur's livery, an expectant expression on his face.

"Billie's still getting ready."

Woody nodded and joined Dillinger at the window. They were silent for a few moments.

"You know," Dillinger said, "sometimes when I look down there at all those people, I wonder what it would be like to just walk out of here and join them, be a part of their world, and blend in. Silly, huh?"

Woody removed his chauffeur's cap and wiped the beads of sweat dappling his forehead with a folded white handkerchief. "Not so silly. Sometimes it's nice to be invisible. Though with a black man that's pretty much what happens most of the time. We don't have no choice." Dillinger turned and gave his valet an appraising look but said nothing. Woody continued. "But with you it's different. You ain't like other people anymore—walk with them and they's just as likely to kill you as love you."

"Well, that's nothing new," Dillinger said with a smirk. "Especially with the hate mail I've been getting."

Woody frowned. "What do you mean?"

"There are mugs out there who don't think I deserve what I've gotten—that I should be rotting in prison . . . or dead."

"How many letters?"

Dillinger shrugged. "The studio sends over a bag of fan mail every day, and most of it's all right, but there's always a couple of bad apples." He stared at the milling crowds far below, then said, "To hell with 'em. It's a nice night for a walk, and I want to show her off."

Woody smiled, his attention diverted by something behind Dillinger. "Nothin' wrong with that. If I was you, I'd want to show her off too."

Noticing the direction of Woody's gaze, Dillinger turned to find

Billie standing a few feet behind them. He didn't think it was possible for her to look more beautiful, but she did. The slinky red gown made her look like a Grecian goddess.

"You like what you see, big boy?" she asked with a throaty purr and a gleam in her dark brown eyes.

Woody squared the cap on his head. "I'll see you two downstairs."

Neither Billie nor Dillinger noticed Woody leave, their eyes riveted on each another. She glided over and nestled against him, his nostrils filling with the heady scent of her perfume.

"Well?" she asked, straightening his bow tie. "Do you like it, or not?"

"Sure, I do," he replied, taking her in his arms. "But if you keep this up, we won't be going to dinner."

"That's fine by me . . ."

Dillinger chuckled. "I figured that. But the Cagneys are eager to meet you."

"And you want to show me off," she said, her smile widening.

"You heard?"

"I did," she said, giggling.

Dillinger grinned. "Well, okay then, let's vamoose."

They left moments later, and during the short elevator ride to the lobby, Dillinger thought about what he'd told Woody. That he received hate mail came as no surprise. He'd known there were those who despised him and everything he represented. Hoover was the undisputed president of that club, but what *did* surprise him was how much it bothered him. Back in his bank-robbing days, he prided himself on being able to charm those he needed to charm. His survival depended on it. Beyond that, he didn't care. Now he realized he *did* care. Either he was going soft, or Hollywood was getting to him. Dillinger chuckled at the absurdity of it all.

"What's so funny?" Billie asked, taking his hand and leaning against him.

"Nothing," he said. "Just thinking about the next picture."

"You and Shirley Temple?"

Dillinger laughed. "Yeah, me and the moppet."

"I think it'll be great."

Billie had read the script and told him he'd be a fool not to do it. As soon as he heard that, he knew everything was going to be okay.

"From your lips to God's ear," Dillinger said as the elevator eased to a stop and the doors opened.

21

Roosevelt Hotel
Hollywood, California
February 10, 1936

All eyes were on them as they crossed the lobby. The women were the most brazen, staring at him with expressions of frank invitation. The men were slyer, giving them sidelong glances as they read papers or smoked their cigarettes, as if they were afraid of rousing his jealousy.

Just as they reached the revolving door, a young teenage couple approached, the boy holding out a small book. "May I have your autograph, Mr. Dillinger?" he asked.

The boy looked no older than seventeen, his blond hair slicked back with some kind of shiny pomade. The girl looked a little younger, dressed in a pastel print dress, her light-brown hair coiffed in a Marcel wave. She gazed at Dillinger with an adorable wide-eyed stare that made him feel better than he had a few moments ago.

Dillinger smiled. "Sure, kid. You staking me out?"

The boy glanced nervously at the girl. "Uh, no, sir. We were passing by and I thought we'd see who might be here."

"I guess it's your lucky night," Dillinger said, holding out his hand.

The boy smiled and handed over the black leatherette book along with a cheap fountain pen.

"What's your name, kid?"

"Charley, sir. Charley Parrot."

Dillinger wrote: *Knock 'em dead, Charley. Best wishes, John Dillinger,* and handed the book and pen back. The boy read what Dillinger had written and his freckled face lit up. "Thank you, Mr. Dillinger. This is swell. So's your new movie, by the way." He then turned to Billie. "Can I have yours, too, ma'am?"

Billie looked nonplused. "Oh, I'm not a movie star or anything."

"Go on, honey, it'll be worth plenty someday."

Billie gave him a dubious look but took the pen and book, scrawled her name, and handed everything back to the boy.

"Thank you, ma'am," the boy said.

"We're going to be late, Johnnie," Billie said, nodding toward the door.

Outside, the Ford rumbled at the curb; Woody stood holding the rear door open.

Dillinger clapped the boy on the shoulder. "See you in the movies, kid."

They exited the hotel and climbed into the car, which slid away from the curb and glided out into the flow of traffic.

Billie seemed subdued, and Dillinger noticed. "You okay?"

She was silent for a moment and then nodded. "Yeah, but I felt kind of silly doing that," she said.

"What, signing your autograph?"

"Yes."

"Why?"

"Because you're the star, and I'm just your date."

Dillinger looked Billie in the eye. "I thought you'd get a kick out of it."

Billie placed her hand on his arm. "It *was* kind of fun, but it's not me."

Before Dillinger could ask her what she meant by that, they made the U-turn on Vine and pulled up in front of the Brown Derby. Woody climbed out and opened the door.

Outside the restaurant, a photographer carrying a Speed Graphic walked up. "Can I get a shot of you and the lady, Mr. Dillinger?"

"Sure thing."

Dillinger put his arm around Billie, and the photographer raised his camera, made an adjustment, and clicked off the shot, firing the flashbulb. Just then someone came running toward them, shrieking at the top of her lungs.

"Johnnie! Johnnie! Johnnieeee!"

Though his eyes were still dazzled by the flashbulb, he saw a woman rushing toward him. She appeared well dressed at first, but on closer examination her garments had a worn, shabby look about them, and her hair hung in lank, greasy strings under a moth-eaten hat. She appeared to be no older than thirty, but there were dark circles under her sad bloodshot eyes that made her appear far older.

"I want to have your baby, Johnnie! We'll be so happy then."

A chill ran up Dillinger's back. The woman was off her rocker—nutsy Fagin, as his old cohort Homer Van Meter would have put it.

Before he could say anything, Woody stepped up behind her and grasped her shoulders. "Ma'am, let me get you a cab. You don't want to be doin' this."

Far from calming her, Woody's gentle words and touch enraged the woman. "You get your dirty hands off me, you fucking bastard!"

Dillinger felt his blood boil. "Listen, lady, there's no call for that. You need to get a hold of yourself."

The photographer, realizing he'd stumbled into a newsworthy moment, slapped a new plate into his camera and fumbled for another flashbulb.

The woman stood staring at Dillinger, tears welling in her eyes. Rivulets of black mascara ran down her cheeks, giving her face the appearance of a fright mask. "How come you never called me? I waited and waited and you never called!"

Behind the woman, the door to the restaurant burst open and two large men dressed in dinner clothes lumbered out. To Dillinger's practiced eye, they looked like hired muscle. That was good, as he had a feeling they were going to be needed in a moment.

Dillinger turned his attention back to the woman. "I'm sorry—"

"Mabel—my name's Mabel. Did you forget, Johnnie?" she said in an eerie sing-song voice. "You used to say you loved my name."

The woman started trembling.

"I'm sorry, lady, but we've never met, and you know it."

The woman suddenly noticed Billie standing next to him. "It's because of this bitch, isn't it! You'd rather be with her than *me*!"

A flashbulb went off, followed by a loud pop as the used bulb shattered against the sidewalk.

Dillinger caught the eye of one of the bouncers and they moved toward the woman. When they took hold of her, she screamed then stamped on the foot of one of the men and elbowed the other in the stomach. Then she ran toward Billie, howling, her red lacquered nails curving like talons. Without a moment's hesitation Billie hauled off and swung at the woman with a roundhouse punch, hitting her chin with a loud smack that echoed off the outside wall of the restaurant.

FLASH! POP!

Stopped in her tracks, the woman's eyes rolled up into her head and she dropped to the pavement like a marionette with its strings cut. Billie staggered back against Dillinger, her composure on the edge of shattering. Dillinger put his arm around her and guided her into the restaurant. They stopped just inside the door and he moved her over to a small love seat and sat down next to her.

"What was wrong with her, Johnnie?" Billie asked, breathing hard. "You didn't really know her, did you?"

"I've never seen that dame in my life. She's crazy, Billie. Bughouse crazy."

"I know, but she seemed so . . . sad, and pathetic too. And then she just comes at me like some kind of wild animal." Billie grimaced, inhaling sharply. "Christ, my hand hurts."

"Let me look at that," Dillinger said, taking her hand in his. "Just relax." He gently moved each of her fingers, which were already beginning to swell, watching her face for any sign of pain. "They're bruised, not broken, and they'll be sore for a few days, but that's all."

A waiter passed by and Dillinger grabbed him by the arm. For a moment, the man looked annoyed, until he saw who it was. "Do me a favor, pal," Dillinger said. "The lady needs some ice for her hand."

"Yes, sir," he said, heading into the bar, returning moments later with a dishtowel loaded with crushed ice. Dillinger took it from him and went to place it on Billie's hand. "It'll stain the dress, Johnnie. It's silk."

"No problem," he said, moving her hand to his leg and easing the ice-filled towel on top of it.

One of the bouncers came in, limping. "That broad sure has heavy feet," he said.

"What's happened?" Dillinger asked.

"The cops took her away," the bouncer said. "She's gonna be spendin' the night in the tank, that's for sure."

The news seemed to upset Billie, and Dillinger caressed her shoulder.

"I just can't believe I did that, Johnnie."

"Well, if you hadn't done it, I would have. She wasn't going to hurt you."

"And the way she talked to Woody was so ugly. Did you see his face?"

"Yeah . . . I'll talk to him later."

That seemed to calm her. A moment later, Dillinger spotted Robert Cobb, the restaurant's owner, approaching. The man looked shaken. "I'm so sorry, Mr. Dillinger, this kind of thing almost never happens here. Is there anything I can get for you or the lady? It's on the house."

"It's all right, no harm done. And I don't need anything, but I think Billie'd like a snort right about now."

"Please," she said, nodding.

"She likes bourbon—neat."

Cobb nodded toward a waiter, who scurried off. Moments later, the man returned with a single cut-glass tumbler expertly balanced on a cocktail tray. He held it out for Billie, who took the glass and drained the two fingers of whiskey in a single gulp. She sighed and placed the empty tumbler back onto the tray. The waiter looked impressed.

"Thank you," she said, flashing the man a smile.

Dillinger gave an inward sigh of relief.

Cobb, who still looked dismayed, leaned over. "The Cagneys are inside at their usual booth. Shall I escort you?"

Dillinger looked to Billie, who handed the ice-filled towel to a nearby waiter. They rose to their feet and followed the owner into the main restaurant.

✖ ✖ ✖

"Hiya, tough stuff! You're looking like a star!" Cagney said, rising to his feet and clasping Dillinger's outstretched hand. He looked tanned and fit from his month in Palm Springs. Then Cagney turned to Billie. "And this must be your better half. Hiya, I'm James Cagney—call me Jimmy."

Billie smiled and shook Cagney's hand, completely disarmed, forgetting—for the moment—the pain in her hand. "So nice to meet you, Jimmy. I've always loved your movies."

Cagney gave her a sly look and turned to a matronly woman seated at the table. "May I present my wife, Frances. Dear, this is John Dillinger and his lady friend, Billie Frechette."

The woman smiled, and Billie felt genuine kindness and warmth flowing from her soft, brown eyes. "How nice to meet you both," she said, extending her hand. Billie shook it and then Dillinger did the same.

"Sit, sit," Cagney said, waving toward the table. "Everything is good here, especially Cobb's salad. You hungry, Billie?"

"Starved. I'm ready for anything except grapefruit."

Cagney's mouth dropped open and then he laughed. "This girl's a pistol, Johnnie."

Frances smiled indulgently. "Ever since that film came out, people would serve him grapefruit everywhere we went. It got to be tiresome, but now we just laugh. Just the other day we had a woman ask Jimmy to push one into her face."

Billie's eyes widened. "You didn't."

"I sure as hell did," Cagney said with a laugh. "The woman was so happy—she even had her husband snap a photo."

A waiter approached. "May I get you and the ladies some drinks?"

Billie ordered another bourbon and Dillinger stuck with ice water. The Cagneys both ordered Manhattans. When the waiter left, Frances leaned toward Billie. "So, I understand you've only been in town for a few days, dear. Where were you before coming here?"

Cagney looked uncomfortable, and Billie patted his arm. "It's okay, Jimmy." She turned to Frances, who now wore a puzzled expression. "Like Johnnie, I was in prison. I was released about two weeks ago."

"Oh, my, I really put my foot in it, didn't I?" She laughed and then posed another question with a wide-eyed innocence that was endearing. "Were you robbing banks too?"

"Frances," Cagney said, his voice tinged with exasperation.

"Shush, dear, I really want to know the scoop, as the reporters put it."

Billie liked this woman. She didn't have a malicious bone in her body, and while Frances was no beauty queen, she understood why Cagney loved her.

"Believe it or not, I was in jail because I was in love with Johnnie," Billie said, placing her hand on Dillinger's arm. "They thought they could flush him out if they put me behind bars."

"That's awful. How long did they hold you, dear?"

"Two years."

Frances shook her head. "James, that is just frightful. That our system of justice would stoop to such a travesty. You should talk to Franklin, dear. Get this woman a pardon."

"Franklin?" Dillinger asked.

"She means FDR," Cagney said. "We're acquainted, that's all."

"Acquainted? Nonsense," Frances said. "You helped him raise all that money for his campaign. He'll listen to you."

Cagney gave his wife a look that said "enough."

"It's okay, Frances, I'm doing fine. And so is Johnnie."

"Isn't he just?" she replied.

The drinks came moments later, and Billie did her best to keep a smile on her face and to participate in the conversation. Despite her brave front, she kept hearing that crazy woman shouting that she wanted Johnnie's baby. To her credit, Frances noticed Billie's mood, but remained silent. Later, as they were leaving the restaurant and waiting for their cars, Frances leaned close and whispered to her, "I hope everything's all right, dear. But if not, we can talk anytime you feel like it. I've been around enough to know a few things."

Billie smiled, appreciating the older woman's gesture. "Like where the bodies are buried?"

Frances laughed. "Especially those."

The Cagneys' car appeared just then, and they all said their goodbyes. A few moments later, Woody appeared with the Ford, and she realized she was glad to be headed back to the Roosevelt. She may have been feeling like a prisoner there the past few days, but now it felt like a safe haven.

Like a hideout . . .

22

H e grinned and slowly turned around.
"I give up, boys!" he said, loud and clear over the clamor of the
streets. "I surrender!"

*In front of him were three Bureau of Investigation agents with
their pistols drawn. To a man they all looked as if they'd seen a ghost.*

*One of the agents, a short, stocky man with a round face and beady
eyes, raised his .45 automatic, taking aim.*

"Agent Hurt! Stand down!"

*Instead of complying, the jug-eared agent grinned and pulled the
trigger.*

Dillinger bolted awake, his breath coming in ragged gasps, his heart
pounding against his ribcage. Letting out a sigh, he ran a hand
through his hair. His palm came away covered with a sheen of cold
sweat, the same sweat that coated his entire body. Throwing off the
duvet and the sodden sheets, he planted his feet on the floor, feeling
them sink into the thick pile carpet, a welcome anchor to reality.

Christ, that was so damned real!

He'd always been inclined toward vivid dreams, ever since he'd been a kid, most of which he could recall in detail the next day. And he'd dreamed of his surrender many, many times since that night in July 1934, but it was never like this—it never varied from what actually happened. *Until now* . . .

This time that agent—Hurt—had ignored Melvin Purvis's direct order and fired his weapon, a killer's grin on his homely face. He could still hear the roar of the .45, and even now he could almost smell the sharp tang of gunpowder, the hot gases burning his—

Dillinger shook the last vestiges of sleep from his mind, recalling the details of the dream. What rattled him was that he now realized he'd been a lot closer to death that night than he'd ever considered in the past. In his spur-of-the-moment decision, he'd never considered that one more step and he would have been lying on that Chicago street, blood seeping from his shattered skull. Dillinger had never seen Agent Hurt after that night, but he'd never forgotten the man's cold, implacable gaze.

The other weird thing, and the only other detail that differed this time around, was that instead of Anna Sage waddling next to him in her bright orange skirt, it was Billie wearing that red Daba gown.

He looked over at her sleeping form and felt a calm wash over him. He still felt something had gone wrong for Billie last night, and it wasn't that poor woman who'd accosted them and then turned on her. It was something else. And he'd tried to coax it out of her after they returned to the suite to no avail.

Stumbling into the bathroom, he took a quick shower then threw on some clothes. Woody was up early, as usual, brewing coffee in the kitchen.

"Mornin', Mr. Dillinger," he said, pouring a cup and pushing it across the counter.

Dillinger took a sip and sighed. As usual, the coffee was perfect. "Johnnie? What are you doing up so early?"

Dillinger turned and saw Billie wrapped in her green silk dressing gown, eyes still puffy from sleep. She stifled a yawn and took the empty stool next to Dillinger as Woody poured another coffee and slid the steaming cup in front of Billie.

"Couldn't sleep—bad dreams."

Billie shrugged and sipped her coffee. "Did you get the paper, Woody?"

Dillinger saw the valet's cagey reaction.

"What is it?" he asked.

With a resigned sigh, Woody pulled the paper out from beneath a folded towel and handed it to Billie. Frowning, she took it, opened it, and sat staring at the front page, her eyes flooding with tears.

"Oh my God," she cried, covering her mouth.

Dillinger grabbed the paper and his blood ran cold. A photo of Billie took up four columns above the fold with an inch-high headline that read:

DILLINGER'S MOLL TAKES CARE OF BUSINESS!

The photo had captured the moment Billie's fist had connected with the crazy woman's jaw, distorting her face out of all recognition. For all the photo's violence, Billie looked cold and detached.

"I'm so sorry, Johnnie," she said, falling into his arms, her voice cracking.

"Hey, hey, it ain't the end of the world, kid. It's just a stupid picture. People will forget all about it by the end of the week."

"What if they don't? They're calling me a moll, Johnnie, a goddamned moll! Like I was some cheap floozie!"

She was working herself into a lather, and a quick glance at Woody told Dillinger that he felt just as helpless to do anything.

Dillinger nodded to Woody, who beat a hasty retreat.

After the valet left the kitchen, Dillinger held Billie close to him, feeling her entire body tremble, as if he were holding a frightened animal. "We'll get past this, honey. We will."

She looked at him with an expression of profound regret. "I don't want to mess this up for you, Johnnie."

※　※　※

Dillinger spent the remainder of the morning studying the script for *The Little Grifter* and making notes, but his concentration was spotty at best. Billie dominated his thoughts, and no matter how hard he tried, he couldn't get the image of her tear-stained eyes out of his head.

Making matters worse, Jack Warner called and ordered that Billie vacate the Roosevelt until the Brown Derby episode blew over. "We can't have this kind of thing happening, John," the older man had said, not bothering to hide the annoyance in his voice. "I've spent my life getting to know the public, and they will not tolerate this."

"But the woman *attacked* her, Mr. Warner. She was defending herself. *I* would've clocked that crazy dame if she hadn't."

There was a long silence before Warner spoke. "Well, thank Christ you didn't!" Warner stopped speaking and Dillinger could hear the man take several breaths. "You know, Fox almost pulled out of the deal."

"Because of Billie?"

"That's right, and I just spent half the night smoothing things over."

"That's nuts!"

"Maybe so, but that's the business we're in. And it's no crazier than my getting you out of prison and putting you in the movies, John. I spent a lot of money to make that happen, and you're not going to fuck it up!"

Dillinger remained silent for the rest of Warner's rant, an impotent rage building in his gut. When the older man hung up, he smashed down the receiver and left the room, heading down to the Roosevelt's bar, where he ordered a Scotch and soda and brooded. Not only would Billie have to vacate, but her new accommodations were to be paid by Dillinger, Warner making it clear this was a part of his penance. He decided that he would put her up at the Beverly Hills Hotel, as it was relatively close, and Billie deserved the best. At least Warner hadn't forbidden him from seeing her. If he had, he would have quit right then, told the old bastard to take his money and go to hell. Dillinger smiled at the thought, then sighed as the reality sank in. He *wanted* this career, he just didn't bank on working for someone who was proving to be as tyrannical as J. Edgar Hoover.

What Dillinger couldn't reconcile in his mind was Warner's rage at how he had handled a bad situation. Perhaps Warner, who considered himself infallible, expected that attribute in his associates. Dillinger didn't see it that way; he always played the hand he was dealt.

Returning to the room, Dillinger found Billie in the bedroom and gave her the bad news. She took it better than he'd expected. Instead of a lot of cussing and carrying on, she simply nodded, her eyes downcast. Seeing her so depressed made it all the harder, and he silently cursed Warner again.

"You know this will only be for a while," he said, holding her against him. "Just until this next picture is done, and I'll come by as often as I can."

Billie looked up at him, a lone tear tracking down the line of her

this

jaw. "But what am I gonna do, Johnnie? I can't stay cooped up in there all day long!"

"Nothing's stoppin' you from going out shopping, or anything else for that matter. And while I'm working, Woody will take you anywhere you want to go."

"I can only shop so much, Johnnie, and I don't know anyone."

"You know Frances Cagney, don't you?"

"Yeah, but we only just met, and I can't just move in on her, you know."

Dillinger grinned. "No, but give her a call. Once this picture starts, I'm going to be out of here all day long and memorizing lines at night. I'd be just as busy if you were staying here."

"So how are you gonna find time to visit me, then?" she asked, some of the fire returning to her eyes.

The grin returned. "I'll manage," he said.

23

1408 Tamarind Avenue
Hollywood, California
February 13, 1936

Robert Butler parked the LaSalle directly across from the small white house with its picket fence, then reached into the backseat for his jacket and notebook.

"You ready to go, Scoop?" he asked, smiling at the pretty twelve-year-old girl seated next to him.

"Do you think Mr. Dillinger will remember me?"

Butler gave his daughter, Lizzie, an indulgent look. "Honey, I don't think he'd *ever* forget you."

That brought a smile to her face that reminded him of her mother's, more and more.

"All right then, let's go. Time is money."

"You always say that," she said with a grin.

"That's because it's always true."

Lizzie giggled and gave her father a peck on the cheek.

They crossed the street and marched up the half-dozen wooden steps to the front door. The yard had just been watered, and the cement walk in front of the house was riddled with puddles. The smell of fresh-cut grass hung in the air. He only had to knock once before a petite woman with the bluest eyes he'd ever seen opened the door. She smiled and said, "You must be Mr. Butler." She offered her hand and Robert took it. "I'm so pleased to meet you."

"Likewise, ma'am, but please call me Bob."

The woman's smile widened. "Bob it is. And who is this pretty thing?" she asked, turning to his young companion.

"I'm Lizzie, and I'm a writer too!"

The woman laughed. "Well, my name's Rosanne, and I'm not a writer, but I'm married to one. Come on in." She opened the door wider and beckoned them inside.

She led them into a book-lined study where Butler spotted Melvin Purvis seated behind a desk fit for a pasha, leafing through a stack of manuscript pages, a sharpened red pencil stuck behind his right ear. When they entered the room, Rosanne cleared her throat and Purvis looked up. He put the papers and the pencil down and stood up, an easy grin creasing his face. Butler had forgotten how short and slight the former FBI agent looked—maybe five-five in shoes and a hundred twenty-five pounds.

"It's good to see you again, Mr. Butler," Purvis said, extending a hand. "And under far less onerous circumstances, I might add."

Butler shook Purvis's hand, suppressing a smile. The former agent's subtle humor was a welcome change from his taciturn behavior the first time they'd met back in Indiana.

"As I told your wife, you can call me Bob."

"Please have a seat. Our other guest has yet to arrive, but we do have some refreshments in the meantime."

Rosanne turned to Lizzie. "Would you give me a hand, honey?"

"Sure," she said, following the older woman into the kitchen.

They reappeared moments later with Rosanne carrying a platter of roast beef sandwiches in one hand and plates and napkins in the other, while Lizzie hefted another tray containing a pitcher of iced tea surrounded by four empty glasses. Purvis made room on his desk, shoving his typewriter to one side.

"All right, then," Rosanne said. "I'll leave you three to get acquainted—"

Just then a sharp knock sounded at the door.

"Oh my, he's here," she said, wiping her hands on her apron and looking nervous for the first time.

"It's all right, Rosie, he's not going to bite," Purvis reassured her. "Go on and let him in."

The man was silhouetted in the doorway, but Butler knew immediately it was Dillinger. The former outlaw removed his fedora and smiled. "Good afternoon, ma'am, I'm John Dillinger."

"Of course you are," she said. "I'd know you anywhere!"

"Must be the wanted posters," Dillinger quipped.

Rosanne laughed, waving him into the room. "Come in, come in!"

Dillinger grinned and moved into the study. His smile widened when he saw Butler. "Bob! How the hell are you?"

"I'm fine, John, no complaints."

"Good, good." Then he caught sight of Lizzie seated catty-corner to the desk. "And how's my little lookout?"

Lizzie rushed over to Dillinger, who swept her up in his arms. "You're not so little anymore, are you?" he said. "You're turning into a real heartbreaker." Lizzie beamed and gave Dillinger another hug. "What are you doing here, darlin'? You playing hooky?"

Lizzie gave him a solemn shake of her head, her blonde curls catching the sunlight streaming in through the window. "I have a writing assignment for the school paper. I got the day off so I could write about you."

Dillinger laughed and set her down. "Well, you can't beat the power of the press, now can you?"

"You look well, John," Purvis said, appraising him with a guarded expression.

"You do too, Melvin."

Dillinger crossed in front of Butler and took a seat between the two men.

"I like to sit facing the door—an old habit." He eyed the tray of sandwiches. "May I?" he asked.

"Rosanne'll be mighty upset if we don't make a dent in these, so please, help yourselves."

The four of them attacked the food, devouring all but two of the sandwiches. After they'd eaten, Butler pulled out his notebook and began the interview.

"Mr. Purvis, both you and Mr. Dillinger have completely changed your lives over the last couple of years. How difficult was the transition for you?"

Purvis looked thoughtful, as if weighing how much he should say. "I would say the transition to civilian life was harder than I expected. I considered numerous employment opportunities, some of them in law enforcement, none of which panned out. Finally, I decided to start writing, something I'd always enjoyed, but never considered as a professional career. I got lucky, I guess."

"So, what are you writing these days?" Butler asked.

Purvis brightened. "Right now, I'm working on two detective novels and a screenplay about a woman scheming to murder her husband."

"Sounds like fun," Butler said with a grin. "I've always had a notion to write a screenplay, and Lord knows I have plenty of material. Never seems like I have the time, though."

"You have to find the time," Purvis said. "Even when I was chasing Mr. Dillinger and the rest of his gang, I would always take the time to write for at least an hour every night. It was my way of unwinding."

"Well, I've read some of your short stories," Butler said, "and I enjoyed them very much."

"Thank you," Purvis said with humble sincerity.

"Now, John, I don't want to leave you out of this. You're starting a new picture this week. Is that right?"

"Yes, it's called *The Little Grifter* and it's about a father-daughter confidence team."

"A departure from Duke Mantee, I would guess," Butler said.

"Yes and no. I'm still playing a mug, but one who sees the light. By the end, he's reformed himself and become the kind of man he never thought he could be."

"Can I ask a question, Daddy?" Lizzie asked.

The three men looked at the young girl, who had a steno pad on her lap and a pencil in her delicate hand. "Do you think you and Shirley Temple will get along?"

Dillinger winked at Butler. "She sounds like a pro, Bob," he said, then turned to Lizzie. "Well, she kind of reminds me of you, honey, so I don't think I'll have any problems. I just need to remember my lines and not trip over the kid."

All of them laughed.

"Any ambitions beyond this?" Butler continued.

"Well, this should probably be off the record, as I don't think Mr. Warner will want to read about it just yet, but I've asked him to let me direct a film."

Both Butler and Purvis looked intrigued.

"But it's not official. He's agreed to look at a script, so I've got to come up with something good."

"What about one of Melvin's?" Butler asked, gesturing toward Purvis.

Dillinger looked surprised. "Well, why the hell not? Got anything you're hot on?"

Purvis looked embarrassed. "Right now, no. Just a couple of short stories that will probably never see the light of day."

"I think you should write about Johnnie," Lizzie piped in.

The three men looked surprised.

"Honey, you mean like '*The John Dillinger Story*'?" Butler asked.

"Something like that?"

The girl nodded.

Dillinger sat back in his chair with a chuckle. "You've got a smart girl there, Bob. I think that's a hell of an idea." Lizzie's proud smile lit up her face, and Dillinger continued. "Not only do I think Warner would go for it, but if we do it right, it'll make a bundle for all of us!"

"What do you mean—all of us?" Butler asked.

"I think the three of us should try working on it together. You just said you always wanted to write a script, so here's your chance. What do you say?"

"I guess I'd be a fool to turn this one down," Butler said with a grin.

※　※　※

After everyone left, Rosanne cleaned up the remains of their snack then announced she was going out to shop for supper. Purvis, pretending to read over his morning's work, accepted her soft kiss then watched her leave. When the door clicked shut behind her, he tossed the pages onto his desk and reached for the phone. It was a call he was dreading, but he had no choice. It rang only once before it was picked up.

"Special Agent Hurt," came the voice with its Oklahoma drawl.

"It's me."

"You're late, Special Agent Purvis."

Purvis swallowed his annoyance. "It couldn't be helped, Clarence. The interview went on longer than I thought. I couldn't just throw them out to call you. And I also had to wait until Rosanne left the house."

"You haven't told her anything, have you?"

"No, I haven't."

The line was silent.

"Anyway," Purvis continued, "there's not much to report—Dillinger wants me to help him write a script. All on the up and up." He deliberately left out any mention of Robert Butler's involvement, as he didn't think it relevant and Purvis didn't want Hurt sniffing around the reporter.

"That's an interestin' development," Hurt said, his tone matter-of-fact. "What's it about?"

"It's going to be called *The John Dillinger Story*."

He heard the agent chuckle. "That's a good one. Maybe you should shoot the ending at the Biograph, too, while you're at it."

"I'm not joking," Purvis said.

"No? Then the fucking joke is on the kids of America."

Purvis sighed. "This is not going to be a whitewash, Clarence. It will be the straight story, with no punches pulled."

There was a long pause and then, "When do you start?"

"It's just an idea that came up this afternoon. Dillinger is starting his new picture tomorrow."

The line went dead, and Purvis muttered an oath as he hung up the phone in disgust. Even talking to the man made his insides roil. What made it worse was that he was feeling a growing respect for Dillinger, something he never would have thought possible regarding his old adversary. And now he was actively involved in Hoover's maneuverings to trap the man, a fate he no longer deserved—and it galled Purvis to the core.

"What a load of crap," he said, reaching into a desk drawer and pulling out a bottle of Old Overholt whiskey and a shot glass. He poured a drink and knocked it back. As the rye whiskey seared its way down his throat, he considered all the consequences of what he was doing. Purvis knew he was playing a dangerous game, but he fully intended to make sure no harm would ever come to Rosanne. He was not so sure about himself.

24

20th Century Fox Studios
Los Angeles, California
February 14, 1936

Woody craned his neck, trying to see to the front of the line of cars waiting to drive onto the studio lot. "I don't rightly know what the hold-up is, Mr. Dillinger."

"That's okay," he said, his eyes scanning the script pages they were shooting that day. "I don't think they'll start without me." A courier had delivered the call sheet the previous night, just as he was about to leave his room at the Roosevelt to head over to Billie's bungalow at the Beverly Hills Hotel. Aside from listing the day's shots, the call sheet also informed him of the time he and the other actors were expected to arrive at the studio for makeup.

For him, it was six o'clock.

Fortunately, he'd remembered to grab his copy of the script along with a change of clothes.

When he arrived at Billie's bungalow, and after a cozy steak dinner catered by the hotel's El Jardin Restaurant, Dillinger reviewed the call sheet. The first scene they were scheduled to shoot was the hospital scene where his character confronts the very real possibility that his daughter might die. It was the most emotional scene in the film, and Dillinger was worried sick that he wasn't anywhere near ready to perform it.

"Christ, Billie, the first damn scene!" he shouted, pacing the floor.

Billie kept her eyes on the copy of *Photoplay* she was reading. "Didn't you tell me they do this kind of thing on purpose?"

"Yeah, I did. They're testing me again. This scene is make or break, honey. I screw this up and they'll be fitting my wardrobe for Eddie Robinson by noon."

Billie looked up and smiled indulgently. "I don't think it's quite *that* bad."

Dillinger sat beside her on the bed and gazed into her bottomless brown eyes. "You don't understand. It feels like everyone's betting I'm gonna make a sap of myself."

"Everyone's *not* betting on that. And you didn't make a sap of yourself on *Petrified Forest*, did you?"

Dillinger let out an impatient sigh. "That's because I was just playing myself."

"You were never that mean," she said.

"I just don't know if I'll be able to cry on cue like the script calls for. It's not easy for a guy, you know, much less a hard-boiled egg like me."

Billie put down the magazine and ran her hand through Dillinger's hair then caressed his cheek. "I know . . . but you're an actor now. And that's what actors do. What would Maria tell you?"

Dillinger shot her a sly look. "You must take some-ting from inside and put it outside for everyone to see," he said in a dead-on Russian accent. "You do that, and it will be the truth."

Billie clapped her hands to her mouth, laughing. "Oh, my God, that's priceless, and she's right, Johnnie. You're going to do fine. I *know* it."

Dillinger kissed her and stood up, moving to where his jacket hung over a hard-backed chair. From the inside pocket he drew a light-blue box tied with a white satin ribbon. "Happy Valentine's Day, sweetheart," he said, handing her the box.

"But that's tomorrow!" she said, her facing lighting up.

Dillinger shrugged. "Yeah, well, I'm a little tied up tomorrow, so I thought tonight would be okay."

"It's more than okay." She laughed and tore open the package, revealing a small black velvet box inside. Her eyes went wide. "Johnnie, what are you doing?"

"Open it," he said, his grin widening.

She flipped open the velvet box, revealing a two-carat diamond set into a platinum ring encircled with smaller diamonds. It caught the lights in the room, sparkling like a tiny galaxy.

"Will you marry me, Billie?"

Billie's eyes flooded with tears and her lips trembled. She nodded her head vigorously. "Yes, yes, yes!"

Dillinger laughed and picked her up off the bed and twirled her around, eliciting a peal of girlish laughter.

"Come on, let's see if it fits." He put her down, grabbed the velvet box, and removed the ring. Billie, still giddy, held out her left hand and let him slide the ring onto her finger.

"It's so beautiful," Billie said, turning her hand this way and that.

"That's just a rock. *You're* beautiful."

Billie hugged him. "You always know the perfect thing to say."

"So, when do you want to make me an honest man?"

"Johnnie, I don't know!" Her eyes widened again. "My God, what about Walter?"

"You mean that no-good jailbird husband of yours?"

"Please don't call him that."

"Fine, he's a prince who's spending the next ten years behind bars. You don't still love the mug, do you?"

"No," Billie said, shaking her head, "I don't think I ever really did, but—"

Dillinger smiled. "No buts. I'll ask around about getting you a divorce. Louis will know."

"Your old lawyer?"

"Yes. Now, do you want some big church affair or City Hall?"

She hugged him again. "I don't care. We can think about it, we have time."

"Yes we do, kiddo, yes we do."

※　※　※

"We're almost there, Mr. Dillinger," Woody said, breaking him out of his private thoughts. He looked up from the script and saw there were now only two cars ahead of them. They were waved through and it was Dillinger's turn.

Woody rolled down the window and said, "Mr. John Dillinger for Stage Twelve."

The guard, an older man, leaned down and stuck his head in the window. "John? That really you?"

At the sound of the guard's voice, Dillinger looked up again, a smile creasing his face. "Cappy! What the hell are you doing here?" he asked, climbing out of the car and embracing the older man.

"I took your advice," Cappy said. "Took my retirement and got out of that hellhole!"

Dillinger leaned back and laughed. "That's the ticket! But why didn't you call me like I said? I could've helped, although it looks like you're doing okay."

"I am, John, I am. And honestly, I didn't want to bother you."

Dillinger shot him a look of mock annoyance. "You'd never bother me, Cappy. I'm glad you're here."

The older man grinned. "Thanks, Johnnie. I'm glad to be here, and I'm the Assistant Chief of Guards, no less."

"Well, that's great," Dillinger said, clapping the older man on the shoulder.

Horns started honking.

"Hey, Mac, I'm gonna be late!" someone screamed.

Dillinger waved to an irate man leaning out of his Ford Model 40 DeLuxe two cars back then turned back to Cappy. "I better get going. Stop by the set if you get a chance."

The streets of the studio were narrow and thronged with cast and crewmembers from a dozen different productions, moving in every direction. Coupled with other vehicles towing racks of wardrobe and flats for sets, it was like a traffic jam at rush hour. Except here it was rush hour from the moment the studio opened until shooting shut down for the night. Dillinger took in all these sights and sounds, feeling the butterflies kicking up in his stomach.

After fifteen minutes of braving the crawling traffic, Woody pulled up in front of the massive sliding doors of Stage 12. They were cracked open about three feet, enough to allow people in and out. A young man wearing thick glasses and carrying a clipboard emerged, spotted the car, and jogged over.

"Good morning, Mr. Dillinger. I'm Hal, one of the assistant directors. I don't mean to rush you, sir, but they need you in makeup right now."

The young man looked anxious, which made Dillinger smile.

"I'm all yours, kid," he said, climbing from the car, his script under one arm. "I'm not sure when I'll be done, Woody. Take care of Billie."

The valet gave a good-natured shrug. "I will, Mr. Dillinger, and I'll be here when you need me."

Hal went to the door and waved Dillinger forward.

"Here goes nothing," he mumbled, and followed Hal.

As soon as he was inside the stage doors, two crewmembers slid and latched the door and a sign lit up: CLOSED SET.

"This way, Mr. Dillinger," Hal said, beckoning him.

Winding his way through the tangle of cables and lights and frantic crewmembers dashing about, he soon found himself at the back of the soundstage. The area consisted of a cluster of six makeup tables on casters lined up, all of them topped by mirrors ringed with incandescent lights. One of the six chairs was occupied by a woman dressed as a nurse, attended to by an older man who was powdering her nose. Two chairs down, a curly redhead wearing a green smock smiled and motioned for him to have a seat.

"After Agnes works her magic," Hal said, backpedaling away from Dillinger, "I'll take you over to wardrobe, okay?"

"See ya, kid." Dillinger moved over to where the makeup artist waited and eased himself into the tall canvas-backed director's chair.

"Sorry to keep you waiting, doll," Dillinger said.

The woman smiled and threw a barber's cape over him and snapped it behind his neck. She then placed tissue paper between his neck and the shirt to protect the collar. "That's okay, Mr. Dillinger, you weren't that late."

Fifteen minutes later, the girl put on the finishing touches just as Hal returned. "Right this way, Mr. Dillinger."

The next stop was a makeshift fitting room where Dillinger traded his hundred-dollar suit for a much shabbier one. There was even a cigarette burn on the cuff.

Minute by minute he felt more and more like his character, Joey Pratt, the down-and-almost-out con man, who is soon to realize his daughter means more to him than just a meal ticket.

They left wardrobe and Hal walked Dillinger over to the set, which consisted of a hospital bed and a couple of chairs surrounded by three walls. A tall man with dark wavy hair wearing a pair of horn-rimmed glasses stood near the camera, giving orders and motioning to others in the catwalks overhead with a set of unique hand signals. They waited until John Ford finished talking to the crew, and when he sat down on a director's chair, Hal motioned for Dillinger to follow.

"Mr. Ford? May I present John Dillinger."

The tall man looked up with a look of mild surprise then he stood, holding out a meaty hand. Dillinger took it.

"Mr. Dillinger, glad to have you aboard."

"Thank you, Mr. Ford. I'm here to do my best."

Ford grinned. "Splendid. Has Hal filled you in?"

The young man looked stricken. "Uh, not yet, Mr. Ford. I wanted to get him out of makeup and wardrobe first."

Ford gave Hal an understanding look and then turned back to Dillinger. "Well, I just wanted to make it clear that when you're on one of my sets, things will run smoothly if you just do what I tell you. Can you do that, Mr. Dillinger?"

Dillinger sensed this was a man used to getting his way, and he had to admit from the films he'd seen, the man knew what he was doing. He also sensed the director's little speech was a test, and the look of expectancy on Hal's young face all but proved it.

"You're the boss of this mob, as far as I'm concerned. I'm just a hired gun. But one thing *I* want to make clear. If I have an idea, I'm going to let you have it . . . in a manner of speaking." Dillinger grinned and Ford laughed.

"We're gonna get along fine, Dillinger. Have a seat. We're just waiting for Miss Temple to finish wardrobe."

Ford motioned toward another director's chair, which Dillinger noted had his name stenciled on the back. He sat down, feeling an odd sense of calm steal over him. He'd heard about Ford being a tyrant, but he seemed to be a down-to-earth guy. He also sensed the gruff exterior cloaked a raging temper that would flare if provoked.

A flurry of activity behind him drew him out of his thoughts. He turned and spotted a young girl dressed in a hospital gown as she headed toward the set, followed by a retinue of attendants, one of them an older woman who had to be her mother. She had an angelic smile on her face, in spite of the bandages swaddling her head and the fake bruises on her face. Though Dillinger knew it was just makeup, it hurt to look at her. He stood up as she approached.

"How do you do, Mr. Dillinger? I'm Shirley. I'm so glad we'll be working together," she said, looking up at him with those blue eyes that had charmed a nation.

Dillinger got down on one knee, which brought them to eye level. "I'm glad to meet you, kiddo."

Quite unexpected, Shirley put her arms around him and gave him a hug. "Watch out for Mr. Ford, he can get grumpy."

Dillinger laughed, and they separated.

Hal stepped forward with a megaphone. "All right, everyone. Places!"

The talking ceased, and Dillinger followed Shirley onto the set, where he helped her climb into the bed. Under the lights, her bruises appeared to blossom, and Dillinger noticed the heat immediately. "Feels like a sauna in here," he said.

"That's because this film's in Technicolor," she said, sounding like an old pro. "They need a lot more light for it." She nodded emphatically, and Dillinger chuckled.

They were joined by Ford and an older man dressed as a doctor.

"Good morning, Mr. Kibbee!"

The older man winked at Shirley. "Mornin', darlin'!"

"All right," Ford said, getting their attention. "As some of you who've worked with me before know, I like to shoot the first rehearsal. Sometimes we get lucky that way. So, we'll go over the blocking, and then we'll try a take. Sound good?" The three actors nodded. "Excellent."

They spent the next fifteen minutes rehearsing their movements, while Hal put down color-coded tape marks for both Dillinger and Guy Kibbee. Dillinger kept the flow of the dialogue in his mind, gauging his movements accordingly.

"Let's do a take," Ford said, taking his seat by the camera.

"Quiet on the set!" Hal shouted through the megaphone.

Somewhere in the building, a bell rang for five seconds and then fell silent.

"Roll camera," Ford said.

"Rolling," the camera operator said in a bright tenor.

"Roll sound."

"Speed," said the sound recordist, his gaze locked onto a bouncing VU meter.

Ford leaned forward and said, "Action!"

25

Roosevelt Hotel
Hollywood, California
February 14, 1936

Dillinger had Woody drop him at the back of the hotel. He wanted to avoid the fans and the autograph hounds who accosted him every time he entered or left. Most of the time, he didn't mind, but tonight he just needed a little peace and quiet.

He watched Woody drive off and then he entered the kitchen. Staffed with black and Latino men busily preparing food, they took no notice of Dillinger as he sauntered through their midst. Emerging into the restaurant, he avoided the frank stares from the nearby tables and headed into the lobby and then the elevator. Even Sid, the diminutive elevator operator, sensed his mood and refrained from his usual banter.

Once inside the room, Dillinger threw off his jacket, loosened his tie, and flopped onto the couch with a sigh, his mind going over the day's shooting. If today's experience was any kind of predictor for the next three weeks, it was going to be rough. *The Petrified Forest* was a walk in the park by comparison. One reason for that was the role. Joey Pratt was a complex character, much more so than

Duke Mantee had been. The directorial style was different, as well. Archie Mayo had been like everyone's favorite uncle, while Ford was more like the mythical Captain Bligh. That aside, the day had gone well. The first scene was shot in four different setups with an average of three takes each. The hardest part was making sure he moved and said everything the same way from shot to shot. Whoever said acting was easy needed a good swift kick.

The phone rang, and Dillinger groaned. Woody, who'd just come in the front door, picked it up. "Mr. Dillinger's room," he said without missing a beat. He listened then put the phone against his chest and turned to his boss. "It's Miss Billie."

Dillinger nodded, rose from the couch, and took the phone from his valet. "Hey, baby, how are you? Ya miss me?"

"Yes, I do, and I'm fine, but you sound exhausted."

"I am, but it was a good first day."

"How did the scene go?"

"I think we aced it, but it's hard to tell with Ford."

"Ford?"

"The director. He's not generous with praise. He just gets on with it, so I assume I gave him what he wanted."

"You coming over?"

A part of him wanted just to soak in a hot tub and go to bed. On the other hand, that bed was awfully empty without Billie. Dillinger grinned. "Yeah, let me get cleaned up and I'll be there pronto."

※　※　※

Instead of having their dinner in the bungalow, they decided to take their meal in the El Jardin itself. That way it would feel as if they were going out without leaving the sanctuary of the hotel. Some of the gowns and a few of the everyday dresses had been delivered from the House of Daba that afternoon, and Billie decked herself out in a black satin ensemble with a rhinestone trim that shimmered in the restaurant's low-key lighting. She was wearing the ring, too, and it dazzled every time she moved her hand.

"I took your advice and called Frances Cagney," Billie said after giving their drink order to the waiter.

"Oh, yeah?" he asked with a cheeky grin.

She chucked him on the shoulder. "Don't be so smug."

"So? Tell me."

"Well, she heard all about what happened at the Derby and she wants to give me a tea next Tuesday."

Dillinger looked puzzled. "Give you a tea?"

Billie rolled her eyes. "You know . . . like an afternoon party with a bunch of gossiping women yacking while stuffing their faces with tea and cakes."

"Ah," Dillinger said, laughing. "Sort of a blowout minus the hootch."

"Oh, stop it," she said with a barely concealed grin. "Frances is inviting all of her friends. She thinks it'll give me a chance to show these women the real me."

The drinks arrived, and Dillinger sipped his Manhattan before answering. "I think it's swell," he said.

"You do?"

"Sure. You need something to break the ice, and this sounds like the ticket. And Frances is right. Once these women get to know you, they'll love you as much as I do."

"I hope you're right."

"If they don't, they're idiots."

※　※　※

Special Agent Hurt watched Dillinger and his moll from a secluded booth across the dark, intimate room. He was too far away to hear

249

their conversation and could only catch a word or two when the woman raised her voice, but they looked happy and that set his teeth on edge. And the only reason he was sitting there watching them was because Hoover had given him an unlimited expense account and orders to the effect that he had *carte blanche*. Not that he'd ever want to be seen in places like this off the job. Not on your life. These weren't real people—they were phonies out to grab whatever they could from a public who desperately wanted to emulate them. Well, to hell with that.

Billie's diamond ring caught the light again, sending a tiny super-nova into Hurt's eyes.

You think marrying her is going to make her any more respectable, punk? Think again.

When he'd read the account in the papers about what Billie Fre-chette had done outside The Brown Derby, he'd laughed until tears ran down his face. Trash would always show their true colors. He'd almost wished it had been Dillinger smacking that crazy broad. That would have made his job a lot easier.

26

Roosevelt Hotel
Hollywood, California
February 18, 1936

The alarm rattled precisely at five a.m., ripping Dillinger out of an exciting dream where he'd made a large withdrawal from a small bank in Indiana. He silenced the alarm with a well-practiced slap and flopped back down onto his pillow with a sigh of contentment. He looked over at Billie, who was sleeping on her stomach, snoring softly. Dillinger smiled, recalling the passion of the previous night. Sex with Billie was nearly always volcanic, a consequence of their chemistry forming a unique and volatile compound. Yet he wondered what their married life would be like now that he'd popped the question. The prospect both thrilled and frightened him. Still, she was the best thing that had ever happened to him—there was no denying that.

The odors of coffee and bacon wafted in from the kitchen, making his stomach growl in anticipation of Woody's fine cooking, and with a tired groan he sat up. Stretching, he turned and saw Billie was awake, staring at him.

"You're not too tired, I hope?" she asked with a soft giggle.

Despite Jack Warner wanting her to stay in a separate hotel, he'd grown tired of running back and forth for his clothes and toilet articles. He'd finally relented and had her stay over last night, after sneaking her in through the kitchen and up the service elevator. A part of him hated to put her through that, but another part of him enjoyed the subterfuge, a reminder of the old days. The other reason he had her stay was that Frances Cagney was holding her tea in one of the private rooms downstairs later that afternoon.

"You nervous?" he asked, encircling her in his arms.

"A little," she replied.

"You'll be fine. Just remember, whatever happens—"

She put a finger to her lips. "I know, 'it's Hollywood.'"

Dillinger showered and changed into a charcoal-gray pinstripe suit. After breakfast, Billie saw him off to the studio, the soft insistence of her kiss lingering long after he left the hotel. All during the ride to Fox he kept seeing her beautiful face and the frown lines between her eyebrows that had never been there before. There was fear in her eyes, too, and he silently cursed the Hollywood press and their razor-edged hypocrisy for putting it there. In the eyes of Hollywood—most of it, anyway—he was now accepted, but only because he was a valuable commodity, and he knew he would be re-earning that acceptance with every successive film. Yet for these reporters and their readers, Billie was perceived as a threat to their precious social order.

And me the one robbing the banks!

When they reached the studio, Dillinger was gratified to see the line of cars was shorter than usual. Perhaps he would have time to call Billie before the first shot of the day, give her another boost of confidence. As it happened, there wasn't time, but Dillinger knew

Billie could take care of herself. After all, she'd dodged a bullet or two in her time.

✳ ✳ ✳

The cream had begun to curdle, and a lone fly buzzed around the delicate pastries laid out on the table surrounding the filigreed copper samovar, the heating flame now sputtering as the fuel ran out.

Billie stared at the floor, not wanting to look at Frances, not wanting to see that expression of naked pity on her face. It was all she could do to hold back the tears. The Roosevelt's vast tearoom was empty, save for the two of them and the three waiters endlessly rearranging silverware and cups that would never be used.

Those bitches! Those goddamned bitches and their judgmental bullshit!

"Billie . . ." Frances said. "I'm—"

Her eyes welled as she stood. "I'm sorry," she said, and fled the room.

She tore down the hallway toward the bank of elevators, avoiding the pointed stares of the other guests who moved aside to let her streak past.

They know, somehow—they know.

An elevator was disgorging a group of hotel guests, and Billie shouldered past a gray-haired matron, who stared at her with ill-concealed contempt. Billie forced herself to unclench her fists.

"Seventh floor, please," she said.

The elevator operator knew enough not to speak, which made the ride upward feel as if it lasted three times longer than it should have.

When Billie reached the door of the suite, her trembling hands fumbled and dropped the key.

"Shit, shit, shit!"

She snatched the key off the floor, shoved it into the lock and threw open the door, racing past a bewildered Woody and on into the bedroom, where she slammed the door. Sobbing, she flopped onto the bed and buried her face in the pillows, howling with anguish.

A few moments later, there was a knock on the door, soft yet insistent.

"You okay, Miss Billie?" Woody asked through the door.

Billie sat up and grabbed a wad of Kleenex from a box on the nightstand and wiped her eyes, the soft white tissue coming away streaked with black mascara. She then reached for more tissue and blew her nose. Her eyes felt as if she'd been swimming in the ocean, the salt in her tears rendering them raw and gritty.

"Miss Billie?"

"I'm okay, Woody, I'm fine," she said, clearing the mucus from her throat.

"Mrs. Cagney is here. She wants to speak with you."

Billie felt her chest tighten, the tears threatening to erupt again.

"Please tell her I'm not feeling well."

A moment elapsed before Woody answered. "I don't mean to butt in, Miss Billie, but I think it might be best if you'd come on out."

Billie sighed and rolled her eyes, annoyed, but not at Woody. Frances obviously wanted to make amends, but this was something good intentions couldn't fix. Still, Johnnie would want her to be polite to the wife of the man he considered his best friend.

"All right, I'll be out in a minute."

After a quick look in the mirror, she decided to forgo putting on more makeup. Frances already knew how upset she was, and there was no point in attempting to hide it. Steeling herself, she left the bedroom and made her way into the living room. She found Frances seated on the couch, her kind face etched with worry. She looked up, her eyes widening.

"Oh Billie, I'm so sorry," she said, rising to her feet. "I really had no idea these women would do such a thing. I assumed they were better than that—I was wrong."

Billie felt a rush of warmth and gratitude as she joined Frances on the couch. "I appreciate you saying that. I just don't know what to do. These women are never going to accept me, Frances. Maybe I should just go back to Wisconsin. I'll be doing Johnnie more harm than good if I stay."

She placed a hand on Billie's arm. "You know that's not true."

Billie nodded, a tear tracking down her cheek. "I just can't shake the feeling I'm going to hold him back, and I don't want that. Johnnie had it so hard growing up. He deserves the chance to make good."

"And he is, but he needs you too, Billie. That much I know. My Jimmy would be lost without me."

Billie smiled sadly. "But at least you have friends out here. I have no one."

"I'm not so sure about those friends anymore, dear, but as for you, you have me."

Billie felt as if she might cry again. "Thank you, but that's only a part of my problem. I don't think I can just sit around like a housewife and do nothing— Oh, God, I'm sorry," she said, noting a change in her friend's expression. "I didn't mean for it to come out that way."

Frances, who still had a hand on Billie's arm, gave it an affectionate squeeze. "It didn't. What you said just made me think of something. It's going to sound a little strange, but I have an idea that might be just what you need."

Billie frowned. "Strange how?"

"What would you think about taking a job?"

Billie looked surprised. "A job? *Me?*"

Frances nodded. "I'm going to tell you something you may have figured out already. Hollywood is a small town, and it's a town that runs on talent. 'Talent is king,' they say. That's why everyone's falling all over themselves for Johnnie."

"And that's why their wives are treating me this way. Because I have no talent and no power . . ."

Frances nodded. "In their minds, you don't count. And I also think they're jealous."

"Of me?" she said, incredulous.

Frances nodded. "Your youth, your beauty . . . and Johnnie."

"Well, that I can understand," she said, shaking her head. "So, you think I should go work in some store? I'd probably make a mess of it."

"No, not a store, and I don't believe you'd make a mess of anything."

They fell silent for a moment and then Frances said, "Jimmy told me you're reading all of the scripts coming to John and that you recommended he take the Shirley Temple picture."

"I did, but since it was already a done deal, it was mostly to put his mind at ease. He thought it was screwy, but as soon as I read it, I knew he should do it."

"And what if you'd thought it wasn't?"

Billie's eyes locked with Frances's. "I would have told him not to do it."

"You see, my dear, you *do* have talent. You see the potential in others and you know instinctively what is best for them. You knew what was best for Johnnie."

"But that's only 'cause I know him so well."

"Of course," Frances said with a chuckle, "but you'll get to know others too."

"What are you suggesting?"

The older woman smiled and patted Billie's arm again. "Jimmy and I have a friend at the William Morris Agency. His name is Johnny Hyde and he's the vice president, and I happen to know he's looking for someone special to groom as a literary agent. And I think you'd be perfect."

"A literary agent?"

"Yes, William Morris represents quite a few of the top actors, producers, and writers, and he's one of the best there. And as my Jimmy has said on more than one occasion, the talent agencies are the powerbrokers of this business. As for the job, at first, you'll probably be running errands and fielding phone calls, taking dictation—that sort of thing. Can you type?"

Billie looked pained. "A little, I guess."

Frances shrugged. "It doesn't matter. The important thing is you'll be meeting people. It's relationships that make the deals in this town, and once you learn the ropes and get to know the writers and the producers, you'll be operating from a position of power. You'll never be treated like you were today. Not ever again."

Billie looked intrigued for the first time. "But will this man take me seriously? I can't imagine there are that many women agents."

Frances grinned. "I think you'd be one of the first. What a lot of men don't want to acknowledge, dear, is that often there are times a woman will hold a much better advantage in negotiations, especially one as attractive as you. Mr. Hyde knows this. He's also a bit of a ladies' man, though I think with you it'll be hands off."

Billie laughed, her mind reeling with the possibilities.

An agent?

It was crazy, yet the prospect of it set her pulse to racing. She hated sitting around the Beverly Hills Hotel all day, every day. It was mind numbing.

"I don't know how my Johnnie will feel about this—me having any kind of job, that is."

"Why don't you talk to him about it? Mull it over and let me know what you want to do. I really think you'd have a knack for it, my dear."

※　※　※

Joey Pratt felt a trickle of sweat run down his back as he watched his daughter Sadie studying her cards.

"Say, is the kid gonna take any cards, or what?"

The gravelly voice belonged to Slappy McGurk, a low-level gangster who couldn't resist the lure of a card game and the chance to take a couple of rubes. Joey looked to his daughter, Sadie, who smiled and winked at him, her amber curls shining in the dingy overhead light.

"Nah, she's good, aren't you, honey?" Joey asked, suppressing his own smile.

Slappy's hound-dog face twisted into a sour grimace. "Gimme two," he growled.

Joey dealt two cards to the surly mobster, who tossed his discards onto the table in disgust. The other two thugs at the table, whose names Joey had already forgotten, followed suit. Joey quickly dealt them new cards and then sat back and waited for Sadie.

"I'll bet twenty and raise you ten," she said, pushing her pile of money into the growing pot in the center of the table. The two gangsters, whom Joey now dubbed Mutt and Jeff, placed their bets. Joey quietly folded, his pulse quickening.

Slappy stared at Joey and chuckled, then he turned to Sadie. "You think you got something, kid?"

Sadie stared back at the ugly gangster but remained silent.

Slappy cracked an evil grin. "Gotta pay to play, kid. I'll see your thirty and raise you a c-note."

The other two gangsters threw down their cards. "I'm out," they said in unison.

"That's fine by me," Slappy said, pushing his pile of cash into the pot. His grin widened.

Sadie stared at Slappy, all the innocence gone from her pretty blue eyes. She pushed her entire stack of winnings into the pot.

Slappy's eyebrows shot upward in surprise.

"Call," she said, her eyes still locked onto the gangster's hollow-eyed gaze.

"Read 'em and weep, kid." Slappy laughed and turned over his cards. "Full house, kings high."

Sadie looked as if she might cry, and Slappy laughed all the harder as he reached for the money.

Sadie's free hand shot into the air, her feigned sadness turning into a knowing grin. "Not so fast, Slappy."

Sadie turned over her cards, revealing a royal flush.

Slappy's eyes bulged out and he leaped to his feet, knocking his chair over backwards. "You rotten little chiseler!" he screamed, and reached for his gun. Joey sprang across the space separating him and Slappy and the two grappled for the gun, causing it to go off and send a bullet into the ceiling.

"Get him, boys!" Slappy yelled as Mutt and Jeff reached for their pistols.

"STOP!"

All the men turned to see Sadie holding a .45 automatic in a two-handed grip, aimed squarely at Slappy's head. Her hands were rock steady, her gaze merciless.

Joey grinned as he collected the guns. Mutt and Jeff stood frozen, unsure of their next move.

"She's a crack shot, McGurk. I taught her everything she knows."

Slappy stared into Joey's eyes. "Yeah, some father you turned out to be."

The confident grin slid off Joey Pratt's face.

❋ ❋ ❋

"Cut!" John Ford shouted. "All right. That's it for today, people. Good work. See you all bright and early tomorrow."

The bell rang and Walter Long, the actor playing Slappy, still stared daggers into Dillinger's eyes. Then the man relaxed, and a warm grin spread across his craggy face. He grabbed Dillinger in a bear hug.

"Good going, my friend," he said, patting Dillinger on the back. Then he turned to Shirley Temple. "And you, my little dear, are scaring the pants off me!"

Shirley raced into his embrace and Long let out a belly laugh.

Dillinger smiled.

Walter Long, one of those actors who would always play tough guys and mugs because of his bulldog features, was one of the warmest men he'd ever met. Still smiling, he turned to make his way off the set and spied his old friend Cappy watching from the sidelines.

"You're lookin' real good, John," he said as Dillinger fell into step beside him.

"You think so?"

Cappy nodded.

Dillinger clapped the old guard on the shoulder. "Thanks, Cap, it's nice to know I'm doing something right."

Cappy laughed and they sauntered through the great sliding doors into the deepening night.

Dillinger found Woody and the Ford waiting in the usual spot. He climbed in after bidding his old friend a good night and they were off. It only took minutes for Dillinger to realize something was off with his valet.

"What's wrong?" he asked, when he couldn't take the silence any longer.

Woody sighed and shook his head. "Nobody came to Billie's tea."

Dillinger sat forward. "What? Nobody came?"

"Just Mrs. Cagney. Billie was awful upset when she came back to the room. It was only after Mrs. Cagney came up and spoke to her that she seemed better."

"What did she say to her?"

"I don't rightly know, Mr. Dillinger, but I expect Billie will be wanting to talk to you when we get back. She's making supper, by the way."

"Billie's making supper?"

"I've been teaching her a few things, here and there. She learns fast."

Dillinger sat back with a smile on his face. Billie was a smart kid, and he liked that about her. Too many women prided themselves on being dumb, or at least giving the appearance of it, and he'd never held with that. Dumb was boring. Then his thoughts turned to the tea and Dillinger's anger threatened to boil over. The nerve of those old broads. He vowed when he got home he'd try to make Billie forget all about them.

※　※　※

The first thing that hit him when he walked in the door was the smell of baking meatloaf. Throwing his jacket on a chair, he made his way into the kitchen, where he found Billie putting the finishing touches on the mashed potatoes, a frilly apron over her Daba dress.

"Hey there," he said, leaning against the doorjamb.

Billie turned and flew into his arms. "I'm so glad you're home."

"It's okay," he said, patting her back. "Woody told me."

She pulled back and gave him a searching look. "It was so embarrassing, Johnnie. No one . . ."

"I know, but Woody said Frances spoke with you and that you seemed to feel better."

"I do, but can we talk about it over dinner? I'm starved. All I had were those damned teacakes and cucumber sandwiches—one burp and you're empty."

Dillinger grimaced and Billie laughed.

"At least you can laugh about it," he said.

Woody bustled into the small kitchen. "Everybody out. You all go sit and I'll serve. Smells real good, Miss Billie."

Billie grinned from ear to ear as she and Dillinger made their way to the dining area. The table had been set with crisp white linen, sterling flatware, and two slender candles already lit, their soft light casting a romantic glow.

As they took their seats, Woody came out of the kitchen bearing a bottle of champagne, which he proceeded to open with great fanfare. He poured two glasses and placed the open bottle into the silver ice bucket next to the table.

"I thought we were saving this," Dillinger said in a low voice.

Billie shrugged. "After that tea party, I need something stronger."

Dillinger nodded.

A moment later, Woody emerged from the kitchen carrying two plates laden with meatloaf, mashed potatoes, and gravy.

Dillinger grinned as a plate was placed in front of him. "My favorite," he said. "Thank you."

Billie smiled, and they began. After eating in silence for a few minutes, Dillinger spoke. "So, tell me, what did Frances talk to you about? I imagine she felt awful, since this was all her idea."

"Yes, she did, but I don't blame her for anything. She was as surprised as I was when after two hours no one showed up. But she did give me something to think about. I'm just not sure how to say it."

Dillinger forked a mouthful of potatoes. "Just spit it out."

Billie put down her utensils, picked up her champagne flute and drained it, then told him about Frances's suggestion. She stopped speaking, reacting to the shocked look on Dillinger's face.

"A literary agent?" he said. "Honey, do you have any idea what those guys do?"

"I think I do. And like I said, they'd be training me."

"But Billie, you don't need to work. I make enough dough for the both of us." He gestured to the room. "I mean, look at this joint."

"I know, and I'm grateful, Johnnie, I really am, but I just don't think I can sit around here all day, doing nothing. And don't say I'm going to make friends, because obviously that's not going to happen so fast." She poured another glass of champagne and knocked it back.

"Hey, go easy on that stuff," he said. "Look, I'm sorry for what happened today. It was just plain mean and rotten, but that doesn't mean you have to go career-girl on me. I don't want you working, Billie, it's not right."

"Not *right?*" she said, refilling her champagne glass.

"Hey, I told you to go easy."

Billie's face flushed, and she picked up the half-empty bottle of champagne and hurled it against the wall, where it exploded, spraying glass and expensive bubbly all over a nearby chair.

"Jesus Christ, why'd you go and do that?"

"Because I'm your trophy, Johnnie, your pretty china doll ready to be trotted out whenever you need to show me off. That's all any of these people think when they see me."

"That's not true, and you know it."

"Yes, it is. I have *nothing* to do all day. *Nothing.* At least if we lived in some cute little house instead of this high-class dump, I could pretend to be a housewife. But I can't even have that—and I don't want it."

"You want to be a goddamn agent."

"Yes."

Dillinger shook his head and Billie sighed. She reached across the table and took his hand. "I don't want to argue, Johnnie. I guess I was hoping you'd be happy for me, for the opportunity. I think I could be really good at it. I convinced you to take *The Little Grifter*, didn't I?"

"Yes, but—"

She squeezed his hand, silencing him.

"As soon as I read that script, I could see you in that part. And I could find other scripts for you too. I know we don't need the money right now, but things have a way of changing. You can't have too much dough, you've told me that yourself." She squeezed his hand harder, almost pleading. "I need *this*, and I think we'd make a great team. It's just like you used to tell me: it's us against them, and we're outnumbered—remember?"

Dillinger squeezed her hand back and stared into her eyes. "I remember . . ." He paused a moment, his gaze shifting to see Woody peering out from the kitchen. "It's okay, the fireworks are over." The valet grinned and moved to clean up the shattered glass. Dillinger returned his attention to Billie. "If you really want to do this, then

264

fine." He shook his head and chuckled. "I guess I'd have to be a grade-A sap to stand in your way."

"Really?!"

Dillinger laughed at her glee. "Yeah, sure."

First Mayo practically breaks my foot, Gable calls me a punk, and now Billie reels me in like a prize trout . . . and they're all getting away with it. I must be getting soft.

She came to him then, sitting in his lap and showering him with grateful kisses. "Of course, he may not hire me. I still have to meet him, and I still have to pass the interview."

"One thing I've learned is Hollywood is full of salesmen, and you just sold me. If this guy doesn't see that, he's a bum."

Billie kissed him on the tip of his nose. "What do you say we have the rest of our dinner in bed?" she asked.

"Just no more champagne."

Billie laughed.

27

The Stargazer Hotel
Hollywood, California
February 21, 1936

Hurt lay on the sagging brass bed, smoking his last cigarette of the day. The hotel's neon sign mounted just outside his window pulsed and flickered in a sputtering multicolored rainbow, casting its tawdry luster across the water-stained ceiling. He imagined some people would find it hard to sleep with that kind of distraction, which was why the room was so cheap, but Hurt liked to watch the sign go through its endless cycle. The low-frequency hum coming through the walls and the kaleidoscopic pattern of the lights relaxed him.

The naked blonde next to him stirred and stretched. Then she raised herself up on one arm, brushing her tousled hair from her gaunt face. She smelled of stale sweat. "You want me to stay the night, mister?" she asked, caressing Hurt's bare, muscular arm with her index finger. "It'll be extra."

He reached for his wallet on the rickety nightstand and handed her a twenty. "I like to sleep alone," he said.

The girl shrugged. "Suit yourself."

She climbed off the bed and pulled on her underclothes and the tired-looking print dress she'd been wearing when he picked her up on Sunset, then slipped into a pair of scuffed patent leather Mary Janes. She moved to the door and gave him one more look then left, the door shutting behind her with a dry click.

Hurt blew out a stream of smoke and then stabbed out the cigarette in an ashtray already overflowing with butts, some of them stained with the girl's red lipstick. He glanced at his watch and realized it was time to call the director. It didn't matter that it was nearly three in the morning in Washington, Hoover would be there waiting for his weekly report.

Coughing, he climbed off the bed, the springs groaning in protest, and slipped on his shirt. He left the room moments later and made his way down the three flights to the lobby. The phone booths sat at the far end of the room across from the registration desk, now attended by an elderly man with a salt-and-pepper stubble on his face, who sat reading a magazine.

Inside the phone booth he picked up the handset and deposited a nickel into the coin slot, listening as it clicked and clanged its way down into the coin box.

"State the number, please," the operator said in a pinched, adenoidal tone.

"This is a collect call," Hurt said, giving her his name and repeating the private number Hoover had made him memorize.

"Just one moment, sir."

There was a buzz and several clicks before he heard the familiar ring.

"Hello . . ."

"This is a collect call from Clarence Hurt," the operator said.

"I'll accept the charges," came Hoover's clipped reply.

Hurt waited until he was sure the operator had clicked off.

"Good evening, sir, I hope this isn't too late."

"It's not, Special Agent Hurt. What do you have for me? Have you recruited Mr. Purvis?"

Hurt couldn't help smiling at that. Even though Purvis had been reinstated as a federal agent, Hoover would never call him a special agent ever again. To him, Purvis was employed on a provisional basis that precluded that hallowed title.

"Yes, sir, but that took some doing."

Hoover gave what passed for a chuckle. "I imagine it did, but he *is* on board?"

"Yes sir; however, there are other developments."

Hoover was silent, and Hurt took that as his cue to continue.

"Purvis called me to report that Warner has agreed to let Dillinger develop a film project and he's decided to do one about his own life. He's planning to star in it, as well."

Hoover sighed. "A film that will no doubt cast the Bureau in a less than favorable light. Anything else?"

Hurt's throat suddenly felt dry, prompting him to cough. "Excuse me, sir. Purvis has agreed to help him write the script."

"Good Christ! Those two working in concert could tarnish the reputation of the Bureau for generations. This cannot be allowed to happen, Special Agent Hurt. You inform Mr. Purvis that he is now going to 'change his mind' and beg off the project."

"Sir, I don't think that's wise."

"Oh, you don't!"

"If you'll permit me. Purvis is solidly on board, as he knows we can put him out of work and keep him permanently unemployed. Having him work with Dillinger will give us access we wouldn't normally have, and he can be persuaded to keep the Bureau in a favorable light, or at least a historically accurate one."

"That's what I'm concerned about."

Hurt ignored that. "I also think this film could be used to our advantage."

"Oh, and how is that?"

Hurt hesitated a moment.

"I'm waiting, Special Agent Hurt."

When he outlined his thoughts, Hoover laughed out loud, and Hurt's heart sank.

"You'll have to forgive me for laughing," Hoover said after he'd calmed down, "but that is the best idea I've heard in a long time. Make it happen, Special Agent Hurt. Make it happen and your future in this Bureau will be a golden one."

Hurt hung up the phone, feeling an odd mixture of joy and despair, a feeling that had become all too familiar. He would call Purvis in the morning and tell him what to do, and he would do his best to make his plan a reality and make Hoover proud. He just prayed his best was good enough.

28

Roosevelt Hotel
Hollywood, California
February 24, 1936

It was just past noon when Rosanne dropped Purvis off in front of the Roosevelt Hotel.

"How will you get home?"

Purvis smiled and patted her hand. "It's a nice day, I'll walk."

"It's over two miles, Melvin."

"It'll be good for me."

His wife rolled her eyes and kissed him. "Have fun."

"I'll do my best." He grabbed his yellow pad of paper and climbed from the car. He watched her disappear into the lunch-hour traffic and then he turned and entered the hotel, crossing the crowded lobby to the elevators. One was opening just as he reached it, disgorging a half a dozen guests. When the last one emerged, he stepped in and turned to face the door. The elevator operator, a middle-aged man with freckles who had to be under five feet in height, closed the doors and asked, "Floor, sir?"

"Seven," Purvis replied.

The elevator man's eyebrows shot upward. "Goin' to see Mr. Dillinger, sir?"

The last thing Purvis wanted was chatty banter with a stranger, but he realized the man could be a valuable ally. And at the very moment that thought occurred to him, he felt a flash of self-loathing. That bastard Hurt had him over a barrel, and he hated that helpless feeling. The latest request—order, rather—was ridiculous. He'd tried to tell the man he couldn't guarantee Dillinger would like the idea, much less Jack Warner. He could only suggest it. "Do your best," was all Hurt said before hanging up on him.

"Yes, Dillinger," Purvis said.

"He's popular today. I took up another fella just a little while ago."

That would be Butler.

"Here you are, sir," the man said, opening the doors. "Straight down the hall and to the right."

Purvis gave the man a half dollar.

"Thank you, sir. The name's Sid, by the way."

"Thank you, Sid," he said, and exited the elevator. The doors slid closed behind him. Purvis made his way to room 722 and pushed a brass doorbell button adjacent to the doorknob. Moments later, a tall, middle-aged black man wearing a black suit opened the door. "You must be Mr. Purvis," he said with a smile. "Come on in, they's waitin' for you in the living room."

Purvis followed the man in and found Dillinger and Butler lounging in overstuffed armchairs surrounding a low coffee table made from polished steel and glass. The view through the windows behind them was a spectacular vista of downtown Hollywood.

Dillinger waved and then stood. "Welcome to my hideout," he said, clasping Purvis's hand. The twinkle in his eye belied his serious tone. "Every time I wake up I still have to pinch myself."

Purvis nodded agreeably then turned to Robert Butler. "Mr. Butler, it's nice to see you again. Where is your charming daughter?"

"At school, I'm afraid."

Purvis nodded. "How did she do on that writing assignment?"

"A-plus!" Butler replied.

Dillinger grinned. "Hey, that's great. I want to read it, if she'll let me."

"She'd kill me if you didn't."

The three men sat back down, Butler and Dillinger on the two white armchairs and Purvis on the jet-black couch. Purvis was just noticing the two drinks on the glass coffee table when the valet spoke. "Would you gentlemen be wanting more iced tea?"

Dillinger looked to Butler, who shook his head. "You want some tea, Melvin?"

"That would be fine."

"Just a glass for Mr. Purvis."

The valet nodded and disappeared into the kitchen. A moment later he emerged bearing a tall, sweating glass of iced tea. Purvis took it, thanked him, and had a sip. It was sweet, cool, and had just the right tinge of lemon.

"Bob and I were throwing the bull about the script before you came in. I think it helps if you have an actor in mind for a role, so let's think about casting for a moment. I'm playing myself, so that's easy. Who do you think could play your part, Melvin? Any thoughts?"

Purvis contemplated this for a minute, as he'd never really considered it. Then he said, "How about Clark Gable?"

The other two men burst out laughing.

"Sorry," Dillinger apologized, "but that mug's got more ham than a meat truck. And I don't think Mr. Gable would be interested. Let's just say he and I don't see eye to eye. Anyway, he's at MGM, and we'll need to look around the Warner lot first. How about Jimmy Cagney?"

"He's good," Purvis admitted, "I was just hoping for someone a little . . . taller . . ."

Butler couldn't resist. "How about Durante? He's taller and hasn't done much since he broke up with Buster Keaton."

Dillinger grinned and took the bait. "Say, how about Keaton? He's good. I've met him, a nice guy when he's sober . . ."

Purvis saw where this was going. "I guess Cagney is tall enough, but will he do it?"

"He's my pal," Dillinger said. "He'll do it. And what's more, I'm betting Warner will go for it, too."

"Shall we get started?" Butler asked.

"Yes," Dillinger said, rising to his feet. "Follow me."

The three of them grabbed their drinks and headed into the dining area, where a pristine Underwood portable typewriter awaited at one end of the table, a ream of typing paper and a box of carbons lying next to it.

When he saw Purvis's expression, Dillinger laughed. "You didn't think I was expecting you to lug that clunky thing of yours, did you?"

"Uh, no, but I figured we'd just be bouncing ideas around today."

"We will," Dillinger said, "but the sooner we knock this out, the better. The other reason I brought in the Underwood is because I don't want to risk any of the pages getting out to the wrong people. We're keepin' this on the QT, so all notes and pages stay here. Anyone have a problem with that?"

Both Butler and Purvis shook their heads.

Dillinger indicated for them to sit. "All right then, let's get cracking."

They all sat at the table, Purvis in front of the typewriter. Grabbing two sheets of typing paper, he made a carbon sandwich and fed it into the platen.

"And one other thing before I forget," Dillinger said. "We've gotta do something about the title."

Bob looked surprised. "What's wrong with it?"

"Too run-of-the-mill."

"How about this?" Purvis asked, his fingers punching the keys of the Underwood in a rapid staccato. He turned the typewriter and showed the other men the single line at the top of the page:

```
"Dillinger: Public Enemy No. 1"
```

"That's the ticket!" Dillinger said, clapping his hands.

The Underwood's action was smooth and fast, and Purvis felt real satisfaction as words hit the page. For the next four hours the three men talked, and Purvis typed. And while there were a few false starts, in that short amount of time they worked out a rough plot for the script.

The afternoon was winding down and everyone, while exhausted, felt they were off to a good start. As they stood up from the table, it hit Purvis that this was the perfect opportunity to broach his idea—or was it Hurt's? Ever since his conversation with the agent, he'd thought about the man's off-the-cuff remark, liking the sound of it more and more.

"Maybe I'm getting ahead of myself," Purvis said, "but here's a thought. Suppose we shoot the ending, the scene where you surrender, at the actual Biograph Theater?"

"On location?" asked Butler. "In Chicago?"

"That's a hell of an idea," Dillinger responded, "but I'd have to sell Warner on it. He likes to keep things on the lot—it's cheaper. His idea of location shooting is a soup kitchen in Burbank."

"Think about it, John," Butler said, offering a newspaperman's perspective, "you can't buy that kind of publicity. Warner will love it."

Dillinger invited the men to stay on for a drink, but Purvis, though wanting one, was anxious to leave. As they shook hands goodbye, Dillinger confided, "Something's bothering you, Melvin, and I think I know what it is. An actor playing you on the screen . . . it's a queer feeling, ain't it? Just keep remembering we're on the same side now—I've got your back. And if we hang, we'll hang together."

Purvis couldn't push that thought out of his mind as he walked home that afternoon, and as soon as he arrived at the house, he reached for the bottle of Old Overholt, taking a deep draught. While the whiskey provided a pleasant little fog, it did little to ease the guilt. He kept hearing Dillinger's voice: *If we hang, we'll hang together.*

And perhaps that had been Hoover's plan all along.

29

The William Morris Agency
Hollywood, California
April 6, 1936

Billie finished the script with a sigh and placed it on the growing pile of material destined for rejection. It was hard to believe today marked her one-month anniversary at the agency, and what amazed her the most was just how average most of the submitted scripts turned out to be. Fortunately, she only had to write coverage reports on the ones she felt deserved further consideration, but if she read a hundred, maybe *one* was worthy. Still, she loved the job.

True to her word, Frances had called Mr. Hyde and arranged a meeting a few days after she'd broached the news to Dillinger. With less than a week before the interview, Billie used the time to work with Salvador Daba to design a wardrobe for work. It was her idea to use the charcoal-gray pinstripe wool common to men's suits and have the designer create a female version. When she'd tried the outfit on for Johnnie the night before her meeting, he'd looked at it appraisingly then whistled. "You look smart, Billie, real smart," he said.

The next day, Frances picked her up and they made the short drive to the agency's offices on Vine. Johnny Hyde received them with a gracious bow at odds with his thick New York accent. Billie could tell the agent was impressed with her businesslike appearance, something the secretaries also noticed with thinly veiled astonishment. Seated around his desk, they made small talk for a few minutes before Hyde got around to the business at hand.

"Frances tells me you have quite an eye for a good story," he said.

Billie proceeded to recount her tale regarding the Shirley Temple script. When she finished speaking, the older man smiled. "As Frances told you, I'm looking to hire someone with an eye for good storytelling. What I would like to do is give you five scripts to read and have you write what we call 'coverage.' Basically, you write a brief description of the plot and then your opinion as to the strengths and weaknesses of the script. Once you've completed them, we'll meet again. How does that sound?"

Billie caught a look from Frances and she cleared her throat. "I'm grateful for the opportunity, Mr. Hyde. I won't let you down."

"Terrific! See Peggy on the way out," he said, rising to his feet.

The meeting was over. As they left, Billie stopped by the desk of Hyde's secretary, who handed her the five scripts bound together with hemp twine and said, "When you have these done, please give me a call and I'll have a messenger come and pick them up, along with your coverage. And by the way, I love your suit."

Back at the Roosevelt, Billie changed into more casual clothes and got to work. She read the first three scripts in a little over six hours and her intuition kicked into high gear. It was obvious Mr. Hyde was stacking the deck. Overall, the scripts were competent and somewhat entertaining, but she had a feeling Hyde wanted her to find the one diamond hiding among the rhinestones.

She made notes on each one as she finished them and had read the last one by late evening. As fate would have it, the fourth script turned out to be the golden child. It was called *My Man Godfrey* and was a romantic comedy about a socialite and her butler. It had loads of charm and humor, some of it bordering on slapstick, as well as a solid undercurrent of romance she knew would make audiences fall in love with the story.

Billie waited until the next day to start writing her coverage; her notes turned out to be invaluable in helping her recall the crucial details of each script. And she was glad Johnnie had brought in a typewriter.

When she called Peggy at the agency later that day, Hyde's secretary was stunned. "You really read all five of them and wrote them up already?"

The awe in the young woman's voice made her confident Mr. Hyde would be impressed.

The messenger arrived an hour later, and then it became a waiting game. Johnnie was supportive, but as the days clocked by, Billie began to worry her confidence may have been misplaced.

The call came at the end of the first week of March. She was in, and not only that, she now shared an office with Peggy, who managed the office. The clincher had been her analysis and enthusiastic recommendation of *My Man Godfrey.* When they met again, Mr. Hyde told her the script was due to start production in a month over at Universal.

"The director is one of our clients," he said.

The other four scripts were non-starters and were there only to give Hyde a broader look at her analytical skills.

Billie's thoughts returned to the present, and she debated about typing up her morning's work before lunch, but her growling stomach clinched the decision. She now regularly took her midday meal at the Brown Derby, with Mr. Cobb never failing to be kind and solicitous. His fawning attentions were almost embarrassing, but she accepted them as a perk of the job.

Most of the time she dined alone and would read a script and make notes while she ate, and today was no exception. However, this script was different. It was the first draft of *Dillinger: Public Enemy No. 1*. Johnnie had handed it to her the night before, asking her to read it and be blunt. He thought it was good, but felt he was too close to the material to be objective. She'd put off reading it until lunch, as she wanted no distractions.

By the time the coffee was served, she turned the final page and sat back, expelling the breath she'd been holding.

It was good.

No, it was more than good, and it ended on an uplifting note. There were some rough spots, but these could be fixed. A couple of tweaks and it would be ready for Jack Warner.

※ ※ ※

When she arrived back at the Roosevelt, Woody was cooking up something that smelled Italian and Johnnie sat with his own copy of the script, making notes on a yellow pad. He looked up when she walked in. "How's my favorite agent?" he asked with a cheeky grin.

She threw off her high-heeled pumps and joined Dillinger on the couch, giving him a long, passionate kiss. "She's doing just fine. I read the script."

Dillinger gave her a penetrating look.

"It was terrific, Johnnie, but there are a few spots you could tighten up."

"Oh?"

"That first scene with Baby Face Nelson."

Dillinger nodded.

"Yep, it's slow, and that pompous little pipsqueak was never slow.

Okay, now tell me, is there anything you especially liked?"

"There's a *lot* I liked, but I really enjoyed that scene at the Biograph where the little girl asks for your autograph, especially the part where after you surrender you blow her a kiss and say, 'See ya in the movies, kid.' I loved it."

Dillinger chuckled. "Yeah, I like that too. You know, that kid is making quite a name for herself now."

"I know. She's one of the agency's clients. Which is why I think we should see if she'd be willing to play herself in the film."

"You know, sometimes you impress the hell out of me."

They fell silent for a moment and then Dillinger changed the subject. "By the way, I got a call from Louis Piquett today."

"And?" she said, turning serious.

"He said it's all gonna come down to money. Walter wants a payoff, or he'll contest."

"Wait a minute, Louis spoke with him?"

Dillinger nodded.

"And how much does the bastard want?" she said, her anger flaring.

Dillinger held up his hands. "Calm down. Louis thinks we can get him down to maybe five grand."

"That's too much for him." Billie sulked. "He's playing us for saps, Johnnie."

"Look, I don't want to pay the guy a plugged nickel, but you need to realize that even if I do have to pay him, you're worth it."

Staring into his loving eyes, she knew without a shadow of a doubt there wasn't another man on earth she'd rather be with.

30

The Pasadena Theatre
Pasadena, California
April 29, 1936

"The picture's already started, mister. It's a preview, *The Little Grifter*," the box-office girl said in a bored monotone.

Dillinger leaned closer to the glass separating them and smiled. "That's okay. One, please."

The girl tore off a ticket and handed it to Dillinger, who placed a quarter on the marble countertop. "Don't spend it all in one place."

The girl gave him a puzzled look, which began transforming as recognition set in. Dillinger's grin widened, and he held a finger to his lips. "Mum's the word, doll."

She nodded, stunned, as Dillinger slipped into the theatre. He debated about grabbing some popcorn, but his stomach was doing flip-flops, so he bypassed the concessions and entered the darkened theatre. He found a seat on the aisle in the last row, two seats away from an overweight woman chomping on Milk Duds. She gave him a passing glance then returned her attention to the screen. It was nearly a full house.

He'd only missed the first ten minutes, and since he knew the story so well, he spent his time studying the other members of the audience. People seemed to be enjoying it, laughing in the right places and hushed during dramatic moments. The problem started in the poker scene when Shirley Temple drew the .45 automatic and aimed it at Walter Long. Dillinger heard a collective gasp from the audience, and several women stood and walked out, muttering to themselves. And when Walter delivered the last line of the scene, a portly man across the aisle called out, "Yeah, what kinda faddah are ya?"

"Go back to robbing banks, you mug!" another man screamed.

Others laughed and joined in with pointed jibes of their own, drowning out the dialogue in the following scene.

What the hell is wrong with these people?

Fortunately, subsequent scenes calmed the audience, but another dozen people stood up and left. Dillinger's stomach gurgled, and he felt a trickle of sweat run down his back, and the damned place was air-conditioned. He turned and saw the fat woman staring at him with a look that told him she now knew who he was. She shook her head, a sad, offended look in her eyes. She turned back toward the screen, cramming more candy into her bulging cheeks.

The final straw came during the hospital scene near the end of the film where Dillinger's character—Joey Pratt—breaks down, begging a God in whom he's never believed to spare his daughter. The audience started booing, and several more people shot to their feet and made for the exits.

When the picture ended ten minutes later, the houselights came on, and what remained of the crowd filed out of the auditorium.

There was no applause.

Dillinger estimated that at least a quarter of the audience had walked out during the show. The palpable silence in the auditorium made it feel like a tomb, which he supposed it was. The woman seated near him stood and brushed his knees as she bulled past. "You should be ashamed," she said, and waddled up the aisle and out the door.

Thank Christ Billie wasn't here to see this.

He'd wanted her to come, but she'd complained of having a headache and stayed in.

He'd figure out a way to tell her, but the real question was how Warner would react during their meeting in the morning. Dillinger turned at the sound of the cleanup crew entering the auditorium, and he headed for one of the theatre's rear exits, finding Woody and the Essex waiting curbside at the mouth of the alley. To the valet's credit, he said nothing during the ride home, sensing his charge's pensive mood.

※　※　※

Jack Warner greeted Dillinger cordially, motioning for him to take his customary seat. As usual, Warner asked him to be there at seven in the morning. On the spur of the moment he decided to bring the *Dillinger* script with him. The title page listed only two authors: Melvin Purvis & Robert Butler.

Now here he sat in Warner's plush, wood-paneled office, the manila envelope containing the script resting on his lap. Warner didn't appear to notice, getting right to the point.

"As you know, Fox had a sneak preview of *The Little Grifter* at the Pasadena Theatre last night. I'm afraid the comment cards were not favorable."

Dillinger sighed and shook his head. "I was there, Jack. They hated it . . . and me."

Warner's eyebrows shot upward. "Not everyone."

"What do you mean?"

"At least a quarter of the audience turned in response cards, and more than a few said you were good. The big problem is the kid."

In Dillinger's mind, he could still hear that gasp when the tyke pulled out the pistol.

"Nobody liked seeing cute little Shirley Temple as a gun-toting con artist," Warner continued. "Fox miscalculated badly, and now they're beside themselves because there is no way in hell they're ever going to release the film."

"Jesus, we worked damned hard on that picture."

"I know, John, but that's the business. You try to do something different and the audience stays away in droves. It's terrible, but that's the way it is."

Dillinger leaned forward. "That was just one audience, Mr. Warner. Maybe we can make some changes. They could re-shoot Shirley's role with Jane Withers; she always plays a brat."

Warner shook his head. "Shirley Temple is sacrosanct, John. How would it look if she had to be replaced? Fox is not going to do anything to put her star power at risk. I hate to say it, but *The Little Grifter* is dead on arrival."

"So, what do I do now?"

"We're looking for scripts. When we find one, I'll let you know."

As disappointed and angry as he was about *The Little Grifter*, Dillinger realized now was the perfect moment to broach his project.

"You remember a few months back we talked about me directing a film?"

Warner nodded. "Yes, and why do I think you're about to spring one on me?"

Dillinger grinned and tossed the manila envelope onto the older man's desk. Warner leaned forward, unwound the string holding the envelope closed, and slid out the script, his expression guarded as he scanned the title page. *"Dillinger: Public Enemy No. 1"*?

"Think of it, Jack, the straight scoop on everything that's happened. They'll be on the edges of their seats. And we don't have to worry about little kids."

Warner chuckled. "I'm truly sick about what's happened, but I'd be less than honest if I didn't say I'm glad it's someone else's problem. They're going to lose over a million dollars on this."

"We still get the loan-out fee?"

"Yes. There's nothing in your contract that gives them an out. You played, now they've got to pay."

"That's something, anyway." A silence fell between them, each man lost in his thoughts. Finally, Dillinger stated what was uppermost in his mind. "So, the script . . . you'll look it over?"

Warner stood and held out his hand. "I'm looking forward to it."

✄ ✄ ✄

"Jack, are you coming to bed?"

Warner looked up from the Dillinger script, momentarily disoriented. He saw Ann silhouetted in the doorway of his study. She was wearing one of her filmy negligees, the kind that reminded him he still had a pulse. The effect was especially arresting this evening, as the light behind her shone through the thin fabric, giving him a glance at what he was missing.

"I've got nine pages left, honey, I'll be right in."

He saw the shadow of a smile on his wife's face.

"You'd better, or it's the doghouse for you." She turned and sauntered away.

Sighing, Warner pushed thoughts of marital bliss from his mind and concentrated on finishing the script. These writers were terrific, and to think one of them was the ex-FBI agent that had run Dillinger down and taken his surrender. He had to smile at the serendipity of it all. When he'd finished, he closed the script and laid it down on the coffee table, his mind reeling with the possibilities.

There was no doubt in Warner's mind the resultant film would be a box office bonanza. His thoughts went back to those poor schmucks at Fox with a million-dollar film they couldn't release.

Warner shook his head.

As for Dillinger, his story would be a hit. There was only one problem, and it was a *big* one.

Hoover.

The writers put the man in the worst of possible lights. If Warner greenlit this film, he'd be taking on Hoover's full wrath. There was nothing he wouldn't do to keep that film off the screen, including unleashing the IRS on the studio. His own taxes were above reproach, but there were things a man running a studio had to do, things that wouldn't bear too close a scrutiny. And the dirt he had on Hoover would only go so far.

Warner exhaled the breath he'd been holding and rubbed his eyes. The thing to do was to sleep on it, see how it looked in the morning. Well, maybe sleep was the wrong word. He laughed and headed upstairs to the waiting arms of his much younger wife.

31

William Morris Agency
Hollywood, California
May 1, 1936

She'd barely started on the second script of the morning when the phone rang. Peggy answered it then turned to Billie. "It's Mr. Dillinger on the line."

Billie tossed the script onto her desk and picked up her extension. "Hi, sweetie, to what do I owe the pleasure?"

"He passed on the script, Billie."

The smile died on her lips. "Warner?"

"Yeah, can you believe it? He gave me a whole song and dance, telling me this, telling me that, saying that he's going to make it up to me."

"What did you say?"

"What *could* I say?"

"But he promised you."

"He's the head of the studio. He can do whatever the hell he wants."

"I know he's the head of the studio, but—"

"That's not everything . . . I didn't want to tell you before . . . but now it doesn't matter."

Billie didn't like the sound of this. "What, Johnnie?"

"Fox is shelving *The Little Grifter*."

"Oh my God, *why?*"

"Apparently, the test audience hated Shirley Temple conning people and pointing guns at them."

Billie sighed. "I don't know what to say, Johnnie. That's awful."

"There's nothing *to* say, kiddo. It's done. The irony is that test audience liked my performance. It's just too damn bad no one'll ever see it."

"What are you going to do?"

"I don't know. Warner says they're looking for scripts for me, but it sounds like a load of bull. Christ, Billie, my career might be over."

"Don't say that."

"Why not? Once the word gets out about the Temple picture, they'll put the blame on me, rather than their own stupidity. They sure aren't going to blame that sweet kid. And now Jack passes on my script."

"Fox won't say anything, not unless they want to risk a lawsuit. They'll make up some vague reason to satisfy the press and then they'll shove it under a rug."

The intercom buzzed, and Billie frowned. "I've got to go, Johnnie. How about we give Woody a break and go out tonight, maybe the Trocadero."

Dillinger sighed. "Maybe you're right. The last thing I need to do is sit around feeling sorry for myself. We'll paint the town red, honey."

32

1408 Tamarind Avenue
Hollywood, California
May 3, 1936

The knock on the front door came just as they sat down to dinner. It was not a polite tap, either, but a rhythmic pounding that rankled the nerves.

"Why does that man keep bothering us, Melvin?" Rosanne whispered.

"He can't hear us in here, dear."

"I don't like him one bit. What does he want with you?"

Purvis stood and tossed his napkin onto the table. "I'm sorry, but I can't tell you. Please don't ask." His wife bristled. It was uncommon that he would keep anything from her, but Hurt's threats—both stated and implied—were not to be taken lightly. "I'll be back in a minute."

Purvis left the kitchen and traversed the front room, just as the pounding on the door resumed. He wrenched it open to find the Oklahoman lounging against the porch railing.

"Nice evenin', isn't it?"

Purvis stepped outside and gently closed the door. "It would be a lot nicer if you weren't interrupting our Sunday supper."

"My apologies," Hurt said without a trace of sincerity, "but this couldn't wait. I've heard you've finished the Dillinger script."

"Yes. What's that to you?"

"The director would like a copy for review."

Purvis sighed. "You know, Clarence, this is getting old. Mr. Hoover cannot have the script because I don't *have* the script."

"What do you mean, you don't have the script?"

"Because we worked on it in Dillinger's hotel suite exclusively, and the pages never left the premises. It was a condition of the job, a security measure. So, I don't have it. By the way, I'm surprised you didn't hear that Jack Warner took a pass."

"Took a pass?"

Sometimes the man could be obtuse.

"It means Warner Brothers turned it down. They won't be making the film."

Hurt remained silent, but the more disturbing thing was the fleeting look of naked desperation on his face, a look quickly subsumed by his usual hard-boiled countenance.

"This is not over, Special Agent Purvis," he said, marching off the porch. "Stay on point."

Hurt banged through the picket fence gate and strode off, heading south.

Purvis remained on the porch for a few minutes, listening to the sounds of the night: the crickets chirping in Rosanne's flower boxes and the steady swish of traffic on Sunset. *Stay on point*, the man had said. It meant be ready for anything. Somehow those three words scared Purvis more than anything.

With a sigh of disgust and frustration, Purvis returned to the kitchen and told Rosanne everything. She sat and listened without interruption, and when he was finished, she grasped his hands in hers.

"I'd be lying if I said I wasn't afraid of that man," she said, staring in his eyes. "I am. But the one thing I know is that—no matter what—you'll do the right thing."

Purvis's heart swelled with pride, gratitude, and love. He didn't know if he was truly worthy of her confidence, but he knew without a shadow of a doubt that he would rather die than ever let her down.

33

1801 Angelo Drive
Beverly Hills, California
May 4, 1936

The private line rang just as Jack Warner was settling into his favorite easy chair with the latest financial reports. He hated reading them, finding them tedious in the extreme. The only redeeming factor was being able to confirm the company was on solid ground, which was usually—and thankfully—the case. Once he signed off on the reports, they would be published to the stockholders.

The phone rang again.

"All right, hold your horses, goddamn it," he said, tossing the documents onto the table. He snatched up the phone. "This had better be good."

"Good evening, Jack."

Warner frowned. "What the hell? Is that you, Hoover?"

"Who else would be calling you on your private line at this late hour?"

Knowing there was no way he was going to avoid the conversation, Warner forced himself to calm down. "Okay, what do you want?"

"I heard you turned down the Dillinger script."

Warner's pulse kicked up a notch. Only a handful of people even knew about the script, and Warner wondered for a moment who he would end up firing tomorrow.

"Are you there, Jack?"

"Yes, I'm here."

"Did I hear correctly? Did you pass on the script?"

"Yes, I did."

"I think that was unwise."

Now Warner was thoroughly mystified. Shaking his head to clear the evening cobwebs, he said, "You'll have to forgive me, Edgar, but I'm not sure why you feel that way. That script is not kind in its depiction of you or the Bureau. I should think you'd be happy I turned it down."

"The Bureau has to play rough when we're fighting crime. And I assume it will be a fairly honest depiction of events. The Bureau catches Dillinger and he is jailed, am I correct? Use your influence to make sure we are depicted fairly, that's all I ask. You know me, I'll do anything to protect the Bureau, and in the balance, I think this will work in our favor."

Warner's eyes widened in disbelief. "Well, I wish the hell I'd known this the other day. If I reverse my decision now, I'll look like an idiot."

"No, you won't."

"You don't understand—nearly everyone who sees this script is going to run the other way. And they're going to do that because they're afraid of *you*."

"If that's your concern, you have my permission to announce that Warner Brothers, with the full approval and cooperation of the Federal Bureau of Investigation, will be producing *Dillinger: Public Enemy No. 1*."

"That makes no sense."

"It does to me." Hoover paused, letting that sink in, and then continued. "Jack, I think it's ultimately good for the Bureau and will make money for your studio. For once we're on the same side; don't screw this up."

Hoover hung up a moment later and Warner sat there holding the phone in his hands for a full minute before replacing the handset onto its cradle.

Rising from the chair, he walked over to the dry bar and poured himself a finger of Scotch, then doubled it. He drank it down in one gulp.

Why was Hoover so insistent he do the film? Maybe he was confident that the Breen office, the industry's self-censorship agency, would make sure the script showed the Bureau in a favorable light. Maybe the egotistical bastard wanted to see himself portrayed on the screen by a famous actor. Or maybe it was just because Warner had passed on it, and Hoover wanted to wield his power once more.

Was he going to do what Hoover asked? Of course he was. He'd be a fool *not* to do it. The irony here was that he was going to do it for the same reasons he'd turned the script down in the first place. It seemed where J. Edgar Hoover was concerned, he couldn't win for losing.

Jack L. Warner is proud to announce that

Warner Bros. Studios will be producing

"DILLINGER: Public Enemy No. 1"

Directed by and Starring John Dillinger

in a historic association with

J. Edgar Hoover

&

THE FEDERAL BUREAU OF INVESTIGATION

Principal Photography will begin July 1, 1936

34

As Woody piloted the Essex through the Cahuenga Pass, Dillinger watched the passing scenery with a smile on his face, the *Dillinger* script—with its myriad scribbled annotations—clutched in his right hand.

This is going to be a hell of a day!

Dillinger's smile widened, and he found himself marveling in the sights he normally chose to ignore: the sun sparkling through the leaves of the trees, a hawk circling overhead, its wings spread to catch the thermals, and a pretty blonde on horseback who greeted him with a friendly wave.

It all felt right.

And when Woody steered the car onto the Warner lot, he smiled again, happy to see Cappy Hauser installed in his new job at the main gate.

Dillinger rolled down the window. "Looking good, Cap."

The old guard beamed. "First day of pre-production, Johnnie?" he asked, shaking Dillinger's hand.

"That's right."

"Well, I know you're gonna make a hell of a picture. I'm bettin' dollars to donuts."

"Yeah, well, just don't eat too many."

Cappy laughed and moved closer to the car. "And by the way, thanks again for getting me the job here. I was real worried, Fox lettin' me go and all. Just wasn't right."

Dillinger studied the older man, seeing the anger and resentment in his eyes.

"Think nothing of it, pal," Dillinger said. "I'm just glad you called me this time."

"I didn't want to be no burden—"

"To hell with that. We both know Fox canned you 'cause of me, though you'd never get those bastards to admit it. Besides, you're my good-luck-charm, and you belong here with me."

Cappy laughed again.

"I appreciate that, Johnnie, I really do." He fell silent, and for a moment he looked as if he might say something else when the vehicle behind them honked.

Dillinger turned and saw it was the Wells Fargo payroll truck. He gave the driver a thumbs up. The man stared back at him with a blank expression then honked again.

Chump.

"Gotta go, Cap," he said, pointing over his shoulder. "Can't hold up the money, now can we?"

Woody dropped him in front of the one-story adobe-style bungalow at the far end of the lot, which now housed the production staff of *Dillinger: Public Enemy No. 1.*

Inside the reception area, he greeted his new secretary, Adele, an elfin girl with big round eyes and dimples when she smiled. She handed him a sheaf of pink message slips. He flipped through them, seeing that most of them were calls from the various department heads regarding their assignments on the film.

Christ, it's the first day and they're already piling it on!

The phone rang.

"Dillinger office, good morning," Adele said.

I like the sound of that.

"Yes, he just got in."

Dillinger could hear the muted drone of the caller's voice but couldn't make out the words. "Yes, sir, he's standing right here, shall I put him on?"

Dillinger frowned and reached for the handset, and Adele held up a hand. "Okay, I'll tell him," she said and hung up. "Mr. Warner wants to see you right away."

Dillinger sighed and handed her back the messages. "Go ahead and call these mugs back and set up meetings with each of them. Okay?"

The girl nodded, a cheerful smile lighting up her face. "Will do, Mr. Dillinger."

He left the bungalow and caught a ride on one of the electric carts passing by, reaching Warner's office building a few minutes later.

He found the older man on the phone as he entered his office.

"I don't give a damn what he said," Warner shouted. "We're paying him more than enough. I want him on the lot and doing the job he contracted for or I'll get someone else and the schmuck gets bupkis." Warner held his hand over the receiver and motioned for Dillinger to take a seat. He slid into the high-backed chair facing the desk and waited while the older man finished his tirade. When he hung up, Warner rolled his eyes toward the ceiling.

"Why, God? Why me?"

Dillinger's eyes twinkled with amusement. "Trouble in paradise?"

"You don't know the half of it." Warner reached for the large bottle of Milk of Magnesia sitting on a nearby credenza. "It's always something, Johnnie, always something. Putting out fires all day long. Comes with the territory." He twisted off the bottle cap, took a swig of the chalky-white stomach remedy, and sighed. "You know the sad thing? I'm actually getting to like the taste of this stuff."

Dillinger chuckled. "That *is* sad, Jack. I thought pictures were supposed to be fun."

"Fun?" Warner made a face. "You have the fun, I get the headaches. That's my job. That's what I do."

Dillinger raised his arms in surrender. "Okay, okay, you win. So, what's going on, why'd you need to see me? I'm barely on the lot five minutes and I've already got a full day of meetings."

Warner sighed. "I know, I know, but I had to see you. And there's just no easy way to say it. I'm gonna put Archie Mayo on as director."

Dillinger's stomach took a roller coaster plunge. "Jesus Christ, Jack, *why?*"

The studio head spread his hands, as if to say, *what are you gonna do, it's business.*

"I'm concerned that you might be biting off more than you can chew with this picture."

Dillinger shook his head. "That's malarkey, Jack. Who knows more about my life than me?"

Warner nodded impatiently. "That's beside the point—you have no experience as a director. There are so many things you've got to be on top of, and that takes experience you just don't have yet . . ."

"I would if you let me."

Warner acted as if he hadn't heard. ". . . and this picture's gonna cost a lot of money."

Dillinger stood and approached the desk.

"If it's money you're worried about, you can put my salary back into the budget. I'll do it for nothing."

"That's all well and good, but again, that's not the point. I'm sorry, but it's got to be this way. There's too much at stake."

"Mr. Warner," Dillinger said, leaning over the studio head's massive desk. "You liked my first film so much, you busted me out of stir to work for you. You and everybody else loved me in *Petrified Forest*, and you're enthusiastic about this script. I can do this, Jack. I can. Just give me one good reason why I shouldn't direct?"

Warner said nothing for a few moments, his eyes smoldering. "I could give you a dozen reasons, but I don't need to explain myself to you. You're forgetting who's in charge here. Do you know that without me you'd still be rotting in that stinking jail cell? That may seem like a lifetime ago, but that's where you'd be right now if it weren't for my intervention. I got you out and set you up pretty well, Dillinger. Problem is you have a short memory. You owe *me*, not the other way around."

"You sprung me because I could make you good money."

"I can make good money with or without you. Now get out of my office, you fucking ingrate!"

Seething, Dillinger returned to his bungalow, finding Adele with another handful of messages. "Keep 'em," he said, stalking past her and into his office, where he slammed the door. He slumped into the chair behind his desk and sulked for ten minutes, then grabbed an empty cardboard box and began packing up his stuff. At least there wasn't much. Christ, maybe he'd pushed it too far, but Warner had no right to call him a fucking ingrate.

Still, the man had a point.

There was no denying that Dillinger owed him—big time. He just wasn't sure he wanted to *be* in that position. He hated the idea of being beholden to anyone, especially someone who kept reminding him at every opportunity. What the hell kind of life was that?

Things have a way of changing.

Dillinger sighed in disgust. That was certainly the case here. He'd told Billie that very thing back in their Chicago days, and she'd reminded him again, by repeating it to him word for word before he'd started work on *The Little Grifter*. Sometimes he hated it when she was right.

Half an hour later he had three boxes ready to go and was reaching for the phone to call Woody when a studio messenger arrived bearing a sealed envelope. Dillinger signed for it then sat there staring at it.

"My pink slip. Just in time," he said, tearing it open.

Dillinger's eyebrows shot up.

Dear Johnnie:

I wanted to say how sorry I am about what happened in my office earlier today. I was overly harsh. I've had time to think and I wanted to let you know that I've reconsidered. If you're willing to have an experienced director on-set with you on "stand-by," I believe having you as the credited director would be in the best interest of the film, and that's all I really care about. I do have faith in you, so let's go out there and get 'em!

Yours Truly,

Jack Warner

Dillinger read it twice before it all sank in. And while he felt vindicated, he wondered why the man had bothered to bring it all up in the first place. Still, Jack was only human, and everyone made mistakes. At least he was man enough to admit it. He could just do without the Jekyll and Hyde routine.

35

Warner Bros. Studios
Burbank, California
June 1, 1936

Dillinger had to get away from the phones.

That was the thing about a working production office. There were lots and lots of phones, and they all kept ringing—all day long. Shutting the door to his private office did little to stem the tide, as his own phone rang off the hook. That's why he'd gotten into the habit of getting up from his desk every day at precisely ten fifteen, leaving the bungalow and taking a long, leisurely stroll around the lot. Despite the hubbub of a normal workday, with casts and crews dashing about, he found this private time did wonders to clear his mind and relax his body. And the best thing was nobody bothered him.

Now, a week after the blow-up with Warner, Dillinger was reminded of something his stepmother used to say: *Be careful what you wish for, Johnnie, you just might get it.* She was right. Directing his little prison newsreel had been a cakewalk compared to what he now faced. And while he still had to worry about acting, once the cameras rolled, he now was responsible for choosing the crew, casting the actors, and on and on and on. And while he enjoyed every minute of it, he was only too happy to lean on the experience of his producer, Hal Wallis, to make most of the below-the-line decisions regarding the production. He'd seen the man operate while working on *The Petrified Forest* and respected his cool head under fire. The fact that Wallis had eschewed a credit on the finished film bewildered Dillinger, but he was sure the man must have his reasons. It didn't matter. Dillinger had requested him, and Wallis was eager for the opportunity.

"How ya doing, Mr. Dillinger!"

Dillinger smiled and waved at a young man emerging from the writers' building and kept moving. At least the air was cool this morning, or he'd be sweating bullets by now.

He headed toward the backlot, where the exteriors of three Midwestern banks were under construction, although "construction" was a loose term in this case, as the crew were redressing the "New York" street to look like the streets of towns in three different states.

As fate would have it, these sets would be used later in the shoot. Much to Dillinger's surprise, Warner had okayed shooting the climax of the film at the actual Biograph Theater in Chicago. While expensive, Hal Wallis convinced the studio head it would be an efficient, controlled, and fast shoot. Exteriors only—the lobby and theatre interior could be recreated on the backlot. Two nights and they'd be on their way back to Hollywood. And Dillinger had argued the publicity would be worth every bit of the added expense. Warner had listened and given his assent.

But why, Dillinger pondered, did it have to be the first scene shot? Just like the situation with *The Little Grifter*. He thought he knew the answer.

They're testing my abilities as a first-time director. If I'm going to make unusual requests like this one, they want to know from the get-go if I don't have the crust.

Dillinger was pulled out of his thoughts when he heard a familiar voice.

"Mighty impressive, if I do say so." He turned to find Melvin Purvis standing next to him, a red pencil stuck behind his ear.

"Yeah, it is . . . but not half as impressive as yours and Bob's script. I think we've got a winner."

"Your name belongs on it too, Johnnie."

"My name *is* on it," Dillinger said.

"That's not what I meant."

Dillinger laughed. "I know . . . I'm kiddin' with you. Just thought it would be too much, and I didn't want it looking like I was wearing too many hats." He was silent for a moment, then asked, "Working on anything?"

Purvis nodded. "My tawdry little murder mystery seems to be gaining steam, although it's not really a mystery. You know who's doing what from the start. The enjoyment comes in seeing them get their comeuppance."

"Is that the one with the woman scheming with her insurance agent to kill her husband?"

"Yes, and I finally came up with a title: *Devil in a Red Dress.*"

"That's a good one."

"I'm even thinking it might make for a good book, too, but if the studio buys it . . ." Purvis shrugged. "It'll be out of my hands."

"Sounds like you need a good agent."

"Oh, yeah, you know anyone?" Purvis asked, a glint of humor in his eyes. "I hear Billie's doing well at William Morris."

"Yes, she is," Dillinger said with pride.

"You think she'd consider representing me?"

Dillinger shot his old foe a grin. "Can't hurt to ask."

They fell silent, watching the crew methodically aging the facade of the Sioux Falls bank to make it look more like the real thing.

"You know, I was going to ask Billie to show the script around when Warner changed his mind."

"That took me by surprise, as well."

"And he wouldn't tell me *why* he changed his mind. Said something like 'I reconsidered my decision,' and clammed up. And then those ads appeared two days later in *Variety* and *The Hollywood Reporter.*"

"You think Hoover put him up to it?"

Dillinger's gaze locked onto Purvis's face. "I do. But I also think Warner passed on it to begin with because he was afraid of what Hoover might do."

"He was wise to think that way."

"Maybe so, but that only makes what happened even more odd. Why the hell would Hoover ever want to do me a favor? What's his angle?"

Purvis turned away from Dillinger, but not before he caught the look of guilt on the ex-agent's face.

"What is it?" Dillinger asked.

"I'm sorry, you'll have to forgive me, but I really don't like talking about that man." He glanced at his watch. "And I just realized I have a meeting in about five minutes. Sorry to rush off."

"Not a problem."

"Anyway, I just wanted to stop by and see how the sets were coming along." Purvis stuck out his hand and Dillinger took it.

"If you want, I'll talk to Billie about representing you."

"I'd appreciate that."

He watched Purvis striding away, feeling an unaccountable sadness creep over him. Something was bothering Purvis, Dillinger was sure of it, but it could be anything. As extraordinary as it was, he'd come to view Melvin Purvis as an ally, something unimaginable just two short years ago. And he was saddened because he was dead sure his new friend had just lied to him.

36

Warner Bros. Studios
Burbank, California
June 17, 1936

"Who's next?" Dillinger asked.

Hall Wallis consulted the typed list of actresses auditioning for the role of Billie Frechette. Most were crossed off, and some had notations next to their names. "Joan Blondell," he said.

Dillinger nodded, glancing at his watch. It was nearly three in the afternoon, and they'd been auditioning actresses since ten o'clock. Most were adequate, but none of them exceptional. The problem was, while these actresses were all beautiful, none of them were Billie; none of them had that spark of impudence that made her unique.

"How many after her?"

"One more, and that does it for the contract players." Wallis sighed, his bushy eyebrows creasing in a frown. "I still don't know why you won't at least consider Bette Davis. She'd be great—and you've worked with her."

"That's the problem."

"What do you mean?"

Dillinger's expression was carefully neutral. "Let's just say our off-screen chemistry would be an issue."

Wallis met Dillinger's level gaze, a wry grin spreading across his face. "Ah, got you. No Miss Davis."

"Christ, maybe I'm too particular," Dillinger said, after a moment of silence.

"I don't think so. But I do believe she's out there, somewhere."

"What if she's at another studio, can we get a loan-out?"

"Who'd you have in mind?"

Dillinger shrugged. "I have no idea. I was hoping you might."

Wallis looked thoughtful. "Since we already have Garland for the Biograph scene, we could try going back to MGM—but only if we strike out here first."

Dillinger nodded. "Okay, if we go back to Metro, then how about Joan Crawford? Can we afford someone like her?"

"I thought you had no idea."

Dillinger laughed. "Can't blame a guy for dreaming."

"You have good taste," Wallis said with a grin. "But to answer your question, I believe we can. Warner was more than generous in giving us a four hundred thousand dollar budget. Because of that, I think we'll have some wiggle room on that end if it comes down to it."

Dillinger's admiration for his producer rose another notch. Wallis was smartly dressed in a black and white herringbone jacket that complemented his rugged good looks, looks more often associated with an actor than a movie producer. A slightly receding hairline sat above dark, wide-set eyes. Behind those eyes lay a glimmer of warmth, of which he was keenly aware and often used to his advantage. Hal Wallis was a straight shooter, a tough dealmaker, but a man of his word.

Wallis turned and signaled to the young assistant at the door, which he opened, letting in the next actress.

Joan Blondell strode in with a confident smile, her platinum blonde hair gleaming in the overhead lighting. "Hello, Hal, how are you?"

Wallis stood and hugged her. "I'm fine, fine. No complaints. How's Dick?"

"He's great; he's finishing up *Stage Struck* over on Twelve."

"Aren't you working on that, too?"

Joan nodded. "I have a couple of days off, so here I am."

"Well, that works out nicely. Joan, let me introduce you to our director, John Dillinger."

Dillinger stood, and Joan turned on her thousand-watt smile. She offered her hand and Dillinger took it, impressed by her solid grip. "You know, people are saying you look like my husband, and I thought it was baloney—but you really *do!*" She laughed, and both Wallis and Dillinger joined in.

"Did you get the pages we sent over, Joan?" Wallis asked, turning the meeting back to the business at hand.

"Yes, I did, thank you."

"Any questions?" Dillinger asked.

They all took their seats and Joan said, "The only question I have is, what was Billie really thinking when you and she first met?"

"I have no idea," Dillinger said slyly. "Probably that I was too full of myself."

"Did you want to refer to the pages, Joan?" Wallis asked. "We have a set if you need them."

She pointed to her head. "It's all up here."

Dillinger was impressed again. Most of the actresses, while reading competently, hadn't bothered to memorize their lines. "The scene we'll try takes place the night before the holdup in Sioux Falls, and it's the first time we ever fought about what I did for a living."

Joan's eyes widened. "Really?"

Dillinger nodded. "She's worried because Baby Face Nelson is a punk and can be trigger happy. She's right, but I don't want to hear it because it's a plum bank and promises a big payoff. As the scene begins, you're sitting staring out the apartment window as I come in."

"Got it," she said.

"So, let's take it from the top." Dillinger stood, leaving his own pages behind, and came around the table as Joan took a chair and placed it near the room's only window. She sat and gazed out, her expression turning melancholy.

Dillinger went to the door, opened it slightly, then closed it.

※　※　※

"You okay?" he asked, his expression troubled.

Billie turned from the window where she'd been watching the rain, her eyes red and puffy. "No, I'm not okay."

Dillinger threw his hat and coat onto the bed, crossed the room, and joined her. "You still mad about Nelson?"

"He's crazy, Johnnie. You know he's crazy and you're letting him lead you into a trap."

Dillinger took her hand. "We cased every corner of that bank, honey. It's a knockover—a cinch. We'll be in and out. Nobody's gonna be waiting for us. You'll see, it's going to be fine."

Billie stood up and moved toward the dresser, her tears flowing freely. "Now I know how a cop's wife feels, every time her man straps on that badge and gun. Wondering if he's gonna come home that night, or whether he's—"

She broke down and Dillinger took her into his arms.

"Listen," he said, stroking her dark, lustrous hair, "I know how you feel about Nelson. You're right about the mug, but he knows banks. There's over fifty grand in that joint, just waitin' for us. One more job after that and we can get out of here, go south."

Billie's tear-stained eyes gazed into Dillinger's.

"We could go now, Johnnie."

"We need more dough, honey, or we'll be down and out before we know it. Trust me."

Billie grabbed Dillinger and kissed him passionately.

⚜ ⚜ ⚜

"And . . . cut," Wallis said, but it was another couple of seconds before Joan broke the kiss.

"You even kiss like Dick," she said breathlessly.

Dillinger thought of a bawdy retort but reconsidered.

They moved apart, and Dillinger returned to his seat behind the table. Wallis, a bit unsettled by the intensity of the scene, smiled and said, "Thank you for coming in, Joan, we'll let you know once we make a decision."

"That's fine," she said, standing. "I really enjoyed meeting you, Mr. Dillinger, and I hope we get to work together."

She turned and left the room a moment later.

The two men remained silent for a brief time then Wallis cleared his throat. "I thought she did really well, John."

Dillinger's head was bowed in thought. "She was great. The only thing I'm concerned about is that in some ways she's too sweet. That smile of hers certainly is."

"Too sweet? I've seen some of her films, and she can play it as tough as a two-bit steak."

"I agree, I'm just not sure, Hal." Dillinger sighed, picking up his pencil then tossing it back down onto the table. "She's the best we've seen, that's for sure, and she certainly kisses well, though I wouldn't mention that to Billie."

Wallis laughed. "No, I think I'll keep my own counsel on that, too. All right then, let's get this last one over with and we'll call it a day." He motioned to the boy by the door, who let in their final audition. And in walked Billie, only it wasn't.

"Hi, gents, I'm Glenda Farrell," she said, giving Dillinger a saucy once-over. "I hear you know how to treat a lady."

The resemblance was astounding. Normally a blonde, Glenda had found an appropriate wig. Even her makeup included Billie's preferred shade of red lipstick. She'd done her homework.

Dillinger stood and said, "Miss Farrell, thank you for coming."

She took his hand, and the warmth of her skin infused him. "Have a seat," he said, indicating the empty chair.

Even the way she sat down was sexy, crossing her legs at the knees to display the curves of her calves to their best advantage. "I do have a couple of questions," she said.

"Shoot," Dillinger replied.

She looked into his eyes and gave him Billie's lopsided grin.

Jesus Christ!

After answering her questions, a few of which were somewhat intimate, they ran the scene. As with Joan, Glenda had memorized her lines, but Dillinger felt as if he were wired to an electric dynamo as they reached the point in the scene where he takes her into his arms.

And then Glenda did something different. She caressed his face then pulled him closer, her gaze burning with fire and passion, her lips quivering.

"I love you," she said with breathless urgency. Then she crushed her lips against Dillinger's. Unlike the scene with Joan, he felt a sharp stirring in his loins. He held her tighter against him and she kissed him harder, as if she never wanted it to stop.

Just like Billie.

37

Roosevelt Hotel
Hollywood, California
June 23, 1936

"Mr. Dillinger, Miss Billie?" Woody called out from the kitchen. "Mr. Butler is on his way up."

"We'll be right out!" Billie replied. Turning back to the vanity mirror, she put on the final touches of her makeup and nodded with satisfaction. "You need help with your tie?"

Dillinger stood in front of the full-length mirror with a frown of frustration on his face, the bow tie for his dinner clothes tied in a clumsy knot. Billie shook her head, smiling affectionately, then rose from the vanity and stood behind him. She reached around Dillinger's neck for the ends of the tie and began knotting it expertly. "I like it when you tie it this way. It's sexy."

"Yes, it is," she breathed into his ear, "but it's also the only way I can do it."

Billie and Dillinger emerged from their bedroom just as Woody opened the front door to admit Robert Butler, his wife, and Lizzie. Lizzie's eyes bulged as she took in the room's luxurious décor.

"Hey, Bob, thanks for coming!" Dillinger said.

Butler handed Woody his hat then shook Dillinger's outstretched hand. "Glad to be here, John." He turned to his family. "I don't think you've met my wife, Millie. Honey, this is John Dillinger."

"How do you do, Mr. Dillinger?" she said, extending her hand. Dillinger took it, marveling at its softness. Her heart-shaped face was framed by naturally blonde hair, and her dark brown eyes evinced warmth and kindness.

"It's nice to finally meet you, Millie. And please call me Johnnie. And this is my fiancée, Evelyn Frechette."

"Everyone calls me Billie," she said, stepping forward. Millie smiled and shook hands with her.

"And how's my little lookout?" Dillinger said, bending down to Lizzie. The young girl grinned and gave Dillinger a big hug.

"Not so little anymore," Butler said.

Dillinger gave Lizzie an appraising look, realizing she was wearing a touch of makeup, perhaps for the first time, and in the adolescent planes of her face he caught a glimpse of what she would look like as an adult. "You look real pretty, sweetheart," he said, eliciting another radiant smile from the young girl.

Dillinger led the way into the suite. "Can I get anyone a drink? Bob, Millie?"

"Scotch," Butler said.

"Seltzer for me," Millie added.

"And what about you, Magoo?" Dillinger asked Lizzie. "I'll bet Woody could scare up a Coca-Cola. Would you like that?"

"Please," Lizzie replied.

"All right, everyone, take a load off. And if you're hungry, Woody has put out some horse ovaries to hold you until dinner."

"Horse ovaries?!" Lizzie said, horrified.

Billie shook her head, trying not to laugh. "Johnnie's just being funny, dear. He means *hors d'oeuvres*. Finger food."

Lizzie laughed and followed Woody into the kitchen, returning a moment later with her drink.

The phone rang, and Dillinger answered.

"Mr. Dillinger? This is the front desk. The rest of your guests have arrived."

"Send 'em up, Gilbert. And thanks."

Five minutes later, there was a knock, and Dillinger moved for the door. "I'll get it." When he opened it, he found the Cagneys and the Purvises laughing about something, having become acquainted on the ride up in the elevator.

"Come on in, folks," Dillinger said, opening the door wider.

After everyone was introduced and drinks served, they sat around the coffee table while Woody put the finishing touches on the meal.

"I want to wish you the best of luck, Johnnie," Cagney said. "You've come a long way, and it's only going to get better. Top of the world!"

Dillinger lifted his champagne glass in salute. "I appreciate that, Jimmy. And I'm glad we're finally working together. You and Melvin get a chance to talk about your role?"

"Not yet," Purvis said.

"Then you can do it on the train, I've got a berth booked for you on the Chief."

"I appreciate that, John, but my part of the work is done. You don't really need me there."

"That's beside the point. I *want* you there—it's important to me. I think maybe you'll bring me good luck."

Butler sipped his Scotch. "My old paper wants me to cover the shoot, so I'll be there too."

317

"That's great." Dillinger smiled. "I have a good feeling about this, boys, and I owe much of it to my co-writers. So, I want to toast Bob Butler and Melvin Purvis."

"Hear, hear," Butler said, clinking glasses with Purvis.

The phone rang, and Dillinger heard Woody answer it. A moment later he stuck his head out of the kitchen. "I think you should take the call, Mr. Dillinger."

"This better be good. Excuse me, everyone."

As he passed the kitchen, Dillinger pointed to the bedroom, and Woody nodded.

He picked up the phone and sat on the bed. A second later he heard Woody hang up the extension.

"Hello, Mr. Warner. I hope to see you on the set next week."

"I don't think that's very likely, Johnnie."

Dillinger frowned. It wasn't Jack Warner, as he had assumed. "Who is this?" he asked, annoyed that someone was interrupting his dinner party.

"It's J. Edgar Hoover, Johnnie."

"You're kidding me, right?" Dillinger asked, already knowing the answer. "So, to what do I owe the pleasure?"

"I wanted to wish you luck in Chicago. I hear the town is rolling out the red carpet for you."

"You want to wish me luck?"

"I do. I think it's high time we put the past behind us."

"Is that why you convinced Jack Warner to change his mind about producing my film?"

"Yes. I thought you, of all people, would tell the truth."

Dillinger laughed. "The truth? I would think that would be the last thing you'd want on that screen."

"That surprises you."

"You could say that, Edgar."

If Hoover had a problem with Dillinger being so familiar, he gave no indication.

"Nevertheless, I want to let bygones be bygones. Again, good luck."

There was a click on the line and Hoover was gone.

"This is nuts," he said, mumbling to himself. He replaced the receiver and rejoined his guests as Woody announced the meal. As they settled in around the dining room table, and Woody served plates heaping with Chateaubriand, potatoes *au gratin*, and green beans, Dillinger found his thoughts returning to the phone conversation. Was it possible Hoover was actually burying the hatchet? He'd seen the agent shadowing him, and while it was annoying, he knew he had nothing to fear because he wasn't guilty of anything. He was now a movie actor and soon to be a director, why on earth would he do anything illegal to mess up the good life?

※　※　※

"Dig in, everybody," Billie said, lifting her fork and knife. She took a bite, feeling the tenderloin melt in her mouth.

"My God, this is delicious," Millie Butler said.

"And how," Cagney echoed. "Let's have a toast to Woody." Everyone except Dillinger raised their wine glass. Lizzie raised her second bottle of Coke.

Woody bowed in gracious appreciation. "Thank you all. Just mind you save room for dessert," he said, before disappearing back into the kitchen.

That was when Billie noticed Dillinger picking at his food. "Johnnie, is the meat okay?"

"It's fine," he said, taking a bite. "Just an odd phone call."

"Odd? How?"

Dillinger, who'd kept his eyes on his plate, lifted his gaze to meet Billie's. "Because it was J. Edgar Hoover."

The clatter of utensils dropping onto a plate startled everyone.

"Sorry," Purvis said. He picked up his knife and fork and resumed eating, but Billie couldn't help noticing his discomfort.

"What the hell did he want?" Billie asked.

"He said he wanted to wish me luck on the film, telling me the past was the past and bygones were bygones."

Purvis picked up his wineglass. Dillinger noticed his trembling hand, the Bordeaux sloshing back and forth inside the glass.

"That sonofabitch really had the nerve to call?" Cagney blurted out, incredulous.

Frances placed her hand on her husband's arm. "Jimmy, please, we have children present."

Cagney rolled his eyes. "Sorry, Lizzie."

"That's okay," she said, obviously enjoying the moment more than anyone else.

"Perhaps he's sincere," Frances offered.

Or maybe he's trying to rattle Johnnie, Billie thought. *Set him up for failure while appearing to have had a change of heart.*

Dillinger held up a hand. "Next week we're going to start making our movie, and I don't give a damn what Hoover thinks. Now let's enjoy this meal or Woody is gonna kill me."

Everyone laughed, and the mood was broken, except for Melvin Purvis, who remained silent throughout the rest of the meal.

38

The Stargazer Hotel
Hollywood, California
June 23, 1936

Hurt tossed his cigarette onto the sidewalk then stepped into the hotel lobby. "Any messages?" he asked the grizzled old man behind the registration desk.

The man shook his head, his turkey jowls quivering. "Nothin', mister, nothin' at all. Was you expectin' something?"

Hurt stared at the old man, his amber eyes narrowing. The old codger was jittery for some reason, his knotty hands shaking, and he stank even worse than usual of stale tobacco.

Hurt turned and headed for the stairs.

"Don't you worry none, I'll let you know if I hear anything," the old man called out as Hurt mounted the steps.

He stopped climbing as a feeling stole over him, a tingling at the base of his spine he could never ignore. The old geezer had never been anything more than indifferent to his guests, treating them all as if they were nuisances, as if he couldn't be bothered to put in more than the minimal effort. Now he was being helpful.

Hurt returned to the desk, leaning close to the old man, who took an involuntary step back, his bloodshot eyes widening. "Has anyone been here asking about me?"

"No, sir, ain't been nobody here askin' for you."

The man's voice rose in pitch. He was nervous—and he might as well have been wearing a neon sign like the one outside the hotel.

Without another word Hurt returned to the steps, taking them two at a time. When he reached his floor he scanned the halls, finding them deserted as usual. He pulled his Colt 1911, racked the slide back as quietly as possible, and moved toward the door to his room. He halted when he saw the door was ajar and the light inside was on.

He felt his face flush with anger, his mouth twisting into an ugly sneer. Creeping forward, he put his ear to the door and listened.

Nothing.

The knuckles on his gun hand turned white as he moved in front of the door and bashed it open with a swift kick, his gun ready.

"Good evening, Clarence. Nice night, isn't it?"

Purvis sat on the sagging easy chair near the window, the hotel's neon sign splashing its array of colors all over him in its never-ending cycle.

Still aiming the pistol at Purvis, Hurt approached.

"You can put that way, I'm not here to hurt you; that's why I left the door open and the lights on," Purvis said.

Hurt didn't move a muscle, staring at his former boss with naked contempt.

"How'd you find me?"

Purvis smiled and Hurt trembled with rage. "I followed you after one of your surprise visits to my home, and you never had a clue."

"Fine. And I supposed that old goat in the lobby was only too happy to give you my room number."

"I showed him the badge you gave me; it does come in handy."

"What do you want?"

"Mr. Hoover called John Dillinger this evening to wish him luck. He even said, 'no hard feelings.' I just wanted to know if that's true. Is it true, Clarence?"

Hurt's face remained a mask of stone as he moved toward Purvis, the gun still gripped tightly in his hand.

"Stand up and open your coat . . . slowly."

Purvis complied and Hurt nodded. He did indeed have a gun, but it was holstered.

"You never answered my question," Purvis said, re-buttoning his jacket.

"The director does not see fit to confide in me." Then Hurt dropped a bomb. "He's pulling me off this case, and your assistance is no longer required, *Mr.* Purvis. Now hand over that badge."

Purvis remained outwardly calm. "Why the change of heart, Clarence? You and I both know Hoover will take a vendetta to the grave. Give it to me straight."

For the first time since they worked together two years before, Hurt dropped his tough-cop act. "Hell, I don't know. I just take orders," he said, shoving his .45 back into his shoulder holster. "Trying to second-guess *why* Hoover does anything will drive you nuts. You more than anyone should know that."

Purvis remained wary. "On the level?"

Hurt nodded. "I'm leaving for Chicago tomorrow."

"Chicago?" asked Purvis. "Where Dillinger's shooting the first scene of his movie, at the Biograph?"

Hurt rolled his eyes, a pained look on his face. "On other business. From there to Washington, or wherever the Chief sends me." Then the anger flared in Hurt's voice. "Christ, I'm telling you what you've been hoping for, what *I've* been hoping for, and here

323

you are looking for reasons to jinx it! Think whatever the hell you want."

✖ ✖ ✖

Purvis tried in vain to make sense of what he'd just been told as he reached into the inside pocket of his jacket with a slow and deliberate action, removed the badge, and handed it to the sullen Oklahoman.

"Good," Hurt said, slipping the badge into his pants pocket. He moved to the window and pulled aside the gauzy curtain, the light from the neon sign throwing his body into silhouette. "I'm leaving tomorrow, and I hope I never see this fuckin' town again." He turned and faced Purvis. "Dillinger's a heel—a goddamned road apple—and I don't suppose he'll ever get what he deserves. He'll get what he gets."

An awkward silence fell between them, and Purvis didn't even bother to say goodbye to the man who had once been his comrade-in-arms, who at one time had his back. He just turned and walked out the door.

As he walked home, his swift footsteps slapping against the concrete, Purvis kept replaying the conversation in his head. Despite what Hurt had said, he knew in his gut something was off. It had all made sense until Clarence piped in, "He'll get what he gets."

Maybe I'll take Dillinger up on his offer to go to Chicago.

And maybe it's a good thing Clarence didn't think to take back my service revolver.

39

2432 N. Lincoln Avenue
Chicago, Illinois
June 30, 1936

From his second-floor perch in the building directly across the street, Clarence Hurt watched with measured patience as the *Dillinger* film crew swarmed over the Biograph Theatre and the surrounding area, erecting scaffolding and platforms for lights and multiple cameras. A cadre of grips adjusted massive banks of Klieg lights, all of them trained on the Biograph Theatre entrance and its adjacent buildings. There were even lights mounted on the roof of his building, and the entire effect made the street glow. On the sidewalk below, crowds watched from behind sawhorses, hoping in vain for a glimpse of Dillinger, and the traffic was a permanent snarl. Horns honked, tourists yammered—a cacophony that was music to Hurt's ears.

He chain-smoked and took in the entire tableau, counting the hours. The details of his plan had formed in his mind during the train ride back to Chicago. It was a stroke of luck that the building right across from the theatre had a vacant apartment on the second floor, which he'd rented for an entire month. His ringside view of the entrance to the Biograph thirty yards away was perfect.

He stabbed out his latest cigarette and picked up the brand-new Winchester Model 70 off the table, admiring the gleam of its blued steel. Boasting a smooth bolt-action modeled after a German Mauser, it was chambered for .30-06, a proven high-powered round that could drop a buck at two hundred yards. Here, distance wasn't an issue. He'd spent the previous afternoon in a deserted field sighting the scope, adjusting it for a far closer shot.

Lifting the rifle to his shoulder, he sighted through the scope, watching the young brunette counting receipts in the theatre box office. She was close enough to kiss; the detail so sharp he could count the pores in her perfect porcelain skin. Hurt lowered the rifle and grinned. This was going to be a turkey shoot.

"Tomorrow night, you're mine, John. And you'll get yours."

40

Billie smoothed the lipstick on her lips, gave herself one last appraisal, and rose from the vanity. "How do I look?"

Dillinger grinned. "Like a million bucks, kiddo."

She giggled and gave him a peck on the cheek and strode out of the bathroom.

In the lobby, the concierge met them and guided them out to the sidewalk, where the studio-provided car, a sleek, black Packard, stood idling at the curb.

Cagney, seated on one of the jump seats, leaned out the door. "Let's get a move on, Dillinger, your destiny awaits."

Dillinger grinned and settled into the cushy seat next to Billie, the two of them facing Cagney and Melvin Purvis.

"So, how's it feel, Mr. Director?" Cagney quipped.

"Pretty damn good," Dillinger replied. And it did. Despite Jack Warner's initial reluctance to film at the actual Biograph Theatre, he'd seen the merits of Dillinger's argument. He'd called Mayor Edward Kelly and made a personal appeal. It didn't hurt that Kelly had

seen *The Petrified Forest* and was a fan. The necessary permits were
rammed through, giving the cast and crew the run of the 2400 block
of N. Lincoln Avenue until six o'clock a.m. on July 2nd. To top it off,
Chicago's finest would be providing security. Dillinger found it iron-
ic that the very cops who would have gunned him down two years
ago would now be protecting him.

The ride to the Biograph took longer than he expected. And as
they drew closer to N. Lincoln Avenue, the traffic worsened.

"Is this going to be a problem, Johnnie?" Billie asked.

"Once we're at the location, the cops will block off both ends
of the street. No one will get in or out for the next twelve hours."
He turned to Purvis, who was staring out the window and had been
quiet for the entire ride. "Everything okay, Melvin?"

Purvis turned and smiled. "Just thinking about how we've come
full circle."

"Yeah, ain't it a kick?" Dillinger laughed. "Is Jimmy ready to be
a G-Man?"

"The only thing he lacks is a law degree," the former FBI agent
said, looking at Cagney.

The excitement in the car grew as the Packard reached the intersection of Halstead and Lincoln. Dillinger leaned forward and saw
the cops had already blocked off the street. As they approached, a
sergeant raised his arm and motioned for them to keep moving. Dillinger rolled down his window.

"Hey, Sarge, we're here for the fun."

The cop nodded when he recognized Dillinger, and he turned to
the other policemen behind him, signaling for them to move the sawhorses blocking the street. They passed through and headed toward
the glow of the studio lights.

Billie gave out a low whistle. "This is amazing."

Dillinger was watching something going on across from the theatre, where crewmembers were positioning a camera crane under the watchful eye of Hal Wallis.

"Hey, driver, pull up here," Dillinger said, "and keep the engine running."

The Packard eased to the curb just south of the theatre and Dillinger leaped out, crossing the street with quick strides. He found Wallis in conference with the cameraman. "Hey, Hal, what's going on? Why is the crane just getting here now?"

Wallis turned to Dillinger, a tired yet jovial expression on his face. "Everything's under control, John." He looked up into the sky. "It'll be fully dark in about forty minutes; by that time, we'll be ready for rehearsal. Wardrobe and makeup are waiting for you in the trailer." He patted Dillinger on the shoulder.

Smiling with relief, Dillinger rejoined his party standing under the Biograph marquee, which now included a fourth member, Robert Butler.

"I can always count on you showing up," Dillinger said, shaking Butler's hand.

"I wouldn't be much of a reporter if I didn't."

"You bring my little lookout with you?"

"She wanted to come in the worst way, Johnnie, but my wife put her foot down."

"Well, you're all invited to the premiere if we ever get this show on the road."

"Mr. Dillinger?"

Everyone turned at the sound of the voice, which belonged to an earnest young man clutching a clipboard. "We need to get you and Mr. Cagney into makeup and wardrobe."

"Okay, kid, lead on."

The four of them followed the young assistant director to a sleek, shiny Airstream Clipper trailer parked just past the alley. The young man held open the door, allowing Billie and Cagney to enter first. When Purvis hung back, Dillinger said, "You're welcome to come in and sit with us, Melvin."

Purvis held up a hand. "That's okay. I think I want to walk around and get a feel for things."

"Old habits dying hard?"

Purvis smiled. "Something like that."

Dillinger watched him melt into the crowd, that odd feeling returning. Something wasn't right.

※　※　※

As Purvis walked away from the Airstream trailer, he kept to the theatre side of the street, his eyes scanning the crowds of extras being organized into random groups by the various assistant directors. He counted a total of five cameras, including the one being mounted to the late-arriving crane. He turned his attention to the crowd of onlookers lining the sidewalk across the street, trying to see if Hurt was among them, but the studio lighting blinded him, making it nearly impossible for him to make out individual faces.

※　※　※

The makeup girl examined her handiwork with a critical eye, turning Dillinger's face first one way and then the other.

"Am I pretty yet, Maggie?"

The young woman laughed. "You'll do, Mr. Dillinger."

Dillinger leaned his head back as someone rapped on the trailer door.

"Come in."

Hal Wallis walked in, closing the door behind him. He took a seat next to Dillinger, his expression grave.

The smile slid off Dillinger's face. "What, what is it?"

"Archie Mayo's outside. Warner's ordered him to take over."

"What!" Billie said, the script she'd been holding falling to the floor with a loud slap. "He can't do that—"

Dillinger held up his hand and Billie fell silent. "Is this some cockamamie joke the crew came up with, 'cause it's not funny."

The producer sighed and shook his head. "I wish to hell it were."

"So, Warner decides to wait until now to spring this crap on me?"

"Near as I can tell, it was all last-minute."

"Bullshit! It would take Mayo at least three days to get here by train. Warner's been planning this all along."

Dillinger stole a look at Billie, whose forlorn expression mirrored his own feelings. Warner had reneged on their deal, had stabbed him in the back.

Hal interrupted his thoughts. "Mayo wants to speak with you."

Dillinger clenched his fists, closing his eyes for a moment, then looked the producer squarely in the eye. "Fine, tell him to come in."

Hal looked pained. "He wants you to come out."

Dillinger banged his fist on the arm of the director's chair and rose to his feet, pulling the Kleenex from around his collar. He glanced at his reflection in the mirror, noting the Clark Gable mustache the makeup girl had just applied. It looked just like the one he'd once sported. The rest of the wardrobe was a perfect match to what he'd worn that fateful night: white silk shirt, a gray tie flecked with black, white canvas shoes, and gray flannel trousers. Everything was just like it was, even his mood. He reached for the straw boater and placed it on his head, seating it with a gentle tap to the crown.

"I'll see you out there, Mr. Dillinger," Maggie said, avoiding his eyes as she slipped out the door.

Billie joined him at the mirror, encircling him with her arms. "I'm sorry, Johnnie."

She began to cry, and Dillinger's anger boiled over. It was bad enough Warner was reneging on their agreement, but he found himself hating the man even more for making him look like a fool in front of Billie.

She pulled away, sniffling and wiping her tears. "Christ! Now I'm a goddamn mess."

Dillinger kissed the tip of her nose. "I'm going to go talk to Mayo, maybe there's a way to salvage this thing."

She shook her head. "I don't think so. I've got one of my feelings."

"I'll be fine," he said, kissing her again. "You go and put your face back on and come on out. Frances Cagney's in the VIP section with the mayor and the rest of the stuffed shirts."

That seemed to make her feel better, and Dillinger left the trailer.

He found Archie Mayo standing at the mouth of the alley, watching the crew making their final preparations. Dillinger forced himself to remain calm. Warner was a rat bastard, but Mayo was a right guy. Maybe he would listen to reason.

Sensing his presence, Mayo turned and smiled. "You've set these cameras in just the right places."

"I learned that from you."

The older man nodded, accepting the compliment. "I'm sorry about this, John—it's nothing personal. It's just business."

"Funny, that's what Murder Incorporated says," Dillinger responded, not bothering to temper his sarcasm.

Mayo remained silent.

"When did Warner assign you?"

"A week ago."

Dillinger let out a sigh then turned to the older man. "Despite what Warner thinks, I can do this, Mr. Mayo. It's all up here." He pointed to his temple.

"I'm sure you can, and if it were up to me you would, but Mr. Warner was quite emphatic. You're out as director."

"And what if I refuse to accept that?"

Mayo's expression saddened. "You'll be placed on suspension and they'll bring in another actor. Everyone's replaceable, John—everyone . . ."

"Everyone except Jack Warner . . ."

Mayo again remained silent.

Jeff, his first assistant director, moved up behind them, his posture making it clear that he now knew who was calling the shots. Mayo turned to the young man and said, "We're going to rehearse this a couple of times before we roll camera. Five minutes."

Jeff nodded and ran off.

"John, when we get back to LA, I'll tell Warner personally that I think you're up to the task, but if we're going to get through tonight, we're doing it his way."

"Do you really think you'll change his mind?"

"No . . . I don't," Mayo said, shaking his head and walking away. "I'll see you on set."

Steeling himself, Dillinger emerged from the alley. All eyes turned to him and the assembled crowd began to applaud and cheer. Dillinger smiled, nodded, and waved as he continued walking, feeling as if he was walking that "last mile."

Studio guards held back the crowd as Dillinger made his way into the VIP section, where special guests waited along with principal cast members. He shook hands with Mayor Kelly and the city council. Cagney stood with his wife, looking every inch the G-Man.

Frances Cagney gave him a hug and a kiss. "Best of luck with this, Johnnie."

"Thanks, Frances."

"Where's Billie?"

"She'll be along in a minute."

He gave Frances another hug and then turned to find Cagney watching him with a huge grin on his face.

"You ready for this, Johnnie?"

"Me? I'm always ready."

Cagney frowned, sensing Dillinger's somber mood. "What's wrong?"

"Nothing."

"Now, don't give me that. I know a load of malarkey when I hear it."

Dillinger gazed at his friend then shook his head in disgust. "Warner's replaced me with Archie Mayo as director."

Cagney's eyes bulged. "Warner's replaced—why, that dirty rat!"

Dillinger grasped Cagney by the arm and leaned closer. "There's nothing we can do, Jimmy. If I refuse, I'll be out altogether. Let's just get through tonight, and I'll deal with Warner later."

Cagney nodded.

Jeff had climbed onto the platform for camera one and raised his megaphone. "Stand by for rehearsal!"

"That's our cue," Dillinger said.

The two of them made their way to the front of the Biograph, and Dillinger watched as Archie Mayo took the megaphone from his assistant and stepped up onto the crane.

"I want to thank you all for coming here this evening." The crowd cheered, and Mayo waited for quiet. "I also want to thank the crew for all their hard work in prepping for tonight's scene. We're going to rehearse this a couple of times, so keep your powder dry."

Mayo motioned for the actors playing the Bureau agents to come over as he stepped off the camera platform. "All right, you three and Mr. Cagney will be waiting by the streetlight as the theatre crowd exits. When you spot Mr. Dillinger leaving the theatre with Anna and Polly, you'll follow. He'll stop and surrender just before they reach the alley. When Hurt raises his gun, Agent Purvis will order him to stand down. We'll cut there. Everybody got that?"

The four actors nodded. Mayo turned to Dillinger, who nodded, doing his best to look amenable.

"All right, then, let's do this," Mayo said.

✖ ✖ ✖

Purvis watched as Dillinger and the two actresses playing his companions disappeared into the Biograph.

"All right, this is a rehearsal. Everyone quiet!" came the amplified voice of the assistant director. The chattering crowd obeyed, falling silent in less than fifteen seconds. Other than the light whistling of the wind and the rumbling engines of the cars waiting to drive past the theatre, there were no other sounds.

"Background . . . Action!"

Immediately, the cars at either end of the street and the extras started moving.

"Principals . . . Action!"

Extras spilled out from the theatre lobby onto the sidewalk. Some turned left toward the alley, while others veered right, chattering away as if they'd really seen the movie. A few even dashed directly across the street, causing cars to brake and honk their horns.

A shiver ran up Purvis's spine. This was more than a severe case of *déjà vu*. It was a replay of history—one that could result in a decidedly different outcome. He was the random element, the variable that would determine the true outcome. The real question was, would he even be able make a move to stop it?

❋ ❋ ❋

Hurt tensed as Dillinger and his two consorts emerged from the theatre and began to stroll south toward the alley. He brought the Winchester to his shoulder, placing the center of the crosshairs on the back of Dillinger's head. He exhaled, his finger caressing the trigger—

And then everything changed as the massive camera crane rose up to its full height, deftly blocking his entire view of the street.

"What the hell is this?" Hurt growled, lowering the Winchester.

After a few moments, he heard someone yell, "Cut!" and the crane descended to its starting position. Dillinger returned to his first position inside the theatre—his chance was gone.

Angry, Hurt slammed the rifle onto the table and stood, pulling out his Colt 1911 and racking a round into the chamber.

He'd have to wing it; get down in the crowd and pick off Dillinger if he had the chance. And who knows, he might get lucky and get away in the resulting chaos.

If I don't pull this off, Hoover will make damn sure my life isn't worth living, anyway.

With one last glance at the Winchester, he dashed out of the apartment.

When Hurt reached the street, he nearly barreled into one of Chicago's finest. He reached into his lower coat pocket and flashed his badge.

The ruddy-faced cop gave him a curt nod and moved away. Hurt turned toward the Biograph. The assistant director was back on the camera platform.

"Everyone back to their number-one positions for the second rehearsal!"

The extras began retracing their steps, and Hurt felt a trickle of sweat running down his back. It wasn't as hot this night as it was two years ago, but it was hot enough.

He noticed James Cagney and the other actors reaching their starting positions near a lamppost. He smiled and shook his head when he spotted the actor playing him. Not even close.

"Places, everyone!" the assistant director shouted.

Crossing the street, Hurt worked his way into the throng of extras who were waiting for the rehearsal to begin.

✖ ✖ ✖

Time was running out. From his vantage point north of the theatre, Purvis watched as Dillinger and the two women disappeared into the Biograph. He felt a trickle of sweat running down his back, and his hands were sticky. Turning, he scanned the crowd across the street one last time.

And then he saw him.

Hurt was crossing the street in a mad dash.

A few moments later, the assistant raised his megaphone.

"Background . . . Action!"

The extras and the cars started moving.

Purvis dived into the crowd of extras, trying to keep Hurt in view, and cursing his lack of height. The Oklahoman was now only a few steps back from where Cagney and the other actors waited.

"Principals . . . Action!"

Purvis moved closer, his eyes locked onto Hurt, who fell into step behind Cagney and the three other actors as they began to move.

Just then Dillinger and his two dates emerged from the Biograph lobby. Purvis kept one eye on the former outlaw and the other on Hurt, who seemed to be relishing the moment.

Step by inexorable step, they drew closer to Dillinger and the two women walking on either side of him.

And then Dillinger halted in his tracks and raised his hands.

In a flash, Hurt pulled his .45 and leveled it at the back of Dillinger's head.

※　※　※

"I give up, boys. I surrender!" Dillinger said, turning to face the actors behind him. The smile died on his face.

Behind Ward Bond, who was portraying Agent Hurt, stood the *real* Agent Hurt.

When the call to cut didn't come at the expected moment, the extras slowed their pace, milling about, unsure of what to do next. To Dillinger, it almost seemed as if time had stopped, the end of the barrel of that .45 yawning like the pit of Hell.

It was his nightmare come to life.

※　※　※

When Hurt pulled his .45 and pointed it at Dillinger, Purvis reached into his jacket and drew his .38 revolver, aiming it between Hurt's shoulder blades. "Stand down, Agent Hurt."

"Game's over, Melvin," Hurt said, without a trace of alarm. The agent's gun hand remained rock steady, aimed at Dillinger's head.

Dillinger remained silent and watchful.

"I mean it, Clarence. Stand down, this isn't going to happen."

There was a moment of quiet, as if a blanket had dropped over the world. And then, in a blur of movement, Hurt turned and fired.

※　※　※

Dillinger had to call on every reserve of will to resist the urge to attack and disarm the man. At this range, he wouldn't hear the blast. It would be like switching off a light.

"I mean it, Clarence. Stand down, this isn't going to happen."

338

Dillinger saw Hurt's expression darken and his eyes narrow as—for a split second—his hatred turned toward another target. He spun around and fired the .45. With a groan of agony, Purvis clutched his side and collapsed to the pavement, where he lay curled in a fetal position.

A woman screamed, and extras moved away from Hurt and Dillinger in a concentric wave, as if parted by giant hands.

Before Hurt could turn his attention back to him, Dillinger tackled him to the ground and pummeled the man's face with rapid-fire punches. In moments, the agent's face was a mass of blood and bruises.

A half a dozen police closed in, their pistols drawn. "Everyone, freeze!" one of the officers demanded.

Dillinger climbed off Hurt and stood, his chest heaving. "You just couldn't let me live my life, could you?"

Hurt coughed and spit blood on the sidewalk as two cops pulled him to his feet and cuffed him. "You don't *deserve* a life," he said, his voice dripping with venom.

"Someone call an ambulance!" Dillinger shouted. "Right now!"

One of the cops ran into the theatre, where a phone awaited. Dillinger turned and knelt by Purvis, whose pallor was as pale as new cream.

"Hang in there, pal. Can't have you dying on me now."

Purvis nodded and coughed.

Just then Billie pushed her way out of the crowd, her eyes wide with horror.

"Oh my God, Johnnie," she said, throwing herself into Dillinger's arms. "I heard the shot, but I couldn't see anything from where I was. I didn't know what to think."

"I'm okay, but we need to take care of Melvin."

Ten minutes later, the ambulance arrived along with a police paddy wagon. The police shoved Hurt into the back and slammed the armored door with a clang. The agent's gaze never wavered from Dillinger as the cops drove him away, as if he thought he could somehow will his enemy's heart to stop beating if he stared hard enough.

Dillinger and Billie watched as the ambulance attendants strapped Purvis to a stretcher and loaded him into the back of the ambulance.

"Where are they taking him?" he asked the driver.

"Passavant Hospital. 303 East Superior."

When the ambulance left, Dillinger turned to his first assistant director.

"Tell Mr. Mayo I want to go for a take," he said, hating himself for putting the film before his friend. They got the shot on the second try. The rest of the shoot went smoothly. After Mayo called for a wrap just after four o'clock in the morning, Dillinger rode to Passavant Hospital with Billie and the Cagneys in silence.

When they arrived, Dillinger headed straight to the admissions desk and bulled his way to the front of the short line.

The nurse, a stout middle-aged woman with bright red hair, glared at him. "Sir, you need to wait your turn."

Dillinger leaned over the counter. "Nurse, I appreciate that you're busy, but I need to know about one of your patients, Melvin Purvis."

The woman pursed her lips, as if tasting something rotten. "And I told you," she said, pointing, "the end of the line is back there."

Anger flared and then dissipated under the weight of his weariness. "Listen, ma'am, he was hurt because of me. It's my fault, see? And he's a friend. Maybe the best one I've ever had. If you could just tell me if he's okay, I'll go."

The woman's hard shell softened, and she reached for a clipboard hanging from a nearby hook and studied it for a moment. "He's in recovery. But the doctor's not allowing visitors until the morning . . . and only then if he okays it."

Dillinger thanked the woman and they left soon after.

Back in their suite at the Drake, as they undressed for bed, Billie took him into her arms. "I'm sorry about Melvin, Johnnie," she said, caressing the back of his neck.

"I know," he replied after a long pause. "He took a slug to save me."

He broke the embrace and sat down on the bed, sighing with disgust. "Hoover was behind this."

Billie's expression turned from sympathy to alarm. "You don't know that."

"I do. That man never forgets. Melvin told me Hoover personally kept him from getting another job, until he lucked into getting hired by Warner. He's like a dog that won't let go of your pants leg. Hoover wants me dead, and he's never going to give up."

Billie sat next to him. "Listen to me. You've had a long, tough day. But you got the scene in the can."

"And Melvin's in the hospital with a hole in him."

"He would have wanted you to get the job done, Johnnie. That's the way he is."

Dillinger chuckled despite his dark mood. "Yeah, you're right about that. You know, between Warner and Hoover, I'm beginning to wonder if this business is worth the trouble."

41

Passavant Hospital
Chicago, Illinois
July 3, 1936

Purvis awoke from his nap, the pain in his side a dull throb compared to its fiery glory two days before. From what the doctors told him, it was pretty much a miracle bullet that managed to drill completely through his body without damaging any major organs or severing any arteries.

"All in all, if you're going to suffer a wound like this, Mr. Purvis," the surgeon intoned, "you couldn't ask for a better trajectory. And while there may be some residual pain due to some minor nerve damage, you should make a complete recovery."

Rosanne had wept with joy, making Purvis promise that he would get rid of the revolver and stay away from anything having to do with the FBI or law enforcement. It was an easy promise to make.

"How are you feeling, Melvin?"

Purvis turned his head and found Rosanne staring at him intently. He sighed, a rush of emotions bringing tears to his eyes. He also felt a debt of gratitude to Jack Warner, who had personally chartered a plane to bring his wife to his side.

"We nearly lost each other, didn't we?"

Rosanne nodded, clasping his hand between hers. "I don't know what I would have done, Melvin. And I don't ever want to find out."

Purvis squeezed her hand in return.

There was a knock on the door, and a second later in walked Dillinger and Billie, their expressions etched with equal measures of hope and concern.

"We tried coming to see you yesterday," Dillinger said, "but they wouldn't allow any visitors. I'm glad to see you beat the rap."

Purvis nodded then turned to his wife. "Honey? Do me a favor and crank me up."

Dillinger held up a hand. "I'll do it. Say when."

Dillinger grabbed the crank and slowly raised the head of the bed so that Purvis was now resting in a sitting position.

"That's good. Thank you."

Rosanne stood and moved to Dillinger and hugged him. "Thank you for saving Melvin," she said with a sob.

Dillinger patted her back then squeezed her shoulder. "I couldn't let my partner in crime go down without a fight, now could I?"

Rosanne laughed. "I won't forget, and neither will Melvin."

Dillinger shot a glance at Purvis, who nodded solemnly.

"Now, I'm going to see if I can find some coffee and let you three have a visit."

"You don't have to go on our account," Billie piped in.

"I'm not," she said with a smile, and left the room.

Dillinger waited until Rosanne had left then turned to Purvis. "You'll be happy to know Hurt's rotting in a cell at the county jail. Ain't that a kicker?"

"I heard," Purvis said. "I've also heard Hoover's disowned him, calling him a 'rogue agent bent on a personal vendetta.'"

Billie shook her head. "That snake."

"What's going on with the film?" Purvis asked, changing the subject.

"We got the Biograph scene in the can, but we're on hold for a couple of weeks. I told Warner I'd do things his way, but I needed some time off before I dive back in. I've been going like gangbusters for over a year, so Billie and I are hightailing it down to Ensenada to soak up some sun, maybe do a little deep-sea fishing. Just have to take care of a little business in LA before we go."

Purvis looked wistful. "If I didn't have this hole in my side, I'd go with you."

"Now that would be something." Dillinger's eyes twinkled with mischief. "Except if you went swimming with that hole in your gut, you'd probably sink."

The three of them laughed, and then Purvis yawned. Dillinger frowned. "We're tiring you out. Sorry about that, kiddo."

"It's okay. The doctors say I should be ready to go home after the weekend."

"That's great," Dillinger said.

Rosanne walked back in, carrying a tray with three cups of steaming coffee. "I didn't know how you liked your coffee, so it's black. I hope that's okay."

"What about me?" Purvis said with mock indignation.

She gave him a look that said *not on your life* and placed the tray on a nearby table.

"Thank you, I appreciate that," Dillinger said, "but truth is Billie and I have a plane to catch. I just wanted to stop by and see how he was doing."

Rosanne nodded, her expression tinged with disappointment. "We're glad you did."

As Billie and Dillinger headed for the door, Purvis called out. "You stay out of trouble down there, you hear?"

Dillinger looked amused. "Trouble? I wouldn't dream of it."

Purvis chuckled as his friend left the room. After they were gone, he settled back on the bed and fell into a deep and dreamless sleep.

42

The phone rang, and Purvis had every intention of ignoring it. Ever since they'd arrived back home the day before, well-wishers had called at all hours of the day and night to give him their regards and sincere hopes for a full recovery. He'd let Rosanne fend off most of them and stayed in bed until late in the morning when the boredom became too much to bear. Thankfully, the pain in his side had dwindled to a dull throb, and the doctor had advised that he get up and move around at least a little bit, so he'd put on his robe and gone into his study. He'd spent the last hour rereading the pages of *Devil in a Red Dress*. It was good—better than good—and it was destined for the capable hands of Raoul Walsh, who promised to give it careful consideration.

The phone rang again.

"Melvin, please answer it!" Rosanne called from the kitchen. "My hands are covered with flour."

"Okay, okay, I've got it," he said, reaching for the handset. "Hello?"

"Good morning, Mr. Purvis, I hear you're doing much better."

Purvis closed his eyes as a wave of nausea rushed through him.

346

It was that bastard Hoover.

He swallowed the bile in the back of his throat then took a deep breath. "Why are you calling me?"

"Aside from my genuine concern for your well-being, I thought you'd like to know John Dillinger has absconded to Mexico with the entire Warner Brothers' payroll—six hundred thousand dollars! He pulled it off with two confederates, one of them a studio guard, and the other his goddamned valet! You see, I was right all along, and all you fools refused to believe me."

"If any of that is true, you and your bloodhound drove him to it, you son of a bitch."

"Oh, it's true, all right," Hoover replied with breathless intensity. "He even sent me a telegram. Would you like to hear it?"

"Do I really have a choice?"

"'Dear Edgar: Just wanted to let you know Billie and I have taken a powder and we're not coming back STOP If you want me that badly, you'll just have to come and get me STOP I'll be waiting with bells on STOP And Billie says you should go to hell in high heels FULL STOP.'"

For a moment, Purvis couldn't think, and then the absurdity of all that had occurred over the last two years caught up with him and he began to laugh, a belly laugh he felt down to his sutures.

"What the hell is so funny?" Hoover blustered. "You stop laughing right now, and that's an order!"

That only made Purvis laugh all the harder, clutching his wound in delicious agony.

And he was still laughing when he took the phone and slammed it back in the cradle, hanging up on the high and mighty J. Edgar Hoover.

DILLINGER DOES IT AGAIN!

Robert Butler
Dateline: Chicago, Illinois

It was LIGHTS, CAMERA, and ACTION, as John Dillinger made history again a fortnight ago, recreating his famous surrender at the Biograph Theatre in the heart of Chicago's Lincoln Park District for the upcoming Warner Brothers film: "Dillinger: Public Enemy No. 1."

When asked before shooting commenced if he felt the weight of history, Dillinger characteristically said, "We're here to do a job the best way we know how. We could have shot this on the backlot, but we wanted to give the film every bit of realism we could."

John Dillinger, former bank robber and acclaimed film star, can now add psychic seer to his list of accomplishments. Before cameras rolled, the situation became a little too real when screenwriter and former FBI agent Melvin Purvis was wounded in a gun accident on the set. Mr. Purvis was transported to Passavant Hospital and filming commenced a little while later with Warner stars James Cagney as Melvin Purvis and Ward Bond as FBI agent Clarence O. Hurt.

There are unconfirmed rumors that the production is on hold while Dillinger vacations in Mexico. According to producer Hal Wallis, due to unforeseen circumstances Dillinger may be replaced in the production as both director and star. Archie Mayo has been approached to direct, and Warner contract player Humphrey Bogart, who played Duke Mantee in the stage production of "The Petrified Forest," is being considered for the Dillinger role.

About the Authors

BILL WALKER is an award-winning writer whose works include novels, short stories and screenplays. His first novel, *Titanic 2012,* was enthusiastically received by readers, and Bill's two short story collections, *Five Minute Frights* and *Five Minute Chillers,* are perennial Halloween favorites. A highly-respected graphic designer, Walker has worked on books by such luminaries as Ray Bradbury, Richard Matheson, Dean Koontz, and Stephen King. His his last two novels, *Abe Lincoln: Public Enemy No. 1* and *Abe Lincoln On Acid,* were published in 2013 and 2016 respectively.

BRIAN ANTHONY is a writer and award-winning film maker. His first feature film, *Victor's Big Score,* was praised by *Variety* as "A tremendous calling card for writer-producer-director Brian Anthony." As a writer-producer Anthony has contributed to shows for American Movie Classics, Arts and Entertainment, and Fox Syndication, including *Beneath the Planet of the Apes* and *Lost in Space Forever.* A veteran film historian, Anthony has been interviewed on network television regarding film history, and co-authored the acclaimed biography of the film comedian Charley Chase, *Smile When the Raindrops Fall,* in 1998. Brian is an expert art and book restorationist, and you can see his work at Anthony Restorations.

Other Books by Walker & Anthony

Abe Lincoln: Public Enemy No. 1

Abe Lincoln On Acid

Beautiful Monsters